This book is dedicated with love to...
Enoch, Troy, Tara and Bethany

"To everything there is a season,
and a time to every purpose under the heaven:
A time to be born, and a time to die; a time to plant,
and a time to pluck up that which is planted;
A time to kill, and a time to heal;
a time to break down, and a time to build up;
A time to weep, and a time to laugh;
a time to mourn, and a time to dance;
A time to cast away stones, and a time to gather stones together;
a time to embrace, and a time to refrain from embracing;
A time to get, and a time to lose;
a time to keep, and a time to cast away;
A time to rend, and a time to sew;
a time to keep silence, and a time to speak;
A time to love, and a time to hate;
a time of war, and a time of peace."

Ecclesiastes 3: 1-8

CHAPTER ONE

THE STATELY BUT aged Guggenheimer Nursing Home stood before her. Recently restored, it dominated the steep hillside rising up from the Lynchburg Expressway. Joellen Farrar pulled into the parking lot beneath tall oak trees and couldn't help but think of the irony of life!

The sprawling, grassy lawn led out to Grace Street and to the bridge, or rather overpass, that was adjacent to the nursing home. That was where her mother's home had been, where she had lived and left when she married as a young girl. It had been torn down years ago to make room for the expressway. And now, after all these years, she had returned. Her mother had returned to Grace Street to die...next to where she had roller skated as a young child.

Joellen shook her head and slid out of the SUV, ridding herself of such pensive thoughts. She took a deep breath, mentally preparing herself, and marched up the wide, old steps of what used to be the Guggenheimer Memorial Hospital for Children, but that was when her mother was also a child. Strange, she thought, now it's a nursing home. She pulled open the door and smiled at the two women at the front desk and spoke cheerfully to several others as she made her way down the long corridors, while her stomach churned within, dreading the daily visit.

"Hello there. You comin' to see Miss Meredith today?"

"Yes, ma'am," she patiently replied. Without fail, the elderly, frail lady, straddling a wheelchair in the middle of the hallway, asked her the same question every day.

"Hope she's doing better today, honey," she added, then dropped her head onto her sunken chest.

"Yes, ma'am. I hope so, too." She glanced back at the old woman, but already her eyes were closed to the world around her. Joellen hurried down the long corridor. Miss Meredith...her mother's name was Meredith Leone Thaxton. Such a pretty name, she thought, but her mother had once said that she wished she had been called Margie. Funny how a lot of us would change our name if we could. She certainly would have. She would have picked something more graceful or regal, something like Christianna or maybe Alexandra. Yes, Alexandra would have been nice.

She arrived at Room 55 and momentarily stood by the door, reluctant to enter, listening for any sound from the other side, and then quietly eased into the small room. Her mother lay beneath a tautly stretched sheet, and all Joellen could see were her swollen fingertips clutching the top hem.

"Mama...."

Silence.

"Mama," she repeated softly.

Silence.

"Mama, it's me, Joellen."

Gradually, in slow motion, the sheet lowered, exposing her mother's large, brown, doe-like eyes as they peeped over the white edge.

"Mama, why do you have the sheet over your head?"

At first she thought only her mother's lips were moving, but then she heard a faint whisper, and she leaned closer.

"…because…because he's out there. He's trying to kill me…he wants to cut off my head!'"

JOELLEN DROVE OUT of the nursing home parking lot and turned left onto Grace Street, jumbled thoughts racing through her head, half-baked thoughts, thoughts that had a way of dredging up the past and kidnapping any ray of sunshine. She must put the picture of her mother out of her mind. She must erase those words she'd just heard. It was too painful, and there wasn't anything she could do about it. There wasn't anything anybody could do. She pushed the stereo button.

Get out in that kitchen and rattle those pots and pans.…

She nodded in sync with the rhythmic beat that transported her back to the fifties, back to cousin Betsy Jeanne's basement as the old, familiar sound blasted forth, filling the SUV, surrounding her, captivating her soul. Betsy Jeanne's gray painted concrete floor felt refreshingly cool to her bare feet as they danced to the frenzied beat bouncing off the diminutive record player piled high with forty-fives. Their youthful energies kept pace as the little records dropped down one after another until the last one, and they dropped with it, giggling uncontrollably.

Those were the days, she sighed, as she maneuvered down the narrow city street, past the old fire station. But where did they go? She glanced into the rearview mirror; how in the world could she be pushing sixty!

The narrow street curved sharply and descended to Twelfth Street, and she turned right onto it, and then left to Court Street, glancing over at the Lynchburg Historical Foundation building, previously Bragassa's Toy Store, her mother's favorite place as a child. She envisioned small children pulling long strands of brown taffy in the little store like her mother used to do.

Climbing the hill, she looked to the right and to the left, not wanting to miss either side. It was another old, narrow street, now in the historical district, with cars parked on both sides. Her mother's grand old church stood with dignity on the right, The First Baptist Church, where she had been baptized, and her mother's school, the John Wyatt School, on the left. Of course, its school days had long since gone. Although all of these things were way before her time, she strangely felt an affinity to them.

Normally she would have continued on up Court Street to Fifth Street on her shortcut home, but involuntarily she steered the SUV toward Clay Street, one street up. Occasionally she did this, just to pass over the old brick streets and reflect on her own past.

Lynchburg was originally built on a series of steep hills. A small band of stout-hearted Irish men and women under the leadership of John Lynch started the town upon the sharply rising slope of the James River way back in 1786. Since that time, of course, it had grown significantly, proudly marching up those hills and beyond. Joellen's mother arrived in Lynchburg at the age of six, and her family settled on one of those hills called Diamond Hill. She traipsed those downtown streets for years, but her mother wasn't the only one. So had she. Of course, her mother's footsteps were many more. Meredith Leone had grown up down here, spent all of her days as a youngster on these narrow, hilly streets. Joellen had only spent a few years, but years that were indelibly imprinted in her memory.

The bumpy brick street and fenced-in reservoir, with its statue of a water bearer, were oddly familiar, like yesterday. Joellen remembered walking down the tree-lined street beside the reservoir and wishing she could see the water, but it had been covered over with asphalt the year before she moved there. It had supplied downtown Lynchburg's water since 1883, and the dubious water bearer stood on the wall separating the two basins, but no water poured from the jug on its shoulder. And whether or not the bearer was male or female was immaterial, but it used to puzzle her as she strode back and forth.

Reluctantly, she looked across the street at the old Henderson place on the corner of Sixth and Clay and remembered Mr. Henderson, the last family member of five generations to live there. Pulling over to the side of the street under tall, shady trees, she switched off the ignition and just stared at it. It had been restored in the seventies to its original grandeur, and a business was actually located within it now. Officially it was known as the Price-Turner house and was listed on the National Historical Register. Mr. Price had bought the lot from Lynchburg's founder, John Lynch, in 1814 and built the Federal style house on it that same year. He sold it to the Turner family later on, and they kept it for all those generations. But Joellen referred to it as the Henderson place for she had lived in one of the apartments in the big yellow tenement house next door that Mr. Henderson also owned.

But everything looked different back then.

She recalled the day she'd gone to visit the old guy about buying his typewriter. It was one of those big black metal things with exposed keys reaching up to you like spidery fingers, beckoning you to the challenge. In fact, she'd seen a few like it in antique shops lately. She couldn't remember how much he'd wanted for it but more than it was worth. She had decided against it, finally purchasing one of those cheap, little portable things.

5

As she sat staring at the vacant lot beside the old Henderson place, she could almost hear the metallic click-click-click bouncing off the chrome kitchen table to the high plaster ceiling. The old yellow tenement house was gone now, and she was glad—too many memories. The only thing left was the hitching post out front, a unique relic of the past, a past beyond her past. Suddenly in the photos of her mind, she could see her little boy, Ryan, standing there, holding onto that hitching post. It was Easter morning, and he was all dressed up in his little blue suit with the short pants, clutching his Easter basket as she snapped his picture with her Brownie.

She choked up.

Slowly the old yellow tenement house began to materialize before her eyes, emerging out of history's haze, out of a dense fog. Yellow clapboard slapped back in place, long windows crystallized and vacantly gaped at her. Front steps dropped down, and there she sat in the gently falling rain. The wet sidewalk glistened in misty pools of streetlight, and she stared up into the darkened sky and pondered.

Within the midst of it, the midst of it
Oh such peace and tranquility
As on these darkened steps I sit
The rains so gently fall upon me

A closeness it is, yes—a closeness it is
To that something—that something great
Which thru my years, I've seemed to cherish
But could not reach—nor could not take

Strange, she thought, how she'd composed such words during a time when she was *anything* but close to God, not a Christian, not even a churchgoer, just a young girl in her early twenties seeking purpose in life, a purpose that seemed so illusive in those days. Suddenly she could see the back porch, with its rattling screen door, and then that night flashed before her as if it were yesterday.

She was fleeing from the yellow tenement house out into the cool October night, and her heart was racing, her eyes darting left and right. Was he following? A heavy blackness closed in around her. She must run! She must hide somewhere!

The uneven sidewalk beneath her bare feet was cold and slippery with the night's dew, and frantically she struggled not to trip. It stretched out ahead of her, a beckoning grayish white in the moonlight, leading her on. Abruptly it stopped. The corner!

Which way?

The steep hill to the left led downtown. She turned right instead and found herself at the gate of the church courtyard, the elegant St. Paul's Episcopal Church that embraced the entire Sixth Street block of Clay Street. Her feet automatically led the way through the gate and to the boxy church rectory shadowed in front of her. Instinctively she climbed its steep steps up to an elevated back porch, a good six feet off the ground. Collapsing on the rough, wooden floor, she stared up at the quarter moon, breathing long, deep sighs. For several minutes, she lay still, trying to calm herself, and decided to stay there until it was safe to return home, when he was asleep, passed out.

But then she heard voices, strange voices approaching. She heard the rise and fall of varied monotones coming nearer, and knew they were males, black males. New fears surfaced! Lying prostrate on the porch floor, she stared into the darkness and, to her horror, saw three figures, tall figures, swinging through the gate into the courtyard. Instantly she realized that unwittingly she had placed herself in a most precarious spot. The courtyard of the church rectory, situated on the corner of Sixth and Clay, was a favorite shortcut for many of the locals who regularly passed through it rather than walk all the way around the corner. And the shortcut led right beside the rectory's porch!

Her heart pounded and her breathing quickened. The voices grew louder, so loud she could actually make out their conversation had she had the state of mind to do so. Intense fear seized her, blocking out all but the sounds of the approaching men.

She pushed the horrid thoughts away, thoughts of racial hatred, racial fights and murders, not to mention…no she wouldn't think of that! They were coming right toward her—their heads level with the porch. All they needed to do was turn slightly, and they would see her. *Dear God, help me!*

SPRING OF LIFE

As tiny wildflowers push upward
through a stubborn sod
So a newborn leaves the womb
to face a world so hard

CHAPTER TWO

JOELLEN

SHE WAS BORN on a cold January day in 1944, the product of two very different worlds. Heavy rains poured, pounding the hospital's flat roof without mercy.

"What a day for giving birth!" exclaimed the head nurse, hurriedly entering the sterile delivery room. Young Meredith Leone Thaxton struggled to help the unborn child fighting its way down the unyielding birth canal.

"Not a good day to be born period!" Nurse Franklin added, peering over thick-rimmed glasses, her starched white cap perched atop a head of wiry, gray hair. "...what with war raging everywhere!"

Beads of perspiration formed across Meredith's smooth forehead as she pushed and strained, pushed and strained. Silently she wished the two nurses would just shut up. Good day or not, she had to get this baby out! And she was scared. She was scared to death! Suppose she couldn't get it out? Suppose she died giving birth? Then what? Who would take care of her little girl back home? Who would care for the baby if she died? She didn't want to die!

The door pushed open, and Dr. Randlett entered, rushed as usual but pleasant as always. "So what do we have here, Mrs. Thaxton? A baby boy or another little girl?" Meredith stared at the kind doctor with her large, frightened eyes,

11

unable to answer, as another pain rocketed through her trembling body.

The drum of incessant rain continued to beat upon the roof and hammer the large windowpanes as the long hours slowly ticked away. And unbeknown to anyone in the sterile delivery room, two celestial angels, God's secret agents, sat perched on the windowsill, totally invisible to all and apparently just a bit impatient. *"Should be just about now,"* Celeste said to Victor.

"You think so?"

"Just you watch," Celeste added.

Suddenly a shrill baby's cry pierced the delivery room. *Celeste eyed Victor. "I think our job's just begun!"*

Nurse Rawlings swept into the delivery room in her usual take-charge manner. "My goodness, who laid this baby over here by this cold window?" she scolded, "...rainy and damp as it is."

Gingerly leaning over the naked little newborn, the angels cautiously examined her. *"Doesn't look like much to me!"* *Victor analyzed.*

"She'll grow...don't let her fool you. Sometimes these little ones can be the worst, you know...keep us busy day and night!"

Feeling the cold draft seeping underneath the window, Nurse Rawlings grabbed the infant up. "Goodness...goodness! Wrap'er up in this here blanket."

LYNCHBURG LAY IN the Piedmont of Virginia. The Piedmont, a broad plain of gently rolling to hilly land stretching from the tip of New York to Alabama, set between the Appalachian Mountains and the Atlantic Coastal Plain, was where European settlers came. They saw the similarities to their own homeland and named it

12

"piemonte," which meant "foot of the mountain." Its rich land had yielded over half of the total production of tobacco in America, and Lynchburg was proud of its contribution. It rose up at the foot of the ancient, gently sloping Blue Ridge Mountains and, like most other towns, had not escaped the snares of war. It, too, had succumbed to its tentacles—rationing, blackouts, and daily bombardment of war news. It had also sent its men, young and not so young, off to combat. The world was at war...for the second time, and it raged on many fronts. Scores of young men, husbands and fathers, were gone, but Bennett Thaxton was still at home, and it was eating at him like a cancer.

He paced nervously back and forth in the small waiting room of Lynchburg General Hospital and stared at the closed doors. Why was it taking so long? Who said it was easier the second time around? It was just as hard as the first time! He thought of his little golden-haired daughter at home and wondered what she was doing. An older gentleman sat complacently in a corner, puffing on a large cigar, reading a crumpled newspaper. Bennett wondered how in the world he could be so relaxed. As if hearing his thoughts, the older gentleman shook out the paper and folded it up neatly and laid it on the table cluttered with magazines. He nonchalantly nodded at Bennett, propped his head against the chair and closed his eyes. Bennett frowned and reached for the paper to take his mind off what was going on behind those closed doors. The headlines jumped out at him.

"Reds Within 10 Miles Of Polish Border; 1,000 Tons Of Bombs Rained On Berlin." He squirmed in the straight-back chair as he continued to read... *"Army Makes New Landing In Pacific...General Douglas MacArthur landed veteran American*

13

Army troops, including elements of the 32nd Division, on the beach at Saidor on the north coast of New Guinea, without opposition yesterday to strike the third lightning blow in 18 days against the Japanese in the Southwest Pacific area...."

The familiar rush, the excitement, the magnetic pull that he had been struggling with for some time, was there again. He wondered what was going on with his older brother Otha right now, who was in the Navy Seabees. Bennett had always admired Otha, his gentle ways, his kidding, but now he really admired him.

Oh, well. He would soon be a father of two! How could he leave his sweet Meredith and two babies? But still the nagging thoughts were there. If they didn't win this horrible war, what kind of world would his children grow up in? And his grandchildren? And everyone was going...everyone but him, it seemed. He anxiously flipped through the newspaper. D. Moses & Co. advertised *Victory in 1944.* Guggenheimer's Department Store declared *Our New Year's Wish—Peace in '44.* Leggett's proclaimed *Start the New Year Right. Buy War Bonds.* He shook his head. It was everywhere—you couldn't get away from it.

He continued to read absently...*All Fronts Find Nazis In Retreat.* It sounded like things were going in the right direction, but when would it end? It had been going on for several years now, and he had watched his friends leave, and his best friend, then his brother. Everybody but him!

He glanced back at the closed doors.

Poor Meredith. She was awfully frightened on their drive to the hospital, gripping the dashboard until her knuckles turned white. But she had been scared to death for the last nine months, just like before. He couldn't understand it. Of course, he realized giving birth was no small matter, but other women seemed to take it in stride. His brothers'

14

wives certainly did, and his sisters, and from all accounts, he knew his mother had. He, being the youngest, was no witness to that fact, but she had had eight babies!

The double doors flew open and Nurse Rawlings appeared. "Mr. Thaxton, you have another daughter!" His face lit up in relief, glad it was over! He suppressed his disappointment, but there would be others, and the next one might be his son. Young Bennett Thaxton loved children and yearned for a houseful.

"Thank you, ma'am. Thank you. Can I go in now?"

Several days later they walked out of the hospital, down its wide front steps and out onto Hollins Street where Bennett had parked his Chevrolet sedan. Meredith glanced back at the imposing hospital with its large round columns and hoped it was the last time for her! The small bundle in her arms stirred and stretched, and she wondered what Janet would think of her.

Just two-and-a-half-years older, Janet curiously watched her parents enter the small cottage at the top of Creek Hill, located in Amherst County, just across the river from Lynchburg. She held onto Grandma Isabelle's hand and studied the wiggling bit of red flesh that her mother was holding and wondered why everyone was so interested in her, even Grandma Isabelle.

WINTRY WINDS HOWLED outside while the rocker rhythmically creaked and baby Joellen slept. Grandma Isabelle proudly snuggled the tiny bundle to her breast, another one—this would make six grandchildren for her now. She glanced out the window. The rains had stopped, bringing the raw, cold weather and terrific winds that buffeted the weatherboard cottage.

Meredith was pleased to have her mother with her for a few days. Not only because she needed her help, but she dearly loved her mother. She was all she'd ever had.

Grandma Isabelle slowly rocked the infant, listening to her soft, sucking sounds. She seemed hungry, and she wished Meredith hadn't decided to nurse her. She wondered if she had enough milk by the way the baby kept crying. It was taking its toll on Meredith, too; she could tell. She worried about Meredith, her youngest from her first marriage. There had been four children, and they had all seen hard times, but Meredith seemed to have been affected the most. She was a tender, delicate soul...and now with children of her own?

Meredith shuffled into the room, clutching the door knob and bracing herself. She looked extremely weak.

"Why don't you sit down, dear. You just had a baby!"

She eased onto the davenport.

"You know it takes awhile to get your strength back."

"I know." She remembered how long it had taken with Janet. "Guess what I read in the paper just now."

Isabelle knew she had been quiet for some time in the kitchen, engrossed with the newspaper. "What, dear?"

"There's going to be an immediate reclassification of all fathers...it's already been ordered."

"Well now, I wouldn't go to worrying about that. Even if Bennett were to be drafted, I reckon for sure he could get a deferment...because of his work at the hosiery mill. They need workers like him to stay home and produce the supplies they need. I just heard the other day about another fellow working at the mill that was probably going to apply for a deferment."

"I know...I know that...but Bennett's got something on his mind...."

16

"What do you mean?"

"Well…he's been awfully thoughtful lately, like in another world. I think maybe…maybe he *wants* to go."

The rocking chair stopped.

"It's happening all the time, you know," Meredith continued, "married men with children going. I just now read about one joining up that had *eleven* children…and he was inducted into the Army."

Her mother's mouth fell open.

Meredith kept talking, as much to herself as anyone. "I can understand Bennett thinking about it, though… everywhere you look, you see the war. It's all around us…in everybody's faces. Everything you read says *Back the Attack*. This ol' war has been going on so long now, and it's hard on a man…you know…left at home…especially a man like Bennett. People have a way of saying things that…well… you know…makes a man feel like he's not doing his part if he's still here…."

Her mother understood. It was true, but she certainly hoped Bennett would get a deferment.

"…especially since Otha left, he's been awfully moody."

"…and look what's happened to *him*!"

Her mother was referring to the fact that his older brother Otha had joined the Navy Seabees when he heard that they needed skilled carpenters to rebuild Pearl Harbor, and he wanted to do just that. He was a master carpenter, and they would need his skill in the rebuilding. Otha was in his late thirties and figured that he wouldn't be in any danger, and they certainly wouldn't send someone his age into battle. But he didn't go to Pearl Harbor. Instead he was shipped out to some of the deadliest fighting areas in the Pacific, where airstrips had been knocked out—temporary airstrips located in tangled jungles on islands that had not been fully taken. It was his job, along with his fellow Seabees, to rebuild these airstrips midst the hellish fighting and bombing. Bennett worried about his older brother. Otha was a mild, complacent sort of fellow, and he couldn't imagine how he was holding up under such conditions.

SIX MONTHS LATER, in the heat of summer, Bennett Thaxton was inducted into the Army, and Meredith and the children went to stay with his folks on their rolling country farm. Having grown up in the city, country life was a startling revelation to Meredith, especially on the Thaxton farm. They were hard-working, Scotch-Irish people, and strictly religious.

Sensitive Meredith watched her stoic mother-in-law deftly wring the chicken's head off without a thought and drop it into a ready pot of boiling water. She watched her pluck its feathers out one by one, exposing its naked white body. She cringed, turned her head, and fought against the sickening fowl odor, feeling deathly nauseous. They hadn't been able to afford chicken very often on Grace Street, but she just as soon not eat any as to have to get it this way!

She struggled to keep up with the elder Mrs. Thaxton, cooking on the large wood stove, which heated up the kitchen and the rest of the house unmercifully on those long, hot summer days. She swept and scrubbed the two-story house, and vigorously washed the family's clothes on the scrubboard outside, the strong lye soap burning her tender hands. She also helped to make the awful raw soap, stirring and boiling it over the steaming hot fire adjacent to the back porch.

Still Meredith never felt like she quite measured up to her mother-in-law's expectations. Maybe it was a look out of the corner of her eye or the way she seemed frustrated at times. Not that Mrs. Thaxton meant any harm. She was a good woman, a caring woman, but she wasn't used to someone like Meredith either, someone who would rather read a book or go to a theater than scrub and clean and cook. Why, those movies were the devil's work, causing folk to be downright lazy and spending good time looking at foolishness instead of doing what they oughta be doing! She prided herself in efficiently running her household, working from daybreak till sundown, and she fully expected others to do the same. Married at the tender age of sixteen, she was well used to the demands of a large family and the never-ending tasks of a working farm.

But the theater is what young Meredith longed for the most. She had grown up in them, considered them her haven, while her mother trudged to work every day, leaving her to fend for herself. She would cheerfully skip down the familiar cobblestone streets, or skate down the rough sidewalks to one of several matinees always playing, pay her dime and sit through several times. She figured she got her money's worth that way, and besides it filled the long hours before her mother would return home. That's what she lived for—her mother coming home from work and the theaters. Whether it was the new Paramount with its elite art-deco interior, or the older Trenton or Isis, she was happy and content hunkered down in the comforting darkness with those tantalizing shafts of hazy, silver light mysteriously shooting over her head. And the big screen up front! It had transported her to far away places, far from the small town of Lynchburg.

Young Meredith's head was crammed full of Hollywood names, names of plays and songs, and glamorous movie stars, and all this she yearned for as she grappled with the hardships of farm life.

Winter came early in the year of 1944, particularly in the Virginia countryside. It was the middle of November, and Meredith stretched to pin the heavy work clothes on the long, double clothesline. Roughly jabbing down the wooden pins, she braced against the fierce wind that whipped the cold, wet clothes around her ninety-eight pounds, entangling her thick dark hair in its raw dampness. The wet clothes immediately succumbed to its harshness and stiffened to its touch. At last she was finished. Her hands red and stinging, she hurried back to the house as Papa Thaxton's overalls and shirts, already frozen stiff, stretched out as if he were in them. Glancing back, she stifled a laugh and raced to the porch. She could hardly wait to get back inside, to the hot wood stove, to the sweet smell of dinner cooking, but Mrs. Thaxton met her at the door and thrust another tub of wet clothes at her. Her face fell.

BY EARLY 1945, the Allies had closed in on Japan, largely due to superiority at sea and in the air. Japan had already lost vast amounts of its empire and the majority of its aircraft and cargo ships. Most of its warships were gone, too. American B-29 bombers were hammering its industrial base, and American submarines were fast sinking crucial supplies that were headed to Japan. Maj. Gen. Curtis E. LeMay had taken over command of the air war against Japan in January and had beefed up the raids and began flying in low at nighttime. They had also begun dropping incendiary bombs, setting the Japanese cities afire. Then a massive raid in March destroyed the heart of Tokyo, but its fierce leaders wouldn't give up.

It was decided that more bases were necessary in order to increase the bombing against their determined resistance. The Allies selected Iwo Jima and Okinawa, two Japanese islands, for these much needed bases, and American Marines began landing on Iwo Jima in February, but it was slow going. The Japanese hung on desperately until the middle of March. In the end, approximately twenty-five thousand Marines were killed or wounded.

The next stop for the Allies was Okinawa, the largest and most important island of the Ryukyu Islands, about 350 miles from Japan, an easy flying distance. The island was mountainous, and jungle covered much of it to the north. Low, rocky hills made up the southern portion, where most of its people lived in the subtropical climate. Allied troops began to pour onto its shores the beginning of April, and Bennett Thaxton was one of them.

Meredith couldn't sleep at night. What was happening to Bennett? Would he come home to her? Would she be left a widow like so many others to raise her two little girls alone? She was afraid to voice her fears, afraid they might come true. Instead she carried them heavy on her heart as she strove to get through the long days tending to her young daughters. They had left the Thaxton farm and moved in with Bennett's older sister Anna and her family. Though she was exceedingly pleased to get away from the farm, she struggled to please Anna and not be too much of a burden on her; however, Anna seemed perfectly happy having them there, especially the children. Like Bennett, Anna loved children and wanted to tend to the baby all the time, which certainly made life a lot easier, but there was something about her in-laws that caused Meredith to feel uncomfortable. Anna must be like Mama Thaxton, she thought, able to work circles around her. She wished she could stay with her own mother, but there was no room in their tiny house.

Joellen, still bald but plump now with winsome dimples, had celebrated her one-year birthday without her father, but she wasn't aware of it. She didn't even remember having a father, but three-year-old golden-haired Janet did and she missed him terribly.

THE WAR CONTINUED on into the summer, and loneliness and anxiety were taking their toll on Meredith. She tossed and turned during the hot, still night, her cotton gown damp and sticking to her. Janet was pressed up against her, sound asleep, her warm body heat making her even hotter. The upstairs bedroom had heated up like an oven during the day, and it still hadn't cooled off. She was downright miserable. She tumbled out and pushed the small castiron bed over to the open window, hoping for a breath of air. The baby stirred and whimpered in her crib. Quietly, she crept back to bed. She wished it was winter. She wished Bennett would hurry and come home. When would it all end?

The answer hung in the pregnant summer air.

The United States, Britain, and China had issued a statement threatening to destroy Japan if it didn't surrender. In spite of the announcement, Japan resisted and kept on fighting. Then on the sixth day of August, an American B-29 bomber by the name of *Enola Gay* dropped the first atomic bomb on the city of Hiroshima, killing somewhere between seventy thousand and one hundred thousand people. Still the Japanese leaders would not respond, and a second bomb, a larger bomb, was dropped on Nagasaki on August the ninth, killing approximately forty thousand more people.

On the fourteenth of August, Japan agreed to end the war.

The news broke with jubilant activity far and wide. The long war was finally over! People couldn't believe it—so long they had lived under its hideous cloud. Meredith could hardly contain her excitement. Bennett was coming home! But soon she found out that he wouldn't be home quite yet, not for a while anyway. At least he was out of danger. He had survived the Okinawa hell where approximately fifty thousand Allies lost their lives and roughly one hundred and ten thousand Japanese, including many civilians who chose to commit suicide rather than surrender. It was a ghastly bloodbath.

Bennett was shipped out to Korea for the duration of his enlistment, and Meredith patiently mustered her strength for the long months ahead, another lonely Christmas and New Year. Finally in the frigid month of February, he came back, bringing with him shrapnel in one leg that would irritate him for the rest of his life, but he counted it a small price to pay to be back home.

Nine months later, Meredith gave birth to the son Bennett had dreamed of midst the ravages of war, and they named him Daniel. Papa Thaxton and Bennett's older brothers helped him build a small four-room bungalow across from the family farm for his growing family. Bennett was happier than ever as he squatted down and brushed the milky whitewash on the new picket fence. The war was over, leaving him a strong sense of pride having fought in it. No one could say he hadn't done his part, no one could say he didn't serve his country!

He gazed down into the face of his infant son. One day when his children were older and the wretched war was history, they would be proud of him. And his grandchildren…he grinned to himself. They would be proud of him, too.

Though the war was over in reality, it still hung on in Bennett's subconscious, periodically surfacing in hideous *dreams,* nightmares that swept him back to Okinawa, to the gruesome pictures he struggled to erase, sights he fought to forget. When would they stop? Such was the Friday night in the spring after his return. Meredith awakened to a loud commotion outside. It was the *chickens.* Something must be in the chicken house!

She grabbed her robe and throwing it on, wondered where Bennett was. His spot was empty. Janet and Joellen were bawling in the next room. They must have heard the ruckus, too. "It's okay…everything's all right!" she called out while racing to the door that was standing ajar to the dark night. Her fears increased. Where was Bennett? Why was the door open? The sounds from the chicken house grew louder, shrill cries and wings flapping and fluttering. The chickens were going crazy!

She dashed outside and couldn't believe her eyes. In the moon-lit night, a dark silhouette was swinging a large stick at the terrified chickens that darted this way and that, bouncing off the chicken wire and chaotically colliding with one another. It was Bennett. In his underwear, he ranted and raved, flailing the stick at the frightened chickens.

"I'll kill you Japs…you hear that…I'll kill you…no more Japs! I'll kill you, you hear! You won't kill us anymore…not my friends…not my…."

"Bennett…Bennett…" She ran to him. "No…no… Bennett…stop…stop!"

He turned to her in confusion. In the slight moonlight, she looked into a stranger's eyes and shuddered.

Hesitantly, she stood there.

He stared down at the stick hanging limp in his hand and at the chickens beginning to settle down. When he looked back up at her, it was Bennett. And she realized that he had been asleep, walking in his sleep, fighting in his sleep! He reached for her, and they clung desperately to one another, trembling in the moonlight midst white chicken feathers floating about.

THE SEASONS PASSED into years, and Bennett Thaxton's nightmares became less frequent, and his children grew. They enjoyed their little home that faced Papa Thaxton's cornfield, tall with rustling stalks and fat ears of corn. Hours were spent hiding between its long rows, intoxicated with childish privacy, lost in its imaginary world. And in the fall when it waned, draped with colorful morning glories, they basked in its beauty of blue and white, beaded with the glistening early morning dew.

And when springtime flooded the Virginia hills again, with its warm south winds, rustling the deciduous forest and its unfurled, pea-green leaves, the child Joellen sat at the edge of the woods smoothing the spongy green moss beneath her. She had had her fourth birthday, and her senses were keen now, alive to the myriad sights, sounds and smells of the world around her. She inhaled the fresh air and felt the invisible wind blowing her wispy, baby-fine hair into her eyes.

She sat spellbound as fragile blue fairies danced about her, masses of them, delicate bluets waving in the gentle spring breezes. Their pale blue faces, stamped with minute yellow hearts, simultaneously swayed, hundreds of them, thousands of them. She gingerly ran her pudgy palm across them, careful not to break them, and looked around for the wind. She could feel it. Where was it? Where was the wind that caused the tiny bluets to sway?

Celeste smiled at Victor.

CHAPTER THREE

PRESENT

JOELLEN'S ADRENALINE WAS flowing with a heightened sense of expectation, as she wheeled her SUV around the trying curves leading up the steep mountain. It was morning. There was something about morning that set it apart from the rest of the day, purity, freshness, anticipation, and hope.

Her creative juices were surging, a sense of suspense, lifting her higher and higher, beyond earth's daily troubles, challenges, and concerns. Unable to contain the magic mood, she smiled visibly as she made her way up to the Peaks of Otter to work on her new book. The National Park Service was allowing her to peruse their archived files, stacks of them, drawers full, packed together. She couldn't wait! This way she could place her story in the authentic settings she desired. She loved fiction, the art of creating, but people often had the wrong idea of fiction, thinking it all pretend, an imaginary world when, in fact, it was simply truth rearranged, a little bit here, a little bit there, all intertwined to make up the whole. But at the same time, she was fascinated with history and had discovered that by subtly weaving the two together, she could enjoy both. She hoped others would, as well, and she firmly believed that history should be remembered and preserved.

Birds fluttered in lush treetops as she rounded curve after curve, a deer timidly stood in the side brush innocently watching her pass, and a squirrel zigzagged across the mountain road. She glanced up into the clear blue morning sky above the treetops. No matter that she was pushing sixty—she felt sixteen! And why not? Life was good, and all her children were well and doing okay, also her grandchildren. Everybody was doing okay...well, almost everybody. Thoughts of her mother clouded her world again, but she must not let that happen. Why, she had the whole day to devote to her writing, and it was still early.

Normally at this time she would be firmly situated behind her office desk, her door shutting out the magnificent morning, shutting out the early songs of birds, shutting out the fresh air and shimmering dew, shutting out the warm morning sun. She recalled that first day after she left the working world. She had opened the front door and walked outside. The grass was still wet with dew, and the purity of morning air had embraced her. It was a revelation.

Why, she had missed all her mornings!

ENTERING BLUE RIDGE PARKWAY

The familiar sign welcomed her, and the SUV climbed past the dense forested campground that looped around the mountainside to the left, where they often camped. Topping the mountain road, the sprawling valley with its Park Service buildings came into sight: the Visitor Center and Restaurant and Lodge muted in soft morning clouds. A misty fog rose steadily from Abbot Lake. The miniature island, with its thick stand of trees and brush, was almost invisible in the midst of it. She pulled into a parking space in front of the visitor center and shut off the engine. There was hardly anyone there but the workers. A little too early for most visitors, just the way she liked it. Glancing at her watch, she realized, in fact, that the visitor center hadn't opened yet. Good, she would take her hike first.

The bracing mountain air welcomed her as she started down the leaf-strewn path that led from the visitor center across a slight wooden bridge and over to the trails. The narrow path paralleled the Blue Ridge Parkway for a ways, though mostly hidden from sight by the lush fall foliage, providing a unique sense of privacy. The tapering path glowed in the early morning sunlight, wet from the previous evening's shower, and millions of raindrops glistened atop the abundant foliage. Fine, silky webs crisscrossed her path, and she brushed them aside, making her way gingerly down the forest trail. Birds rustled in the thicket that sandwiched the trail, busily seeking their breakfast.

She approached the crossroads of the trail: to the right would take her underneath the Parkway, a low dark tunnel over one of the many creeks that wound beneath it, and to her left were the beginnings of two lengthy trails. Suddenly she stopped in her tracks!

She was immersed in an almost ethereal world.

Hazy morning fog hung low and heavy, a heavenly mist enveloped the now widened pathway, but it was pierced by bright sunrays in long, rainbow shafts. Towering oak trees and cucumber magnolia trees hugged it, sheltering it with a canopy of dripping leafy foliage. It was surreal. The produced effect was likened to what Joellen had always imagined one's last walk might resemble. She shook herself for reality and glanced at her watch—better get back to business.

Loaded down with the thick, bulky files from the Park Service Archives, she settled beneath a spreading oak behind the visitor center and began to read page after page of documentaries, accounts told by those now gone on, those who had lived and loved and worked and died in the aged mountains. She read their accounts with tears and laughter, and was reminded that everybody has a story, some seemingly more interesting than others, some happier, some sadder, but everybody has a story. She sighed…even her mother. Once again, those large doe-like eyes stared at her, and last Sunday was fresh in her mind.

She had decided to spend Sunday morning with her at the nursing home instead of going to church. Somehow, she figured God would approve. She had stuck the *Smoky Mountain Hymns* tape into the TV that hung from the ceiling, and the soothing sounds of a mandolin, dulcimer, and banjo pleasantly filled the small room. Her mother's swollen fingers began to gently tap the white sheet that covered her, and she slowly moved her head with the music. Then with closed eyes, she began to lip sing…

Some glad morning when this life is o'er
I'll fly away
To a home on God's celestial shore,
I'll fly away.

Suddenly Joellen felt sad, not for the memory of that Sunday morning, for that was a happy memory, one that she would cherish, glad that she'd taken the time to go. The sadness was for her mother's life, and again she wondered why. Why did some people have such heartbreaking lives? She figured there were things she would never understand in this life, but couldn't help but wonder why there were those born into a life of comfort and security while others, like her mother, were born into just the opposite. Fatherless at a young age, Meredith had been forced into a life of dearth and insecurity. Her father had been institutionalized at Western State Hospital when she was barely six years old, and he remained there until he died an old man. Meredith was raised by her mother, she and her three older siblings. It had been a hard life for all of them, leaving permanent scars.

Joellen had grown up hearing the stories. Her Grandma Isabelle had worked at a bakery to support them all, the Lynchburg Steam Bakery. She had heard how they wouldn't have survived if it hadn't been for the generosity and charity of the graceful old First Baptist Church on Court Street where Meredith and her mother attended. She had heard the stories of how Meredith and her brother followed the railroad tracks down by the James River to pick up the fallen coal for their stove in frigid, icy weather.

Perhaps this was enough to rob her mother of future happiness, dragging her down to the depths of depression. But was there more?

There were times when her mother seemed happy, times when she told little jokes or mimicked people, not in a malicious way, but in a funny, jovial sense. She had a real knack for impersonation, a talent, in fact. Having lived around a number of people with varying ethnic backgrounds, she had deftly picked up their particular accents and lingo, and could at any moment lapse into their unique style of speech, a real treat for the children. And sometimes she sang when she was happy, and she knew all the words to most of the popular songs.

Sitting under the shady oak tree, Joellen could hear the old, familiar tune and her mother's soft voice...

How much is That Doggie In The Window?
The one with the waggely tail;

31

How much is That Doggie In The Window?
I do hope that doggie's for sale...

Forgetting her research, she settled back to the soothing resonance of the rustling autumn breeze and drifted back to her childhood.

1953

SHE PICKED UP the large round *I like Ike* pin and spun it across the small wooden kitchen table with its peeling white paint. Joellen didn't know much about Ike, but she knew he made her folks happy.

Dwight D. Eisenhower, riding on the wave of his enormous popularity from his significant and successful role in World War II, had been inaugurated as thirty-fourth president of the United States. At first he had refused to run for president, arguing that it was necessary and wise for professional soldiers to abstain from seeking high political office. But large groups sprang up all over the country called IKE clubs. They wanted him as president! Finally he decided that a soldier's duty might also include service in the White House, and his campaign got off to a slow start. He particularly didn't care for all the reporters, especially when they focused on his wide grin instead of his extensive military experience.

Soon he jumped in, however; and just before the election he pledged, "I shall go to Korea" to help end the war, the war which had begun in 1950 and was as bloody a war as any. He received almost thirty-four million popular votes, 55 percent of the ballots and went to the White House as the first Republican president in twenty years. Bennett was among the happy voters. Although a strong

Democrat like the rest of the Thaxton family, he had voted for Ike, holding him in high esteem as did most veterans. They especially appreciated his role in Operation Overlord, as supreme commander of the Allied Expeditionary Force, which had led the invasion on Normandy, the turning point of World War II.

Life seemed good to nine-year-old Joellen. She was hardly aware of the Korean War that was being brutally fought overseas—there was nobody really close to her in the war. She also didn't realize that they were considered poor by some because most everyone she knew was the same, except for her best friend and cousin, Betsy Jeanne. She listened to the static song emanating from the little radio on top of the ice box. *I love Paris in the springtime*....

Life seemed good, that is, to everybody but her mama. Ever since she had gotten big and pregnant, her mother didn't seem happy, and every two weeks she had to go to Charlottesville to the hospital. Once she had stayed for two whole weeks. Her daddy said it was her nerves, and so did Aunt Anna.

Her mother sat at the table across from her, reading the newspaper. *From Here to Eternity* was playing in the theaters across the country, and Meredith yearned to be a girl again, aimlessly spending the day in the theater, watching all those Laurel and Hardy movies or the Tarzan shows with Maureen O'Sullivan and Johnny Weissmuller. She had adored them, and also Mary Pickford and Douglas Fairbanks. She had loved the old silent movies, too. And she missed seeing all the other stars—Myrna Loy, William Powell, Leslie Howard, Claudette Colbert, Clark Gable, Betty Davis, Mickey Rooney, and Jimmy Stewart and so many others. She wistfully followed their stardoms in the paper, escaping the drudgery of housekeeping, which she couldn't keep up anyway, and away from the constant bickering between the children, away from the dismal gray of winter.

She flipped the page over, and the new queen of England stared out at her, Queen Elizabeth II. Her father, King George VI, had died early the previous year, and Elizabeth Alexandra Mary was suddenly thrust onto the throne at the tender age of twenty-five. What would it be like to be queen? Meredith fantasized and waddled over to the hot wood stove for the kettle of water to wash the stack of dirty dishes piled high in the sink. She hated having to heat water all day long. She didn't miss the crowded city, but she did miss the conveniences and again wondered why the Thaxtons didn't. Grandma Thaxton didn't seem to mind any kind of difficult task or trouble. Leaning her bulging stomach against the hard porcelain kitchen sink, she marveled at her strong mother-in-law's capacity for hard work. *Strong constitution,* she thought to herself, while pouring the hot water into the basin. That's what it is. I guess I just married into the wrong family!

She glanced over her shoulder at Joellen, still spinning the Ike pen around on the table, the irritating sound grating on her nerves. "Joellen, why don't you go into the bedroom and play."

She shoved the pen aside and idled into the next room, the bedroom she shared with Janet, and peered under the sagging double bed, looking for her turtle. She pulled the heavy piece of iron out from under it, sliding it on the worn linoleum. Actually it was a foot off an old discarded stove, burned and rusty, salvaged from the trash pile out back, but imaginatively her turtle. She rubbed its head and slid it back under the bed alongside her grandmother's footstone.

Grandma Thaxton had given them her footstone for safe-keeping, but Joellen didn't know how it had ended up under *her* bed! Probably because they were cramped for space, of that she was well aware. That's why Daniel slept on the couch in the living room, and she didn't know where they were gonna put the new baby!

She grabbed her coat off the nail behind the door and headed outside.

"Where you going now?" Meredith asked.

"Outside."

"But it's cold outside."

She pulled open the front door. "I've got my coat on."

Meredith shook her head and tried to scrub the pork chop grease off the iron skillet. Already the hot water was lukewarm, and the grease held stubbornly. Where was Janet? Janet always helped her. Probably still over at Grandma Thaxton's. Thank goodness Bennett had taken Daniel with him to the ice factory. He and Joellen had been in and out, in and out all morning, fretting and squabbling until she had taken the switch to both of them. Now Joellen was pouting.

Joellen caught her breath at the onslaught of the bitter wintry air and struggled to button the top button of her coat. Heading around the side of the house and down the sloping hill to the back yard, she pulled open the heavy, creaking door to the basement, her eyes slowly adjusting to the dim interior. Dark and gloomy, the sunless cellar had a couple inches of muddy water standing on the red dirt floor from the last rain. Now it was partially frozen. The basement had been half dug out, one of those projects her father had started. Busy working two jobs and taking care of his growing family, Bennett Thaxton was not one to worry about muddy basements and fences needing white-wash and such. Joellen stepped onto the two by six wooden plank that lay atop the water and carefully marched across it, delicately balancing herself. She stared down at the crystallized muddy water that formed around the long plank, and tried not to fall off.

Maybe her mother would bake some of that tapioca pudding she loved. She could see it now, its bubbly surface resembling that of poison oak covering her arms in the summertime. She could smell it, too, and her mouth began to water. But she doubted it. Her mother hadn't been baking much since she'd returned from the hospital. Instead, she spent a lot of time in bed with the door shut. It must be her nerves, she thought.

She paused on the plank, and then gingerly stepped over to the next one that took her to her own private world. She reached in the corner behind the earthen jar on the rough hewn shelf and pulled out a large key, then climbed up on the tall metal stool that her daddy had given her. It had been given to him, most likely, but it was just the right height to reach her "secret compartment." That's what she liked to call it. Actually, it was just a large board that her daddy had hinged onto the bottom shelf and locked onto the top shelf. The shelving was nailed onto the rough cinderblock wall, but it made a perfect place for Joellen to keep her valuables. Although Bennett Thaxton was not one for worrying much about whitewash or finished basements, people were high on his list, and his family held the top spots. He struggled to make them happy and provide their needs, even such whims of his very private young daughter.

She turned the key in the large padlock, *and Victor grinned at Celeste.*

The heavy door fell down, revealing her "other family." The open side of a tin dollhouse gaped at her, sparsely furnished with eight or ten pieces of plastic furniture scattered within, a miniature pink bed and playpen, and a white table and chairs. However, it wasn't the dollhouse or its furniture that beckoned Joellen, and it didn't bother her that she had no dolls for it. She much preferred her own diminutive paper people that she had painstakingly drawn and cut out. They afforded far more flexibility, standing when she leaned them against something, stretching out on the bed, taking turns, of course. They could even sit on kitchen chairs when folded straight across the middle of their flat abdomens. But it wasn't even the tiny paper people that intrigued Joellen enough to come down to the dark, cold basement day after day.

It was the *story.*

The story was in her head, bursting to come out, pressed in between her school studies, her concern for her mother, and her wonder of life. Daily she played it out through her myriad paper people that steadily grew to more than twenty-five: boys, girls, babies, mothers, fathers, grandparents, and friends.

An hour passed and she emerged from her make-believe world, from the dark basement and pulled open the door, squinting in the bright sunlight. That should make her mother happy. The sun was shining! She should tell her, but remembered the switching, and it wasn't her fault either. It was Daniel's. She wandered over to knock on her grandmother's door instead. Maybe her grandmother was making some peanut butter candy.

"Come on in, child," she called out. "Janet just left."

Joellen stepped into the small house trailer that sat be-side their house. Once Papa had died, Grandma Thaxton had given up the homeplace and bought the second-hand trailer, immediately making it her home, warm and cozy. She glanced around at her grandma's open sewing box with a rainbow of embroidery thread streaming out of it. No cookies today! She flopped down on the small couch.

"Lookin' for somethin' to do?" her grandma asked, while carefully stitching a pillowcase.

She nodded, unable to fool her.

"Well, your picture's yonder in the drawer. How 'bout you doin' some paintin' on it?" Before she could answer, Grandma Thaxton reached around her, fetched it out of the drawer and slapped it down in front of her. Joellen reluctantly sat down and spread out the miniature plastic containers, grabbed a tiny brush and began to stir the hard-ened paint.

"Don't reckon you have too much to do before you'll be finished," her grandma coaxed.

Joellen didn't mind painting the picture, but it was so mechanical. The color-coded canvas of a lone bird dog was only half-done, no matter what Grandma said. She dipped the brush into the thick, oozing brown paint and began tediously filling in the teeny numbered spaces. She was quickly bored, but determined to finish it, or rather Grandma was determined for her.

"Aunt Anna's got your home permanent ready...said she's gonna give it to you the next time you go down there."

Joellen nodded. She certainly wasn't in the mood for that!

"What've you been doin' today?"

"Oh, nothing much." No use telling her about the switchin', and for sure she couldn't tell her about the story down in the basement.

"Playing with that stove turtle, I bet," Grandma chuckled, reaching for more embroidery thread.

"Some."

"Still keepin' it under your bed, I s'pose."

Joellen nodded.

"You still got my footstone under there, don't you?"

Joellen nodded again a bit impatiently. At least once a week she asked her the same question.

"That's good. I reckon I might need it one day."

WINTER WORE ON, and Meredith was lost in a shadowy world of darkness and anxiety, a world that she was unable to cope with more and more. The doctors didn't know why. She was a mystery to them. They concluded that most likely her problems stemmed from her very early years. Perhaps there were skeletons hidden in her subconscious unable to be freed, but able to torment her in subtle ways. She lay in her darkened bedroom in the middle of the day with drawn shades, unable to coax herself to get up.

Life was just too much.

She was sad, everything was sad. There were too many worries, too many problems. The children needed this and the children needed that, and now she was going to have another one! Not that Meredith didn't love her children, she did, but life was simply too heavy for her, heavy like the baby she was carrying.

The third day of April Meredith gave birth to another son, and they named him Brian. Bennett was beside himself—two sons! Such a proud father, he felt like strutting all the way to the fertilizer mill. If only Meredith could be happy, then he would be the happiest fellow in all of Virginia!

Spring gave way to summer, and Joellen watched the iceman pull up out front and walk around to the back of his black panel truck, open the doors and heave out a huge chunk of ice with his heavy iron tongs. She sat on the sidewalk and watched him lumber across the yard, panting and making funny wheezing noises as he carried it to the house. She watched the dripping ice leave a trail of water spots on the sidewalk, and she inched along behind him, poking her finger in each cold wet spot before it evaporated beneath the hot sun rays. She watched a big red ant shoot out from the dusty dry grass edging the sidewalk toward one of the water spots, and remembered her and Betsy Jeanne stomping a whole pile of them awhile back, trying to make the sun shine. But they wouldn't dare stomp a black one! No way, then it would rain even more—at least that's what Grandma Thaxton said. Her daddy said it was so dry now, maybe they should stomp a few, but she figured it was just another old wives' tale because it never did stop raining that day.

Betsy Jeanne appeared out of nowhere, and they took off to the woods, coming up on their uncle's hog pen. Joellen leaned over the rough rail fence and poked one of the big fat hogs with a long stick. He grunted and wallowed in the oozing muddy pen, relishing the attention. Two equally whopping hogs sidled up to the fence, grunting and seeking her favors. She breathed in the stinking odor of the foul pig pen, and laughed. Betsy Jeanne grabbed another long stick and began to scratch one's back. It squealed in delight, and she giggled and scratched that much harder. "Want to go with us riding after lunch?"

"Where to?"

Betsy Jeanne shrugged. "Don't know, but Mama said to ask you if you want to come." Joellen considered her options, hanging out at the pig pen or going home. "Yeah, I'll go." She enjoyed riding in Betsy Jeanne's large new Oldsmobile. Her father traded often, keeping nice vehicles, and they always started! She could count on it, not like her daddy's old Chevrolet that spit and sputtered and cut off, sometimes to restart and sometimes not.

Joellen and Betsy Jeanne curled up on the sizeable back seat, staring out the windows as the Oldsmobile rolled down Creek Hill. Then Joellen pulled out a small tablet and pencil, and Betsy Jeanne watched.

"Whatcha writing?"

"Oh nothing."

Betsy Jeanne shrugged. She was always scribbling something.

After riding for a while, they pulled up in a generous parking lot adjacent to a mammoth redbrick building. Joellen leaned out the window and read the fresh new sign. *E. C. Glass High School.*

She stared blankly at Betsy Jeanne.

"Why're we stopping here?" Betsy Jeanne asked.

"We just want to see it, that's all," her mother replied. "This is Lynchburg's brand new high school, and everyone's talking about it. We thought you girls might enjoy seeing it, too." They frowned at one another. The new high school was situated on a prominent corner, Memorial Avenue and Langhorne Road, two of Lynchburg's significant streets. They climbed out and strolled across the sprawling, grassy lawn and up the wide steps, dazzled by shiny, new floors, strong smelling paint, windows galore

41

and a huge cafeteria. It was something to see! Slowly, they shuffled along with the large crowd of pleased onlookers, and then sat down at one of the long narrow tables in the cafeteria. Betsy Jeanne's parents chatted with other guests while they waited impatiently. But Joellen couldn't imagine going to such a school! It was far too intimidating, and she was suddenly glad for her little two-room school house under the tall oaks on Wright Shop Road. Of course, this would be her last year at Oak Grove School. It only housed the first four grades, and she was well aware that next year she would have to transfer to the big school—Madison Heights School. It was big enough, but this one!

When they pulled out of the parking lot, she stared back at the impressive school and wondered whether or not to tell her mother about it. Of course, she probably already knew. Even though she was sick, nothing seemed to escape her. Most likely because she read the papers, Joellen thought to herself. She knew her mother had attended the old E. C. Glass High School and decided not to mention the visit and how shiny and new everything looked, and how big and pretty. No, she wouldn't mention it.

CHAPTER FOUR

1956

THREE YEARS LATER, Joellen was growing up—turning twelve years old, a pivotal age for boys and girls. Her thoughts wouldn't take form, vacillating, darting around. Some days they half-heartedly took the form of play, spending long, summer days in the forest and pastures, climbing trees, wading creeks, catching tadpoles and crawfish, or playing with her paper people in the basement with her day-to-day saga. But then there were days when her thoughts exploded, creating within her a strange restlessness like warm summer breezes that blew through the forests. She had no way of knowing that this was the time that occurs in everyone's life—when suddenly all seems different, though everything around her seemed the same—quiet and peaceful.

And it was so. The devastating ills of the Great Depression in the thirties and the wretched war of the forties ultimately created a backdrop in America for the quiet fifties. It was a decade of restoration, relaxation, and happiness for the most part. The exception, of course, being the Korean War, and though it was one of the worst wars in history, it did end three years later on July 27, 1953.

Thereafter, in stark contrast to what had been, the fifties were gentle, soothing, quiet, and comforting. Even the president was comforting. Everybody liked Ike! Well, almost everybody. A disgruntled Taft man did express, "It looks like he's pretty much for home, mother, and heaven." Who could fight that? He definitely embodied the mood of the times.

To my clandestine friend, Joellen wrote in her little Blue Horse composition book, having just discovered a new word. Of course, the friend was fictitious like her elongated stories down in the basement. But this conjured-up friend was one she could confide in, one that only she knew about. She didn't have, nor did she want, a pen pal like some of the kids at school. No, she preferred her own private pen pal, one that could never tell her thoughts or ideas.

I'm totally confused today, and I just don't know what to do. First I thought I would go down to the basement, but it's so dark and damp down there...and so nice and sunny outside...and besides, paper dolls are for children! And I don't know where Betsy Jeanne is. She's usually here by now.

There's a real cute boy in my class, and I think I'm in love! Don't tell anybody, and you'll be my angel!

Victor beamed. "She's writing me a letter!"
"Not you, Victor. She doesn't know you exist."

Joellen was seeing things through a dissimilar lens, like the limp piece of flexible colored plastic that they stuck over the television screen to make it different colors, blue, green, red, or yellow, depending on which color of plastic they slapped onto the screen. They were so excited when they received it from the mail-order company, bragging that now they had color television, but soon the novelty wore off as they tired of seeing everything in one color. It might as well be black and white!

The forests and pastures had also lost their spell; not as alluring as before, they were receding into the background. Instead she wondered about the big world that seemed far more intriguing. The second-hand television set that sat on a rickety table in the living room alluded to such as it filled the small room with static whenever it was switched on. Its black tube would explode into snow, electric vibrating snow...until miraculously there was a picture...a vague picture, but definitely a picture, and a picture of things not on Thaxton's Lane, nor in Madison Heights, or even in Virginia, for that matter.

The happy fifties were magic now!

Young people everywhere were spellbound. Joellen and her siblings were elated that now they didn't have to walk all the way down Thaxton's Lane to their cousins' house to watch *The Howdy Doody Show* with Clarabell and his bicycle horn. Doodyville, with all its puppets and Peanut Gallery of children, was now in their house! No more congregating with all the other neighborhood kids, fighting for the best seat.

JOELLEN SECRETLY HID her little blue book beneath her underclothes in the second drawer of the small chest she and Janet shared, and joined her siblings in front of the television set. She was fascinated to actually see the famous cowboys race across the fuzzy screen instead of just hearing them emanate from the small radio atop the icebox. It was pure joy usually, but today there were those mixed-up feelings. She yanked off her coonskin and turned to the trash can to spit out the hot ball. Just too hot! And that was silly, too! Whoever heard of *hot balls*? Just because everybody else was sucking on them didn't mean she had to!

She headed outside. It was a beautiful Saturday morning, and her adrenaline was pumping. She had to do something! Childhood's pure illusion was fast vanishing. The fantasy to sink deep within its cozy folds and crevices didn't seem real anymore. She was reaching out, stepping onto the hard concrete of adult life. It was cold, alien, unfriendly, and all too soon she would face its sobering reality. But today the slight young girl would hold onto the illusion, a link to happiness before the world crowded in.

She rounded the corner of the house, skipping down the rocky hillside, past her daddy's beehives with swarms of honeybees buzzing in the warm morning sun. She thought of the sticky, sweet honeycomb that she loved to chew on until all the sweetness disappeared, causing it to become hard and crunchy. Skipping on past the trash pile where her father burned the family refuse, where she had found her turtle, having endured the fiery flames, she passed by the john with its door ajar and on down to the woods. Soaring oaks and poplars pressed in against one another in their race toward the coveted sun, and once in the midst of them, she selected a tall, straight poplar and shinnied up until she reached the first limb.

Joellen's strength was also her weakness, her hard-headedness, her father claimed. Often he had warned her of the poplars. But higher and higher she climbed, rising up toward the wide, blue sky, basking in the bliss of freedom. She gazed out over the smaller treetops, gloating over them, inhaling the fresh morning air and wishing she could stay up there forever. She thought about life, her future, and wondered what it would be. A blank page, and the mystery and anticipation intrigued her.

She glanced back up the hill at their small chimney and red roof jutting just above the tree line. Already she was noticing and feeling the embarrassment of their humble lifestyle compared to some around her. Why couldn't they have a bathroom like Betsy Jeanne? And hot water? She marveled at the hot water that gushed out of Betsy Jeanne's bathroom spigot when she turned the crystal knob imprinted with the big letter "H." And why couldn't she buy hot plate lunches at school like her friends instead of the same old sack lunch every day? Especially that mouth-watering cornbread and steaming meatloaf served on Wednesdays. And she hated being singled out when everyone else paid their ten dollars to go to Camp Sacajawea, and she was allowed to go free. Charity? Her independent spirit revolted at what was forced upon her. When she grew up, things would be different. She smiled out over the treetops, then she heard an eerie crack!

"It's your turn, Celeste!"

There was excruciating pain as she plummeted to the bottom limb and lay draped over it, gasping for breath. It was awhile before she managed to climb the rest of the way down, and limping home, she remembered her daddy's warning.

IN THE MIDST of the calming fifties, the placid waters were suddenly stirred. Elvis Presley burst upon the scene—brash, handsome and sexy—bringing with him something tagged rock and roll. Eisenhower America changed, especially for those young people poised for what the world had to offer. The twenty-one year old Memphis truck driver picked up the mike and began to sing "Don't Be Cruel," and Joellen's heart soared along with millions of other budding young girls.

The black sound of rhythm and blues, dubbed rock and roll by New York disc jockey Alan Freed, caught on like wild fire. White teenagers flipped over it, though they didn't understand it and neither did their parents, who reacted in the only way a good parent would—with shock and fear. They were used to the soothing, sophisticated sound of the big bands of the forties, but by the early fifties, the big bands were considered soulless, and the jitterbug was rampant. But when Elvis appeared it was altogether different from anything they had ever seen or heard!

Joellen begged her daddy to let her see his first movie, *Love Me Tender*, when it came to the Warner Theater. Reluctantly, he agreed, and she and Betsy Jeanne melted in their theater seats, struck by his powerful charisma and unmatched voice. They staggered out of the dark theater into the bright sunshine in a daze, wondering what had happened. Elvis filled their world afterwards. They saved their pennies to buy Elvis billfolds and Elvis bubble gum cards and movie magazines with large Elvis pictures plastered over them. They carefully pressed the bubble gum cards into big, fat scrapbooks, and Joellen hid hers underneath her bed beside her turtle and Grandma Thaxton's footstone. Now she was truly in love!

Meredith was pregnant for the fifth time, and life was bearing down hard upon her. They still lived in the small four-room house across from the Thaxton farm. Where would they put this new baby? she wondered. Joellen wondered, too.

She and Janet shared the only other bedroom in the house besides their parent's room. Daniel slept on the couch in the living room, and little Brian, now almost three years old, still slept in the baby bed set up in the living room beside the oil circulator.

There was no place for another baby!

And they didn't have any money for another baby! Joellen silently argued, already differentiating between herself and the other girls at school, comparing her own things to theirs. Maybe her mother really wasn't pregnant after all. She didn't look pregnant! But she had heard them talking, talking about a new baby coming. She didn't know much about God, but the preacher at church said He would answer prayers. So she began praying. She felt a twinge of guilt with each prayer, but her fear of more kids and less money prodded her on.

"Please, Lord, don't let Mama have another baby…we've got enough already…we don't need anymore!"

Victor and Celeste shook their heads.

Meredith was sinking deeper and deeper into the inevitable abyss awaiting her. Not only because of the imminent birth process, which she dreadfully feared, but Meredith was depressed, deeply depressed, trapped with the overwhelming burden of a soon-to-be fifth child.

How could she take care of another one?

Already burdened with guilt, she studied the cluttered house. It pressed down upon her like a weight—the dirty clothes piled high in the pantry, and the floors that needed scrubbing, and she had to get breakfast yet. No sooner was breakfast over than it was time for dinner, then supper. It never ended, and she couldn't keep up. How did others do it? She thought of her mother-in-law. Mrs. Thaxton had everything in control, and it all seemed so easy for her. Her own mother had raised four and worked in the bakery, too. There must be something wrong with me, she thought, grabbing hold of the frying pan underneath the stove and trying not to awaken Bennett, who was sound asleep. He had just crawled into bed after working the graveyard shift at the fertilizer mill.

Brian was fretting to go outside, but it was too cold outside, and she had to help the others get ready for school before the school bus came. Then the laundry had to be gotten up for the laundryman, who would be here soon. She plopped the frying pan down on the stove and shuffled into the cramped living room to rouse Daniel against his protests. Brian stopped fretting and jumped onto the couch with Daniel. Soon they were scuffling.

"Get up Janet...Joellen," she called out. "It's time for school." They were rolled into one big knot in the double bed.

Meredith's heart sank as she stared at the kitchen that she had left the evening before, too tired to clean up. Flour dusted the stove and table from supper's biscuits, and spilled over onto the worn linoleum. She didn't know why flour was everywhere after she baked biscuits. Mrs. Thaxton didn't have that problem.

The round, galvanized tub still sat by the door, filled with dirty water from the children's baths last evening, a cloudy skim settled upon it. She knew Bennett would have emptied it, but he was working two jobs now and was so tired when he came home, he probably didn't even notice it. She glanced at the pantry door standing ajar, and remembered the slop jar needed emptying. She detested carrying that thing down the steep back steps, carefully balancing it so that it wouldn't spill over, and down the path to the outhouse, especially in the cold winter. Once she had slipped on the icy pathway, and well...she didn't want to think about that.

She trudged over to the sink, turned the spigot on to fill up a saucepan with water and set it on the wood stove. At least it was hot. She could always count on Bennett for keeping the stoves banked. They never went cold or hungry. He was a good provider, a good husband, a good father, and he was strong, strong like his mother and father. All the Thaxtons were strong.

Strong stock, she muttered to herself, and sank onto a kitchen chair, brushed the flour dust aside, and reached across the table for yesterday's paper. Absently flipping through it, a small column immediately caught her attention.

Isis Building Being Razed as Parking Lot.

"Oh no," she cried aloud, "...not tearing it down!"

"Tearing what down, Mama?" Janet asked.

"Never mind, you get ready for school." She read quickly. *Razing of the Isis Theater building in 600 block Main Street is underway and when completed in about 90 days will make room for a parking facility. The building floor, which slopes upward from Main Street, will be retained for use by the parking facility. Erected in 1914, it was the first local structure designed and built as a motion picture house. It was unique here because the movie screen was placed in the front of the building with the seats facing Main Street.*

That's what made it special, Meredith thought, suddenly overcome with longing for the theaters downtown and for her mother, and for the way life used to be. She could almost smell the popcorn and the chocolate she snuck in, hidden in a small paper bag. Most of the time she didn't have any money for the candy sold in the theater, so she had carried her own. But those days were gone, and she wearily pushed herself up from the table to fix the kids' breakfast.

GRANDMA ISABELLE FINISHED drying the last breakfast dish, and placed it neatly in the cupboard and remembered she had to iron Mr. Walters' shirts today. Mr. Walters was her second husband, and she tried particularly hard to please him. She glanced at the clock over the stove. There was plenty of time yet to enjoy another cup of coffee. After pouring it, she sat down and spread out the morning paper.

Eiffel Tower Flames But Still Stands. It was the front page headline. *Fire broke out atop the steel-skeletoned Eiffel Tower early today. It was brought under control by firemen who panted all the way to the top of the 984-foot structure on foot.*

"My goodness!"

She turned the page, flipping through the advertisements. Jackson's Drugs had hot water bottles on sale for $1.49. Making a mental note, she continued reading. Grace Kelly and Prince Rainier planning their wedding for after Easter, and there was a large picture of the whole Kelly family posing after the engagement luncheon. Such a beautiful girl.

Her thoughts returned to Meredith. Too bad she couldn't have married a prince. Oh, she liked Bennett Thaxton enough, couldn't have a nicer son-in-law, but country life was not for Meredith—no indoor plumbing or hot water—especially with all the children, and now another on the way! She had just returned from a visit, more concerned than ever. What was going to become of her?

Had Meredith inherited her father's problems? Or could it possibly be that she was suffering from…from memories…memories that no child should have. All those frightening episodes came back, flooding her mind, and she was thrust back to Pearl Street…and there he was. Standing alone across the street, staring up at their house, just standing and staring as black clouds formed overhead! Even now, after all these years, her arms felt an icy tingle at the thought. He had escaped the mental institution again and was standing there staring up at the house. What was he going to do? Little Meredith, just six years old, stood at the window, holding onto the curtain.

"Come away from that window, Meredith—now!" She had grabbed her by the arm, pulling her along, out the back door, out into the thunderous twilight as lightning zig-zagged overhead, cutting a swath of dazzling light across their path. They ran as the blackened sky opened up and rain poured down upon them. They ran across the soggy yard, through the sticky wet brush, into the thick grove of trees. They ran and ran and ran, stumbling over the rocky ground until....

"You gonna iron my shirts today?" Mr. Walters appeared in the doorway, snapping his suspenders.

Grandma Isabelle stood up, the wretched memories falling off like scales from a fish. "I was just fixing to."

JOELLEN WRAPPED THE sticky, woolen scarf around her neck and headed outside to the basement, her Elvis scrapbook discreetly tucked beneath her coat. Already one of her brothers had accidentally ripped a page, and she was going to take care of that. The basement was dry, and she hurriedly unlocked her compartment, hiding the precious book behind her dollhouse. Suddenly, she had the urge to resume her story, and the tiny paper people came alive as did the story oozing from her imagination. But just as suddenly she felt foolish playing with paper dolls and climbed down off the stool.

She locked the compartment, hid the key, and left the basement. A moaning wind had gotten up, rattling the chains of the old swing her daddy had made for them. She had always loved to swing and wandered down toward it. Plopping onto the rough wooden seat, she pushed it back as far as she could and lifted her skinny legs up into the bracing air. The elevation and rush of wind swept her high, not just physically but mentally, creating a tremendous appetite for life!

But what is life? she thought. Can anyone know it? She had lived long enough to grasp bits and pieces: the magic of Christmas with its cedar smell and embracing love, the murky secrets of Halloween and ghostly goblins, the wonder of a new baby in the house, the dark fear of her father fighting a neighborhood fire, the subtle and embarrassing awareness of their social status, the mysterious whispered talk of adults, the bewildering and also frightening news in her *Current Events* about Communists and atomic bombs.

She knew the horror of a squealing hog as it hung from the old cherry tree at slaughter time, its throat slashed and crimson blood gushing out, and also the rank smell of the outhouse. She knew the fear of thunderstorms, and she hated the sound of her mother crying. But she relished her Grandma Thaxton's hot buttered hoecakes and peanut butter candy, and her mother's tapioca and Aunt Anna's chop suey, and she delighted in the tranquil forests and was ever in awe of the changing seasons. She loved them all, spring, summer, fall, and winter.

She especially loved the feeling of freedom the first day of summer, and going barefooted, and the hot tar smell in the road and its spongy, sticky feel oozing between her toes, but she dreaded and hated the first day of school— the fear, the apprehension, the lack of confidence. She knew the sound of fall when blackbirds filled the edge of the forest with a loud clamor, and cicadas began their evening song, and relished the smell of faint wood smoke, and she yearned for the first snowflake of winter, and loved a white sky full of them, and the cozy feeling of a hot fire in the wood stove. And rain—she loved rain anytime, any season, any day and especially at night. And she liked that new found feeling when certain boys noticed her, and she particularly loved the sense of total abandonment when she danced to Elvis's music. But what else was there? she wondered as the swing swept higher and higher, up into the spreading arms of the barren oak. She gazed up into the steel-gray sky and sang…

Que sera, sera
Whatever will be will be
The future's not ours to see
Que sera, sera

CHAPTER FIVE

MEREDITH WATCHED HER children set out, half walking, half running up Thaxton's Lane to catch the school bus. Janet and Joellen rushed ahead, clutching their schoolbooks, and Daniel sought to catch up, his sturdy little legs in full swing.

Meredith was fond of the name Thaxton's Lane because it was named after Papa Thaxton, and she had dearly loved Papa just like everyone else. A saintly man some said, a spiritual man who believed in God and family and hard work. He had set the example for his large family, but he had been gone now for several years, and Meredith missed him terribly. If only he hadn't developed pneumonia, he might still be here, she thought sadly. Papa was the closest she had come to a father.

The children disappeared over the slight knoll and out of sight, and she heard the bus churning to a stop. Just in time, she thought. It was Monday morning, a cold, gray February day. She turned back to the waiting chores and little Brian who was clinging to her skirt, a tenderhearted child, anxious to be near her or his father.

"Now, run along, Brian, and play with your trucks and cars."

She closed the door and stared down at the postcard in her hand, feeling the old, familiar waves of depression beginning to engulf her like dark waters of a massive flood. She fought against them, knowing all along that she wouldn't win, and slumped down on the couch to read the difficult, scratchy handwriting.

Dear Meredith,

Hope you had a nice Christmas. I've been thinking about you and your brother and sisters. I think about you a lot. But I'm fine, fine as can be here with all these crazy people. Maybe I wouldn't be here if it weren't for you. If only your mother still loved me! But she had all you children to love, and she stopped loving me after you came. I don't understand why, but I wish things were different. Maybe I'll get out one day and come to see you.

Your Daddy

Meredith held her forehead and stared down at the wrinkled postcard, a mixture of hurtful emotions reeling in her head: anger, sadness and confusion, feelings she didn't understand. She jumped up from the couch, raced to the kitchen, and shoved it into the wood stove and watched the lapping flames devour it. It curled up and disappeared.

There!

She backed off from the stove. But the flames couldn't erase the memory, the memory of her father nor the place where he lived—where he had lived ever since her mother had him committed. She wished she could erase the memory.

It was a day just like today, she recalled, staring out the window—cloudy and gray. The day they went to Staunton. She had never been there before, and she didn't know what to expect. She had heard things about it. Her older brother and sisters had told her that their daddy was in a place for mean, crazy people. She had often wondered about it, and some of the books she'd read, books about far away places, English moors and such, mentioned them. Some even described such places in vivid detail, and she'd wondered if it would be the same where her daddy lived. She didn't know whether she really wanted to know or not.

But that day, that cloudy, gray day, she found out. She was unsure about going from the start, but Bennett was so insistent about taking her. He thought it would be good for her, that she should meet her father. The last time she had seen him she was barely six years old and couldn't remember much about him. She wondered why. Some people could remember things before they were six years old. Why couldn't she? The doctor said possibly she had suppressed it. Her memory? Was it hidden away? She struggled to revisit her veiled past, but the first memory she had was being lifted out of bed, her grandfather's bed in Petersburg. She always liked to sleep with him, but she couldn't understand what was going on. It was dark, and she thought her grandfather was still sleeping, but he wouldn't move when she touched him, and he felt so cold. He wouldn't answer when she called his name either, and everyone was talking in whispers. She never saw him after that. She was told that he had gone to heaven, and she figured he had because he was such a good grandfather, and he was making her a little trunk because he worked at a trunk factory. He had already made one for her sister, small and oval shaped with intricate little belts and buckles, but hers was never finished. They had moved to Lynchburg right after that, she and her mother and her brother and sisters, and her grandmother, and her daddy…but soon after her daddy was gone, too.

She was told that he had died, also. She guessed it was her mother's way of protecting her, though it caused her to fear that life was very fragile, and she clung to her mother.

But when she was older, she was told the truth…a truth worse than death, a truth that she fiercely guarded. No one should ever know!

But she and Bennett hadn't been married long before he decided to take her. It was about a hundred miles from Amherst County, and they had gone in Bennett's old coupe, which wasn't the fastest. She thought they would never get there, probably because of her apprehension that steadily grew with each added mile, but she didn't let Bennett know. He was so proud to be taking her, feeling that it was his duty. He had laughed and talked all the way up the winding roads and over the mountains. When they got there, they drove around the small town of Staunton looking for the hospital. Finally Bennett pulled over to ask directions.

"Sir, can you please tell me where the Western State Hospital is?"

"You mean the insane asylum?"

Meredith stiffened beside him.

Those words still rang in her head, the shock, the embarrassment, the pain. Sometimes late at night, they rang out loud and clear, louder and louder…*the insane asylum…the insane asylum.* But her daddy wasn't insane. Maybe a little strange, and mean, they said, an alcoholic for sure. But they also said that he was intelligent and liked to read…like her. The hospital said he was schizophrenic, but her daddy wasn't insane.

The directions brought them right up in front of the sprawling hospital. Meredith keenly recalled her reaction— a mixture of surprise, anxiety, and fear. She wasn't prepared for the initial sight of how big it was. Eighty-some acres they said. It didn't seem like a hospital. There was a large dairy barn and cattle on the place, and it had plentiful gardens just plowed up, ready for planting. They were told that the patients worked there and received a small pay for their work. In a sense, it was more like a home than a hospital. She remembered the meandering creek that wound across the large sloping front lawn with overhanging willow trees, their long slender branches drooping listlessly over, dipping into the flowing waters. And there were outdoor brick fireplaces, seemingly ready for large, happy gatherings. She recalled the elegant-looking redbrick buildings, trimmed in white, perched on the hillside. And she remembered the five stately homes that sat on the grounds adjacent to it, homes for the doctors, brick residences, with their own private entrance between rock columns.

She and Bennett had driven into the main entrance with its attractive light posts, and up the driveway with leafy shade trees overshadowing it, and green park benches lining it. A picturesque gazebo stood out to one side resembling the ones you saw in magazines. They had driven up to the stately main building—a beautiful, Jeffersonian brick building with a white cupola and imposing Greek Ionic columns. It was all so charming and welcoming.

Until she went inside.

And all the welcoming beauty vanished! The sterile atmosphere quickly brought her back to reality. It wasn't just a home. It was a hospital and not just any hospital, but a hospital for mental patients. Patients with problems that society didn't want, didn't accept, and readily pushed behind closed doors and heavy iron fences. She could still see the long, black, wrought iron fence that surrounded the place, separating it from the busy streets outside where normal people lived and normal people walked and drove past.

It was early springtime when they went, but it was a cloudy, gray day. She remembered looking up at the clouds, dark and heavy, as they climbed the steps to the imposing main building, and she had wished the sun would come out. And then there was the train whistle! She would never forget it. Standing there on the porch, about to enter, suddenly a heavy rumbling announced the approach of a train, and a haunting whistle sent shivers up her spine. Bennett had hugged her to him as they watched the massive train raucously roll and vibrate over the high trestle that rose to the left of the hospital. Her nerves, already a wreck, shattered. She was ready to turn back, ready to leave and head home, but Bennett led her in.

The place was cold, cold and impersonal, everybody efficiently going about their business. Bennett walked her up to the desk, and after filling out the required papers, they were led through a maze of doors and corridors. The further they went, the more frightened she became. Then they stopped at a closed door.

"This is Mr. Conner's room."

Meredith automatically stepped back as the hospital attendant knocked.

"Come on in," a deep, husky voice answered, and they entered.

Meredith continued to stare out the window and remembered sitting in that room, Bennett close beside her, holding her hand. The man she faced was a stranger. It was the most painful memory of all. She didn't exactly understand why. Perhaps it was the wooden leg. He had even joked about it.

"Comes in handy sometimes," he chuckled, knocking on it repeatedly. "...helps to beat off the insane."

She would never forget those words. They conjured up all kinds of frightful pictures, and she had seen them, the insane, that is. They scared her. Maybe that's what bothered her most, knowing that her daddy had to live with them.

And the wooden leg stuck in her memory like glue.

He had lost his leg before she was born, before any of them were born except for her oldest sister, Mable, who was just a baby at the time. He was only twenty-one himself. Her mother had told her the story: how times were hard and he had hoboed out west looking for work. He was used to hopping freight trains, but he said that he miscalculated that jump, and it cost him his leg. He fell under the train that was crossing over a high ridge. A wheel rolled over his leg, and he tumbled down the steep ravine with his leg hanging on by a shred. He cut off his leg with his pocket knife, but knew he would soon bleed to death. No one knew he was down there! He managed to start a fire, and an old colored man, who was passing by in a horse and buggy, saw the smoke and came to his rescue. The old man took off his coat, wrapped it around his leg for a tourniquet, and took him to the hospital. He saved his life.

But the wooden leg wasn't the only thing that stuck in Meredith's memory. There was something else, something she couldn't put her finger on, something that hung over her as the heavy, gray clouds in the sky. Her daddy was a man she didn't know and wasn't sure she wanted to know. But she knew he had been mean, real mean, and he drank heavier than most men. She had heard the stories of how tough he was. How he often escaped the hospital, and how it took several policemen to restrain him, even with his wooden leg. But yet there was something else as real and tangible there in the room that day as the tall mountains rising up behind the hospital.

Her daddy watched her staring out the window at them.

"That's Mary Gray and Betsy Belle," he said suddenly.

"Who?" Bennett had asked.

"Mary Gray and Betsy Belle."

"I think Meredith's looking at the mountains up there, sir," Bennett explained.

Her daddy nodded, licking his lips. "Mary Gray and Betsy Belle...that's their names," he repeated. "Named after two little girls that got lost in them mountains...never did find'em."

Meredith looked at Bennett, and he saw a strained look in her eyes which he had never seen before. "Well, Mr. Conner, I guess we better be going." He stood up and grabbed her hand. "It's a long drive back home, over the mountains, you know...and it's fixin' to rain."

Meredith remembered that drive back home like it was yesterday. It did seem long, very long, and it rained all the way. And the feelings that she brought back with her, they had never left. She watched the fire in the wood stove. There was no trace of the postcard now.

JOELLEN ARRIVED AT school a little early and pulled out her spiral notebook and pen. She quickly began her rounds in the sixth grade classroom, asking the same question, "Want to join my Elvis fan club?"

"Sure...but did you know that Wynn Carter has a fan club, too?" her friend, Julie Adams, teased. "She's already asked me to sign hers."

Joellen glared at her.

"...but I didn't."

She poked the notebook and pen in front of her. "Who for?"

63

"Pat Boone, of course...*writing love letters in the sand*," Julie mocked in a sing-song voice.

"Oh well, he's pretty good, but too square. He can't hold a candle to Elvis!"

"That's what I said." She scrawled her signature in the notebook, and Joellen hurried off before the shrill school bell rang out.

After school, she decided to meet her cousins at the barn. A number of them lived on Thaxton's Lane, and it was their papa's barn where they liked to congregate. It stood across the road from their house just beyond the garden and the cherry tree and it wasn't being used now but still had a pile of hay stacked up in the loft. She headed toward it, and thought of her papa. She had a vague memory of him walking slowly down the garden path, thin and stooped, with his hands clasped behind his back. She tried to visualize his face, but it kept evading her. She wondered if her cousins had the same problem.

The loft was warm and cozy. Lately they had taken to hanging out there and reading *True Confessions*, hunkered down in the soft, sweet-smelling hay. Her cousin Frankie grinned as he read the risqué story, and Betsy Jeanne sneered at him. Joellen grabbed the magazine and began to read. Caught up in youthful defiance, they giggled and poked fun at the forbidden stories.

"Guess what I have," Cousin Cliff boasted, hoisting himself up into the hayloft and pressing in against them.

They stared at him.

"Well, don't you want to know?"

"What?" they chimed in simultaneously.

He paused for the measured effect, and then presented a crumpled pack of Camels, still half full.

"Where'd you get *them*?" Frankie demanded, his big blue eyes protruding beneath a shock of red hair and surrounded by a mass of summer freckles.

"I'll never tell," Cliff taunted, waving the pack of cigarettes over his head, enjoying his brief moment of triumph.

"Whatcha gonna do with'em?" Betsy Jeanne eyed them curiously.

"Now what do you think I'm gonna do with'em, Miss Brains?" He looked at her as if she had suddenly dropped down from planet Mars. The cousins gawked at one another, their wonder mounting.

"You gonna smoke one?" Frankie questioned, even more wide-eyed.

Cliff grinned, cocked his head sideways, and pulled out a book of matches. There was an audible gasp. He struck the limp match, but it didn't light. The whole book was slightly damp from harboring in his pants pocket too long while splashing through the creek. He tried again, and still it didn't light. "Darn it!"

"It's not gonna light," Frankie chided, and Cliff frowned at him.

Suddenly a wicked flame shot forward, and a sulfurous odor instantly permeated the loft. Cliff lit the cigarette, and languorously took a long drag while all eyes riveted on him. "See, nothin' to it," he bragged, smugly leaning back against a bale of hay.

Obviously intrigued, they stared at him as the smoke encircled his head.

"Who's next?" he challenged.

Each one looked questioningly at the other, while seeking to hide his or her intimidation.

"How did you know how to do it?" Frankie pried.

"Shucks, I been smokin' for years. Well...not cigarettes exactly...but me and Clyde, who lives over on Seminole, we been smoking them monkey cigars ever since he moved in there...you know...they grow on them trees in his back yard."

Betsy Jeanne screwed up her pretty face. "Those trees are full of those ol' black and white caterpillars! I can't stand those fuzzy-lookin' things!"

"We don't smoke the caterpillars, stupid! We smoke the monkey cigars, you know them long, narrow pods that grow on the trees in the summer. When they get dry, Clyde picks them off and hides them under his bed from his folks, and we cut the ends off, light one end and smoke the other."

"Yuck!" she exclaimed.

"Heck, they ain't so bad." He took another long drag and smiled proudly. "But not half as good as this."

"My friend Otis smoked corn tassels one time," Frankie interjected. "It was in the fall, you know when the tassels get all dried up and all. Said he pulled out them dry tassels from the corn ears and rolled them in his papa's old newspaper and smoked it like real tobacco!"

"Were they any good?" Cliff asked, slyly rolling his eyes around, still waiting for a taker.

"Not too good, he said, but it was all he had."

"I'll do it!" Joellen suddenly exclaimed, grabbing the cigarette out of Cliff's hand.

Victor frowned.

She stuck it in her mouth, immediately despising the bitter taste but determined to smoke it anyhow.

"Now, inhale it," Cliff coached like a pro. She didn't really know what inhale meant and gulped a mouthful of smoke, swallowed it, and doubled over coughing while the others broke into laughter.

Celeste winked at Victor.

"Here, give me the dang thing before you burn the whole barn down!" Cliff grabbed the cigarette and none too soon for Joellen.

Dear Secret Angel,

Today was an interesting day—got a lot more signatures for my Elvis Fan Club—more than that Wynn Carter and her precious Pat Boone. I can't understand anyone liking Pat Boone better than Elvis!!!

And I smoked a cigarette! I couldn't let that smart-alecky Cliff outdo me. But just between me and you—it was yucky! But who knows, maybe I'll do it again. One thing, though, those True Confessions*—I think I've got them figured out. They all end the same way, and I'm getting tired of them. I won't tell the others, though, but I might just see what the library at school has in it.*

AS THE YEAR passed its half-way mark, summer settled in over Central Virginia, hot and humid. Not much was taking place to make headlines in the small town of Lynchburg, but there was an insignificant event happening that would later prove to have a monumental effect, not only on Lynchburg but on America and beyond. A young preacher and a handful of men were buying the old theater seats from the Isis Theater since it was being razed. They wanted them for a new church they were starting in the former Donald Duck Bottling Company up on the hill of Thomas Road. They had been busy day and night scraping the thick, gooey syrup off the floor where they were going to install the seats. The young pastor, Jerry Falwell, just out of college, was so excited to be following God's call, and he couldn't wait to get the new church going.

Meredith's fifth baby was born later that July, and they named her Katy. Immediately Joellen was taken with this charming baby sister, and she repented of her many prayers, glad that God hadn't seen fit to answer them. Maybe that preacher didn't know everything.

Summer flew by way too fast for Joellen, and it was September already. The family was sitting in front of the television one cool, September evening—all but Meredith and the baby, who were in the bedroom. The Ed Sullivan show had just come on, and suddenly the small screen came alive with music, motion, and rhythm. Joellen was ecstatic, mesmerized by the wiggling, shaking, singing Elvis Presley, and she jumped up off the couch and began dancing along with him.

"Sit down...sit down...and act like you've got some sense in your head!"

Joellen gaped at her daddy.

The unexpected scolding stung and utterly shocked her. Dejected, she sank onto the sagging couch. Her daddy had never yelled at her. What had she done wrong? She hung her head and fought the tears, confused, angry, and hurt. It was rare for Bennett Thaxton to scold one of his children, but to see his young daughter jump up and start swinging to such wild music...and music coming from a man behaving in such an unseemly way. Why, it was simply more than he could stand! He was not alone. The same fear characterized thousands and thousands of parents as they anxiously watched their adolescent daughters all over America. What in the world was happening to them? Never before had they witnessed such actions on the part of an entertainer...or their children. This must be stopped! It was ridiculous! It was dangerous!

But as a tidal wave picks up speed and power, rolling over more placid waters and ultimately the land, such was the rock and roll movement across America and the world. It had been unleashed, and now it could not be stopped.

Dear Secret Angel,

Daddy really hurt my feelings today, and I don't know why. He's usually so sweet and kind, but he got really upset with me and hollered loud. He's never hollered at me before. He must really hate Elvis!

JOELLEN AWOKE TO the buzz of a fly around her head and slapped at it. She yawned and stretched. Another fly lit on her neck; again she slapped. She hated being awakened by flies in the long, hot summer. She heard one hitting up against the windowpane and pounding the screen trying to get out.

"Dumb fly," she mumbled and rolled over, pulling the thin blanket over her head. She was almost back to sleep when Betsy Jeanne jumped on the bed beside her, the springs creaking loudly. Her cousin often raced up Thaxton's Lane to wake her up, anxious for a summer day of fun. She was more than two years younger, still a kid, Joellen figured, as Betsy Jeanne yanked the blanket harder. Joellen was dealing with this new business of being a teenager. She had turned thirteen in January and was still getting used to it.

"Get up, sleepy head!" Betsy Jeanne giggled, and Joellen reluctantly pulled the blanket off her head, stretched and looked out the open window. Already the sun was shining.

"Yucky...look there!" Betsy Jeanne was staring down in the windowsill at the dead flies.

"So what." Joellen climbed out of bed. She knew there were no dead flies in Betsy Jeanne's window. She pulled on her clothes, and they headed outside.

"You didn't eat any breakfast."

She looked at her cousin. "I'm not hungry." And she usually wasn't until noon, but as they wandered out in the front yard, she spotted the clusters of ripe berries pressing up against the side of it. The adjacent field was full of the low-lying bushes.

The tiny round blueberries crunched in their mouths, hard and sweet, as they walked down Thaxton's Lane, their fists full and staining blue. They headed for the pasture, soaking up the warm sunshine. The gently sloping hills welcomed them with the song of birds, and they ambled down toward the cold, gurgling creek that wound its way through the rolling pasture. Following its winding path through the close-cropped pasture, they eventually approached the little footbridge that crossed it, and flopped down on their tummies, its warmth seeping through their cotton dresses. They gazed down through the cracks in the planks, idly staring at their fluid images waving and bouncing below.

"You think we'll ever get married?" Betsy Jeanne blurted out, tossing a pebble into the water and watching its expanding ripples widen and widen until they disappeared.

"I reckon we will. Most people do, you know...but I don't want to marry just anybody."

"Who then?"

"Elvis."

"Who doesn't?"

"...Tab Hunter wouldn't be bad either."

"He's a doll baby!"

Joellen jumped up singing...

Young love, first love
Filled with true devotion
Young love, our love
We share with deep emotion...

Joining in, Betsy Jeanne grabbed her hand, and they twirled around atop the little bridge...

They say for every boy and girl
There's just one love in this whole world
And I know I've found mine....

Collapsing in complete and delirious abandonment, they shrieked and giggled, rolling over and over, nearly falling off into the creek.

"I wonder when we'll find ours," Joellen sang out to the cloudless sky and the great unknown. "And I wonder who it will be."

Betsy Jeanne stared up with her.

"Ever think about that?"

Betsy Jeanne shrugged her small shoulders.

"Well, I think about it."

They rolled over and were silent for a while, peering down through the cracks, watching the creek waters rush over the smooth, round stones, listening to its soothing murmur.

"Race you to that tree way out yonder," Betsy Jeanne challenged, jumping up and off the bridge. She bounded across the rolling pasture, and Joellen marveled at her speed as she raced to catch up with her. Huffing and puffing, they climbed the hefty branches of the sprawling chestnut oak.

"Y'all want to go with us to the drive-in tomorrow night?" Betsy Jeanne asked, comfortably situating herself in a v-shaped branch.

"Sure." Joellen couldn't wait, and since Betsy Jeanne said y'all, she figured she'd ask her mama, too. She knew her mama loved movies. She always talked about them. They continued to sit up in the old oak for longer than they planned, their random conversations bouncing from boyfriends to marriage to having babies.

"Oh great!" Betsy Jeanne exclaimed.

Joellen followed her eyes downward. The small stud horse had positioned himself directly beneath them. A menace more times than not, they had jokingly nicknamed him Sputnik after the Soviet Union man-made satellite, which had been launched recently. The satellite was the talk of America, and Joellen was well aware of the urgency it had created in people's minds. Coupled with the fact that Soviet Premier Nikita Khrushchev, heading up the dreaded Communist nation, was now the most powerful leader to be reckoned with, Americans were nervous, especially after he promised, *We will bury you.* If the Communists can get into space, maybe they will bury us! Joellen pondered sometimes in the dark of night. The cold war had been going on for some time, but Sputnik had definitely escalated it. However, this four-legged Sputnik was their immediate quandary.

"How're we gonna get down now?" She frowned at their adversary.

Betsy Jeanne scratched her head. "I don't know 'bout you, but I'm stayin' up here." The sun was casting fiery red and amber streaks across the darkening sky before Sputnik ambled off, and they slid down the oak, racing for home.

Joellen excitedly told her mother that they were invited to go with Betsy Jeanne's family to the drive-in. Immediately Meredith brightened at the prospect, taking pains to get ready the next day, pleasant old memories flooding back. She could see Rudolph Valentino's romantic and handsome image boldly plastered on the screen and Mae West's reigning beauty, she could see Jean Harlow and James Cagney…in the old gangster films. It all rushed back to her, and she was back in the darkened Isis, warm and safe.

But when Betsy Jeanne and her parents pulled up, and Joellen went running out, she realized that she had made a mistake…an awful mistake. Another couple sat in the back seat of the large Oldsmobile, and there was only room for her! She hated to go back in to tell her mother.

"It's all right," Meredith said, but her face said otherwise. "You go on ahead."

Joellen and Betsy Jeanne sat in the playground swings below the enormous drive-in screen, but she couldn't enjoy the movie for remembering the look of disappointment on her mother's face. She pushed the swing higher, soaring towards the giant figures moving across the large screen. Poor Mama, she thought, and guilt swept over her for raising her hopes, then dashing them.

CHAPTER SIX

NINETEEN FIFTY EIGHT brought changes, changes that Joellen found difficult and disturbing. They were moving! That was bad enough, but moving to the *country* was the last place in the world that she wanted to go. At fourteen, she was practically grown up! She wanted to be around people, she needed to be around people, lots of people, and young people! And she certainly didn't want to leave the only home she could ever remember, and all her cousins, and Betsy Jeanne.

On the way home from church on a Sunday morning, she dwelled on these gloomy thoughts. Janet walked briskly ahead in the bright sunshine, in a hurry to get home. She wondered why. Her mother was in one of her moods, and she certainly was in no hurry, but she skipped along to catch up anyway.

Maybe she was tired of church, Joellen thought, walking beside her. It *was* pretty boring. The preacher droned on and on this morning, and if it hadn't been for that big painting behind him, she didn't know what she would have done. She had studied it all morning—the blue river and Jesus standing in the middle of it, getting baptized, and that pretty white dove coming down from the cloudless sky. But she wondered why Jesus needed to get baptized. And she wondered why she needed to get baptized. But Aunt Anna said that once she turned twelve, she should get baptized, and so she had. But she didn't feel any different! This whole church thing was a mystery, and, besides, she was tired of going anyway. And she certainly didn't relish going home, but then she pictured that narrow, graveled, country road leading down to the new house and the strong, resinous smell of pines hemming it in on both sides.

"I don't want to move!" she blurted out.

Janet turned and frowned at her. "Well, you don't have any choice, silly. We're moving, and that's that!" she replied impatiently.

"There's nothing down there...but gravel roads and country...and country people!"

"What's wrong with that?"

Joellen shrugged. Suddenly she spotted a row of colorful irises growing alongside the road. "Let's pick some."

Janet glanced at the stately, two-story white house sitting back in the tall trees, nearly secluded from the road. "They belong to the Slaytors. We better not pick them. They might see us, and we'll get in trouble...."

Paying no heed, Joellen edged over to the side of the road and grasped a beautiful purple iris, snapped it off and then grabbed a lovely, soft lavender one and broke it off, too. She hid them behind her skirt.

"You're gonna get us in trouble!"

Joellen laughed and hurried up the road. If they didn't get in trouble stealing from the Rayless store downtown, she surely didn't have to worry about a few flowers! She recalled how cunning she and her cousins had been just last week when they walked out of the store with a whole set of new shorts and tops hidden beneath their own clothes, and the gullible store clerks smiled and wished them a good day! Then she thought of the pretty crystal pin with deep red roses that she had swiped right off Woolworth's counter and proudly given to her mama for Mother's Day. Well...she did have a pang of guilt about that when her mama raved on and on about it. She didn't figure she'd do that again.

When they got home, she grabbed her hula-hoop off the porch. She was going to get this thing down pat or die trying! Already Betsy Jeanne was able to keep hers up longer, and she said they were going to have a hula-hoop contest over at the city stadium soon, and maybe they could enter. But there would be hundreds participating, she didn't know whether she'd be able to beat that many!

"Joellen, Mama said to get in here and eat your dinner!" Janet hollered out the front door.

"I'm...not hungry," she panted as the blue plastic ring whirled around her skinny waist.

"She said to come anyway."

"I said I'm...not...hungry," she gasped between labored breaths as her wiry frame gyrated, and the hoop spun round and round.

"You better come on here!"

The hoop dropped to the ground. "See what you did!"

"I didn't do it," Janet retorted. "You can't keep it up anyhow!"

"I can, too!" Joellen scowled at her. How was she ever gonna get good at it if they wouldn't leave her alone! They said on television that thirty million people were spinning their hoops in America, and she wasn't going to be left out! She grabbed up the hoop and spun it around her waist. *If only I had some hips,* she fumed as the hoop sailed around and around and around.

THE THAXTON FAMILY was ready to move, and Bennett was extremely pleased about it. The opportunity to buy some land from a friend and build a new house elated him. For the first time in his life he was stepping out and would have some land of his own, not just a lot. He couldn't wait. He relished the idea of moving further out in the country, and in some ways away from the homeplace, not that he didn't love his home. But being the baby of such a large family had caused him to strive harder to find his own place, and the new house would accommodate their growing family better with three bedrooms instead of two, and maybe even a bathroom.

But every time they drove down there, a number of miles deep into the countryside, down crooked dirt roads, rutted and butted by dense forest, and hemmed in on both sides with loblolly pines, Joellen cringed.

Dear Secret Angel,

Well, it looks like there's no way out; we're moving! Down in the boonies! Down with all those country hicks! I absolutely hate it! I despise it! I generally detest it!

But move they did.

Joellen found small consolation in the new house, especially when she realized her daddy had run out of money and couldn't finish it! The plain, square cinderblock house had a flat roof, which had become popular for its limited expense, but it would soon prove to be an albatross for her daddy, leaking from then on. The cinder block remained unpainted, gray and rough, and the room for the bathroom remained empty. Joellen's dignity suffered, and she complained.

"You have too much pride for a poor person!" her mother screamed at her.

77

Sulking, she shrank to her bedroom and decided she might be forced to live way down in the country away from all she knew, but she had her own escape. She grabbed a magazine, tearing through its pages filled with handsome rock and roll stars, and Annette Funicello stared out at her with that Mickey Mouse smile and Marilyn Monroe figure. One should be so lucky! She glanced over at her large scrapbook, grabbed it, and sprawled across the bed to paste in more pictures of Elvis. She missed Thaxton's Lane, she missed her old home, and Betsy Jeanne and all the fun they had had…and the pranks.

There was the flashlight! The one that shined several different colors, red, blue, green or yellow, as you slid the colored plastic shield around. Her daddy had given it to her, and she and Betsy Jeanne decided to test it out one night on the next door neighbor. The young guy, in his early twenties, usually came out late at night, just before bedtime and stood at the edge of his back porch. They had seen his shadow before, and though they couldn't really see, they could hear, and they knew what was going on. Joellen giggled all over again recalling the young man's surprise when suddenly the bright green light lit up his private business. A torrent of expletives had exploded, forcing both her and Betsy Jeanne to duck beneath the windowsill, hoping her daddy wouldn't hear.

THE LUMBERING YELLOW school bus bounced over rugged, graveled country roads throwing its tired passengers from side to side. It was a bleak November day, and Joellen stared out the dusty window, streaked with dried rain rivulets. Oaks and poplars raced by, and she thought about school and wished she didn't have to go back. She felt out of place. She glanced down at her favorite green cotton skirt that she and Betsy Jeanne had bought alike, and she had been so proud of it. But suddenly she realized that it was the only thing she had to wear that she was proud of, and she hated Physical Ed! She never knew what was going on with volleyball and dreaded it every day. And softball! She had wished the ground would swallow her up today when she stood there—the last one to be picked again. Oh well, who wanted to play stupid ol' ball games anyway!

The bus jolted to a screeching halt. She motioned for Daniel and Brian to follow as she exited and headed up the gully-filled driveway, wondering how they would find their mama. She opened the front door cautiously, and then remembered. She wasn't home. Daddy had taken her to the doctor. Her heart leaped for joy, and immediately she flipped on the television, turning up the volume as high as it would go.

"Too loud!" Daniel slapped his hands over his ears, running past her.

"S-h-h-h-h," she grimaced at him.

Dick Clark's engaging, boyish smile greeted her as he leaned over the podium and into their living room. She rushed to her bedroom, threw down her books and returned to watch the amazing teenagers who lived in the big city of Philadelphia. They were so cool, not like the square kids at school. She wished she could live in Philadelphia! Of course, she had never been to Philadelphia, but she knew it would be awesome! Suddenly the newest dance craze filled the living room, the one the *Bandstand* regulars had created.

Come, let's stroll
Stroll across the floor
Come, let's stro-oh-oh-oll
Stroll across the floor....

She jumped up, imitating them as they lined up in two long parallel lines, girls to the one side, boys on the other, facing each other, and shifting from left to right, then back again, smoothly keeping pace with the pattern and advancing along the *Bandstand* floor to the popular lyrics. She followed their slow swing and rhythm, mimicking their every move, swaying with the upbeat music, pretending to be one of them, and wishing she could pair off with Kenny Rossi and strut down the middle aisle, all eyes on her instead of Justine Corelli!

If only I could be there!

The *Bandstand* regulars had become an integral part of Joellen's world, more real than those physically around her. She studied the girls in their trendy wool pleated skirts and sweaters, yearning to be like them, popular and pretty, and she meticulously kept track of the hits chart along with Dick Clark.

Whenever her mother happened to be in a good mood, she danced all over the new hardwood living room floor, energized and ecstatic, and sometimes her mother smiled at her. But when she was in what they had come to describe as one of her "moods," which were becoming more and more frequent, Joellen turned the volume way down low and leaned into the set, soaking up its muted beat.

Meredith Thaxton had mixed emotions when it came to her independent daughter. In some ways she understood her need to dance. Why, nobody had loved the Charleston more than her! She used to kick up her heels to it better than any of her friends on Grace Street. But that seemed so long ago, and everything had changed. The world had changed! This crazy rock and roll was something else, and she didn't know where it was going. And Joellen was so determined, so willful. She was going to have her way or else.

The worrisome thoughts muddled her brain as Bennett moved on down Route 29 as fast as the old Chevrolet would go, puffing hard on his cigar. She imagined Joellen was probably having a time right now with the television turned up loud enough for the neighbors down the road to hear. Oh well, she mustn't dwell on such things; that's what the doctor said. Don't worry about the kids, don't worry about the bills, don't worry about the house not being finished, don't worry about anything! She knew she needed to stop worrying. But how do you do that? She wished somebody would tell her. It was easy for them to say, "Stop worrying, Meredith...you need to stop worrying about everything."

But nobody ever told her how!

Joellen painstakingly copied the lyrics to "The Stroll" in her notebook alongside those of the "Hand Jive." She smiled to herself. She had them down pat now. Maybe she would be a dancer and live in a big city one day and....

"I'm hungry!" Daniel fussed, his nose pressed up against the back door window, screwing up his face into an obnoxious stare.

"Me, too, Joellen," Brian chimed in right behind him. "*Bandstand*'s gone off now."

She rose to put her notebook away with her other prized possessions. She'd better get busy. Her folks would be home pretty soon.

THE FINAL YEAR of the magic fifties rang in, and Joellen anxiously but reluctantly turned fifteen, if that was possible. She nostalgically held onto her childhood, yet yearned for a boyfriend like all the other girls. But Joellen didn't look fifteen, more like twelve, to her chagrin.

Obviously overlooked by the young boys with their slick crew cuts or greased flattops and sporting souped-up cars, they searched for girls like those in the beach movies—girls like Annette Funicello, girls who could fill out a sweater like her and walk like her. And that certainly wasn't Joellen. She agonized over it, wondering when she would start to fill out.

The year began to cram in significant events as if knowing the decade was ending. Two more states were added to the Union. Vast Alaska, immediately pushing Texas out of first place. It was the first new state in forty-seven years. Hawaii quickly followed, bringing the total to fifty.

Cuba, just ninety miles off the coast of Florida, was also making historic news. Fidel Castro overthrew the government and took over, becoming its ruler and causing more fear for Americans. And beginning an infamous chain of events, John Fitzgerald Kennedy, a young Irish Catholic senator from Massachusetts, decided to run for the presidency.

But Joellen's life was buried in obscurity at the end of a rutted country road, and she sulked. The one highlight of her week was Friday night, that is, if she could get to Shaner's Skating Rink at Shrader Field with Betsy Jeanne. Gliding across the smooth wooden floor, feeling the rush of wind in her face, and moving to the rhythm of rock and roll music, she noticed the young boys casually leaning on the wooden railing, cunningly eyeing the girls as they skated by, and wondered when her time would come. Unbeknown to Joellen, it was just around the corner.

HE WAS FROM the city, all the more appealing. Not from the rural countryside as most of the boys she knew, not from old MHHS. He was from the west end of Lynchburg and already had a car! His dark shiny hair was stylishly combed back, and his serious good looks and tight-pegged pants mirrored the handsome images in her magazines. He looked like he had just stepped out of one! Not only that, he projected a sense of being wounded by life—the James Dean persona, though it wasn't an orchestrated persona for him, unfortunately. Yet, it was this aura that lured the young girls, especially Joellen. In fact, she saw him as James Dean, Frankie Avalon, and Fabian—all wrapped up in one!

And he was a musician.

This was too good to be true! Rock and roll bands were the ultimate for teenagers, and they were everywhere. In every nook and cranny, there were young boys with guitars strapped to them, surrounded by drums and cymbals, strumming and beating away—in hopes of being discovered, the next rock and roll star. And even if they didn't make it, why, at least they would be surrounded by girls!

The familiar sounds of *The Lancers* wafted out of the old YWCA Building in downtown Lynchburg and into the darkened night. Situated on the corner of Seventh and Church streets, the YWCA had been located there on one of its vertical hills since 1912, part of its mission to empower women and girls. And Joellen was empowered each time she entered its doors, every time she danced out on its shiny floor; maybe not the way it was intended, but she was empowered. The old redbrick building was all the rage, hosting teenage hops, like most every other city in America, but there was always one band that superseded the rest. And *The Lancers* was Lynchburg's band. Hordes of teenagers flocked in from all over Lynchburg and the surrounding rural areas every Friday night to hear them play.

Dale Read Rodman perched nervously on the fold-up chair leaning precariously on its two back legs against the wall. His hands tautly clasped behind his neck, he silently studied the popular band. They were good, and he wished he were up there with them. Music was everything to the slender sixteen-year old, and with an ear for it, he had taught himself to play the guitar. It came easy to him, and he had been playing for a few years, but he yearned to play in a band. Given the chance, he might be as good as these guys!

In fact, Dale Rodman was as good as the guitarists on the platform, but he didn't know it. Or he didn't believe it. His increasingly low self-esteem was one of the reasons why his music meant so much to him. It took him out of himself, out of his dismal environment, out of everything that seemingly pushed him down, and lifted him up on a higher plane. He was fortunate to live behind Ray Pillow, an up-and-coming country music star, who graciously let him sit on the porch with him while he practiced. Dale had vigilantly watched him for years, awed by his nimble fingers and obvious talent. He had played along with him, and afterwards practiced over and over, applying what he had seen his mentor do.

His best friend, Wendell, was busy talking to the other guys that were lined up against the wall, their chairs perched on two legs, as well. Dale was becoming more and more anxious, his eyes darted back and forth, scrutinizing the lead guitarist but also watching the door. He wished they would hurry up and get here. This waiting was making him more nervous! He watched the band's singer, Phil Vasser, grab the microphone. Now, all the girls would swoon, for sure, but he liked Phil, too.

Bennett Thaxton pulled up to the curb beside the YWCA's side entrance, and Joellen and Betsy Jeanne hopped out. "Bye, Daddy."

"Now you said your mama's gonna pick y'all up, Betsy Jeanne?" he hollered after them.

"Yes, Mama's gonna pick us up," she replied, her voice trailing off.

Reluctantly, he watched them approach the little alcove that led into the building. They pulled open the door, and a shaft of bright yellow light spilled out into the darkness, and suddenly a swell of beating drums, blaring saxophones and amplified guitar music shattered the otherwise quiet night. He watched the door close and the light disappear, and listened to the music fade away. His old '49 Chevrolet sputtered and rolled down the steep hill and out of sight. He didn't much like it—his daughter going to these hops, but it was the YWCA!

Joellen could hardly contain her excitement as they stepped into the sizable, brightly-lit room. She rubbed her arms trying to erase the stupid goose bumps. The lively music was bouncing off the walls, and the place was crammed with noisy teenagers. Normally she would be ecstatic, caught up in the music and swooning over the band poised on the elevated platform above them. But tonight was different.

He was going to be here.

They skirted across the dance floor, dodging the spirited dancers.

Wendell poked Dale in the ribs.

"Ouch!"

"There they are!"

Dale glanced up and took a deep breath. He had to be cool…yeah, be cool.

Betsy Jeanne and Wendell were already sweethearts and had been for a few weeks. Now Wendell was setting up his best friend, at least he hoped to. He glanced at the two, who were looking everywhere but at each other.

Joellen couldn't let on how nervous she was! She didn't want him to think her that innocent…or worse still, a wall flower! She glanced at him, and their eyes met briefly before he glanced away. Well!

After the awkward introductions, Wendell and Betsy Jeanne exited to the dance floor, leaving them uncomfortably alone, much to Joellen's dismay. She wanted to yank her back, but this was what she had been waiting for all day! Silently they sat, both tense and unsure, but already this quiet, shy persona was winning Joellen's heart.

Dear Secret Angel,

Guess what. I'm really in love this time! And he's gorgeous! Just like the movie stars…just like James Dean, Frankie Avalon and Fabian and…well, not Elvis…but he's really handsome! And he plays the guitar! Yes, I think it's real this time. I'm in love!!!

WHILE ENGROSSED IN her own private world, the world around Joellen was fast growing out of control. Her mother's condition had been worsening at an alarming rate for the past several years. She had been hospitalized for a short time, then traveled back and forth weekly to the University of Virginia Hospital in Charlottesville for treatments, but still she was caught in the tangled web of depression. Bennett was distraught as to what to do next, but he had to work, work two jobs, in fact, to provide for his large family, and pay the bills, especially Meredith's ever-increasing medical bills. And he had to take on more and more of the dual role of mother and father as poor Meredith found herself incapable. She sought escape, staying in bed day after day, sobbing behind the closed door, but her sobs wafted out to the rest of the house, and the children quietly crept around.

Janet, who had been her mother's helper most of the time, left home, marrying at the tender age of seventeen. Joellen was suddenly thrust into the role of caretaker. She had to take charge while her daddy worked the night shift, looking after the little ones when her mother was locked behind those closed doors. She resented the worrisome responsibility, and she resented her mother's moods. She yearned to be like other girls, like the carefree girls at school. "Your mother is sick," Bennett patiently explained to them, but Joellen wondered. How could she be so mean? Bennett Thaxton sought to make his children understand a situation that he himself didn't understand. He didn't want them to be hurt by her frightening screams of anger and blame.

The chaos at home spilled out. There was turmoil brewing everywhere, it seemed, bubbling over, like the war on the horizon. The Vietnam War, ironically still called a conflict by the government, was escalating. Having begun in 1957, no one knew that it would end up being the longest war in which America would participate. Vietnam, a small country in Southeast Asia, was divided into Communist-ruled North Vietnam and non-Communist South Vietnam. North Vietnam and Communist-trained South Vietnamese rebels were fighting to take over South Vietnam. But the war seemed far away to Joellen and her friends. It would be some time before it would affect them. Instead another war was brewing closer home and daily making the news.

The racial war of America.

Subtly, it had begun before most white folks noticed. But by the end of 1955, in Montgomery, Alabama, something happened that set historic wheels in motion. A weary black seamstress defied the local law and refused to give up her bus seat to a white man. She was arrested, and it was the catalyst for Montgomery's black community. They, including Dr. Martin Luther King, Jr., a scholarly young preacher recently installed in his first church, organized a one-day bus boycott, and on the fifth of December, 90 percent of the black population walked or hitchhiked. But the boycott lasted almost a year, and then the Supreme Court declared bus segregation illegal in Alabama.

Congress passed the first federal civil rights law since Reconstruction, The Civil Rights Act of 1957, and set up the Commission on Civil Rights to investigate charges of denial of civil rights. Actually, the Supreme Court had ruled in 1954 that "separate but equal," the premise for school segregation, was unconstitutional. It later on ordered that all schools be integrated with deliberate speed, but things did not begin to change until 1957.

Even then, desegregation did not come easy. When nine black students attempted to enter Little Rock Central High, mobs attacked, and President Eisenhower ordered troops in. Riots, numerous sit-ins, marches, and the shedding of blood ensued by both blacks and whites. It was the beginning of the Black Americans' emergence, which would meet with powerful resistance and create horrible chaos over America.

But Joellen would not experience any of it, nor the integration. In fact, old MHHS had *Ichabod* written over its weathered door.

CHAPTER SEVEN

"DADDY, LOOK WHAT came in the mail," little Brian ran in, clutching a small brown package.

"Give me that!" Bennett grabbed it, but not in time.

Meredith's big brown eyes grew larger. "What is it?"

"Oh, nothing, probably nothing…."

"Bennett…let me see it."

Reluctantly, he handed it over, and she studied it before untying the yellow string and peeling back the wrinkled brown paper. A box of candy. Slowly, ever so slowly, she lifted the cardboard lid. The individual pieces of chocolate had turned a whitish brown.

"It's old," she half whispered.

"Here, give it to me, Meredith, it's all right. Why don't you finish your coffee?" He gently took the candy out of her hands, and she absently stared out the window, already mentally removed from them. Joellen watched her mother leave the room and shuffle back to her bedroom.

"Here, throw the doggone thing in the trash!" Bennett angrily thrust the box of candy at her.

It was a mystery to Joellen why these things evoked such strong emotions from her mother, but Bennett had learned early on. Coming from such a solid and loving family, it was difficult for him to comprehend at first, but he found out after their trip to Staunton. Though shocked to discover that Meredith's father had been institutionalized when she was only six years old, and she hadn't seen him since, he was even more shocked to learn that he was still there. But that trip had pitched young Meredith into such an emotional state that she cried for days. It was this visit that Bennett thereafter referred to as triggering her depression, and he never took her back.

Joellen carried the box of candy out the back door. The screen door slammed behind her as she threw it in the trash barrel and pushed it way down under so that her mother wouldn't see it later, but she couldn't fathom any of it. Perhaps if she weren't a teenager caught up in her own world, or maybe if someone had set her down and explained it all to her, things would have been different. But depression and mental illness was not something people talked about; instead it was hushed up, whispered about, ashamed of and pretended not to be there. In fact, many things were brushed aside and purposely not faced in the fifties. It was a time of picnics, hula hoops, 3-D movies and soda shops. Anything that challenged the happy-go-lucky atmosphere was stifled, hidden, put on the back burner for another day.

The era would later be tagged "the happy days," and on the surface, it was. But there were strong undercurrents—particularly the cold war with its widespread fear of Communism and the nuclear bomb. The cold war had been ever present in people's minds since World War II. It was on television, in the newspapers, current events, weekly readers, everywhere. And though the fifties would be characterized as the golden age of innocence and simplicity, those that lived through it would also recall the worrisome undercurrents secretly hovering just below the surface.

It was a simpler time, no doubt, before the technology outburst and computer era, before the full-blown Vietnam War, before flower children and hippies, before the violence of the sixties and unrest of the seventies, but it was a lot more complex than most realized. The things that were to follow were simply simmering in the fifties in a huge boiling pot, ready to boil over.

But the people had had enough hard times, and they were seeking the "ideal," immersing themselves in happiness, Norman Vincent Peale's positive thinking, cleanliness, church, and family. Even the best selling books were a testimony to this: *Betty Crocker's Picture Cook Book* was at the top in 1950, and the Holy Bible claimed first place as the best selling nonfiction book in 1952 and 1953 and 1954, selling millions of copies.

Unfortunately, future critics would focus primarily on the materialism of the era; even that was understandable considering the time period. Sandwiched in between two wars, people were tired of rations, hard times, and living in fear from day to day with their loved ones fighting overseas in wars they didn't understand. Finally they could relax, enjoy themselves a bit. They needed to get on with life, to give their children what they didn't have. In fact, many were reliving their own childhood through their children, the childhood they had missed.

As a result, there was an explosion of building, and suburbia boomed! People hurriedly left the cities and the country for new housing developments called subdivisions. Americans were on the move, and over a million houses were built in 1950 alone, most of which were in suburbia. Neat little houses stacked in rows, all looking alike, and sporting new TV antennas. There were television sets in over thirty million homes by 1955, and suburbia back yards were suddenly popular with wavering heat from countless barbecues, shooting smoke plumes high into the air.

Super highways popped up, weaving in and out and all around, crisscrossing the land, making travel such as it had never been to accommodate the late model automobiles that families were rushing out to buy. This was the American dream and, finally, after all the poverty, the Depression and the Wars, people were realizing it. It was a good time, and they would do their darndest to keep the lid on the pot!

But not everybody was on the bandwagon. Meredith Thaxton sank lower and lower into depression, and the family in the little cinder block house at the end of the rutted country road struggled for survival. While the sun shone on all the hundreds of new suburbs, a world of hurt steadily grew in the Thaxton house. Bennett silently and patiently endured Meredith's harsh moods, his stoic nature determinedly persevering, and the children followed his lead. But Meredith suffered the most—an anguish they could not comprehend.

Joellen stared down at the trash barrel and smelled the rank odor of stale food and garbage. She thought about those snobby girls at school and how they had laughed at her. The memory hurt as it flashed before her...and she'd loved that dress, too. That's what made it so hard. She headed back into the house, through the kitchen with its old wood stove and faded oil tablecloth and exposed sink, on into the living room. The polished hardwood floor momentarily lifted her spirits. It was her pride and joy in the new house, and she didn't mind scrubbing and waxing it and did so regularly. Too regularly, in fact, but she didn't know the difference. She simply enjoyed seeing it shine; if only the other floors could have been finished, too. They remained rough and unpainted, and she hated it. But then she remembered her mother's words, "Joellen, you have too much pride for a poor person!"

She'd thought on those words ever since, analyzed them, and turned them over and over in her head. Was it wrong to want nice things like her friends? Like Betsy Jeanne? She knew that pride could be a good thing. People should take pride in themselves and keep clean and so forth, but she also knew that pride could be a bad thing. It could be sin; the Bible said so.

She passed through the narrow hallway where the finished floor met the unfinished, and on past the bathroom that wasn't a bathroom, noticing the "pot." If there was one thing in all of life that Joellen loathed, it was the smelly necessity that Grandma Isabelle delicately referred to as the chamber pot. The only other thing that equaled it was the johnnie house that stood upright out back! At least at the old house, the john was respectfully downhill, out of sight, hidden beneath tall, leafy poplars. Not here!

It stood proudly for everyone to see!

The new property was flat and treeless with no way to hide it, to Joellen's chagrin, but her father didn't seem to mind. In fact, he was probably proud of it, having built it himself, and the others didn't seem to mind either.

Her bedroom was at the end of the short hallway, and in spite of the unfinished floor, she loved it. It was her sanctuary, her own private place except at night when she shared it with little Brian, but that was okay. She loved him dearly along with little Katy. They seemed more like her own than siblings. Her mother was fond of saying that she had two families; the first three born rather close, and there was a stretch of six years before Brian and Katy came.

She began straightening things on her dresser. It was Aunt Anna's hand-me-down, dull and scratched, but a delicate lace scarf donned it, and all of her little treasures were placed strategically atop it—her brush, comb, and mirror, a small bottle of Evening in Paris cologne that she had bought at Woolworth's just last month, her bobby pins, fingernail polish, her light pink lipstick and the little wooden jewelry box that Aunt Ella had given her. And there was Elvis's picture, too, the one of him starring in *Love Me Tender*, with his cowboy hat and charming grin.

She glanced around at the telephone, wishing it would ring, but it sat silently on the small makeshift nightstand that Aunt Anna had made for her out of a bushel barrel. It was covered with a lovely baby blue slipcover that was gathered and draped to the floor. Aunt Anna was so creative. The top was lightly padded and quilted, and there was room for only one thing—the phone, nothing else. That was more than okay. The shiny black phone was the most significant object in the room, in the whole house, for that matter. It was their only phone, and she still wondered how she got so lucky to have it in her room. Of course, she had begged her daddy mercilessly to put it there.

Maybe it was busy. She reached for the receiver.

"Somebody just picked up the phone!"

Guiltily, she put it back down. No wonder he hadn't called. She stared at it, waited a second, then slipped her finger beneath the receiver, slid it ever so slyly over the button, held it down, then lifted the receiver. She waited, then ever so slowly, ever so cleverly released the button and held her breath.

"Did you hear somebody pick up?"

"No…I don't think so."

Joellen smiled.

"Well, like I said, I think it calls for two cups of margarine…no, I believe it only takes one and a half…."

"You have the recipe?"

"I think so…if I can find it."

"You know me. I need a recipe. I'll wait until you find it. By the way, did you ever taste such a good mess of turnip greens that Juanita Fields cooked up last week?"

"Well, I never have! It was delicious…."

Joellen very softly pushed the button down, then rested the receiver on top, shaking her head. Whoever heard such? Turnip greens! If I didn't have anything better to talk about….oh, I wish they'd just hang up! Maybe he isn't going to call anyway. He's probably mad at me again.

She went to her closet and opened the door, gazing at her prized dresses. She gingerly fingered the soft, flimsy material of the first one, then the second one, and the third. She sighed and reached for them.

Momentarily she had second thoughts, but then yanked them out of the closet. She hugged them to her one last time, then looped them over her arm and marched out. She hurried down the hallway, through the kitchen and pulled open the screen door. The trash barrel was already full, but she pushed them down under the smelly garbage, burying them under empty food containers. Retracing her steps, she went back to her closet and gazed at the few remaining dresses, checking the position of the hangers for the umpteenth time, to make sure they were all hanging the same way. In case of fire, she could grab them with one swipe and run for her life. One never knew about such things. She closed the closet door. Oh well, she might not have many dresses, but she still had her pride, good or bad!

Dear Secret Angel,

You know those beautiful dresses I told you about...the ones Mrs. White gave Mama for me...the ones with the pretty little raised flowers and with the ruffled crinolines that went with them...the ones that Bernice White and her snobby friends made fun of? So what if they used to be hers, she didn't have to tell everybody. Well, I'll never wear them again!

CHAPTER EIGHT

IT WAS MARCH, late at night, and a persistent blustery wind ceaselessly banged the screen door open and shut, open and shut. Joellen crept down the dark hallway and into the kitchen to latch it. She hoped not to awaken her mother, who had finally fallen asleep. The wretched hollering and crying had lasted for over two hours. Joellen couldn't understand how her mother could be so angry and say such cruel, hateful things, and it bothered her to think how it affected her three younger siblings, especially baby Katy, who refused to leave her side. A baby needs its mother, she figured, but how in the world did she endure such loud screams and cries? Katy slept with their mother while their daddy worked the night shift, and Meredith wanted her youngest with her. Apparently she found a level of comfort in the warmth of the child's tender embrace, the baby whom she cherished—the baby who didn't question her or turn away from her.

Joellen had tried before to coax her out of the dark, dismal bedroom when her mother was having one of her spells, but Katy wouldn't budge. Stubbornly she lay beside her mother, curled up in her arm midst the wailing, sobs, and screams.

Joellen latched the screen door and crept back to her bedroom. Glancing at the little wind-up clock, she let out a sigh. Eleven fifteen. Softly, she picked up the phone to return his call, slowly dialing each number, holding her breath as the circular dial spun backwards, emitting its distinct sound. She couldn't understand why it outraged her mother to catch her on the phone, so she cautiously picked her times, and usually the call had to wait until very late.

He was waiting.

With the receiver pressed tightly to her ear, she crawled into bed and snuggled down under the covers beside little Brian, who was sound asleep. They whispered sweet nothings of teenage love, and Joellen was happy. The longer they talked, it grew hotter and hotter beneath the heavy wool blankets, but she dared not come out.

"I miss you," he said.

"I miss you, too," she whispered into the receiver.

"I love you...forever," he added tenderly.

"I love you forever," she repeated. "...and I can't wait till Sunday." Sunday was the one day that she was allowed to go out on a date.

"I'll have the top down if it's warm." They loved his trendy convertible, and Sunday it would be April, maybe nice enough. The popular '56 Ford was white with blue upholstery, and it sported a fashionable continental kit out back with blue pinstripes. Joellen had bought a matching blue scarf, and she couldn't wait to wear it.

"That will be really nice."

"Yeah."

"I'll wear my blue...."

Suddenly the light clicked on and before she could move, blankets were being thrown off her, and she was staring into her mother's rage-filled eyes. She cringed as she jerked the phone cord out of the wall, and she heard the line go dead. She jumped out of bed as her mother lunged at her.

Grabbing her arms, it took all of her strength to hold her off, but the look of hatred in her mother's eyes sent cold shivers down her spine. Then the storm of despair raged from within Meredith, hurling forth painful names as she screamed and cursed at her. Joellen stiffened and resolved to be strong, though the cutting words pierced her very soul and took up a permanent lodging. Who was this strange creature that hated her? It wasn't her mother! She glanced back at the bed to little Brian, but all she could see was a small hump under the covers.

Her mother was strong, and she struggled to hold her arms back, but her adrenaline was flowing, matching her mother's. She was angry and afraid at the same time. Then her mother stepped back, and crying out loudly, she returned to her dark bedroom and her tortured mind.

Shaken and spent, Joellen couldn't stop trembling, and dissolved into tears. How could her mama treat her that way? How could she look at her that way? How could she call her those horrible names? She wanted to call her daddy. She needed him! He had instructed her to call him when anything happened, but she gazed at the dead phone lying on the floor.

She tiptoed out into the hall, listening to her mother's angry, wretched sobs slowly subside. She wanted to get Katy out but knew it was impossible and might cause another episode. She could hear little Katy's soothing voice and knew she was okay. Daniel was standing behind her in the doorway, and she signaled for him to go back to bed.

Brian was peeping out from under the hot covers, his hair damp, and his eyes filled with fear. She motioned for him to go back to sleep. The less she made of it, the sooner things returned to normal. Sure enough, he turned over and was soon fast asleep. She stooped to pick up Aunt Anna's overturned nightstand. It had rolled over against the bed, its pretty blue slipcover completely off, exposing its rough wooden exterior. She sat it up and picked up the slipcover, brushed it off, and draped it over the nightstand, and reached for the telephone. With trembling hands, she placed it back on the nightstand, its black cord dangling, and then crawled back into bed herself, but it was a long time before sleep came. When she finally drifted off, her mother's dark, hate-filled eyes stared at her.

THE INNOCENT FIFTIES were coming to an end, but they weren't innocent anymore—the unique decade was culminating in domestic unrest. Blacks and whites were openly confronting one another, a prelude of racial disaster to come, and the submerged undercurrent, the frightening phantom lurking below, the cold war and the dreaded word "communist" were rising to the surface. And the arms race was on. Americans now were very concerned for their freedom.

The controversial Vietnam War, that draft dodgers were frantically seeking to escape, shamed the patriotic veterans of World War II and Korea. They were aghast at such actions and verbally spoke out against it. On top of all this, the age-old generation gap was reaching another level with young boys' hair steadily growing longer while the girls' skirts scandalously hiked up. What was happening to America?

And what was happening to Joellen?

She leaned over the ironing board, deftly painting the words "Hell's Angels" onto her black jacket stretched tautly over it, hurrying before anyone caught her. The white letters stood out, emblazoned sharp and clear...*and Celeste and Victor frowned at one another.*

Some weren't surprised that Joellen turned rebellious, but it was a surprise to Joellen. She didn't know why she was doing the things she was doing—smoking, skipping school, running with the crowd that laughed in the face of authority! But she didn't stop to question it. She enjoyed the daring risk and excitement involved.

Never feeling a part of the mainstream before, Joellen right away enjoyed the camaraderie of the rebellious group. They were different, and she was different with them; they were risk takers, and they were fun. She liked skipping school and spending the day in the old vacant mansion over the hill from it. They didn't damage anything, just explored it and enjoyed it, sliding down its beautiful curving staircase that spanned three stories, and peeping into the dark cellar, wondering about all those hundreds of jars neatly lined up against the wall. She thrilled at the time they considered jumping a slow-moving rail car, but chickened out in the end, and the time they really played "chicken" in their souped-up cars, racing down a dark country road toward each other without any headlights on until one chickened out and swerved off the road.

Bennett was concerned for his willful daughter, especially when the police brought her and Betsy Jeanne home one night past curfew, but he was too consumed with Meredith, and there was only so much he could endure. He had already recovered three bottles of hydrogen peroxide hidden underneath her bed. Each time he had thrown them away, adamantly forbidding her to bleach her hair, she had only bought more. He was bewildered by such determination and such actions. Joellen knew she was walking on the edge, treading dangerous waters, playing Russian-Roulette with her own life, but she had adopted a sense of abandonment. So what?

Madison Heights High School was sweltering in the scorching heat, though it was only the third week in May, nearing the end of school. The old redbrick building was hot to the touch as Joellen and her group of friends lounged casually against it, each trying to conceal their inner fears. The school principal had summoned them to his office. It wasn't the first time, but he had warned that it would be the last.

"I bet Hell's not this hot!" Hilda complained, leaning against the building.

"It's gonna be hotter in ol' Mr. Angersole's office!"

Hilda frowned at Frances, and then broke out laughing with the rest of them as they continued to mask their true feelings.

"I don't care. What can he do to us?" Joellen said.

Nobody answered.

Mr. Angersole sat rigidly behind the large, boxy desk, cluttered with stacks of papers, his dark-brown spectacles resting on his long, angular nose. He peered over them at the small group of rebellious teenagers. His wide, furrowed forehead gave way to thinning brown hair. He was a small man, certainly not an imposing or threatening figure, but the young people were well aware that he held their futures in his grasp. The office was still and hot. The towering windows behind him were raised as far as they would go, but still no breeze stirred. A mousey-gray suit hung limply on his slight frame, and he wiped his damp forehead with a clean white handkerchief, and then cleared his throat. They waited.

After what seemed an eternity, he spoke in his light tenor voice, but it undoubtedly expressed determination and strength. "Well, looks like you're in here again!"

They studied the bare wooden floor.

"I've given this meeting much thought...I don't know what else to do with you. I've suspended you...expelled you, but nothing seems to work. You seem bound and determined to break the rules and ruin your lives!" He paused.

They waited.

"So...I have only one recourse."

They lifted their eyes.

He wiped his damp forehead again, then folded the handkerchief and stuffed it back in his coat pocket and fixed each of them with a cold, hard stare. "You are all aware that final exams are next week. The only way—and I repeat—the only way that I will allow any of you to pass up to your next grade level is...is for you to ace your exams!"

There was an audible gasp.

Each of them knew well that this was next to impossible! The many days that they had missed during the year, and their respective poor grades—why, it would take a miracle!

Joellen's throat tightened. She was scared, really scared. Although she had knowingly and willingly disregarded the rules and her grades, somehow she hadn't entertained the idea that she might *fail!* She walked out of the principal's office, her mind racing. She couldn't fail! To fail, to lose—it went against her very core. Frantically, she delved into her books, studying day and night, telling no one of her plan or purpose. Single-minded and alone, she read, she memorized and doggedly drilled herself into a frenzy—falling asleep in the wee hours of the morning with books scattered about her.

Dear Secret Angel,

Don't have time to talk—got to study, study, study! Boy, have I been stupid! I've really messed up, and I've got to get myself out of this jam. I CAN'T fail!

School ended. Report cards were issued. Most of the group failed, but Joellen had aced her exams and passed by the skin of her teeth. It was a close call, too close, one that she would never forget. Determined to change her ways, to seek out new friends, those on the right path, she surveyed her possibilities. There was Marny, a nice, studious classmate, and Julie, another sweet, polite girl. Above all they behaved meticulously, and they became her best friends. It bothered her somewhat that she had turned her back on her old friends, but this was survival.

It all transpired without a great deal of attention from her family. Bennett was absorbed with Meredith's problems and barely providing for the family, and Meredith was unable to focus on anything but her own depressing plight. But Joellen had made up her mind—she was going to be different, and she was going to be the first one in her family to graduate from high school.

NINETEEN SIXTY USHERED in a brand new decade with new attitudes that wiped out the old. Though things had slowly begun to change in the latter part of the fifties, nobody was ready for the hate and violence nor the moral degradation that was on the horizon. The cold war hung on, but most Americans chose to concentrate on their own personal lives. With suburbia just coming into its own, the stable, old downtowns of America were fast becoming ghost towns. Vacant stores lined vacant streets as major department stores exited to the more popular shopping centers. Pittman Plaza was Lynchburg's, centrally located and built not far from the historic Miller Park. It was an immediate success with its large parking lots. Customers, young and old, were thrilled with the fact that parallel-parking was history. It stole the anchor stores from down-town—Sears Roebuck & Company, Leggett Department Store and J.C. Penney Company. It also boasted its own large-scale grocery, The Colonial Store, not to mention a new movie theater, though theaters were fighting for their own existence.

Television was the thing. Why pay fifty cents when you could stay home and watch *Gunsmoke* or *Wagon Train* or *Have Gun, Will Travel* for free! However, drive-in theaters were the rage for teenagers, allowing them unprecedented privacy, and Joellen and Dale could usually be found parked at Harvey's Drive-In Theater on Wards Road every Sunday night with the speaker hanging onto the window-pane. They were not alone. The graveled furrows were crowded with Fords and Chevrolets and a few Plymouths and Dodges. Even a Thunderbird or Corvette could be spotted occasionally. On very cold nights it was difficult to keep any of them warm even with all the petting going on, and engines alternately switched on and off, much to their neighbors' annoyance.

Joellen turned sixteen that winter, the beginning of 1960, and was a proud sophomore, seriously studying her books. It opened up an exciting new world—a sense of self-worth. Each A or A+ and every "excellent" scrawled in red across an assignment simply impressed upon her to study that much harder. No matter that life wasn't perfect, no matter that her mother was sobbing behind closed doors or screaming obscenities at her, no matter that money was scarce and she couldn't dress like the girls at school, no matter that she lived down in the boonies—she could get the best grades!

She prided herself on this achievement, and its focus quickly became the dominant force in her life, and literature became her favorite subject. She studied Chaucer's *Canterbury Tales* and Poe's *The Raven* and *The Tell-Tale Heart* and *The Purloined Letter* and found herself hungering for more. The pleasing music of words embraced her, and she relished the lengthy poems and sonnets of the great poets even if she didn't understand them, and each new writing assignment presented a welcomed challenge.

MEREDITH WAS MORE than happy that Grandma Isabelle was visiting for a few days, seated prim and proper on the sagging couch, straightening black and white dominos in a little black box. She had just beaten Brian again, but he loved playing the game with her and watched as she carefully inserted the last domino in the box.

"Now, Brian, let your grandma rest some," Meredith said, and he scooted off outside. She turned to her mother. "You ought to read Joellen's school paper, the one that she wrote for her English class."

"Oh-h-h...." Grandma eyed Joellen, whose face flushed red.

"Tell her, Joellen, tell your grandma what it's about."

"Oh, it's just a little story I wrote..."

Meredith chuckled. "...about Mr. Walters." Grandma Isabelle's second husband was known to be quite stern at times.

"I'd like to see it," Grandma coaxed with her keen sense of humor. Joellen reluctantly fetched it from her room and hesitantly handed it to her. She quickly turned away.

106

"*That Cantankerous Character,*" her grandmother read. She looked up at Joellen and laughed out loud, then proceeded to read without pausing. Joellen sat on the edge of the straight-back chair. Her grandmother looked amused. Apparently she was pleased with the story and her granddaughter's insight into the old man. She looked up and smiled. "I think you've got it right, my dear."

Relieved, Joellen settled back in the chair.

The sophomore year flew by, and then it was summer, which dragged much slower. Unable to get a job like most of her peers, Joellen was needed at home to take up the slack from her mother's illness, but the highlight of her week was Sunday. No one went to church in their house, and that was all right by Joellen. She didn't have any religious designs and would just as soon stay home. She could sleep in, and then Dale would pick her up around noon for their weekly date.

They drove out of the country, spinning over dirt roads, with the top down, and the wind lifting her blue scarf lightly, whipping strands of hair into her face. Dale casually drove with one hand and the other draped over her shoulders, a cloud of dust following them to the sounds of Bobby Darin's popular lyrics…

> …*on the sidewalk, Sunday morning*
> *Lies a body oozing life*
> *Someone's sneaking round the corner*
> *Is the someone Mack the knife?*

The controversial words blared out boldly as the white convertible careened around the narrow curves, and an early afternoon sun blazed down upon them. He soon slid off the dirt road and onto the hard surface, and pulled over to the side. She knew exactly what he was up to and watched him ease out of the car and reach for his white handkerchief. He began meticulously wiping the dust off his shiny, waxed convertible, and grinned at her when he climbed back in.

At the end of summer, Joellen prepared for her junior year of school, washing and ironing her clothes, hanging them up neatly in the closet, and getting her three-ring notebooks, paper, and #2 pencils ready. All was quiet except for the drone of the television in the living room, but nobody was watching it. Daniel, Brian, and Katy were outside, and her mother was apparently sleeping. Laying her papers aside, she went to the living room to switch it off, but just as she reached for the dial, a strong, resonant voice stopped her. She stared into the face of the handsome young preacher as he authoritatively waved his large Bible high into the air, expounding the scriptures.

She stood there, transfixed.

Billy Graham's riveting words reached out to her as she stared at the black and white screen. She slid the rabbit ears around in order to see better. He was preaching about giving one's life totally to God in service to Him, and she experienced a strange feeling. He described the need for committed Christians to serve on the mission field in far away places; his piercing eyes stared straight at her and into her soul. The program ended and the invitation was given, and she watched crowds of people leave their seats and start down the aisles, hundreds of them, to make peace with God as the choir sang "Just as I Am." Oddly disturbed, she experienced a strong stirring within and turned off the television. She went back to her bedroom, mulling over what she had just heard.

And the preacher's words lingered with her.

FALL CAME AND school started, and Joellen forgot all about the dynamic preacher and his poignant message. She didn't have time for such profound and disturbing thoughts. Her mother's condition was worsening, her spells becoming more frequent, often merging one into another. Joellen felt like she was balancing a tight wire, struggling not to fall off as she juggled her time between her studies and courtship, while tediously dealing with her mother.

In spite of it all, her grades climbed, bringing immense satisfaction. It was the one thing in her life that she could control, certainly not the situation at home, nor her relationship with Dale, which was spiraling out of control. Their intimacy deepened, though she knew it was wrong. She accepted his engagement ring, but still questioned if marriage was the right thing. She loved him and wanted to be with him, but something wasn't right. They argued, broke up, made up, and then repeated it all over again. Obsessively jealous, Dale constantly vowed his love for her, and she blossomed in it, at least when things were good between them.

Dale Rodman was basically a nice young man, clean-cut, sensitive, though extremely shy and insecure. He was not capable of giving true love—he was searching for a safe haven himself. The oldest of seven, he adored his siblings and enjoyed a strong, close relationship with his mother and one even stronger with his grandmother whom he called "Mama." On the other hand, his father was a distant, cold man that kept himself aloof from his children, centering his attention on himself and his own pursuits. Dale's troubling instability most likely stemmed from this awkward relationship with his remote father. Mr. Rodman had repeatedly pushed him aside throughout his childhood, frequently favoring his younger brother over him. It was not uncommon for him to come home with one candy bar and give it to Dale's younger brother, while Dale stood timidly and tearfully in the background. After years of being made to feel unloved and inadequate, he now searched for that love that had been stolen from him. But this was all too deep and complex for naïve teenagers.

Excitement was in the air that fall as families gathered around their respective television sets to watch the presidential debates between John F. Kennedy and Richard M. Nixon. Something new! For the first time they were able to watch who was running for president and listen to them debate one another on important issues facing the new decade, though most young people weren't so inclined. They were more interested in the electrifying new dance craze that was overtaking America. *The Twist.* Chubby Checker's phenomenal hit had reached number one, and teenagers everywhere were twisting away, including Joellen, who simply couldn't twist enough.

Change was in the air, too. The words segregation and integration were popular topics for conversation, often feeding ill feelings and quarrels. The Food and Drug Administration announced a life-changing decision that would affect millions of people in the future by approving the birth control pill. And in November, the first Catholic president was elected. America was mesmerized with the young family in the White House, especially the beautiful first lady. Jacqueline Bouvier Kennedy brightened up Washington with her stylish clothes and elegant arts, and she supervised an extensive restoration of the White House, while the eyes of America watched in fascination.

People simply couldn't get enough of the new president and his young family. Youth in the White House brightened the future as the president gave his inaugural speech...

Let the word go forth from this time and place...that the torch has been passed to a new generation of Americans.... So let us begin anew....Together let us explore the stars, conquer the deserts, eradicate disease, tap the ocean depths and encourage the arts and commerce....

All this will not be finished in the first one hundred days....The energy, the faith, the devotion which we bring to this endeavor will light our country and all who serve it—and the glow from that fire can truly light the world.

JOELLEN AWOKE TO a steady, pelting rain against the windowpane. It was a bitter rain in the middle of February, and she vaulted out of bed and hustled to get ready in the frigid bedroom, hastily throwing on her clothes. The small kitchen wood stove and oil circulator in the would-be bathroom only heated the kitchen and living room. The bedroom doors were kept shut, and equaled refrigerators in the cold of winter. She reached for her eye makeup on top of the dresser and began applying it, but it was so hard it stuck together. She was purposefully quiet. Her mother was still sleeping, and she must make sure she stayed that way. At least until she got herself and her brothers out of the house. She shook Brian, and he sleepily sat up; then creeping down the narrow hallway on the bare floor, she roused Daniel. She packed their lunches, fed them corn flakes, and sent them scuttling outside in the wet, wintry morning to wait for the school bus, while she raced back to her room to gather her books. At least the rain had dwindled to a fine mist.

The dresser mirror revealed a few strands of mussed hair, and on her way out, she grabbed her brush for a last minute touch up. Running the wide brush through her ginger brown hair, she wished for the hundredth time that she had hair like Betsy Jeanne, instead of such baby-fine hair. Betsy Jeanne had nice hair, thick and wavy, not thin and straight like a poker. Suddenly her mother's bedroom door flew open, and Meredith stood there, her big brown eyes staring wildly.

Startled, Joellen stepped back, slowly laying the brush down on the dresser and reaching for her pink lipstick, which she always carried to school. But her mother grabbed it out of her hand and, with one swift swipe, yanked the lacy scarf off the dresser, throwing bottles, brushes, and mirrors flying across the room and crashing to the floor. Stunned and afraid, hot tears flooded Joellen's eyes as her mother screamed at her. She grabbed up her school books and took off down the hallway past her, hoping to make it outside. She could hear the familiar grinding of school bus gears in the distance. She must hurry and headed for the door.

But not in time.

Meredith, lost in her own dark world, hurled Katy's little rocking chair at her, catching her sharply in the side. The pain shot through her body as she grabbed the doorknob, pulled it open, and fled into the rain. Daniel and Brian were waiting at the end of the long driveway for the bus to stop, their hair already wet and sticking to their faces. Hastily she swiped at her tears as her mother hung in the doorway, yelling after her.

If only she would go back inside!

She didn't want the school kids to hear her. The lumbering bus screeched to a halt right in front of a big, red

112

mud puddle. Gratefully, she heard the door close just as her brothers jumped the puddle and climbed aboard. She followed with downcast eyes.

Of all mornings, he had to be driving!

The handsome blond teenager, her classmate whom she secretly admired, was behind the wheel. Diverting her teary eyes, she quickly brushed past him, found a seat toward the back and pulled open her government book in front of her, pretending to read. No way was he going to see her crying!

The school bus bounced down the dirt road, steady raindrops thrashing its windows, and the pain in her side eased, but not the pain in her heart. Her mother's face and what had just transpired was again before her, and a new rush of tears surfaced. She glanced up to meet those piercing blue eyes in the rearview mirror. Horrified, she raised the government book higher, and steeled herself to read. *The Legislature is the lawmaking branch of government. In the United States, the national legislature is called the Congress. In Great Britain and Canada, it is called the Parliament. In the Soviet Union, it is called the Supreme Soviet of the Union of Soviet Socialist Republics. Most legislatures have the power to pass laws, sometimes called statutes, which all citizens must obey....*

But her mind refused to focus on the boring government facts as they bounced down the rutted roads. Doggedly she pushed the painful memory away, and thought of Dale instead. He had called last night to tell her he was sorry, so sorry for the way he'd acted this past weekend. Just because she had waved at Billy McWane, he had broken her identification bracelet, the one that he had recently given her, angrily yanking if off her arm, stretching it and breaking all the links. Why shouldn't she wave at Billy McWane? He was in her class at school and had been since fifth grade. When that happened, she had broken up with him, but he begged her to come back, repeating over and over how much he loved her and would love her forever.

As the bus rolled on down the wet country road, tender words played in her head, his song for her...

Have I told you lately that I love you?
Could I tell you once again somehow?
Have I told with all my heart and soul how I adore you?
Well darling I'm telling you now

My heart would break in two if I should lose you
I'm no good without you anyhow
And have I told you lately that I love you
Well darling I'm telling you now...

And she needed that love.

But would she be able to put up with his difficult ways forever, his possessive jealousy, and bouts of anger. Mrs. Gilbert didn't think so. She was her home economics teacher, a little peculiar, but she had cautioned her more than once about the rocky relationship. Just the other day she'd warned, while fingering her large orange pop beads, "Joellen, don't fool yourself. His jealousy isn't love, but some deep, underlying insecurity. You're headed for trouble." Could she be right?

Stands of wet, dripping, loblolly pines raced by the window, but it was too late for such thoughts anyway. She was destined to marry Dale Rodman now that they had become intimate. It was only right. She could never marry anyone else!

Suddenly she remembered what today was—the day she had to stand up in front of the whole high school and recite that poem! Anxiety took hold. She hated to get up in front of the class for a book report, much less in front of the auditorium and recite a poem, and a long one at that! But she could do it, she knew she could. She'd studied and studied. She'd memorized it weeks ago, but still she couldn't escape the growing jitters in her stomach.

The noisy auditorium was filling up with boisterous students milling around, jostling one another, punching one another, flopping down in its rickety, old theater-style seats, jumping back up and callously banging them back and forth. A steady hum of busy conversations echoed off the old walls, and Joellen nervously gripped her tablet, intermittently glancing back and forth at the all too familiar stanzas...

But our love it was stronger by far than the love
Of those who were older than we—
Of many far wiser than we—

What did Mrs. Gilbert know? Their love was special, but how could Mrs. Gilbert know that? She was definitely out of step! Mr. Angersole strode across the stage and rapidly tapped his gavel. Joellen's heart was pounding a mile a minute. Would she be able to do it? Or simply go blank? Forget everything? It was her greatest fear. One by one, the students rose from the straight-backed chairs lined across the back of the platform and marched to the formidable podium to recite their particular piece, and her anxiety increased with each one.

"Joellen Thaxton."

Her knees locked, and she just knew her heart was going to stop beating any moment, but miraculously she found herself standing up and moving toward the podium. The aging planks creaked beneath her slight weight, and she could feel her face growing hotter by the second. It must be beet red, she anguished. Glancing out over a sea of faces, she focused her eyes on a far-off classroom door and began to recite.

It was many and many a year ago
In a kingdom by the sea,
That a maiden there lived whom you may know
By the name of Annabel Lee;—
And this maiden she lived with no other thought
Than to love and be loved by me....

SPRING ARRIVED AND with it more worry. The space race between America and the Soviets was common knowledge, both having announced plans to launch satellites in 1955. But when the Soviets launched Sputnik I in 1957, the race took on a whole new force, and when they followed it shortly after with Sputnik II that actually carried a dog, it grabbed everyone's attention. Now they had even topped that, shooting the first human into space in April. The heat was on! The Russian astronaut orbited planet Earth, making history, but not the history Americans wanted to hear. What did the future hold? What would the Soviets do next? Would the Cold War turn hot?

America struggled to catch up, and in early May put its first man into space. Alan B. Shepard, Jr. rocketed outside Earth's atmosphere, fetching beaming smiles from the Atlantic to the Pacific. The Russians were still in the lead, but at least America now had put a man into space. Then President Kennedy announced a determined but challenging plan to put a man on the moon!

"Whoever heard of such?" Aunt Anna exclaimed, as she bagged Bennett's groceries. Aunt Anna and her husband,

Herbert, ran a mom and pop grocery store in the heart of Amherst County and helped Bennett out with his weekly groceries, always adding a few extras.

"Well, if anybody gets there, I hope it's us," Bennett replied. "We sure don't want *them* up there!" His mind went back to the war, dredging up all sorts of ghastly memories. Joellen stood beside him and wondered who would get there first or if anyone ever would. She had heard enough talk to know that whoever reached the moon first would probably control the world, and it was a scary thought to think that the Communists might beat them!

Aunt Anna plopped two pounds of pork chops onto the brown paper and wrapped them up, then marked seventy-eight cents with her smooth black pen. "Paper said it's going to cost nine billion dollars! That's a lot of money."

Bennett nodded. "Like I said, I hope we get there first." He picked up the bags to carry them out to the car, handing one to Joellen.

On the way home, Joellen waited for her daddy to continue the conversation, but he drove silently down the country road. She wished he would talk to her and wondered why he didn't. But Bennett's mind was full of problems, problems concerning bill payments and Meredith's increasing sickness. It was all crowding in on him, and he didn't know which way to turn. She fiddled with the little transistor radio he had given her. The static reverberated, and she held it up to her ear.

A DAUNTING WALL was being erected in Berlin by late summer, made of concrete and barbed wire, to separate the East from the West. This was sobering news. The Soviet Union had renewed its threats. In 1958, Soviet Premier Nikita Khrushchev demanded the Western powers to withdraw from West Berlin and turn their sectors into a "free, demilitarized" city. He threatened to sign a separate peace treaty with East Germany if the West refused. The Western powers rejected Khrushchev's demands. Now it had renewed these threats, and thousands of East Germans had fled to West Berlin. East Germany immediately tightened travel restrictions, but the flood of refugees continued to increase daily. In August, the East German police had begun building the wall to seal off the border. Angry Berliners called it the *wall of shame*.

If the Soviets could do this, Joellen reasoned, what on earth would they do if they reached the moon first? Throughout the summer the hated word "communist" ultimately found its way into every conversation one way or the other. Though Americans went about their personal business, there was always that underlying, nagging worry just beneath the surface. What did the future hold? But Joellen must focus on finishing high school—she must!

She didn't know why it loomed so importantly before her, but it did. Her father had quit school in the seventh grade to help his papa on the farm. On the other hand, her mother had held education in high esteem and had almost made it to the finish line—just one year to go when Grandma Isabelle remarried. Abruptly, Meredith's new stepfather moved them out of the city to "the boondocks" as she often referred to it. With no way to get to school and a certain detachment on Mr. Walters' part, she sadly accepted her fate, though it was a disappointment in her life, one that she never fully got over. Joellen even wondered if her mother might somehow resent her getting the chance.

School started in September, and Joellen could hardly believe she was in her last year. Lost in her studies, she was barely aware of the troubling events in the world stirring around her, or for any event, for that matter, except those thrust in front of her, those unavoidable. But each day that passed, she fretted more that she might not make it. Not because of grades, but her mother was growing more and more depressed, more and more agitated, more and more aggressive. All the children suffered, but for some reason she targeted Joellen, perhaps because she was the oldest, perhaps because of Joellen's stoic, independent ways. Whatever it was, she was catching the brunt of it, especially when her daddy wasn't there, which was most of the time.

Joellen struggled to keep her mind focused on the difficult words of Macbeth. She pressed her hands over her ears, but her mother's hollering grew louder, and her words more volatile. She wished she would calm down and go to sleep. She read and reread the same words over and over.

Is this a dagger which I see before me,
The handle toward my hand? Come, let me clutch thee:
I have thee not, and yet I see thee still…

Suddenly her mother's door flew open, and she stood there with a shotgun in her hands. The long barrel was stuck under her chin, and she screamed out, "I'll kill myself…do you hear…I'll kill myself…."

Joellen vaulted out of bed. "Now, Mama…." She knew the gun was loaded. Her daddy always kept it loaded. Slowly, cautiously, she moved across the bedroom toward her.

Meredith jerked the gun outward. "Stay back…Joellen… I said…stay back…."

She looked into the end of the barrel and backed off.

Meredith shoved it back under her chin. "Nobody understands…nobody knows…I can't live this way…I'd rather be dead!" she screamed.

"Mama…" Joellen pleaded, "please put the gun down. Don't do anything crazy…please Mama…put the gun down…."

But Meredith gripped the gun and hurled obscenities at her that echoed into the night. Brian and Katy watched fearfully, crouching in the corner.

"You want me to call Daddy?" Joellen asked.

"No!" she screamed. "No…don't you dare!"

"Okay…okay…I won't…but please, Mama…let me have the gun…and you go back and lie down. Everything's going to be all right…."

"Everything's not all right…" she bawled. "Everything's not all right…." But gradually she handed the gun over and retreated to her bedroom in a fresh flood of tears.

The children went back to bed, and Joellen lay for over an hour listening to her mother until all was quiet. She opened up her literature book again.

Art thou not, fatal vision, sensible
To feeling as to sight: or art thou but
A dagger of the mind, a false creation
Proceeding from the heat-oppressed brain?

The unfamiliar literature eluded her distraught mind, and she grappled to comprehend the words written so long ago.

The phone rang. She grabbed it. *He knows better than to call this late!*

"Hello," she whispered.

"Joellen," his young voice quivered.

"What's the matter?"

"It's Mama," he began to cry.

"What's wrong?"

"She…she just died…." His voice trailed off, and only sobs could be heard on the other end, heartbreaking, wrenching sobs. Joellen felt for him, wished she could be with him. It was actually his grandmother who had just dropped dead in front of him from a sudden heart attack. His grandparents had always lived with them, and they grew up hearing their grandmother called Mama by their mother, and they did as well. Their real mother was called Lou.

"You mean your grandmother?"

"Yes…Mama…."

Not only was she called Mama, but she fulfilled the role, as well, especially with Dale. Lou was an only child, and when Dale was born, the first grandchild, and a boy at that, his grandmother was ecstatic. They had been extremely close through the years, and now she was gone. But the fact that she had dropped dead in front of him was the clincher—a devastating blow.

In one powerful act, at the tender age of seventeen, he was thrust face to face with death! It gripped him, twisted him, sank deep into his very soul and would remain there for years to come. Death became an obsession. He dwelled on it, imagined *himself* having a heart attack over and over, periodically grabbing his chest and listening, listening for his own heartbeat! And he insisted on being checked out by a doctor to see if he possibly had a heart problem. Death is never easy for a young person to experience, especially the death of someone so close. But for Dale Rodman, it was magnified larger than life. It conjured up all his previous insecurities and fears. Joellen couldn't understand any of it, however. Already developing a stoic spirit in light of her own circumstances, she was acquiring a very low tolerance for weakness and viewed his obsession with death as such.

"You have to go on, Dale…you have to be strong," she encouraged him daily. What else could anyone do? Her strength during this tragic time was a buoy for him, but she wasn't aware of it, nor did she see the pattern they were fast establishing, that one day would boomerang.

SNOW FELL IN early November, much to Joellen's pleasure. She loved it, loved to watch it gracefully descend from the vast gray sky. She was also glad that school was closed, allowing her another day to work on her English paper. She stubbornly determined to get the best grade possible. Off and on all day the thick snowflakes fell, covering the world around her with a heavy white blanket, and she worked on her story. She only stopped to wash a few clothes to hang on the small clothesline stretched atop the oil circulator. Her mother was having a good day, like her old self, telling funny jokes and imitating the vaudeville acts she had seen as a youngster at the Academy Theater. Daniel smiled, and Brian and Katy giggled and laughed, little sponges greedily soaking up their mother's brief sun rays.

" '*Hey mister, you sure do have a nice physique!' a lady said to this man one day,*" Meredith relayed with a twinkle in her eye.

" '*Oh, my goodness! Is that showing?' he answered.*"

Joellen listened to her mother's impish joke and laughed, too. It felt good to laugh. Meredith stirred the pinto beans, the steam fogging up the small window beside the stove, and she began singing…

How much is That Doggie In The Window?
The one with the waggely tail…

Katy and Brian happily joined in, and Joellen felt warm and good inside. It was snowing, the beans were steaming, and her mother was singing. She wished every day could be like this one.

MRS. SOWARD DROPPED the stack of school papers on her kitchen table and plopped down herself, tired and aching. She was getting too old for this. Her white hair, yellowing around the edges, was loosely pulled back in the old fashioned bun she always wore. Her bountiful breasts sagged heavily to her stomach in the straight-backed chair that creaked under her weight. A gust of wind lifted the papers up off the table as her husband of many years entered the house, the screen door slamming behind him, and she grabbed hold of them. He would be hungry for supper, and she had all these papers to grade. Oh well. With effort, she shifted in the chair and started to push herself up when her eye caught the topic of one of the pages.

This Sad World.

Well now, that's noteworthy, but what do any of these youngsters know about that? Her interest aroused, she sank back into the chair.

> *The tree branches swayed gently under the silent breath of wind. The sun was at the point of setting, presenting the forest with a fire-like glaze. The mysterious little creek ran swiftly beneath my feet and tickled my toes that were disturbing the path of its waters. Three nearby pine trees presented me with a trio as they artistically blended their moans. A beautiful robin perched on a delicate twig joined in with her lovely chirping as two tiny wrens began their melodious singing. Last, but not least, an old bullfrog rose up from behind a rock and with pride stuck out his chest and proceeded to croak along with the rest. Among this most beautiful and in-*

123

spiring environment, I was absorbed with happiness. When suddenly I heard a loud "bang"....

"We gonna get any supper around here?"

Mrs. Soward struggled to get up. "I'm getting ready to start it now," she retorted, and her husband frowned on his way back outside. She slowly bent over for the cast iron skillet under the sink, pulled it out, set it down on the stove, and reached for the can of lard nearby. But she glanced back at the paper. A bang? She knew she'd better get supper started, but she'd just take a peek at the ending.

On the way out of the moonlit forest, my ears entreated a lovely sound. It was that of a little bird which had not yet encountered the supreme of all life—man. Hearing the little bird sing so cheerfully, I wanted to say to him,

"Teach me half the gladness that thy brain must know, such harmonious madness from my lips would flow, the world should listen then—as I am listening now."

She smiled. *To a Skylark.*

Shelly was one of her favorites, too. Yes, indeed. That child most likely had never heard any bang or seen any dead bird or experienced any of that. She was a dreamer. Mrs. Soward recognized dreamers, but she also recognized something else, something she had known many years ago—a zeal to create, to pen imaginary happenings in order to mask more deeply hidden feelings. Yes, so many years of teaching young people how to write had given her a keen insight into what went into a paper. Mrs. Soward had had a hard life herself, and her heart went out to young people like Joellen. She recognized her steely character and knew it would serve her well—too well perhaps. The child would make it—she only hoped she wouldn't give up her dream.

NINETEEN SIXTY-TWO arrived and Americans saw their world shifting even more with racial violence, fighting and killing, and they were tired of hearing about the Berlin Wall and its troubles, tired of tensions rising everywhere, and especially in that far-off place called Vietnam where the president was sending more and more of their boys. They were paranoid of the potential lurking dangers by the Communists, the bomb, and possible fallout. The weapon that had been designed to eliminate fear now was the greatest fear of all! Civil Defense shelters had suddenly become a common thing, and students were drilled on what to do and where to go in case of a nuclear attack. "Duck and cover!" they mimicked. Then there were the "bomb shelters!" Even President Kennedy advised prudent families to build one in case of a nuclear war, and some people were doing just that. But Joellen hadn't seen any; though she heard there were some houses built over on Seminole Drive that had one, and that it cost a bundle to build them. She knew her daddy couldn't afford one, that's for sure.

The school bus bumped along, and Joellen glanced down at the *Current Events* that the young student sitting beside her was reading. "What's that?" she asked, pointing to the cover picture.

"A bomb shelter," the little girl answered.

"H-m-m-m."

"Wanna see it?"

"Sure."

She handed the folded paper to Joellen. "It's built underground and has a lead roof…" she explained. "…you're supposed to always keep a lot of food in it, cans of beans and all…and water, lots of water."

Joellen nodded.

"…and a radio and batteries, too. You can't forget the batteries!"

Joellen studied the picture and handed it back to her.

"Wish we had one," the child added.

Joellen shrugged. "We'll probably never need any."

Her eyes widened. "That's not what my teacher thinks."

Joellen stared at her.

"…and she told us where to go if we don't have one."

"Where's that?"

"The school basement…she said we might have to stay down there for weeks and weeks…."

The bus came to a screeching halt, and the little girl jumped up. "Gotta go now. See you tomorrow."

Joellen waved her off, thinking about the *Current Events* picture. It did conjure up troubling thoughts. She had seen instructions on television just last week on how to build one, but her daddy didn't seem too concerned, but then he had his own problems. She kind of wished they did have one just in case. They didn't even have a basement. At least at the old house they had a basement, even if it was filled with water most of the time. The bus was slowing down again, and she could see their cinder block house up ahead. She gathered up her books.

She climbed the wooden front steps and pulled open the door. The house was quiet. Daniel and Brian were already racing around back when she remembered that her mother wasn't home. Daddy had taken her to the doctor in Charlottesville again. She switched on the television to *American Bandstand* as she brushed past, taking her books to the bedroom. The boys bounded in the back door just as "The Twist" reverberated throughout the house.

"No…not again!" Daniel complained, rushing to turn it off.

"Don't you touch that dial!" she yelled out.

"Well, I'm going outside! Come on, Brian." The little fellow trotted behind his big brother, and Joellen turned the dial up louder. The small house rocked with the popular hit that just wouldn't go away…

Come on baby, Let's do the Twist
Take me by my little hand
And go like this…

Joellen twisted around the living room, around and around and up and down, exuberant, caught up in her imaginary world. Agilely, she twisted down to within inches of the shiny hardwood floor, and then twisted back up again. She wanted to dance forever!

But the song ended, and she collapsed on the couch, watching the familiar couples draw close to slow dance, gliding onto the floor, their heads pressed together, and Joellen sighed wistfully. She studied the crowded dance floor and all the customary girls with their bobby socks and white blouses with Peter Pan collars and sweater vests. She dreamily watched the young boys, so handsome in their dark suits. If only *she* could be there!

As always, the time flew by and Dick Clark was signing off with his engaging smile, but promising to be back the next day. Joellen switched off the television. She loved it when her mama was gone and wondered when she would be back. Her daddy had said she might stay at the hospital a week or more this time. She hoped so, and she hoped that the doctors could find out what was wrong with her. Daddy said she was sick, but she didn't seem sick. She just seemed mean.

The house was quiet as she looked around. She hated the place, a miserable place, and she hated living down in the country. She couldn't wait to get away from it all, especially from her mama. She glanced down at her engagement ring and supposed she would marry Dale once she graduated, but even it brought nagging thoughts to mind. Was she doing the right thing? She knew her daddy hoped she wouldn't, hoped she would stay home and be a help to him. Oh well, she'd better get to her school project.

The long, yellowish sheet of meat wrapping paper trailed behind her, stretching out across the bedroom floor and down the hallway. She could hear the boys out in the woods, so she needn't worry about anyone stepping on it, and she arched herself over the paper to sketch Chaucer's Friar by the description he had given in his famous *Canterbury Tales*. Glancing back and forth at her open literature book, she read again the musical words...

And certainly he had a merry note
Well could he sing and play on the fiddle
In songs he easily carried off the prize
His neck was as white as the fleur-de-lis
Yet he was as strong as a champion....

Deftly, she drew her perception of the Friar, reading and sketching, and then stiffly pushed herself up from the floor to study it. She paced up and down the hallway and into the living room, critiquing her work, hoping that Mrs. Soward would be pleased. She'd probably be surprised that she had been able to draw them from the scanty descriptions. Of course she'd had to use her imagination more than once, but she was sure glad her daddy had gotten her that roll of meat wrapping paper from the store. It was just the thing, even though it was a yellowish tan color instead of white, it was the perfect size for the pilgrims. He had asked how much paper she needed, and she told him a lot. She didn't know he was going to bring the whole roll, but it had taken most of it once they started walking across its slick surface. Mrs. Soward asked for the English Literature projects to be turned in, and Joellen handed her the roll of meat paper. She looked at it and up at Joellen, and some of the boys snickered. Joellen pulled off the rubber band, and Mrs. Soward began to unroll and unroll and unroll.

"Here, you hold one end, and I'll pull out the other," she suggested to Joellen, who was already blushing in front of the class. The paper continued to roll out, stretching across the entire blackboard.

"Well, I'll be…all twenty-nine of them, I suppose, on their way to Canterbury!" She was visibly impressed, and at that moment all the work and time and sore muscles were worth it. Mrs. Soward asked two of the boys to come forward and tack it across the top of the blackboard. Joellen couldn't suppress a smile. At the end of class, she asked if she could have it, and Joellen practically floated out the door.

Dear Secret Angel,

You're never going to believe this! Mrs. Soward kept my Canterbury Tales project. She wants to use it to help teach future classes. I really wanted to keep it myself, but I couldn't turn Mrs. Soward down. It's still hanging up on top of the blackboard!

THE CLOSER JUNE came, the more anxious Joellen was. Suppose something happened? Suppose she might not make it after all? She was obsessed with the thought as its reality dangled temptingly close. Every time her mother experienced one of her spells and raged out of control, she feared something was going to prevent her from graduating. And Dale was pushing her to get married at the same time, but she must finish school!

It was the end of March, and the shrill school bell rang out. Joellen settled herself comfortably at her desk, opening up her biology book, as the students shuffled noisily to their seats. Miss Mavis closed the door and sat down behind her large wooden desk. Suddenly Louise Whittaker's hand shot up.

"Louise?"

"Miss Mavis," she began contemptuously. "I have a question."

"Go ahead, Louise." Miss Mavis sounded hurried.

"Can you be elected into the Beta Club in your senior year?"

A hot flush started up Joellen's neck and rapidly climbed higher, and she wished she could sink down into her seat and become invisible. She knew where Louise was going with this. She was well aware that right at this moment she was being considered for membership into the honorary club, but how did Louise know? Who else knew? Everybody? And she had thought Louise was her friend.

The Beta Club thing had come as a surprise to her, too. She hadn't even thought about it, not with the grades she had from the start. Obviously Miss Mavis was caught off guard with the question. "Well...I guess you can," she replied hesitantly, "that is if you have the grades to qualify."

Joellen's scarlet face was glued to her biology book. She figured the whole class was staring at her, when in actuality they had their minds on anything but. She loathed Louise at that moment. How dare she try to humiliate her in front of the class. Well, she certainly hoped she would make it into the Beta Club. That would show her!

Two weeks before graduation, the senior class celebrated with an outing at Riverside Park just across the river and off Rivermont Avenue, a farewell picnic actually. A balmy spring day it turned out to be with a sweeping, clear-blue sky overhead and a promise of a whole new world awaiting the Class of Sixty-Two.

By early afternoon, however, the hot sun was beating down on the hilly park, and Mrs. Soward sought out a cool place in a little gazebo atop one of the hills, catching the frequent breezes from the tall oak trees. She plopped down on the circular bench, fanning herself with some papers as several girls crowded about, including Joellen. She leaned back against the cool wooden boards listening to the chattering, eager teenagers yakking about the end of school and their future plans. Most were headed for college and excitedly exchanged their individual stories about which college and what they would be doing. She noticed Joellen staring off in another direction.

"Joellen, what are you going to do?" she asked softly.

"...I have a job already...at the new General Electric plant," she stammered, trying to conceal her embarrassment.

The look on the old teacher's face spoke volumes, and Joellen turned away. She eased out of the gazebo as Mrs. Soward's attention was drawn into the conversation with the other girls, and walked beneath the aged oaks, feeling dreadfully alone and different. College was out of the question for her. There was no money for college, and her daddy was counting on her to help out at home. Why, he was pleased as punch about her new job! It was better than any job he'd ever had. He still worked the graveyard shift at the old fertilizer mill down by the river, the same one his papa had worked at before, and he drove the school bus in the day plus picked up any small carpentry jobs that he could. She had already promised him she would begin paying the electric bill among other things, and she couldn't let him down. Besides, she knew how fortunate she was to have the job. Why, many people would practically give their right arm to get on with the sprawling new General Electric plant, one of the best paying places in Lynchburg now. Yet she yearned to keep on learning, and she recalled what Mrs. Soward had said earlier in the year.

"When you stop learning, you are dead."

Well, she wasn't dead, that's for sure, and she would keep on learning. There were hundreds...thousands of books in the library!

THE TIME HAD come. Meredith dragged herself out of bed. Already it was hot...more like July than the first of June.

Her daughter was graduating today!

She was happy for her, but yet it dredged up all those past memories—her own school days at E. C. Glass, her own excitement about graduation, and then her wretched disappointment. She was sixteen then, full of hopes for the future, too. What had happened to all those hopes? She felt herself sinking again—down-down-down into the big black hole! No, she mustn't. This was her daughter's day. *She* was graduating, not her...not Meredith Leone Conner! She stretched the name out slowly and painfully. Meredith...Leone...Conner. Whatever happened to her?

The lure of the past pulled her back, and suddenly she could see a small child skipping down the hilly streets of Lynchburg, across Rivermont Bridge and climbing the wide steps of the Jones Memorial Library. A happy, little girl standing on her tiptoes to reach the high shelves crammed with all those books, and she could read any of them free of charge, as long as she returned them on time. She saw her tottering out of the stately building and teetering down its cascading steps, loaded down, a mound of books stacked clear up to her chin and her arms aching by the time she got to her grandmother's front porch on Pearl Street, and she was sitting there on the porch, reading, reading, and reading.

Then a teenager, no longer a child, but a pretty teenager climbing Eighth Street hill, and walking up Park Avenue to school. She had her lunch, her books, and her homework all done in hopes of a good grade. She loved to make good grades, but that was all before Mr. Walters came along and changed everything. The memory conjured up unpleasant thoughts, and she knew she mustn't dwell on them. That's what the doctor said—don't dwell on unpleasant things, upsetting memories, but how disappointed she had been in him. Growing up without a father had been hard. She had always wanted a father like her friends. Maybe then she wouldn't have been so afraid, maybe those bullies wouldn't have chased her home from school with those crawly bugs that had a hundred legs.

She pulled on her worn chenille robe. "But it's 1962, and it's my daughter graduating," she mumbled, shuffling down the hallway to the kitchen. She smelled the coffee on the stove where Bennett had left it. She should be happy today. Why couldn't she feel happy? Why did she feel like crying? She glanced in the small oval mirror above the kitchen sink where Bennett shaved every morning. Her eyes had dark, puffy bags under them; her cheeks were sallow.

"What happened to that pretty girl that lived on Grace Street?" she asked the clouded mirror. Her grandmother had always told her she was pretty, and so had Bennett in those days. All of a sudden she felt weak, so very weak, and sank onto a kitchen chair. Why was she so lethargic? Just last week her mother had encouraged her to get interested in something, watch television, the soap operas. Her mother loved *General Hospital.* "Or read a book," she'd said. "Do something to take your mind off your problems!" But she didn't read anymore.

She didn't know why. She simply didn't want to. A body has to want to do something before it can do it. Where had her "want to" gone? It had been gone a long, long time. Bennett said she should plant flowers like she used to when they had first moved into the little house on Thaxton's Lane across from Papa Thaxton's farm. She remembered those days. She remembered planting flowers, especially those dahlias. They were so tall and sturdy, and the pretty zinnias. She remembered all those different colored zinnias, and they made her happy then. She remembered being happy.

But it seemed so long ago. She knew Bennett would like to see her plant flowers again. She just couldn't muster up the energy, but she had to muster the energy for today. Everyone would be expecting her to be there...and she was dreading it!

Pushing her thick, unruly hair back off her forehead, she was becoming more nervous by the minute. She didn't want to get in that crowd of people with everybody talking at the same time...and talking to her and expecting her to talk back to them. She wanted to crawl back in bed and forget about everything, pull the pillow over her head and sleep. That's what she wanted to do.

Sleep...sleep...sleep.

JOELLEN WAS ANXIOUS. She hoped her mother would be there…and be all right. She checked the time, wondering if she had forgotten anything she was supposed to do. It was early. She was always early, but today she was especially early.

She checked her beautiful white cap and gown hanging on the rack in the school closet, and then sat down at one of the desks to wait for the others. She ran her fingers through the carved grooves, R.B. loves D.S. She wondered who R.B. and D.S. were. She couldn't think of any couple with those initials. They were probably long gone like she would be soon, just a memory like these mysterious initials.

Was she ready?

She looked up at the blackboard and around at the empty chairs surrounding her, all lined up in rows awaiting new students. She felt comfortable here with the smell of chalk and oiled wooden floors, and there was a sense of security in the sameness of every day. One could count on it for the most part, but now? She glanced out the tall windows.

What would it be like to go to work every day? She wouldn't be with students anymore, but grown-ups. She already knew that she would be working in the Wire Area. Though she had good typing and shorthand skills, the factory jobs paid more, her daddy said, and that's what they needed. What do you do with wires? she wondered as she proudly fingered her gold tassel lying in the little white box.

"Joellen, you daydreaming?" Marny rushed in, full of energy, throwing her bags down beside her. "We've got to get going!"

THE GRADUATES LINED up, pulling on their awkward caps, the girls sticking bobby pins this way and that to hold them on, and the boys clumsily pushing theirs down over stiff crew cuts.

"Who ever heard of a square cap?" one of the boys mocked, turning his around and around. "I'd like to know who came up with it! Looks like they could've made them round or oblong or even straight up like a top hat...but square...a square cap for a round head!"

The other boys snickered nervously while watching their families and guests filing into the small auditorium, finding seats, and shuffling around for more advantageous spots. Excited chatter swelled louder and louder as the auditorium slowly filled up, and Joellen strained to see if her parents were out there. The lighting was dim, hard to see, and there were so many people milling about, undergraduates kidding and scuffling with each other, freshmen and sophomores, grandmas and grandpas staring wide-eyed for their particular offspring. It didn't seem possible that....

She spotted them.

Bennett was leading Meredith up the narrow, crowded aisle, one hand out front and one gently on her back. "Here, Mama, sit here." He had begun calling her that ever since Katy was born. With five children crying *Mama,* it was inevitable that he should, too. Meredith followed his lead and began fumbling with the wooden chair seat that wouldn't stay down, repeatedly flying upwards, loudly banging the back. Bennett leaned over and patiently held it down for her, and she slowly sank into it, staring around at all the commotion. Then she looked up front.

The stage platform rose only a few feet above the floor. It was draped on three sides and on top with royal blue and gold curtains, and overhead there was a big gold embossed

"M." A heavy fringe of gold etched the front edge of the royal blue curtain that spanned the entire top of the stage, and three more layers of gold drapery hung overhead, evenly spaced behind the blue. Meredith suddenly remembered her school colors...blue and white...yes, blue and white, she thought, instead of blue and gold. She had loved her school and was so proud of it. It was brick like this one, too, and about the same size. She remembered how she and her friends liked to walk over to the reservoir that was situated beside it and hang onto the fence, looking into the still water. Those were happy memories, but a gloom settled over her as she sat there in the school auditorium. Maybe it was all the excitement of getting here, the effort; everything was such an effort.

After awhile Mr. Angersole strode to the podium and called the crowd to attention. A hush fell over the auditorium as the graduates filed in, one by one, the boys in long, dark blue robes and the girls in white, marching slowly down the aisle.

Bennett leaned over and whispered to Meredith, "She's got a gold tassel on her cap."

She nodded.

They lined up neatly on the platform steps, three rows, the girls in front and the boys behind, and the class of 1962 sang...

> *I believe for ev'ry drop of rain that falls*
> *a flower grows,*
> *I believe that somewhere in the darkest night*
> *a candle glows,*
> *I believe for ev'ry one who goes astray,*
> *Someone will come to show the way,*
> *I believe, I believe*

137

I believe above the storm the smallest pray'r
will still be heard,
I believe that someone in the great somewhere
hears every word
Every time I hear a newborn baby cry,
Or touch a leaf, or see the sky
Then I know why I believe!

Joellen sang out with all her heart, feeling like she would burst with happiness. Yes, she believed! There was magic tonight. The old auditorium had been transformed into a palatial castle of hope, and there was Aunt Anna and Aunt Ella standing out there looking proud, and her poor daddy…he was smiling…and her mama had come. She glanced over at Mrs. Soward, who was beaming from ear to ear. No, she would never forget this night, no matter how long she lived!

Some were wiping their eyes as the inspiring song concluded, and Mr. Angersole arose again. Tonight was more than a turning point for the small group of graduates, he explained. Tonight was a defining point for old Madison Heights High School, which had seen many a graduate walk down its proud aisles.

This would be the last graduating class.

A new and much larger and finer school had been built in Amherst. Joellen really couldn't keep her mind on what Mr. Angersole was saying. Myriad thoughts darted and danced through it, thoughts of the past, thoughts of the future, and thoughts of the present! Before she realized it, it was time for their last song. A lump formed in her chest, and she sang…

When you walk through a storm, hold your head up high
And don't be afraid of the dark,

At the end of the storm is a golden sky
And the sweet silver song of a lark,
Walk on through the wind,
Walk on through the rain,

Tho' your dreams be tossed and blown
Walk on, walk on, with a hope in your heart,
And you'll never walk alone,
You'll never walk alone!

CHAPTER NINE

PRESENT

JOELLEN PACKED UP her box of handwritten notes and returned the files to the Park Service Office, thanked them again, and left for the day. She climbed into her SUV and decided to drive home across the Parkway instead of down Route 43 and through Bedford. The isolation and solace was well worth the time it took, more miles to think and meditate. She was doing that a lot lately. Must be my age, she thought. It's one thing to turn thirty...or forty...or fifty even. She clearly remembered each of those inevitable hurdles, and though she had not welcomed any of them, she had tolerated them.

But sixty!

At forty, she realized she wasn't young anymore. When she turned fifty, she reluctantly admitted she was getting older. "But sixty!" she vented aloud as she wound around the curving Parkway. "Why, my grandmas were sixty!"

And they were old! Did others consider her the same way? It had slipped up on her so subtly, making its irreversible changes. Had she become so accustomed to its comfortable presence that she really didn't see herself the way others did? A scary thought! She peered into the rearview mirror and suddenly remembered her old friend, Dora, who had been fifty-five at the time, and she was only thirty-five. Whenever Dora looked at her with her soft blue eyes, all she could see was her drooping eyelids folding down over them like a tortoise.

She leaned into the rearview mirror again. Doggone that gravity! Its constant tugging, expanding, sagging, and dragging. She stretched her eyes wide open, furrowing her brow upward, erasing the years. Her feathered bangs concealed the orchestrated effect, but she couldn't go around holding it up forever! Of course, she could get a face lift. Everyone was getting one, that and tummy tucks and breast implants—a slice here, a pinch there, a puff here and there. But that was out of the question. Her fear of the knife settled that. Besides, she grinned into the mirror, God is not fond of our vanities. I could come out looking like a freak!

'behold, all is vanity and vexation of spirit….'

Better to go His way. One day it would all be dissolved into death anyway. But the real me—the one who lives within, behind the droop and wrinkles, will never die. It's this person that I need to focus on—the spirit. She settled back to drive. "Actually I don't mind the big six-o," she reassured herself aloud. "What really concerns me is that *time is running out!*"

She stared at the striking fall foliage lining the Parkway—such awesome beauty! She hated to think of leaving it all one day. And though she looked forward to Heaven and knew it was far better, she still resisted the thought of leaving. She loved life…she loved living…she always had! Suddenly she remembered the poem she had written so many years ago, and haltingly began to recite it…

> *Time…oh precious time*
> *Why must you hurry on?*
> *Endless hours cry out in chimes*
> *First, you're here, now you're gone*

My pace is quickened by your hands
which continue round and round
My eyes are blurred by sifting sands
which never cease flowing down

I beg of you...oh precious time
to pause for a little while
If not, my youth will fall behind
and I will tread that last mile

My gosh! I must have been about twenty years old! What in the world did I know about age back then?

She remembered composing it while working on the conveyor at General Electric, bored by the repetition of the job, soldering thousands of resistors, transistors and capacitors into the moving mobile radios. She had hastily scribbled it down, to the irritation of her co-worker, leaning way into her space. That night she typed it up on her little portable typewriter and carried it back the next day for her co-workers to critique, secretly sending it down the conveyor line without the foreman's knowledge. The workers enjoyed the diversion and weren't shy with their comments.

"Why so morbid?"

"Why do you write so much about dying?"

"And growing old?"

"And sadness?"

"How about a little happiness?"

Abruptly her attention was drawn to the paradise trees lining the Parkway. The trees of heaven they were called, dressed in their crimson autumn colors. The sun splashed them, bringing them alive, and also the thick undergrowth of striped maples boasting large, expressive, yellow leaves that created a stunning mural in the darkened forest. Nature is absolutely amazing, she thought to herself. A vast, sweeping canvas painted by the hand of God, literally reaching out to touch us through every sense. And all we need to do is be still.

The SUV leaned into the curves, and she glanced at the digital clock on the dash. 3:30 PM. There was still time to get there.

MEREDITH WAS SITTING up in the wheelchair when Joellen arrived, and a perky young aide was straightening her bed. "Miss Thaxton's doing real good today...but she still won't eat." She frowned at Meredith in a playful way. "I tell her she can't live without eating! Now, maybe I could." Chuckling, she patted her pudgy middle. "Her food is on the table there; maybe you can get her to eat a little of it."

Joellen glanced from her mother to the covered tray beside her. She eased over, lifted the gray plastic dome, and thought to herself that she couldn't eat this stuff either. It was mush! But it was the only way her mother could eat it.

She couldn't tell what it was, but it smelled pretty good. An assortment of little brown plastic bowls held a sallow orange mystery, a pea green, and the last a boring brown. She wondered which one to choose, which one she could entice her mother to eat. Scooping up a spoonful of the orange mush, she poked it at her mother. "Mama, how about a little supper? Smells good...looks good, too," she fibbed, hoping she sounded more convincing than she felt.

Meredith's hand shot up in protest, and she was shaking her head vigorously.

"Don't you want some...food?" She wished she knew what to call it. Janet or Katy would know. They were far better nurses than she was. They were caretakers by nature.

143

Not her. She wasn't comfortable in the role. In fact, there were a lot of jobs in life that she would have enjoyed, but a nurse was not on the list!

Awkwardly she tried again. "If you'll just eat a little of this, Mama, then we'll go for a nice stroll outside. It's a beautiful fall day, warm and sunny. I'll push you out to the little patio, and you'll enjoy it. The trees are turning, too." Again she guided the spoon toward her mother's closed mouth. "Come on, open up, Mama. You need to eat."

"Can't!" She jerked her head away.

"Why, Mama...why can't you eat?"

"Because...."

"Because of what?"

"...him. Because of him," she whispered, peering past Joellen and out into the hallway. "He'll kill me if I eat. He told me so!"

"Who, Mama?"

"...him. He's got a knife."

"That's not true, Mama. Nobody is going to hurt you, come on and eat."

Stubbornly she shook her head, clamping her mouth shut.

Finally Joellen gave up and pushed her mother out of the room, down the long corridors of shiny tile floors, past the gaping doors of the sick and dying, and out into the bright afternoon sun, a welcomed escape from the depressing medicinal atmosphere. A slight breeze stirred the red maples. She eased down on a bench beside her mother, inhaling the crisp fall air. They sat there silently for a few minutes, and she hoped her mother was enjoying it as much as she was.

"Take me back in, Joellen."

"But, Mama, we just got out here...and it's so nice."

"Take me back, Joellen," she demanded.

"You sure…sure you want to go back in so soon?"

She nodded emphatically.

Frustrated, Joellen wheeled the chair around and headed back inside. She pushed her down the long corridor that led by the caged birds and rabbits. Beautiful white lovebirds fluttered their fragile wings and cozily nudged up against one another. An entire area had been cleverly set aside just for rabbits. It butted up to a large plate glass disclosing their natural habitat, and the rabbits were busy burrowing and eating. Usually Meredith enjoyed watching them, but today she didn't seem to notice. Instead, she gestured for Joellen to stop.

"What is it, Mama?"

"Lean down," she whispered. "I have something to tell you."

It was extremely difficult to understand her, and Joellen leaned down real close.

"You see what's in my hand?"

"I can't see anything in your hand, Mama." It was knotted into a tight fist. "Open it up and let me see."

Her mother looked up at her with those big brown eyes. "No-o-o-o." She refused to open it.

"There's nothing in your hand, Mama."

"Yes, there is," she insisted. "Lean back down here, Joellen."

Again she leaned over closely, and Meredith very slowly and very cautiously began to open her fist. "See…it's a big black snake."

"Mama, there's no snake in your hand!"

"Yes, there is, Joellen. Look.…" She was staring down at her hand in a trance-like fashion, as if she actually did

145

see something. "It's moving around…see it…a big black snake."

"No, Mama, I don't see it. There's nothing in your hand."

Meredith clenched her fist again but continued to stare at it in deep concentration.

Joellen reached for her mother's hand, but she jerked it away. "No, don't do that! It'll bite you, Joellen!"

"Mama, there's no snake in your hand. You just think it is, but there isn't."

Like a little child, Meredith answered, "Yes, there is." Then she stared down at herself. "Look, they're all over my lap…crawling all over my lap. See them?"

By now Joellen was completely frustrated, but what could she do? It was evident that her mother could not be convinced otherwise. The hallucinations, or whatever they were, obviously were real to her. However, in light of what she saw or thought she saw, it didn't evoke the natural reaction of horror. She seemed afraid, but not unduly afraid, and after awhile she was able to divert her mother's attention to the pretty lovebirds.

Joellen left the nursing home drained and sad. Poor Mama, she thought. She wished there was something they could do to stop her from seeing those horrible "things." She was already on medicine, strong medicine, to eradicate these ghastly thoughts or hallucinations. But it wasn't working, and they had already changed the medication several times. Strangely, she was being held captive in this invisible prison—this nightmare of nightmares! Joellen couldn't think of anything worse than being in her mother's shoes, believing that there were snakes on you or that there was someone trying to cut off your head.

What saddened her most was that here at the end of her mother's life, she had just turned eighty, she would have to be afraid! Fear had followed her all of her life. She had been scared of everything. From the bugs as a child to when Grandma Isabelle remarried, and she was finally booted out of her mother's bed. Though sixteen at the time, she was frightened and slept on the hallway floor up against their bedroom door. Then there were the superstitions—her world was filled with them. Where did they come from? Her mother's strong Irish background, perhaps; Irish culture was steeped in superstitions. They had grown up with them as children, and woe to them if by happenstance they opened an umbrella in the house, or if a mirror was accidentally broken. Meredith would fear that her life would become even more burdensome, and they were regularly admonished to avoid crossing the path of a black cat or walking underneath a ladder. But her greatest fear was thunderstorms. They literally terrified her, and unfortunately Virginia was known for its violent electrical storms. They beset her so much that she dreaded spring, and would crawl into bed at the first clap of thunder, burying her head under the pillow. No matter how hot, in the middle of July, she curled up in a fetal position with the pillow crammed over her head. Helplessly, Bennett tried to comfort her.

"Meredith, please take the pillow off your head. You'll smother yourself!" he vainly pleaded, but she fought him off if he tried to remove it.

And Joellen vividly remembered all those intense, raging storms when she was small, she and her mother and her siblings all huddled together in the corner of the pantry where she herded them. They would crouch there throughout the shattering thunder and streaks of lightning, with the smelly slop jar and dirty clothes piled high. Quietly they would huddle there until the storm passed over, until the lightning ceased, and the thunder moved off into the distance.

As Joellen drove down Grace Street, she remembered that her mother hadn't eaten. She would tell Janet when she talked with her. What a powerful thing the human mind is, she reasoned, and when it gets off-kilter, it can essentially become dangerous. There was no question that her mother firmly believed in what she was saying—that someone was trying to kill her or that snakes were crawling all over her, or crawling in the shower stall when they gave her a bath, or that someone or something was ordering her not to eat! She believed it so completely that she was afraid to go against this mysterious voice in her troubled mind.

Meredith was a diabetic and had been on insulin for some time. In the past few years, she had had many touch and go physical challenges as a result of her diabetes. Fluid build up around her heart also caused multiple problems. At one point, she had developed a severe problem with food particles getting into her lungs, which caused serious complications, and a stomach tube was inserted for months in order to feed her. All of this would seem enough for one poor soul to endure, but the cruel tricks her mind was playing on her was the greatest plague of all.

Joellen headed home through the old familiar downtown streets, pushing the depressing thoughts away. But as she glanced up Clay Street, another autumn forced its memory upon her.

CHAPTER TEN

IT WAS 1964, late October, but it was unseasonably warm. Even the tall oak trees that lined Clay Street seemed in no hurry to discard their leaves. They hung brown and listless. Its brick-lined streets that had seen better days had shifted with the times, and the rambling old houses were converted into tenements, providing homes for two, three, or perhaps four families. They no longer exuded the prominence of the past, but struggled for survival with peeling paint, crooked shutters, decaying steps, and people within also fighting for survival.

Clay Street ran parallel to the famed James River, a ways up the steep, climbing hill. First there was Jefferson Street running close beside the flowing dark waters; then Commerce one street up the hill, its name appropriately describing its function from its origin. Main was next, the hub of downtown, and Church and Court streets followed. Of course, Court Street boasted the historic courthouse that dominated the steep hillside, keeping watch over the city since 1855.

Clay was the sixth street up from the river, and once had claimed a panoramic view, but now all one could see were grimy rooftops scaling the sharp hills, one on top of another. In the days of its prime, the small city bustled with success. Known as "Tobacco City," it was considered the second wealthiest city per capita in the country. It grew the popular golden leaf and was dotted with tobacco warehouses in the 1800s. Several were located on Commerce, close to the river—Spring Warehouse, Liberty Warehouse, Lynch's Warehouse and Martin's Warehouse. There was Planter's Warehouse on Main Street between Fifth and Sixth streets, and Bowman and Moore Tobacco Factory in the 1400 block of Main. Friend's Warehouse was on Church Street between Ninth and Tenth. Blackwater Warehouse was below Williams Viaduct, and Cabell Street had Ammon Hancock Tobacco Factory.

It had been a genteel time, full of grace, a time to proudly record in the history books. But the tobacco warehouses were gone, along with the elite residential downtown. It had seen the exit of the more affluent, and experienced what most downtowns across America had experienced—the flight to suburbia, leaving the charming old homes to less fortunate dwellers, and the chipped paint, crumbling sidewalks, and porch dividers were a clear testimony to that. The big yellow tenement house on Clay Street was once a proud white with a gentle veranda gracing the front. Now it was covered over by a sallow yellow, and the front yard was sliced down the middle by a yellow picket fence separating the two tenements, with a solid wooden wall dividing the old veranda. Sadly, its prominent stature had been reduced to a pitiful presence.

Joellen and Dale Rodman occupied one of its four apartments with their young son, Ryan.

A lot had happened since Joellen walked the aisle of old MHHS proudly sporting her gold tassel. Ambitious plans, gilded hopes, and naïve aspirations all spilled over and out of the Irish pot of luck and hopelessly ran down the rivers of time, aimlessly adrift.

Unfortunately, the new decade had not brought new beginnings either; instead it had deepened the country's woes. Even the young president's optimistic inaugural speech had fizzled to a more realistic assessment by the end of 1962, when he spoke to the nation, "*The responsibilities...are greater than I imagined them to be, and there are greater limitations upon our ability to bring about a favorable result....It is much easier to make the speeches than it is to finally make the judgments....*"

He had inherited from the Truman and Eisenhower regimes a commitment to prevent a Communist takeover in South Vietnam, and he immediately increased the amount of aid. Then he authorized U.S. helicopters to fire on the enemy, and a year later authorized strafing missions. The war escalated!

A run-away locomotive of racial turmoil was also hurdling down the tracks of time, hurdling to unknown destinies and in the summer of 1963 had climaxed in the Capital, with two hundred thousand demonstrators marching on Washington, and Martin Luther King, Jr. boldly declaring, "*I have a dream....*"

And later that year in the cold month of November while Joellen was soldering parts onto a transistor board as the conveyor line lurched forward, the young president was assassinated! The hope of America was gone, and the country was thrown into chaos.

LITTLE RYAN RODMAN, just over a year old, was taking his afternoon nap. In Joellen's world, he was the most important thing that had happened. Not the headlines, the speeches, or the marches, not even the presidential tragedy—but this small, sleeping child.

An autumn storm had just passed with sudden gully washers, but now had trickled out to a steady drizzle. Joellen watched the little rivulets of water seeping down the large windowpanes of the apartment as she pressed the last side of the white sheet draped over the ironing board. She wondered why it was necessary to iron sheets. But the girls at work said they ironed theirs, so it must be the thing to do, and she wanted to be a good housekeeper. She could see ironing pillowcases, but sheets?

Oh well, she slid the iron back and forth, back and forth, the hot steam rising, forming beads of perspiration across her forehead. She hoped Ryan would stay asleep. The little fellow had been playing so hard all morning. He needed his nap. Her thoughts went back to the day she discovered she was pregnant.

It was the end of summer, that eventful summer of 1962. She had just graduated from high school with high hopes. Even though she was working in the Wire Department at General Electric, she still had hope. Why, she was just eighteen and had her whole life ahead of her!

She had finally summoned the courage to take control of her life, and told Dale that she would rather postpone the wedding and work for a while. She was confused and didn't know about marriage just yet, but Dale was tired of waiting. The argument ended in an awful breakup, and she gave him back the engagement ring.

But it was too late.

She was pregnant. Unaware of it, she threw herself into work, glad to have something to focus on, glad to at last be free of her worries about marriage, and glad to be away from home.

It was right afterwards that Meredith got the news about her daddy. Joellen was at work, stripping and soldering wires. Bennett was sound asleep, having worked the night shift, and Daniel, Brian, and Katy were down in the woods trying to build a tree fort when her sister called from Hampton. Meredith had always wondered what it would be like when she received the news, but now that it had happened, she just felt a big hole inside. So much so that she didn't feel like moving. She had been sitting there at the kitchen table ever since she hung up, and she couldn't remember how long she had been sitting there. It seemed like a long time, and she couldn't stop crying. She didn't understand why she kept crying. She didn't even know him!

She should get up and wash the breakfast dishes, but she just couldn't. She could barely hear shouts and laughter coming from down in the woods, but she knew they would be in soon, hungry for lunch. They were always hungry, but she couldn't drag herself up. And it was so hot. She wiped her eyes again, and she wiped her forehead, and every time she lifted her arm off the oil cloth to do so, that sticky sound grated on her nerves. She wondered if he had been alone. They said he had just eaten his supper in the cafeteria and was going back to his room. She watched dust motes sift through the shaft of sunlight filtering through the screen door. A fly buzzed over her head, and then flew off, straight toward the long yellow strip of fly paper hanging from the ceiling. She watched it smack into it, then buzz wildly but vainly, trying to pull itself off. They said he dropped dead right in front of the elevator. And she had never gone back to see him.

She remembered that day when she and Bennett went. She remembered sitting there in his room, and she remembered the queer feelings. She remembered him knocking on his wooden leg, and those large mountains out his window. What were their names? They were named after those two little girls…Mary Gray and…Betsy Belle. Yes, she remembered now, but most of all she remembered wanting to get out of there.

Brian burst through the screen door, his hair damp from the sultry heat. "What's wrong, Mama," he asked, edging up close to the table. She didn't look up. Her head was in her hands, and she was crying.

"What's wrong, Mama?' he repeated worriedly.

"My daddy died."

By the end of summer Joellen realized something was wrong, dreadfully wrong. Though she didn't understand what being pregnant felt like, by putting two and two together, she finally concluded it must be so. She couldn't go to her mother. Meredith had been even worse for the past few weeks, and she couldn't bring herself to go to her daddy either. She was too embarrassed to go to Aunt Anna, and how could she go to Dale after breaking up with him? She didn't have the courage to reveal her secret to anyone. Somehow, she must work it out. For days and weeks she struggled with her dilemma, unable to sleep, tossing and turning, fearful of the future, embarrassed and ashamed; what was she going to do?

Swallowing her pride, she finally decided to call Dale. They were married within a few weeks in the church parsonage, the same one her parents were married in, and only her daddy stood up for them. No one suspected the reason for the sudden marriage, not even her daddy for they had been dating for so long plus engaged for a year, and everyone was used to their up and down courtship. But her daddy's words still rang in her ears, "As soon as I get one grown where I think they can help me out a little, they up and leave me." That hurt the most.

She slid the hot, sputtering iron over the last corner of the heavy sheet, and heard Ryan stirring in the bedroom. He would be up soon. She thought of her new friend at work, Virginia, whom she called "Virgie," and what she had said just the other day.

"Why, you just jumped out of the frying pan and into the fire!"

She had glared at Virgie, realizing the truth of her words. Virgie worked on the opposite side of the large boxy partition that separated the two of them—the only two castings spot-welders at the large General Electric facility. Positioned directly across from one another, an open passageway carried their voices loud and clear to each other, but no one else could hear. With perfect acoustics, it was an ideal setup for two young women to bond permanently. They talked incessantly throughout the day while nimbly welding the small coils into the never-ending castings, the first step of what would become mobile radios for police departments, fire departments, and such. Joellen was glad that they had moved her to this job. She liked it fine, but she particularly enjoyed her friendship with Virgie. They were the same age, both married young, and both had a toddler. Virgie's little girl, Lydia, was only one year older than Ryan. They had just about everything in common, except for one thing. Virgie was black.

This was an entirely new experience for both of them. Joellen and Virgie had attended and graduated from segregated schools. Although integration had begun in its embryonic stages that winter in Lynchburg, it did not affect the old schools across the river, so Joellen's exposure had been from a distance. Nice colored people had lived on Wright Shop Road not terribly far from Thaxton's Lane, but they didn't socialize together. For the most part, the colored kept to themselves and the whites kept to themselves. She had never given much thought to it one way or the other. It was just the way things were.

Joellen finished ironing the sheet and folded it up. She smiled to herself thinking of Virgie and remembering her slip or near-slip last Christmas when they were discussing the things they liked most about the season. The merry conversation had jumped from Christmas trees to fruitcakes to holiday nuts in just a matter of minutes.

"My favorite nuts are walnuts. I love walnuts!" Virgie announced eagerly.

"Well, my favorites are...are..." Joellen's face turned beet red. *She couldn't say that!*

Virgie leaned forward. "Brazil nuts?"

Joellen looked dumbfounded. *What the heck are Brazil nuts?*

"...they're shaped like this." Virgie held up two fingers showing the length. "...and they're black...the shell is very hard, but the meat is delicious."

"...that's them...Brazil nuts...I love Brazil nuts!"

Virgie smiled at her and a moment of understanding passed between them, the beginning of a long and deep friendship.

Joellen laid the ironed sheet to one side, thinking to herself that she had never called them anything else to this day. She pulled one of Dale's wrinkled shirts from the basket, looked at it, and sighed. He had had this shirt on the night he came in drunk, and she had locked him out. Shivers ran up her spine at the thought.

Her daddy had made her a special lock for the large solid door because he was concerned for her safety after hearing of Dale's drunken escapades. It was a crude night latch, a heavy piece of metal about four inches long, the size of a large primary pencil, and that night she had placed it in position. She was tired of him coming in drunk. She was going to teach him a lesson!

Lying awake, unable to sleep, she heard him stumbling down the long hallway. She listened to him vainly jiggling his key in the keyhole. The door was adjacent to their bedroom door, and she could see it clearly from their bed. He banged on it a few times, but she didn't budge. Then she heard something being dragged across the hallway. Suddenly she realized what he was doing! Like most old Victorian homes, there was a small glass window above the door. It wasn't latched and was slightly ajar. Even in the dark, she could see the window slowly push out, and then he was squeezing through it. He dropped to the floor and yanked the metal pen out of its latch and angrily threw it at her.

She heard it whiz by her head.

"Curved it!" Victor bragged to Celeste.

It hit the pillow with a dull thud, narrowly missing her head. It still chilled her to think of such a close call. It was the last time she used it.

After that Virgie renamed Clay Street and started calling it Clayton Place for the popular *Peyton Place* that was number one on weekly television. But unfortunately there had been too many of these incidents. As she smoothed out the shirt, spraying it lightly with starch, she remembered the other time she had locked him out just before they moved downtown. They were still living in their first

157

apartment, the two rooms in West End, and it was a cold, raw night the first of December. Dale had come home in the wee hours, and she had locked their bedroom door. It was an improvised upstairs apartment. Mrs. Dunford, an elderly lady, rented out her upstairs for extra income. The house had four rooms down and two rooms up, a typical farmhouse built in the twenties, although it sat directly on a city street. Three upstairs windows faced the street, resting on the oblong tin roof over the front porch. A stairwell led up from the small downstairs foyer to the second landing. Turning left, one entered the kitchen, right led to the bedroom. A small open hallway separated the two.

Joellen had been lying in bed for over an hour crying, disillusioned with her crumbling marriage, when suddenly she heard the familiar loud music coming down the street. She knew it was him—he always kept his automobile radio blaring.

When he entered the front door and climbed the steps, he found the bedroom door locked, and it infuriated him! He went into the kitchen for a few minutes, then came back to the bedroom door and banged on it. She refused to open it. Locking him out was her only way of fighting back. With every bang, she hunkered down under the covers and hoped the baby wouldn't wake up. Ryan's crib was in the corner of their bedroom. She heard a strange, squeaking noise and realized he was opening the hall window, which led out onto the top of the front porch.

Then she heard a footstep on the tin roof.

Suddenly, to her horror, she saw him on top of the porch, silhouetted in the full moonlight, weaving back and forth in his underdrawers.

And he was swinging his boot toward the window.

"*NO!*" she shrieked.

CRASH!

The big black boot sailed through the bedroom.

Glass splintered all over the bed, bits and pieces stinging her arms. She jumped up and ran to the crib. Ryan was crying. The noise had startled him, but otherwise he was all right. In disbelief, she watched her young husband climb through the large jagged hole, oblivious to the sharp slivers of glass, and flop down on the bed. Immediately he was out cold, sound asleep. She stood there aghast, shocked and crying along with the baby, as the cold wind whistled through the gaping hole, bringing the raw December chill with it.

"Joellen…Joellen…what in the world…." Mrs. Dunford hurriedly dragged herself up the steps. "What on earth?" She gasped at the broken window and the sheer curtains blowing straight out over the bed. Joellen, crying uncontrollably and hugging the baby to her, was already pulling the crib out of the bedroom and through the narrow hallway to the kitchen. Muttering to herself, Mrs. Dunford held the door for her, "I don't believe it! I just don't believe it!"

Scared, confused and totally embarrassed, Joellen lay the baby back in his crib and closed the kitchen door to keep out the cold. Mrs. Dunford stood by, wringing her hands. "We've gotta put something over that window!" she exclaimed as the cold winds howled outside. "I'll go downstairs and get some cardboard and tape. You wait here. I think I know where some is." With that the small, wiry lady hurried off.

They boarded up the broken window with heavy cardboard, shutting out the cold and wind, and scooped up as much glass as possible from the bed while Dale slept peacefully.

"You and the baby...y'all come on downstairs and sleep," Mrs. Dunford said. "You can sleep on the couch, and I'll help you get the crib down. We'll finish cleaning this mess up in the morning."

"We'll be all right," Joellen stammered. She just wanted to be alone.

"Where you gonna sleep?"

"I don't expect to get much sleep...but I'd rather stay up here."

The old lady shook her head, and after a few more tries, shuffled back downstairs. "This is too much for an old woman!" she sighed as she wearily climbed back into bed.

Joellen switched off the kitchen light and dropped down onto a chair to collect her thoughts. Ryan fell back to sleep in his crib, while silver moonlight spilled into the kitchen, in a straight beam across the linoleum. With her chin cupped in her hands, she leaned onto the table and stared out the darkened window. What was she going to do? Where could she go? How could they live like this?

But she couldn't go home.

The thoughts of home were still too fresh, the hurt, humiliation, and unhappiness. In fact, she had begun having nightmares of going back home, and each time that she awoke, she was determined to make the marriage work. She would never go back!

Suddenly she felt utterly exhausted and sleepy. Where *was* she going to sleep? She glanced around the small kitchen, her eyes falling on the playpen under the window. Oh well, why not? She climbed over the high, wooden sides, curled up in a fetal position, and fell into a fitful sleep.

JOELLEN PAINSTAKINGLY HUNG up the shirt on the clothes hanger and reached for another. She wondered where Dale was now. She simply couldn't understand him. Throughout their long courtship, he had hounded her to marry him, to even quit school and marry him, and then immediately after they married, he began acting like he was single again. But when she confronted him and asked him if he wanted to separate, he wouldn't hear of it.

And the drinking! She had never known him to drink before. Obviously, he had a drinking problem, but it had come as a total surprise to her. How he had been able to conceal it all the time they were dating was certainly a mystery. She recalled the first time he had come home drunk. They hadn't been married a month, and he had come in very late and immediately threw up all over the kitchen floor. Thinking he must have the flu and feeling sorry for him, she had rushed to his side, soothing him, and cleaned up the mess.

Since then, she had learned that alcohol wasn't his only problem. It simply masked a much deeper problem—a problem too complex for her to understand. Often she awoke in the middle of the night to the soft strains of his guitar. He couldn't sleep. Then he lost his job, the beginning of many. She grew accustomed to paying the rent and the bills, and was thankful for her good paying job at General Electric. She knew that he loved her in his own way, and he loved little Ryan, as well. But that was not enough—not when she never knew what might happen, like the other night when she had to flee the apartment and his angry threats and had found refuge, or at least thought so, on the elevated porch of St. Paul's Episcopal Church Rectory. Chills still raced up her spine when she thought of that close call, and she well knew had any one of those young, black men turned their head ever so slightly, he would have looked directly into her terrified eyes as she lay there in the quarter moon—so vulnerable. But they didn't! Maybe they wouldn't have hurt her, and maybe they would have. She would never know because *angels hovered between.*

She pressed the shirt sleeve and remembered how she had jumped up as soon as their voices disappeared into the distance and shot off the porch, leaping down two steps at a time and out into the courtyard, swinging through the open gate, dashing across Sixth Street and back to the tenement house. She remembered how she had eased up on her own back porch and cautiously peered through the plastic kitchen curtain. All was quiet by then, still she slumped down on the porch to wait, utterly exhausted.

But then she grew angry.

What in the world was she doing out there—afraid to go in her own apartment…and she paid the rent…and just having escaped only God knows what!

She sighed and hung up the pressed shirt, and wondered when he would get home. She yanked the cord out of the socket, immediately feeling guilty.

If Mrs. Gilbert saw that!

How many times had she lectured them on how to pull a plug out, by holding onto the plug, never yank it out by the cord as she had just done. Suddenly she felt sad. She couldn't believe that she actually missed school.

Ryan awoke from his nap, toddled into the living room, and wanted to go outside to play. Out back there was a very small yard, surrounded on three sides by a ten-foot fence, and you couldn't see over it or around it. Joellen appreciated the privacy, though it gave her a closed-in feeling. All the same, Ryan enjoyed playing in the black dirt with his little trucks and cars.

The rain had stopped and the sun was shining, and she decided to hang out the few items she had washed. Ryan followed after, pushing his rubber truck through the wet, loamy soil. Then she heard a door open and shut. He must be home! She was thrilled. He had come home in the day-time, which meant he wanted to be with them. She knew the routine; he would come to her, beg her forgiveness and try to kiss and make up, and she wanted him to.

But he didn't come.

What?

She heard a door shut.

"I'll be right back, Ryan." She raced up the back steps and through the apartment, jerking open the front door to look up the long, dark hallway just in time to catch a glimpse of his new, red mustang driving off. Puzzled, she wondered, why did he come home? She glanced around the apartment, looking for a clue. She searched the kitchen, living room, and bedroom. Then she looked in the bathroom. The bathroom sink was empty. Where was her pearl ring?

The one he had given her.

Tears flooded her eyes as she sank down on her knees. How could he?

"Mama," Ryan had followed her in, his baby cheeks smeared with dirt and his eyes questioning. She wiped her tears and hugged him to her. "Let's go back outside to play." She took him by the hand, but the rest of the day she pondered why Dale would take her ring. To pawn it...or....

AS 1964 CAME to a close, Joellen was completely im-mersed in her own problems, only vaguely aware of the growing unrest that was creating havoc in the country. That much she couldn't escape, but her own turbulent life was all she could deal with at the time. She would be turning twenty-one years old, but she already felt much older. Her out-of-control marriage and financial worries drained her energy most days, and she welcomed the night. Often she went to bed alone and fell asleep to the radio in the little alcove of the headboard. Although radio was increasingly being replaced by television, still night radio hung on, mostly for the young people, and they loved it, especially *Night Train*. Joellen turned it down low, skeptically listening to the new sound.

She loves you, yeah, yeah, yeah
She loves you, yeah, yeah, yeah

Along with all the other changes taking place in the sixties, the music was changing, too, and she wasn't so sure about it. Nostalgically she thought back to her last year of school. It was called the year of the dance, bringing out "The Peppermint Twist," "Mashed Potato Time," "The Loco-Motion" and "Monster Mash," and she had loved watching them all on *American Bandstand*. But now there were strange looking teenagers emerging, dressed in wild clothes with unusual combinations of colors and textures, adorned with flowers. What had happened to the pleated skirts and Peter Pan collars? And they were singing songs laced with sarcasm and rebellion that literally frightened the older generation, as they helplessly looked on. The guys wore long hair and adorned their greasy heads with crazy hats and dirty red bandanas. Some even grew long beards. They had adopted the Volkswagen bus as their favorite transportation and were crudely painting them with peace symbols and fitting them with old mattresses. And the girls were throwing away their bras, much to their mothers' dismay.

It was a unique youth movement that had grown out of the innocent fifties rock and roll in America, then spread to Canada, Great Britain, and many other countries. They were called Hippies and rejected the status-quo, the customs and traditions of society, and set about making their own. They wanted a world of love and peace, and they were tagged "flower children" for giving away flowers to communicate this. The extremists lived in communes, parks, and cars, and turned on with marijuana and acid. Their motto was "Make Love, Not War." The Beatles, the popular English group, were helping to spread the movement with their mesmerizing music.

Joellen didn't mind the Beatles' music, though, and even enjoyed some of it. The four mop-haired young men from Liverpool had literally burst upon the rock and roll scene, dominating the record charts. Their music was novel just as Elvis's had been in the fifties, but times were changing, and now it was their time. Parents had been outraged with Elvis, but now, not only parents, but most adults were outraged. The winsome words poured out of the little radio above Joellen's head and carried her into dreamland.

I wanna hold your hand
I wanna hold your hand

She and Dale were young teenagers again holding hands, and she was warm and happy. But those days would not return.

PRESIDENT LYNDON JOHNSON signed legislation revolutionizing American life forever with The Civil Rights Act, to eradicate all forms of segregation in the United States, but it also initiated race riots, including New York where the National Guard was called in. A week later, the bodies of three missing men in Mississippi were recovered. Following that, race riots erupted in New Jersey. And this was just the national news. All over America, desegregation was igniting racial turmoil. Much of it never made the news, especially in small-town America, but nevertheless, it was creating mayhem for many, not to mention fear and unrest on both sides.

It did not affect Joellen, though she did experience something that profoundly bothered her two weeks before Christmas. The festive holiday spirit was contagious in the sprawling General Electric plant, and cakes, cookies, and bourbon balls were being discreetly passed around. Excitement was in the air, and Joellen looked up as Patricia Johnson approached her. Patricia also worked in the Mobile Department, but in another area. She glanced sideways at Virgie as she approached with a pad in her hand and motioned Joellen over.

"We're having a Christmas party at the Fort Avenue location—thought you might like to come." She warily glanced back in Virgie's direction, and Virgie immediately lowered her head to her soldering.

Patricia whispered, "If you do, just let me know. I'm getting a list together of all who want to come."

Joellen nodded, wondering why the secrecy. She returned to her station and sat down in front of Virgie, who pretended to be busy soldering coils into the casting in front of her, but she was unusually quiet and brisk about her work.

"They're having a Christmas party next week."

Virgie nodded without looking up.

"You going?"

"I didn't get an invitation," she answered abruptly, "...
but that's okay. I didn't want to go anyway." She reached
up and hastily repositioned her safety glasses that had slid
down on her nose. Grabbing the solder in one hand and
the welding iron in the other, fiery sparks flew left and
right.

"But that's not right...it's not fair!"

Virgie looked up. "Don't worry about it! It's not the first
time."

"But it's not right!" Joellen insisted. She was indignant.
How could they shun her friend, someone as good and
honest and noble...even Christian-like? She went to church
every Sunday, and quoted the Scriptures to *her* every chance
she got. How could they leave her out...just because she
was black?

But she was left out, and Joellen wouldn't go either.

Americans were so caught up in the unrest at home that
they were not paying a lot of attention to what was going
on overseas. Most people had never heard of Vietnam
until a few years prior, and even then they pushed it out
of their minds, except for those directly affected. A survey
conducted in early December of 1964 revealed that one-
quarter of Americans did not know there was any fighting
going on in Vietnam.

By the end of the year, however, the word was that although none of the combatants had formally declared war,
it was undeniably a full-scale war being waged in Vietnam
and the adjacent territories of Laos and Cambodia.
Approximately twenty-three thousand American military
personnel were in South Vietnam, all still designated "military advisors," and Americans for the most part were proud

167

of what they were doing for the free people of Vietnam. Americans stood for freedom!

Shortly after President Johnson's inauguration for his second term, he pledged to support South Vietnam in fighting Communist aggression, stating that "For ten years now, US Presidents have pledged the help requested by the South Vietnamese; and secondly, our own security is tied to the peace of Asia." He soon ordered air strikes against North Vietnam, and the new forces were not termed "advisors" anymore, but combat troops. Americans perked up.

The president decided to implement Operation Rolling Thunder on the thirteenth of February—the sustained bombing of North Vietnam that he and his advisors had been discussing for some time.

A STUBBORN, RAW cold settled over Lynchburg by the end of February, refusing to let go, and there was snow in the air again. The last snow had barely melted, but the wheels of industry continued to turn. Lynchburg's shoe factories clicked on, its garment factories hummed rhythmically, and the new General Electric plant never closed, no matter how cold or how much snow piled up. It had radios to build—thousands! Virgie and Joellen hurried back from break.

"Sure hope it doesn't start before we get home."

"Me, too," Virgie agreed. "You think everything's gonna be all right...I mean at...Clayton Place tonight?" she teased with a twinkle in her eye.

"Who knows."

"Well, you be careful, you hear."

Joellen nodded.

Dale was out again. She thought of his wallet and the imprint of his wedding ring in it. She had suspected almost from the start of their marriage, and when she discovered the obvious imprint, her suspicions were confirmed. But what baffled her was why he wanted to stay married and still behave like a single guy.

"He wants to have his cake and eat it, too!" Virgie exclaimed, throwing her hands up in the air.

That evening turned out to be a disaster when Dale stumbled in half-drunk. Still unable to recognize his state of imbibing, whether sober, drunk or half-drunk, Joellen was the catalyst for it. He had an unusual ability to sustain large amounts of alcohol without it being immediately apparent to others, but at the same time being definitely intoxicated. Joellen thought he was fine until she pushed him about his whereabouts, and he became angry. She quickly backed off, but he followed her into the kitchen, cornered her, and grabbed hold of her neck. She broke loose.

"I'm leaving." She ran to the bedroom to get Ryan, who was awake and crying. Grabbing him up in her arms, she headed for the door.

"You're not going anywhere!" He blocked the door. His laughter was threatening, and she knew she wasn't dealing with Dale Rodman. It was the stranger again. What was he going to do?

"Put him down!" he demanded.

Alarmed and frightened, she lowered Ryan to the floor. Sobbing, the little fellow ran back to the bedroom, and she panicked. An empty coke bottle sat on the end table, and with a quick thrust of her right arm she grabbed it and whammed him over the head. He fell to the floor as glass shattered, and tiny fragments flew all over the living room. She had to get out! She grabbed up Ryan, yanked open the door and flew down the long dark hallway, her heart racing.

Was he coming after her? Fleeing the old tenement house, she raced out into the cold dark night and down the uneven sidewalk. Without thinking, she headed for Aunt Myrtle's house, two blocks down Clay Street. Her back ached as she bounded down the dark street with Ryan bouncing on her side. Heavy, grayish-white clouds hung low above the tree tops, and she was thankful it wasn't snowing yet.

Aunt Myrtle wasn't really her aunt, but everyone called her Aunt Myrtle. An elderly widow, a God-fearing lady, revered by all who knew her, she was Ryan's babysitter. Her livelihood was baking and keeping children, and she was in the midst of baking a large coconut birthday cake when she heard the loud knock. Hastily wiping her hands on her apron, she hurried to the door. Now, who could that be at this hour? she wondered, cautiously cracking the door.

"Why…what in the world?"

Joellen burst through the door in tears. Aunt Myrtle, a tall, bony lady with thin, graying hair, grabbed Ryan and hugged him to her. She loved him like her own. "Now calm down, child," she said to Joellen, "…and tell me what happened."

"I hit him…."

"Hit who?"

"Dale." She was sobbing uncontrollably. "I hit him with a coke bottle…because…because he wouldn't let us leave!"

"Where's he now?"

"…at the apartment…I left him…lying…on the floor."

"Is he hurt bad?"

A new flood of tears gushed out. "I…I…don't…know. I just took off…I was scared…."

"Try to calm down now…we probably need to call the police…."

170

Joellen nodded, wiping her eyes.

Aunt Myrtle went to the telephone. "Here, I'll call them." She dialed the number and hugged Ryan closer.

Suppose he's dead! Joellen thought, trying to stop the raging tears.

Within minutes a tall, erect officer was standing at the door. "Can you tell me what happened?" he asked Joellen, and she blurted out the story between sobs.

"How bad do you think he's hurt?" the officer questioned.

"I…I don't know…I was afraid to go back…afraid he would…."

"You did the right thing, Miss. I'll go back with you."

She glanced at Ryan in Aunt Myrtle's arms.

"Don't worry about him," she said softly.

Nervously, she climbed into the officer's car. Was it all a bad dream? How could it have come to this?

The officer pulled up in front of the tenement house and walked her to the door. "Now, I'm not going to say anything," he coached her. "You go up to him like you have just come back to check on him, and I'll be right behind you. Understand?"

Joellen nodded, though she really didn't understand, but did as he instructed. They walked down the long hallway, she a few steps ahead of him. The apartment door was still ajar as she had left it, and she could see him lying in the same place. His eyes were closed. She began to sob again and leaned down over him. "Dale…are you…."

He jumped up to grab her.

"Just as I thought." The officer dashed in between and grabbed hold of him. "You were just waiting for her to come back, weren't you, big man?"

The officer carried him off.

"You did a good job, Victor."
"That was some coke bottle!"
"But you softened the blow."
Victor beamed.

AS THE PIVOTAL year of 1965 concluded, America was being steadily ripped apart between racial strife and the hotly controversial war in Vietnam. Riots were breaking out all over the nation. The riot in the Watts ghetto of Los Angeles lasted for five days and resulted in thirty-four deaths and about forty million dollars in property damage. The tide had changed on Vietnam, too; skepticism that had slowly started the previous year had grown to noticeable proportions. Older Americans, who were used to fighting wars, were baffled. They couldn't understand it, and they became less and less convinced as more of their young men were drafted and killed.

The war protests escalated, and a crowd of twenty-five thousand marched in Washington, DC. The year ended with 190,000 U.S. troops in the tiny country, and General Westmoreland made it clear that he wanted another 250,000 in the coming year. Over 1,300 American fatalities were listed, 150 missing American soldiers, plus 5,300 wounded. It was estimated that some 36,000 North Vietnamese by now had infiltrated South Vietnam, most coming down the Ho Chi Minh Trail. The picture looked dismal! And world leaders were desperately seeking to find some solution to the widening war. President Johnson stopped the bombing and offered peace, urging Hanoi to respond positively and agree to peace talks. The first of January, Senator Strom Thurmond of South Carolina spoke up and declared that the United States should use nuclear weapons in Vietnam if victory could not be achieved any other way. As a sharpened knife cuts decisively, the war was clearly dividing the country, and college students nationwide actively took to demonstrating against it. Toward the end of the month, Ho Chi Minh attacked American peace overtures, refusing to comply, and after thirty-seven days of ceased bombing, the air raids against North Vietnam resumed.

Joellen was now well aware of the increased fighting. After three-and-a-half years of failed marriage, she had insisted on a separation in the spring of 1966, and Dale moved out. Although he was unable to accept the role of husband and father, he lost hope when they separated and declared, "If I can't have you, I will not stay in Lynchburg." He joined the United States Air Force and soon thereafter was sent to Pleiku, a small town centrally located in South Vietnam. Immediately upon arriving, he realized his awful mistake. He had enlisted as a baker, assuming he would escape the worst, but the Air Base at Pleiku daily shook with exploding mortars, and each one shattered Dale Rodman's already fragile emotional state. In a never-ending nightmare, he shuddered with each explosion, merely waiting to be blown up. Then he was ordered, along with his peers, to take on the grotesque duty of meeting the constant helicopters that flew back and forth to unload the wounded soldiers and the dead. He carried their twisted, mangled, and bloody bodies, covered with flies, with life oozing from them. Wretchedly sick, he wondered when his time would come, and bitterly wished he were back in Lynchburg, Virginia.

Joellen found herself alone, really alone, for the first time in her life. There was no one telling her what to do and what not to do, no one to be afraid of, no one mistreating her.

It was a revelation, but she experienced mixed emotions. Failure and defeat were difficult, and she was discouraged and unhappy. Although she had initially declined to marry Dale, once she did, she totally gave herself to the marriage. She would make it work, and married life was nice when things were good. She enjoyed the domestic scene, keeping the apartment clean, taking care of Dale's clothes and meals. And when little Ryan was born, all seemed complete. She wanted nothing more than to fulfill her role of wife and mother for the rest of her days. But her dreams of a long, happy marriage had quickly crumbled.

THE DANCE HALL was dim, and the soulful country music filled every crevice. Bennett Thaxton had preached to his children for years that such were the devil's den, and they must stay out of them, but there sat Joellen in the darkened booth. She was ready to defy everyone, even her daddy. Her marriage was over, and life was a farce, she thought, puffing nervously on her cigarette.

She had readily agreed to come with her friends when they invited her. Not that she liked country music particularly, but it didn't matter. It was Wednesday night, and the loud music was vibrating off the low ceiling. Her friends chatted excitedly, but she felt very strange. She was shaking!

Celeste and Victor watched disapprovingly.

Teenage hops were one thing, but this was another. A long bar across the dance floor seated a row of young men—drinking liquor! She couldn't stop shaking. It's Daddy's fault, she thought to herself.

"You all right?" her friend Patty asked.

She nodded awkwardly.

"You sure?"

Again she nodded, afraid to speak, afraid her voice would betray her. The others were laughing, drinking, and enjoying themselves, gliding back and forth from the booth to the dance floor, but she was scared to death someone was going to ask her. It had been so long since she had danced and never in a place like this! What in the world was wrong with her?

Then it happened. A young, sandy-haired guy strode over to the booth. She was all alone, and she could see him coming out of the corner of her eye. Her hands were trembling, and she clasped them firmly beneath the table.

"Would you care to dance?"

She shook her head. "No…thank you."

He shrugged and walked off.

Patty appeared out of nowhere. "Why didn't you dance?"

"I…I just didn't want to."

She shook her head in disbelief. "Well, you're not going to stay in the booth all night, are you?" But that's exactly what she did.

However, the carefree atmosphere and lively country music sparked something within her—something that she had missed. She was ready to be lighthearted for a change. Nobody needed to feel sorry for her anymore, and flinging caution to the wind, Joellen Thaxton Rodman could be found every Saturday night in some dance hall, feeling young and very much alive. She wasn't a victim anymore, she was in control, and nobody was ever going to mistreat her again!

Virgie just shook her head.

Joellen laughed.

"You're sowing to the wind, my friend."

"So what?"

"You're headed for trouble!"

"I've had trouble all my life."

Virgie didn't like to see her cutting such a destructive path, but she understood her better than most. In fact, she was probably one of the few who did.

Soon she was dating, and a whole new role of single life opened up. A young man by the name of Paul Andrews came upon the scene, someone who loved to dance as much as she did, and she couldn't wait for the weekends to see him, to spend hours waltzing over the sprawling dance floor as he swept her along on a magical carpet straight out of a fairy tale. She danced, she partied, and she took off to the beach with her friends while Aunt Myrtle kept Ryan. She felt guilty leaving him, but she was caught up in a whirlwind, a spiraling whirlwind that made her feel good most of the time, as long as she kept spinning. If she stopped, the mystical aura would begin slipping, but she didn't want it to. She relished her new freedom!

"NO VACANCY," RHONDA complained as they drove up and down Atlantic Avenue.

They had arrived at Virginia Beach just before noon after driving for several hours. The sun was high overhead, boiling down upon them. Hot and tired, but full of anticipation, they anxiously sought a hotel. Hordes of scantily-clad beach goers crowded the sidewalks, and lively music spilled out of the little gift shops. A salty breeze blew in off the rolling ocean and across Atlantic Avenue.

"No Vacancy."

"No Vacancy."

"No Vacancy."

"No Vacancy."

"It's hot!"

"Wait...there's one...see it...Vacancy!"

The small sign hung crookedly outside a boxy, gray-weathered shingle house, with generous windows facing a sprawling grassy lawn leading down to the boardwalk. Joellen thought she could see thin, white curtains blowing in the upstairs window.

They dropped their luggage and checked out the fairly large room with two double beds, a rollaway cot, and a tiny bath off to one side. Just as Joellen had imagined, a cool ocean breeze blew right through the large screened window, and there *were* white curtains! She leaned past them, eyeing the swells of never-ending waves. "This is really nice."

Rhonda laughed. "It'll do."

"Let's hit the beach!" Charlene was pulling off her clothes and heading for the bathroom, clutching her new, two-piece swimsuit.

It was a perfect beach day—hot and sunny, tempered with refreshing, salty breezes, but the breezes were deceptive, disguising the heat of the day as the girls stretched out, soaking up the warm sunrays. They laughed and talked, and Joellen almost fell asleep. As the afternoon waned, she rolled over stiffly, and pulled herself up as the others grabbed their beach paraphernalia, heading back to the hotel.

"Hey, wait for me!"

"O-o-o-o...Joellen, looks like you got too much sun!" Charlene was glaring at her from head to toe, and she glanced down at her pink legs. This was the first time she had been in the sun that summer, and realized too late that she had overdone it. After a hot shower, the pink turned a bright red, and she was nauseous.

"Joellen, your legs are swelling up!"

"Maybe you should stay in tonight, keep'em up."

"Y'all crazy!" she retorted. "I didn't come all the way to the beach to sit in some hotel room. I'm coming with you!"

"Suit yourself."

They traipsed up and down Atlantic Avenue among throngs of other young people, in and out of the various nightspots, and Joellen was determined not to be left behind, but as the night wore on, so did the swelling. Pacing painfully slow and stiff-legged, she struggled to keep up. Her legs had lost all shape, completely swollen, and each time they came to the end of a block and had to step off the curb and back up, she winced in pain. Unable to bend her knees, she would awkwardly swing her leg straight out. It looked ridiculous, and one minute her friends were sympathetic, the next they were roaring in laughter.

They ended up at the Peppermint Lounge on 15th Street, and they sat at the bar, eating mounds of fried shrimp and drinking cold beer. Music and laughter bounced off the walls, but Joellen's head was spinning. She had to get out and get some fresh air. She awkwardly climbed down off the barstool and walked to the door, her eyes drawn to the dark swells surging forth in the night, breaking into white caps and rhythmically pounding the long sandy shore. She stood there in a trance, her first time to witness the ocean at night, and quietly studied its constant churning and crashing waves. Stepping out into the strong winds, she inhaled the salty air as the powerful ocean reached out to her.

The next morning she rose from the narrow cot and stared out the large window, rehashing the night. She held her head and lay back down on the pillow, glad to be alone. The girls had already left for the beach without her. Though her legs were better, she knew she must take it easy.

She rested awhile longer, then eased off the cot and reached for the Solarcane, the only thing that gave her any relief. She smoothed it over her legs and arms, enjoying the cool, soothing sensation, then sat down at the small desk under the window, opened a rickety drawer and found a tablet and pen. Grabbing her pocketbook, she pulled out the napkin from the Peppermint Lounge, and began to copy her scribbled words.

Oh, how powerful, how powerful
These magnificent waters of might
Oh, how beautiful, how beautiful
These glorious waters of light

The night is dark and so very still
Except for the comforting, but frightening roaring
If this seems absurd, it is what I feel
Midst surrounding waves, coming and going

Its peace engulfs my very soul
As all the world drifts away
And spreading my arms, I wish to enfold
Its inspiration till the coming day

She stared out the open window at the immeasurable ocean, stretching as far as the eye could see.

But I cannot help but feel that of fright
My being so small and insignificant
Beside the vastness of the ocean at night
And its waves bursting forth so defiant

Nothing seems important to me as of now
Except the maker of these waters of might
And loving its peace, yet loving its power
Makes the ocean to me—waters of light!

THE DAY WAS fading and so was summer as Joellen meticulously dressed for the evening, poking at her bouffant beehive with a small wire pick and admiring herself in the bathroom mirror. "Vanity of vanities," she whispered, then pushed the thought aside. Her dyed hair contrasted with her ivory skin, creating the effect she sought, and she couldn't wait to get to the dance…he would be there! He made her feel beautiful and special, and he must care for me, she told herself, recalling how he'd fallen down on his knees and begged her not to go off to the beach because he would miss her. "And he's so charming," she whispered, carefully applying the soft green eye shadow. She grabbed her sweater. Rhonda would be there soon.

She waited outside on the darkened porch. Sonya, the young girl in the other side of the tenement, already had Ryan occupied for the evening. She was such a good babysitter and didn't mind staying as late as necessary. Joellen pulled her cardigan together against the cool of the night and looked up into the sky. Clusters of twinkling lights danced in the far-off heavens, and she silently studied them. Suddenly a car pulled up to the curb across the street, and she watched a man in a dark suit climb out, two of them, in fact. They walked up the sidewalk and mounted the few porch steps to the house and stood there, ringing the door bell. Joellen slid behind the porch pillar. It was Jerry Falwell and another man. She recognized the preacher—he had visited her in the hospital when Ryan was born. He must do a lot of visiting, she thought, pressing in quietly behind the pillar, and wishing Rhonda would hurry up!

The loud country music made it difficult to hear the conversation at the table, and she sat languidly sipping bourbon and smoking one Winston after another. She was bored. He wasn't there, but occasionally he had to be out of town on business. Soon the bourbon lightened her spirits, and she joined in the dancing. Hayward, an older guy and regular at all the dances, asked her to dance, and he arrogantly spun her out over the crowded dance floor.

He slowed to a waltz and eyed her mockingly. "Where's your boyfriend?"

"Out of town…on business."

He smirked. Hayward thrived on other people's business, other people's misery, and he seemed to always know everything about everybody. She didn't exactly feel comfortable around him, but he was a smooth dancer.

"Why are you smirking?"

He grinned.

"…and why are you looking that way?"

He continued to grin.

"Well?"

"You really believe that bologna?"

"What bologna?"

Amused, he shook his head and again swept her around the crowded dance floor.

Catching her breath, she demanded, "What are you getting at?"

He chuckled, obviously enjoying her dilemma. "You don't really believe your charming boyfriend's out of town, do you?"

A knot formed in her stomach, and she glared at him. *He's trying to tell me something.*

"He's not out of town, and he's not working either!"

"What are you saying?"

He was taking great pleasure in his revelation. "He's at home with his family!"

A cold chill raced up her spine to her neck.

"Your boyfriend is at home with his wife and kids tonight."

She stopped dancing. "I don't believe you!"

"Have it your way." He glanced around, obviously feeling uncomfortable standing in the middle of the dance floor while others awkwardly maneuvered around them.

"Are you serious?"

"I can prove it."

They drove away from the dance hall, away from town, a good many miles out into a rural area to where a neat bungalow stood beneath a grove of maples. Joellen stared as the silver moonlight bathed it midst the darkened shadows.

"That's where he is," he declared.

The porch light illuminated a small pink tricycle parked on the grassy lawn, and it was parked right beside his car! Suddenly she felt sick. "Take me to a phone booth!" she demanded.

"What? You're not going to call him!"

"Just take me to a phone booth, now!"

"Whatever you say."

He pulled up in front of a Seven-Eleven, and she jumped out and ran to the empty phone booth, squeezing through its half-open doors. She flipped through the curled-up pages of the damp phone book, and wondered why she had never bothered to check before. But the thought had never entered her mind. She dialed the number.

A woman answered.

She hung up and returned to the car. "Take me back to the dance."

"Sure thing. Did you find out about your charming boyfriend?"

She didn't answer.

Her thoughts were swirling. How could he? He was such a sweet person, and he acted like he really cared! But then she remembered the times he had been gone on business, and the whole thing fell together like a puzzle. Was she ever naïve! Warily, she noticed that the landscape was becoming quite wooded, and she didn't see anymore houses.

"Where are you going?" she asked.

Now it was his time not to answer.

"Where are you going?" she repeated, her tension mounting.

She could see his creepy smirk even in the slight moonlight, and suddenly she was alarmed. How could she have been so *stupid* to get in the car with him? The narrow, wooded road became gravel and wound down, down, down. Her fear intensified as she sat on the edge of the seat. Where was he taking her? The area wasn't familiar at all. She thought of jumping out of the car, but it was moving too fast, the gravels spinning beneath its tires.

He drove on. There was nothing but darkness and trees. Her heart beat wildly. When he came to a dead end he stopped and switched off the engine. She thought she could hear water running. There must be a creek nearby, she thought, or a waterfall.

"I don't know what you're thinking," she insisted with all the courage she could muster. "...but you better take me back right now!"

He laughed aloud. "Not scared, are you?"

"Of course not," she lied, struggling to mask her fear. "But I want to go back to the dance."

He slid across the seat and grabbed hold of her. She wrenched away. "No. Take me back!" Her trembling voice broke into a cry.

SEVERAL WEEKS PASSED before Joellen could summon the courage to go out with the girls again. Bitter and hardened, she determined not to tell anyone. It had shattered her feeling of control, and she silently accepted the blame. If she hadn't been at the dance hall in the first place just like her daddy said. Then why was she going again? But she knew she had to prove to herself that she wasn't the victim. She would be strong. It would never happen again!

Rhonda drove them toward Appomattox, the historic Civil War town adjacent to Lynchburg, where the nation had been reunited. The secluded dance hall, located just out of the small town, was another place they sometimes frequented. That evening, she enjoyed dancing for the first hour or so. Then a dark gloom subtly descended upon her, and she quietly sat at the bar. She tilted her glass, inhaled her cigarette and murmured, "…vanities of vanities, all is vanity."

"Do what?" the guy next to her turned and asked sarcastically.

"Oh nothing."

He eyed her strangely and returned to his drink.

What was she doing here? Where was she headed?

Pushing the drink aside, she swept across the large dance floor. She pulled open the heavy door and was instantly met by a gusty wind. Rhonda's car was parked beneath a grove of dark, shadowy pines, and she headed for it. It was a fierce wind, and she shivered in its grip. It seized her and reached deep into her soul as lonesome strains of country music wafted out of the dance hall. *What is life?* She pondered. *What's its purpose? What's my purpose?*

She glanced back at the closed doors. "Shells they are," she cried into the howling wind. "All empty shells seeking something, but they won't find it in there! That much I've learned. Laughing and bragging on being free spirits, they're just a bunch of actors like me!"

Initially she had admired their spunk, their freedom, their independence, but she had seen behind the stage curtain. The angry wind whistled through the dark pines, creating its own eerie music. But what else is there? she wondered, and shivered in the threatening force that swooped down upon her.

I hear your angry voice—
a'howling, a'howling, a'howling
a'howling with a mighty force
Could it be for me a warning

I seek refuge behind these doors
amidst a world of sin
I plant my feet upon the floor
and dare you to come in

But your howling cry does not cease
What is it you want from me?
Why can't I laugh with others in peace
And let this life be what it be!

CHAPTER ELEVEN

ANOTHER YEAR PASSED, shedding turmoil within and turmoil without. By the end of 1966, the Vietnam War had come to dominate the world's thoughts and actions. American troops had escalated to approximately 400,000, with over 6,000 listed as dead, and Operation Rolling Thunder was in overdrive. Dale was writing, his letters increasing, and she didn't have the heart not to reply. Her feelings for him had all but vanished, but she knew he needed them. She also knew that she would have to reveal her true feelings sooner or later, but this was not the time.

The chrome kitchen chair squeaked as she leaned over to glance up at the ceramic, octagonal clock hanging above the stove. It was past midnight. All was quiet except for the metallic pecking and the occasional clanging of the old radiator pipes as hot steam pushed through them, but realizing how cold it was outside, the noisy pipes were a comfort. It was mid-January, and she had just had her twenty-third birthday.

She typed the last line to the poem and returned the carriage, rolling the paper upward and out. There! She critiqued it and laid it aside, and reached for another sheet, stuck it in the typewriter and wound it around the carriage bar until she had it aligned just right. She typed a few more lines, then absently reached for the half pack of Winstons and tapped it on the chrome table. She pulled out a cigarette, grabbed the matches and struck one, the strong sulfur smell encircling her, and leaned back as far as she could on the straight kitchen chair to inhale.

"Doggone it!"

She winced at the burning sensation searing down her throat and tried again, but it burned even more, setting her throat afire. She had planned to stay up longer. Thoughts were racing through her head, feelings that needed to be put to paper, but now she would have to quit and go to bed. Frustrated, she rose from the table. After a whole day of smoking, her poor throat simply couldn't tolerate anymore, but she couldn't stay up and not smoke!

She crawled into bed and switched on the radio, turning the volume way down low in order not to awaken Ryan in his little bed beside her. The soothing music softly reverberated against the headboard, and she drifted off to sleep.

The next morning she awoke to an unusual quiet, but she could hear familiar, distant sounds, the start up of Trailways buses nearby on Fifth Street, church bells tolling on Court Street, and the sound of an occasional car passing, but it was all muffled. She jumped up to look out the window.

Snow!

The world outside was blanketed in white, and it was still snowing. She couldn't wait for Ryan to get up, but it was too early to wake him. She tiptoed around the large bedroom with its sealed-up fireplace and wondered what it would be like to have a fire blazing in it. The damp, snowy air seeped beneath the large windows, sending a chill throughout the bedroom, and she pulled on her robe, glancing over at the little bed. He was hunkered down under the warm covers.

Easing out of the bedroom, she cracked the door, crossed the living room and flung open the curtains. The apartment's rooms were of noble height and quite spacious, and all its windows were positioned on the east side, for the opposite side butted up against a large, common hallway. She stood transfixed at the frosted windows, shivering in the draft, as the cold air met the warm. The hardworking radiators hissed and tinged, struggling to heat the huge old tenement house. Although the house was right smack in the middle of downtown Lynchburg, one would have thought it was far out in the country if they happened to be looking over her shoulder. Old Mr. Henderson's back yard, with its numerous trees and lush green shrubs that flowered profusely in the spring, now was laden with fluffy-white snow lying heavy upon every branch and every leaf.

A long, rambling picket fence separated his yard from the tenement house. Usually a faded yellow, it was now topped with mounds of pristine snow, and intermittent white peaks perched atop each picket. On the opposite side a tall, private, wooden fence separated it from Sixth Street that perpendicularly climbed the hills and leveled off on Clay. She heard an unseen automobile motoring past on the other side, a muffled chugging up the hill. But it wasn't the fence that drew Joellen's gaze. It was the little shack beside it. Normally the drab, weathered cabin was a sore spot deteriorating in the midst of such pleasing surroundings, but not today. Its slanted roof was laden with the new fallen snow, and its aged windows and door were etched in white.

Joellen recalled the nice black lady she had met last year when she was interested in Mr. Henderson's old typewriter. There had been a knock at her door one day, and, when she opened it, there stood Mrs. Lewis. "Good morning," she said. "I have a note from Mr. Henderson about the typewriter you were interested in buying." She thrust the folded-up piece of paper at her.

"Thank you." She opened it and read the price. *No way.* "Well, I appreciate you bringing this over, but please tell Mr. Henderson that I think I might wait on awhile."

"You're not interested?"

"No ma'am. I think I'll wait."

She nodded.

"How's he doing...Mr. Henderson?"

"Fairly well, as well as can be expected, I guess. I come in about three days a week...cook and clean for him."

"That's nice." Joellen told her about the incident the previous fall, thinking she should know. Mr. Henderson had fallen out back and couldn't get up. It was a cold day, and the young lady in the first apartment heard someone calling for help, though hardly audible. She asked Joellen to go with her, and they had gone over to the back yard and found him lying on the cold sidewalk just outside the kitchen door. They lifted him up and got him back inside.

"I didn't know anything about that."

"Have you worked for him long?"

"Well...my family and his family go way back." She looked past Joellen, to the little shack. "That's where I was born...me and my father before me. You see, my family were slaves to his family originally."

"Is that so?" Joellen's curious nature was bursting with questions, but she held her tongue.

"After the war, my folks stuck with the family and worked for them...and I'm the last one."

"I see."

Mrs. Lewis left, and Joellen leaned against the cold, damp window, watching the snow fall. She stared at the little cabin with renewed interest. *Why are you still standing there? Oh, little shack of slavery.*

DALE RODMAN LEANED down to lace up his boots, his hands trembling as mortars exploded all around the base. He hated the place! He wondered if he would ever get out! He wondered if he would ever see America again? Virginia? Joellen and Ryan? Even if he were lucky enough to make it out of this dreadful place, he probably wouldn't be with them!

He touched the letter in his pocket. At least she was writing, but he could tell that things weren't right, though he pretended not to believe it. He wasn't a dummy! A helicopter started up, and he listened to the familiar whir. "I don't know why she's even writing," he muttered to himself, but deep down inside he knew. "It's pity, that's all." Suddenly he remembered the day they were married, and she was standing there in that white dress, even though it wasn't a wedding dress. It was still beautiful. What happened?

It was that nagging question that had hounded him ever since they met, never giving him any peace! *Does she love me?* The deep insecurities that Dale Rodman had fought all his life only deepened with marriage. He couldn't escape the fact that she probably wouldn't be with him if it weren't for Ryan. And Ryan was everything to her. Sometimes he wished he could mean as much. He had lived in fear that she would leave him, and his fears had come true! If only he hadn't been such a fool. The helicopter lifted off, and he dreaded its return.

JOELLEN INHALED A long, satisfying drag and then looked up into Virgie's watchful eyes. "What're you looking at?"

"You."

"What for?"

"At all them cigarettes."

"So?"

Virgie welded her coils quietly.

"You think I oughta quit, don't you?"

"I didn't say that."

"But you think it."

Virgie kept soldering. The hot, shiny solder melted, coursing around the tightly-wound metallic coils, spreading out, encircling them. Joellen knew what she thought of smoking and drinking and dance halls. She knew what she thought of the boyfriends, too. Virgie was a churchgoing girl, and she sang in a gospel singing group, though Joellen had never heard her. But she heard her humming hymns throughout the day.

"Well..." she took another long drag, "...they make me feel good."

"I reckon they do."

"Course I probably smoke too many...."

"How many?"

She glanced up at her friend. *This will knock her pants off.* "Two-and-a-half packs a day."

Virgie whistled. "Joellen!"

"What?"

"Great day in the morning...you gonna kill yourself with those Winstons!"

"Maybe so," she agreed.

"Why don't you quit then?"

"Why should I?"

"Well, you know you don't have to smoke and drink that ol' liquor...and go to them ol' dances...and all...."

Joellen grinned at her. *She's really trying to help me. She's my best friend.* "Then what would I do?"

"You could start going to church…that's what the good Lord wants you to do."

"I suppose…but I tried being good, remember, and it didn't work either."

Virgie shook her head.

JOELLEN BROWSED DOWN the long aisles, enjoying the abundance of linens, comforters, and blankets of all sorts and sizes. She was in the terrace level of Pecks. She loved shopping in the downtown stores even if she didn't have much money to spend, but simply purchasing a small item like the colorful bowl she clutched in her hand was a delight. She recalled all those shopping trips with Grandma Thaxton, pounding Main Street in search of a new dress, in and out of every store! Sometimes her grandma would buy one after trying on most of them, but usually she would only buy a little something for her hat. "Makes a body feel good," she explained to her one day on the bus ride back home. "Makes a body feel good to buy a little something new."

Every Friday Joellen asked her carpool ride to drop her off on Main Street, and she cashed her weekly check and paid her bills. There wasn't a lot left over, but she always managed to have a few dollars, and she'd browse the stores, mostly Woolworths and Kresges. Leggett's, Baldwin's and Snyder & Berman were too expensive. But Pecks was her favorite. It had been Guggenheimer's Department Store, a landmark on the corner of Seventh and Main for decades. Now it was converted into this new discount store, and it had a number of items that Joellen found affordable.

She wandered over to the side entrance that faced Seventh Street, and a city bus was hurtling down to its entrance, its powerful gears grinding to a noisy stop, bringing with it childhood memories. She and Grandma Thaxton always caught the bus home right here after a full day's shopping. It had been a bus stop for as long as she could remember. Several passengers stepped off and two got on. Then the doors folded in, and she listened to the sound of the brakes letting off and then its gradual picking up of speed as it rolled on down Seventh Street toward Williams Viaduct. She watched it disappear out of sight and recalled sitting up beside her grandmother as the bus crossed the river and turned right, thrusting into low gear to pull the steep incline known as Rocky Hill. She vividly remembered holding her breath as it neared the top, afraid it just might not make it, afraid it would go tumbling backwards, down, down, down the steep hill and into the dark river. In fact, she had had nightmares of that very thing—almost reaching the top of a steep hill to find that the vehicle couldn't make it and suddenly plunging backwards to a frightful end! Too much imagination, her grandma said.

She felt a pang of guilt as she recalled how she didn't visit her grandma like she should have during her last days, and her grandma had always been there when she was growing up, just like the sun coming up every morning and the moon at night.

Unable to change the past, she pushed the guilt away, remembering her grandma's hats—hats with feathers, hats with birds, hats with flowers. And every season, she had taken special pains to change the particular paraphernalia that adorned them to accommodate the new season, while Joellen sat on her bed, watching the transformation. Grandma Thaxton loved to dress up, and she especially loved her hats. Joellen didn't know of anyone who wore hats today, except maybe Virgie. Virgie said she wore a hat to church every Sunday.

She wondered if Virgie had ridden the bus to town when she was a kid and gotten off here at the same bus stop. She had almost forgotten how the colored passengers had to sit in the back and get off by the back door. That must have been hard for Virgie.

BENNETT'S CHEVROLET SEDAN bounced over the giant washboard that winter rains had created, and whimsical birds flitted back and forth. Joellen watched them, jolting from side to side. Ryan leaned over the back seat between them on his tiptoes, peering over her shoulder. He loved his granddaddy and the wide open fields of his granddaddy's place. It was good for him, she thought, and only hoped her mother would be in a pleasant mood. Meredith Thaxton still fought her battle with depression, though it had subdued somewhat as the children grew.

The old sedan laboriously trudged up the graveled road, jostling over the deep, furrowed rows. Whenever Joellen returned home, she vacillated, wanting to come, but yet apprehensive. Every Sunday, however, her daddy patiently drove out of the wooded country for miles and miles, across the James River, and up the hills of downtown Lynchburg to pick up her and Ryan. It was his desire to have all his children and grandchildren with him and Meredith on Sundays. Well, almost all of them.

"Have you heard from Daniel?" she asked.

He shook his head. "Not since the first time." He fell silent again.

It was the end of February and 1968 had brought more worry for Bennett Thaxton. In addition to the unrelenting burden of a sick wife and his never ending financial concerns, now he had to worry about Daniel, who was also in Vietnam. He wondered what it was going to do to Meredith.

The past year had seen a continual buildup of forces on both sides of the war as hostilities intensified. By year-end, approximately 600,000 American troops were across the seas with almost 16,000 casualties, and opposition to the war was pressing in on all sides. College students demonstrated nationwide, and campuses were vehement with sit-ins and strikes. Draft cards were being burned to the dismay of older veterans, and induction centers were picketed. The Marines were finding it increasingly difficult to find and retain qualified officers and non-commissioned officers, not to mention troops for the frontlines. Daniel was one of those on the frontline. He had left awhile back, and Bennett had received word that he was now in Da Nang. Bennett was well aware of what a dangerous place that was, and his worry increased.

As they pushed up the country road, he did not know that his son was now involved in Operation Houston, a 1st Marine Division in the Thua Thien Province, that would last until the fall and claim over 700 enemy casualties. Daniel was with the Special Landing Force, dangerously paving the way for the troops.

But Bennett smelled garlic!

Amazingly he could still smell it. He smelled it lying in bed sometimes at night, at the fertilizer mill, and even driving up these country roads. It subtly took him back to Okinawa, sitting in the dark with his buddies, outside watching movies, the only thing they had to look forward to when there was a lull in the fighting. And suddenly they smelled it…he smelled it…the garlic. And his buddy yelled

195

out, "*There's a Jap in here!*" The lights were thrown on, and chaos resulted as they scrambled to capture the enemy. But then the sounds of bombs and guns and screams of agony came flooding back, and he struggled to push the thoughts away as he wound his way home.

He hated garlic!

And he couldn't bear to think of his own son in the midst of such horror. He had been proud to serve his country...but he never imagined that *his* son would be doing the same, or even worse. And this war was different, different from anything before—different from anything he had known. You can't win a war with one hand tied behind your back! he thought tiredly, and according to the papers, half the time, they didn't even know who the enemy was. It was a rotten war!

The Chevrolet sputtered, breaking the tangible silence that stretched out between them. Joellen knew her daddy was worried and that he had a lot on his mind, but she wished he would talk to her.

"You know Dale's younger brother, Roy, is in Vietnam, too, now...Saigon," she said.

"That right?"

Joellen nodded, thinking it strange indeed that all three of them were there at the same time. Ryan began whistling, and Bennett smiled up at him in the rearview mirror.

GENERAL ELECTRIC POSTED a string of new job openings in March—clerical jobs. Thoughtfully soldering her coils into the never-ending castings, Joellen considered the postings. She had been working in the plant for six years now, in a number of different departments, a variety of jobs all over the sprawling facility. She liked welding the coils, and soldering the resisters, transistors and capacitors, building radios and control units. She had enjoyed watching the hot solder lithely snake its way around and across the intricate small boards. And she derived a certain amount of pleasure challenging the fast-moving conveyors, but she was bored and had been for a long while. It was time, she thought, time for change. But she glanced through the open passageway. She hated to think of leaving her friend.

It all happened quite fast, however, faster than she expected. She peered up from the bulky Royal typewriter at her new surroundings. Granted, she knew she would be working in another department, perhaps in another building, but another location! Some miles away from the main site where she had been since she was eighteen, she found herself in an antiquated redbrick building. General Electric had leased the old cotton mill some years prior for additional space and located a number of its departments there, including the Service Parts Department, where Joellen was assigned. The old building had a rich history, dating back to 1888, and formerly comprised part of Lynchburg's initial industrial base, employing hundreds up until 1957 when it closed down. But now it was cold and damp, even on good days, even in springtime.

Joellen didn't mind. The new job was interesting and stimulating. It had been years since she had taken typing and shorthand at old MHHS. And though her grades had been high then, the years had taken its toll, her skills were embarrassingly rusty. Fortunately, she had kept her speed up somewhat with her little portable typewriter at home, typing her poetry. Now, however, her poetry composing on the job was over, too.

Still she wrote. Whenever a budding spring flower bathed in sunshine reached out to her, or sweeping clouds soared overhead, or rains washed the world pristine clear, she found herself on the side of the road jotting down what her soul could not contain, urges that swelled within; but she wanted to write more than poetry. She responded to an ad for a Writing Correspondence School, though she didn't know how she could afford it. Nevertheless, in a rare buoyant moment, she filled out the form and mailed it in.

THE KNOCK AT the door surprised her. It had only been two weeks, but here was the Correspondence School representative standing before her, a born salesman. When he left, he not only had her signature, but future designs, as well.

When Joseph Blands initially showed up at the yellow tenement house, his hopes were daunted. He would never make a sale in this old place! But when Joellen opened the door, his fears vanished, and he quickly summoned up his subtle sales talents coupled with enthusiastic encouragement for her writing dreams, and he easily had her convinced to enroll in the correspondence course.

Joseph exuded a polished and persuasive manner, but beneath this smooth exterior he was a very troubled young man, living in an imaginary world he had created. He told her that he was a widower and the son of a Methodist preacher, and Joellen never dreamed that he had a secret and troubled past. Very intelligent and well educated, he impressed her at once. In reality, he had actually been mixed up with selling weapons on the high seas, and he had an estranged family, a wife and two little boys living somewhere in Florida. But floored by his charisma, particularly his interest and expertise in writing, Joellen gullibly hung on his every word, and he continued to follow up with her, soon asking her out.

Maybe, just maybe there could be a future here, she reasoned, a future with someone successful, someone she could share her innermost dreams with, a fellow writer, no less. He did tell her about the wife and two little boys, sadly explaining that they had all been killed in a tragic automobile accident. Obvious tears surfaced as he emotionally described the horrid affair in detail, and Joellen's heart was touched. The poor young man!

She began her writing assignments with enthusiasm and vigor, only to be discouraged when she received the big manila envelopes with her returned assignments splashed in red. It was disheartening to have her work thus critiqued, but she continued on. And so did Joseph, smitten with such a dreamer. He pursued her, bought her flowers, dined her and way too soon was asking her to marry him, even offering to pay for her divorce. Confused and concerned by his aggressive pursuit and swift declaration of love, Joellen wavered. She was tired of carrying the load, but it all seemed just too good to be true. She stalled, and he became more persistent.

On the Saturday before Easter, she received the largest, most beautiful orchid corsage she had ever seen. But what was she going to do with it? She didn't go to church! She thought of Aunt Anna, who never missed. In fact, it was Aunt Anna who had taken her and Janet to church when they were small. It was Aunt Anna who had suggested it was time for her to get baptized when she turned twelve, and she did so just to please her. So she called her and offered her the beautiful orchid corsage, and Aunt Anna made a special trip to town on Easter morning to pick it up. Aunt Anna was impressed with Joseph Blands, too, and had high hopes for this courtship. But soon after Joellen had a conversation with his father, the preacher, and discovered the truth. It was all lies, and the end of her short-lived dream.

THE SALVATION ARMY bus drove slowly down Clay Street, and Joellen sorely wished she hadn't agreed to come! Her neighbor, Sonya, had been pestering her for some time, and she had been so good to them, babysitting Ryan on Saturday nights. She could always depend on her, and in a weak moment, she had given in. Sonya sat beside her and Ryan, smiling from ear to ear. Laughter and chatter grew louder as the old bus rolled on, and then they began to sing.

Love lifted me!
Love lifted me!
When nothing else could help, love lifted me....

Dazed, Joellen stared out the window at the wet city streets as a fine, cold mist fell. She was miserable; her head throbbed! Had she forgotten that Sunday morning followed Saturday night? She wished she were back home in bed. What a stupid idea to be riding down Clay Street on this noisy church bus!

They pulled up in front of the building and filed out into the cold, wet rain, and then into the packed church. She and Ryan sat down on a back pew along with Sonya and her friends. All of a sudden the lively band started up...with drums beating furiously, reverberating off the walls. The jubilant atmosphere swelled around her...and her head pounded harder.

CHAPTER TWELVE

BY 1968 AMERICA was an angry land, with war protests growing more violent every day. Over 10,000 more combat troops had been sent to Vietnam by President Johnson. Drug use was escalating, and racial violence was steadily growing, but in spite of all the wildness and uncertainty facing the nation, springtime blossomed, luring young and old alike out into its beguiling presence.

It blossomed in downtown Lynchburg, heady with the sweet perfume of lilacs permeating lush yards, embracing old Victorian homes. Wisteria climbed profusely up latticed walls and over gabled roofs and porches. Myriad colorful tulips, hyacinths, sweet peas, primrose and hollyhocks filled old, lower gardens and imbued the climbing streets with pleasant fragrances. Even vacant lots added their contribution with pink, blue, and white morning glories draping the overgrown brush. The heavy scent of roses hung over the old city, and birds of all descriptions sang as they flitted from treetop to treetop, from gable to gable.

Joellen could hear them. She was washing dishes at her kitchen sink beside the open window, and the sweet fragrance of Mr. Henderson's back yard wafted in, but her mind was elsewhere. She scrubbed the sudsy dishes, and the last few years reeled before her. Dale had returned safely from Vietnam, but the marriage was over, and his military orders had taken him far north to Minnesota. The dance halls, parties, and boyfriends had proved to be a great disappointment. All the laughter and music was empty. There had to be more to life!

She dried her hands on the dishtowel hanging by the sink and picked up the burning cigarette lying in the ashtray. She took a long drag, and then went back to washing the dishes and remembered the bumper sticker again.

Only one life will soon be past
Only what's done for Christ will last

Coming up on it while driving down Fort Avenue, the words had literally jumped out at her. Why, she was twenty-four years old, and her life was in shambles! Overcome with the fact that she had only one life, and so far she had messed it up, she experienced an overwhelming sense of urgency to do something. But she had tried everything, except....

God.

The answer was there, as real as the floor beneath her feet, as real as the springtime outside, and she couldn't escape it anymore. For a long time she had been feeling that He was drawing her to Him, through the rain, through the wind, through the snow, through the vast, deep ocean, through all His magnificent creation. He had been reaching out to her, but she had run.

She was tired of running.

She didn't exactly understand what was happening—only that she was turning away from it all...away from her past...away from the world...and turning to Him. So walking around her kitchen table, she began to sing...

I've wandered far away from God—Now I'm coming home
The paths of sin too long I've trod—Lord, I'm coming home

Coming home, coming home, Never more to roam
Open now Thine arms of love—Lord, I'm coming home....

And there was joy midst the angels....

"I'll Never Dance Again"

The wind bloweth where it listeth,
and thou hearest the sound thereof,
but canst not tell whence it cometh,
and whither it goeth:
so is everyone that is born of the Spirit.

CHAPTER THIRTEEN

PRESENT

JOELLEN SAT COMFORTABLY in the large RV, staring out the window as they passed milepost 107, leaving Roanoke, heading south. Tall sycamores lined the Glade Creek area, rising up to the height of the bridge they were crossing. Vibrant autumn colors embraced them, and she was delighted to be starting out on their annual Parkway trip. Though a misty rain was falling and a cloudy sky hovered overhead, the color was breathtaking!

They had actually entered the Blue Ridge Parkway at Otter Creek, milepost 61, only nineteen miles from their home. They had spent so many nights in the little campground by the creek throughout their married life, and she had so looked forward to every one of them—eating dinner in the small rustic restaurant nestled by the creek and breakfast in the morning. She glanced over at Wade sipping his coffee.

They had crossed over the James River, its flowing waters cutting through the mountains, and had driven the twenty-two miles to Peaks of Otter. They didn't stop this time but drove on to Roanoke through the Jefferson National Forest.

"Look—more bluebird houses!" Wade pointed to the simplistic, boxy houses that systematically lined that stretch of the Parkway, numbered in sequence by small, white signs. They were nailed onto fence posts that held up rusted barbed wire fences.

"They look like little johnny houses to me," Joellen joked.

"Well, I'm glad to see them. The bluebird's one of the prettiest of all birds in my opinion, and they were almost extinct before they began doing this."

"Who?"

"The North American Bluebird Society."

"How did you know that?"

"Just smart."

"Right. I saw you reading that bird book."

He chuckled.

She was glad that they had decided to leave all the work back home and come to the mountains. They had been making these fall trips ever since they married, pushing twenty years now.

Distant cattle lazily grazed on their right, solid black dots against the green pastures. Joellen watched them as the RV slowly and laboriously wound its way around the winding Parkway. It swayed to the left and swayed to the right, but held its own against the challenging curves and steep inclines. Rustic railed fences appeared, dividing the Parkway from the rolling pastures and deciduous forests, flashing bright yellows and crimson reds. They passed over the Roanoke River, and Wade peered over the lofty bridge to the waters below with huge, smooth boulders. He didn't like height.

Familiar stonewalls hugged the Parkway, low and picturesque. They were relatively new, replacing the walls built by the CCCs in the thirties. The old walls had massive stones, quarried close by. The original architect wanted the finished wall to blend in with the natural setting and appear as a work of nature. Tons of rock was broken up by hand by the young CCC enrollees, and then trucked to the site, and they used the largest stones for the foundation or for capstones. They built wooden forms and set them up for a guide for the miles and miles of walls. It was backbreaking work, but what a result! Visitors had enjoyed the charming rock walls for decades, but now they were crumbling and sinking into the earth. Joellen hated to see them replaced but realized the necessity.

They passed a number of other campers—pull trailers, coaches, and class Cs like their own, and Joellen watched the falling leaves scud across the curving Parkway between them. It was as if she were in another world, and all her troubles had been left behind. But had they?

They passed Milepost 128, and the RV lurched forward, pulling up the mountain. Joellen listened to the gears changing as they climbed higher, driving into a veil of fog. Rocky mountain walls rose on their left, and steep drop-offs appeared suddenly on their right. Wade switched on the lights. The colorful trees up ahead immediately disappeared into the gray mist. They could only see about 200 feet ahead as the RV wheeled slowly around the mountain, and occasionally a pair of headlights appeared out of the fog.

"Be careful, Wade," she warned uneasily.

The road snaked around the crest of the time-worn mountains and steadily continued upward, with patches of thick green rhododendron sandwiching it. The Parkway, basically a shelf carved out on the side of the mountains, followed the lofty ridges, and where the shelf was impossible, tunnels were chiseled through, but they were mostly on the southern end. Wade focused on the double yellow lines in the center of the road, and Joellen's ears began to pop.

She couldn't help but remember another autumn. The autumn before her daddy died. Bennett Thaxton had been the glue that held the family together, the tower of strength they all depended on. And even though he was a small, spindly man, he was very large in the eyes of all who knew him, but the ravages of emphysema brought him down, and ultimately grew a deadly tumor in his lungs. In his last days, weeks and months, the oxygen was not getting to his brain, and he was not himself anymore. She remembered taking him for a doctor's visit that fall, and the color was just like this—awesome!

"Look't yonder!" he'd exclaimed, pointing to the forest of trees edging the country road leading from his home. She had smiled and uttered something pleasant. But he kept pointing and repeating, "Look't yonder, see them?"

She sadly recalled the doctor's visit. Like a little child, he had looked to her for answers to the doctor's questions. Their roles had been reversed, and it had broken her heart. She remembered going down to see him later that fall, to play her guitar for him. He loved string music, and she had just mastered a few country ballads. Relatively new at it, she had only decided to take up guitar when she turned fifty. He tapped his foot happily to the music and smiled at her. But after she left, he asked Meredith, "Who was that lady? I enjoyed her playing."

But the memory that lodged stubbornly within her mind was the morning the ambulance came to take him away from the home he loved, the little, cinder block house he had built for his family. He was already unconscious and gasping for breath when the rescue squad arrived, bringing the stretcher in, but they couldn't get it through the bedroom door. They had to lift him up in a sheet and carry him out to the hallway to the stretcher. He looked so small and frail. Following behind, she had held his head up—afraid it would fall back too much. She remembered hearing Janet and Katy and the preacher talking in subdued tones, comforting Mama in the kitchen.

Daniel rode up front in the ambulance, and she had followed behind. She could still see its flashing red light as it drove up the familiar country road, the road she had always hated. She was hardly able to see it that morning though—her eyes were so flooded with tears. She knew it would be the last time he would travel it. The ambulance wove its way up and down the slight knolls and around the curves, its siren blasting. Thoughts of her childhood whirled in her head, thoughts of him working so hard to make a living down at the fertilizer mill while it turned his nickels, dimes, and quarters black and ate mice-like holes in his pants; thoughts of him repairing her blue bicycle after a crash; thoughts of him piling blankets on their bed in the frigid winter nights; thoughts of him pretending to be Santa up on the rooftop at Christmas.

The ambulance crossed over the two small bridges, and she strained to see her daddy, but could only see the rescue person sitting beside him. Soon they were passing by Triangle Market, and she remembered all the times she and Janet and Daniel as children had crouched down on the back floorboard of his old car, hiding from him until he pulled up at the country store. Then they would pop up. "Surprise!" Patiently he would scold them, but let them come along. The ambulance passed by Thaxton's Lane, and the lump in her throat grew larger. Soon it was rolling down Creek Hill and back up, on the way to town. It had been a heart-wrenching time, and she could still hear the siren, loud and shrill.

"What're you thinking about, Hon?" Wade asked.

"Oh...oh nothing," she replied, pushing the gloomy thoughts back into her memory.

The fog lifted slightly, and they could see large, round bales of hay lying in adjacent fields behind old fashioned rail fences; next followed more barbed wire and pastures. A quaint old farm house with all its outbuildings sat lop-sided from age. She leaned back against the seat, enjoying the tranquil feeling as they drove through the Virginia mountains, over the narrow two-lane road indiscriminately cutting through the solid mountains. She pulled off her shoes, propped up her feet on the large dash and dropped the armrests.

"Comfortable?" Wade kidded.

She nodded.

"How about a tootsie pop?"

"Sounds good."

He plucked two from his shirt pocket, and she peeled off the wrappers, sticking the chocolate one in her mouth, then twisted off the stick of the orange one and handed it to him. He preferred the whole thing at one time.

"Wow!" she exclaimed. They were driving through a tunnel of color created by the overhanging trees, one of those murals you see painted on walls. They emerged, and Wade pointed to another old house sitting forlornly down in a field, brown and decaying, with tangled foliage growing up out of its ripped tin roof. Its windows and doors were gaping vacant holes where once some family had entered and watched the snows fall or the sun rise in the morning, where once babies cried, and a couple snuggled midst winter storms. Now it only hinted of such things.

They passed milepost 153, and crisp poplar leaves skirted and danced across the road. Although the poplars and walnuts were almost bare, usually the first to lose their leaves, the maples and hickories were peaking. But the oaks would hold out to the end, strong and stubborn.

"Smart View Overlook, that ought to fit me. Want to stop?"

"No. Let's keep driving," she replied. "I'm enjoying the ride too much." A long stretch of split rail fence enclosed white-faced cows that languidly lifted their heads and stared blankly at them, contentedly chewing their cuds.

"Looks like you are," he joked. "Wish we didn't have these birth-control seats, you'd be able to slide over close to me." She laughed as three deer leaped across their path, one following the other, and then vaulted over the ridge, their distinct white tails soaring out of sight.

They approached Rocky Knob, just past Milepost 167, with its sign *Bear Country—Protect Your Food and Property.* The campground was situated directly across the road from a sprawling, hilly cow pasture. They had camped there many times. It was now covered with a fresh new layer of fallen leaves.

"Looks full," Joellen said.

"Probably is this time of year…we'll have to come back, besides my stomach's talking."

"Mine, too."

"Can't wait for those pancakes!"

The RV switched into second gear as they left the campground and climbed higher, with cows lowing as they passed. "Reminds me of Grandpa's farm," Wade commented. He had grown up on a large farm in Amherst County not too far from her papa's. Soon they approached Mabry Mill, an old restored grist mill beneath shady trees, offering a look into the past with liquor stills, a primitive sawmill, apple butter making and other interesting relics. It also offered a place to eat.

Wade pulled out the chair for Joellen, scraping it across the slate floor, and the tantalizing aroma of cornmeal cakes, country ham, and fried chicken permeated the back porch restaurant. Joellen glanced around at the bank of open screened windows that were edged by rhododendrons, poplars, and hickories. She inhaled the crisp autumn air drifting in as the friendly waitress took their order and disappeared behind rows of windows, latticed with white shutters. The busy rattle of pots and pans and kitchen utensils could be heard from behind. She glanced at the sun-dappled floor and then up at the white ceiling fans whirring against the dark rustic ceiling. The waitress soon returned with their lunch. Wade happily reached for the small pitcher of maple syrup, pressed the little metal top, and thick dark syrup poured out, smothering his stack of cornmeal pancakes.

Continuing south, they passed Groundhog Mountain, then Orchard Gap. They passed cabbage fields with huge, greenish-white heads, and an old farmer in blue coveralls and red plaid shirt bending over a wheelbarrow full of them.

Milepost 217 was soon left behind and so was Virginia. They had crossed over the North Carolina line and passed the exit to Mt. Airy, the real Mayberry, Andy Griffith's home. They had been there a few years back and purchased the RV they were traveling in. It was their third one. So many happy memories, why was she spending time dredging up the past?

Perhaps it was her mother's condition, and all those unresolved feelings she had pushed back into the corners of her mind for so many years. Now they were resurfacing and demanding attention.

CHAPTER FOURTEEN

1968

A LINE WAS drawn that spring when Joellen walked around her kitchen table singing "Lord, I'm Coming Home." She returned to work the next day and told her friends that she would not be going to anymore dances. They laughed.

"Sure, we'll see."

"Why, you're the life of the party!"

"Nobody enjoys dancing more than you!"

"See you on Saturday."

She smiled at them and walked away, remembering her vow to God. "Lord, I will never again go to a dance! Please take me home with you if I do."

The new job brought her in contact with a whole new world. The department had a fairly large staff, but there was one young girl who immediately befriended her. Lindsey was single, sports-oriented, and quite pretty in an all-American way, and there was something about her that Joellen liked, even though they didn't have a lot in common. Right away Lindsey invited her to church. Joellen had been considering starting Ryan in Sunday school, and she readily accepted the invitation.

Lindsey attended the relatively new Thomas Road Baptist Church, located on the opposite hill from the two-room apartment where Joellen and Dale had first lived. The church had outgrown its original Donald Duck building and now enjoyed a beautiful new sanctuary, but that Sunday services weren't in the sanctuary. Instead a large white tent had been erected for a revival meeting, and Dr. Oliver Greene was fiercely preaching.

Joellen stood in the thick sawdust, staring all around, silently sizing up the crowd beneath the huge tent. She listened to the earnest preacher as he powerfully expounded the scriptures, though not much was digested; instead she was absorbing the feel of the place. Afterwards the crowd mingled under the tent, spilling outside, and eating dinner on the grounds. Joellen experienced a calming peace.

She didn't miss the parties and dances and her old risqué lifestyle, but giving up the Winstons was another story. Held captive by the little three-inch sticks, she was convicted each time she held the Bible in one hand and a cigarette in the other. She realized that smoking wasn't the worst thing in the world, but she also knew that it was the one thing she wasn't willing to give up—the one thing standing between her and God. But how could she stop? She had been smoking since she was fifteen, and she couldn't imagine life without a cigarette!

Another young lady in the Service Parts Department befriended her. Miriam Elder was also a Christian and a member of the same church. They became fast friends and one evening decided to ride out for something to eat. Joellen was behind the wheel of her new Corvair. Not brand new, but new to her, and it was her first car. Both she and Ryan were delighted with it. He stood proudly in the back between her and Miriam.

"Let's go to the Southerner," Miriam suggested. She liked it because of its curb service. Joellen had previously spent many an hour sitting there with her friends, playing their radios, and watching to see who was riding through. She circled, looking for an empty spot and pulled in, noticing a few old partying friends, and waved to them. As Miriam rattled on about what to order, suddenly she felt very uncomfortable. The feeling increased until it felt like a hot poker creeping up her back.

"You want to order pizza?" Miriam asked. Joellen loved pizza. She had had it for the first time there just a few months back. Miriam continued, "I think that's what I want. It's really good how they…."

"Let's go!"

Miriam stared at her. "Go…why?"

"I…I don't know why…I just need to leave…."

"But I'm hungry, Mom," Ryan said.

"We'll go to Hardees."

Confused and somewhat annoyed, Miriam watched Joellen back out and head out of the parking lot. They drove on in silence for a bit. "Why'd you do that?" she finally blurted out, unable to hold it any longer.

"I don't know…but I just felt that I shouldn't be there."

"What's wrong with the Southerner?" Miriam was completely perplexed.

"I didn't say it's wrong…it's just not right for me anymore."

IT WAS LATE summer, and still Joellen struggled with the cigarettes. Not only the cigarettes, but a much larger issue loomed over her. More and more, she wanted to stand up and be counted for the Lord. She read in the Scriptures.

"That if thou shalt confess with thy mouth the Lord Jesus, and shalt believe in thine heart that God hath raised Him from the dead, thou shalt be saved." She wanted to confess…to let the world know that she had made a decision, an eternal decision. But when she did, she knew it had to be all or nothing.

But the cigarette between her yellowed fingers stood in her way!

How could something so small, so seemingly insignificant, hold her captive? She wouldn't allow it and decided to go forward the next Sunday morning, walk down that aisle and publicly give her life to the Lord. Yes, that's what she would do!

Sunday came, and she pulled into the upper parking lot, taking a long drag off her cigarette, supposing it to be her last. But when the invitation was given, her feet planted themselves solidly on the floor, and she clutched the songbook, her heart beating wildly. She wanted to go! A giant magnet was drawing her, but she couldn't move. With bowed head, she peeped around at the crowded pews. There were so many people!

She silently chastised herself all the way home and decided it would be next Sunday. But when the next Sunday came, her heart beat even more wildly, and she clutched the pew in front of her, but couldn't move! She just couldn't find the courage to step out. This went on for weeks, the desire, the plan, the fear, and lastly the disappointment, and though she had more than her share of strength and independence, walking down that church aisle was awfully intimidating. She prayed and prayed and asked God for the courage.

It was mid October, and she pulled into her usual parking place, took a long drag off the Winston, and again determined in her heart that it would be the last. She was

219

tense all during the service, anticipating the invitation. And then it came.

Just as I am, without one plea
But that Thy blood was shed for me
And that Thou bidd'st me come to Thee
O Lamb of God, I come, I come

Her heart was pounding, and she was visibly shaking, but she let go of the pew and put one foot in front of the other and stepped out. Before she knew what was happening, she was moving down the long red-carpeted aisle, and the people in the crammed pews didn't matter anymore.

Afterwards she picked up Ryan from Children's Church and drove up Thomas Road to Langhorne Lane, and on out to Memorial Avenue to Hardees. She felt like she was floating on air. They ate their hamburgers and fries, and she headed on to her folks, still in a daze. Though she couldn't explain it, she knew her life would never be the same.

Her brothers and sisters would be at her folks, too, including Daniel, who was back safely from Vietnam. She couldn't wait to tell them what she had done. The narrow country road hadn't changed much. A few more houses dotted the rural landscape, but for the most part it rather looked the same. About half way, there was the steep hill and two small bridges that spanned the winding creek, and the graveled road curved down toward them. Joellen pulled over to the side of the road next to the first bridge.

"Whatcha doing, Mom?"

"Come with me."

She opened the door, and he jumped out. Ryan was five years old, and unquestioningly mature for his young age. He looked at the water and back at her. She opened her pocketbook and pulled out the half pack of Winstons, and he quietly watched her pitch them into the flowing creek.

"What'd you do that for, Mom?"

"I'm not going to smoke anymore...I gave my life to the Lord today."

He smiled up at her and scampered off toward the creek.

THAT SAME NIGHT she stood in the elevated baptismal waters, dressed in a white robe and nervously listened to the preacher's solemn words, "*I baptize you in the name of the Father and of the Son and of the Holy Ghost...buried in the likeness of His death...raised in the newness of life...*." She went down under the waters, and when she came up, she knew she had truly been baptized.

The next day she returned to work and received more than enough curious stares.

"What happened to your hair, Joellen?" Normally she had it fixed weekly at a beauty shop where they washed it, dried it, teased it and wove a black and white wiglet into it, and the end result was quite dramatic. It stayed that way all week until she went back to have it redone. But when she went under the baptismal waters, that took care of the hair.

As the day wore on, her co-workers noticed that she didn't have a cigarette in her mouth or burning in the ashtray.

"Where are your cigarettes, Joellen?"

"I quit smoking."

"No way!"

"I don't smoke anymore."

"Why?"

"...because I gave my life to the Lord."

"Really...."

A few days later Lindsey approached her, full of laughter.

"What's so funny?"

"The guys...the guys out in Shipping. They said they sure were thrown a curve."

Joellen looked at her questioningly.

She was still laughing. "They said...that they encouraged your boss to hire you instead of the other candidates...because they thought you were cute, single...and looked like you might like a good time."

Joellen frowned at her.

"But now you've gone and got religion!"

JOELLEN EXPERIENCED A zealous urge to tell everyone what had happened. If only they could know the peace and joy that she had found. While sitting in the pew the Sunday after, she watched the choir as they sang up front. Why not? It was the best way she knew of to stand up for the Lord, but how could she go about it? She didn't know anybody in the choir, and she didn't even know if she could sing.

She decided to learn some hymns before she approached the choir director. Every night she studied and memorized the old hymns, and soon she could sing quite a few. Then she called the choir director and asked if she could meet with him. He was a big man, a boisterous man blessed with a deep baritone voice, and he was also a kind man. Though intimidated, she met with him the following Wednesday night and asked if it would be possible to join the choir. She pulled out her list of hymns. "Do you want me to sing them?"

He looked at her curiously and shook his head. "You didn't need to memorize all these...."

She blushed.

"...but that's okay...just be at choir practice tomorrow night a little early if you can."

The powerful words rang out...through the airways... over the televised Old Time Gospel Hour...and Joellen sang from her heart.

I'll tell the world that I'm a Christian
I'm not ashamed His name to bear;
I'll tell the world that I'm a Christian
I'll take Him with me anywhere....

CHAPTER FIFTEEN

PRESENT

JOELLEN SNUGGLED UP close to Wade and gazed into the night sky. The wide window spanning the back of the RV brought the outdoors in, and shadowy oaks and hickories hugged it. A slight mountain breeze blew gently, and occasionally a lone acorn turned loose, plopping onto the top of the camper, and then bounced off. She loved camping. A friend said to her just last week, "You call that camping?" She knew it didn't compare to sleeping on the ground with only a piece of canvas separating you from who knows what! But it was a world of difference between it and sleeping in a motel. Being able to back up to a rushing mountain stream or to the edge of the ocean or deep into a dense forest just the way they were now enabled them to essentially become part of nature.

Two other spacious windows on either side of their bed were opened to the night, and she listened to the familiar hum of cicadas. It reminded her of when she was a child and slept on a pillow resting on the windowsill. There was something about the quietness of night, when the world slept and nature's lesser creatures took over.

"Thank you, Lord, for all this," she whispered into the night. "...and especially for autumn." So many significant events in her life had occurred in the fall, including her commitment to the Lord. And both of her daughters were born then. She thought of her youngest, so much like herself, independent, strong-willed, determined to find her own way in the world regardless of the risks. Her heart was heavy for her, hoping she wouldn't have to go through all that she had before she found the truth. The past few years had been such a challenge, torn between her concerns for her willful daughter and the struggles with her mother. What did they call it? The sandwich generation?

A screech owl pierced the darkness with its shrill cry, and tree branches rustled in the night breeze, gently scraping the window. Wade turned, wrapping his arms about her, and she fell asleep as the crescent moon passed over.

The next morning they were on the road again, but it was a wet road. A fine misty rain was falling. It had begun just before daybreak, and already a light hazy fog was settling in over the mountainous landscape. Before leaving Doughton Park Campground, they had enjoyed a hearty breakfast of bacon and eggs with hot biscuits and apple butter, and Joellen felt rested and full.

They passed by Milepost 240 as the soft gray fog enclosed them. The Parkway curved around the mountain ridges, up and down, in and out, and the rain steadily fell. The spectacular washed colors were breathtaking as they continued through the fog. Raindrops beaded the windshield, and the wiper blades hypnotically crisscrossed back and forth, causing her to lapse into a semi-sleep when suddenly a flock of wild turkeys noisily scudded across their path. Wade braked just in time. They smiled at one another and continued on. The Northwest Trading Post appeared out of the thickening gray fog, and Joellen scrambled for her shoes. It was always a delightful break from the winding

Parkway. Filled with interesting and authentic gifts, crafts, and pastries made by local residents, it was a favorite stop.

They stepped up on the inviting porch, and heavy chimes resonated in the cool mountain breeze. Bluebird houses dangled above them, and Wade pulled open the screen door, pleased to find fresh-baked pastries waiting on the counter.

They left with a loaf of home-baked sourdough bread and a bag of lemon tarts that she couldn't wait to bite into. However, she stashed them in the cupboard above the table until after lunch. The curtain of fog hung low and heavy as they continued south. A surreal mood surrounded them, cutting them off from the rest of the world, and only the edge of the colorful forest was visible as the RV sliced through the foggy mountains. They were traveling in a capsule.

Just like life, Joellen thought. Each of us traveling in our own capsule, rocketing forward, blasting ahead, caught up in our individual lives—oblivious to what's up ahead or what's left behind—never grasping the full picture. Then one day we discover more of life is behind us than ahead, and the past is slapped before us.

She thought back to when she had gotten religion, as the guys out in Shipping said. Immediately she was pressed to share the truth that had been revealed to her, the peace she had found, but she was ill prepared for the response. Even her daddy put her off when she began talking to him about Bible prophecy.

"Oh...they've been talking that stuff as far back as I can remember, ever since I was a boy and nothing's happened yet. I really don't need to hear about it."

She had been crushed. She couldn't understand his attitude and was hurt and taken aback. Then she approached her brother Brian, who was caught up in the sixties hippie movement with long hair and a Volkswagen bus with colorful flowers plastered on it. Certainly Brian needed help! She read to him from her new Scofield Bible and carefully explained what God had done for her. Brian listened patiently and respectfully, then apologized, "I hope you don't mind, Joellen, but I'm not ready yet."

Why couldn't they see it? What was wrong with them? she puzzled, but quickly remembered how long it took her, how long God had worked on her.

The fog thickened.

Wade leaned forward to see. He was a skillful mountain driver, and she was comfortable with him behind the wheel. She relaxed, and remembered again her zeal to witness for the Lord, but she had learned over the years to be a little more patient and wait on the Lord.

"So then neither is he that planteth anything, neither he that watereth; but God that giveth the increase."

Perhaps she could water a little.

She didn't approach the subject again with her daddy, but prayed for him every day, and it took years, almost twenty years. But the day came when Bennett decided to attend a little country church not far from home because the pastor had visited and invited them. Her daddy was an old man by that time, but he and Meredith attended faithfully, and Bennett Thaxton changed. He was a new man.

She remembered singing in the choir, and it had satisfied her longing in one way, but still she felt led to do more. Shortly after, she was approached by the Sunday school director in a hallway and asked if she would be interested in teaching.

Teaching!

How could she teach? She didn't know anything about the Bible!

But soon she was standing up in front of a roomful of first grade boys teaching them and herself the Word of God. She smiled at the memory as the RV wound around the mountain. She wasn't intimidated by the little boys. They were mostly bus children, part of the church's strong bus ministry that was growing by leaps and bounds. Immediately they won her heart, often unkempt and starving for attention, they were little sponges soaking up God's love. One of them, Jerome Williams, a little black boy from downtown, came to mind. At the start of Sunday school, she had asked the question, "Do you know who died for your sins?"

His little hand shot upward, and he was shaking it vigorously.

"Yes, Jerome?"

"Abraham Lincoln!"

And she realized her work was cut out for her. Another picture flashed before her, a candid picture, crystal clear. She was teaching boys and girls by that time, and it was the little blond-haired girl standing in the front row who wasn't singing. All the kids were singing but her. Instead she was staring down at her feet, clad only in a worn pair of flip-flops, and she glanced back and forth from her feet to the little girl beside her, who wore a pair of shiny black patent dress shoes with ruffled white socks. The look of sad realization in the little girl's pretty blue eyes was indelibly imprinted in Joellen's memory.

"What're you thinking about, Hon?" Wade asked again, while carefully maneuvering up a sharp incline.

"…just about life, I guess…and some of the kids I used to teach."

"You miss teaching?"

"Not really." She had taught for over twenty years, eventually following the bus ministry to downtown where it moved to be closer to the children and called itself *The Good Samaritan Center.* Initially she was against the proposed move away from the church and splitting up the children, but after seeing the look in the little blond-haired girl's eyes, she realized that sometimes it was just better to do things a certain way.

"Just wondered," Wade added.

"No. It was time, and now I have a new mission." She thought of the story forming in her head.

View Mt. Jefferson, Elevation 4550. Well, that was impossible. The heavy fog encircled them, but they knew it loomed high over the town of Jefferson.

"I read that it once was called Negro Mountain," Wade mentioned.

"Why?"

"…because the run-away slaves used to hide out here when they were fleeing up north."

Joellen stared thoughtfully into the fog.

They pulled off the Parkway and onto an overlook for lunch. Joellen dropped down on her knees to light the gas oven, and watched the tiny blue flame ignite. She buttered some sourdough bread while Wade sliced a juicy red tomato. They sat across from one another at the minuscule table, and Wade gave thanks for the meal, the beautiful season, and their safe trip thus far through the fog. A gentle drizzle trickled down the large windowpane over the table.

Afterwards Joellen washed up the few dishes, and Wade took off in the rain.

"You're going to get wet and catch cold," she hollered after him. He ignored her and returned with two beautiful sugar maple leaves, her favorite, and laid them atop the dash. "These are for you."

She curled up again in the front seat and smiled at him. "Thank you."

"You're welcome, Sweetheart." And he started the engine. For such a rugged man, he had a sensitive side that never failed to touch her. She examined the leaves—bright yellow, orange, and red. Only a sugar maple could boast of such!

The coziness of their moving house, the passing parade of trees, and the gently falling rain created a cocoon-like feeling, and she returned to her past.

CHAPTER SIXTEEN

1969

JOELLEN AND RYAN moved out of downtown Lynchburg, away from Clay Street, all the way to the mountains of Amherst County, to a place called High Peak, part of Tobacco Row Mountains. The tiny four-room house they rented was beautiful to them with its shiny hardwood floors and pretty knotted-pine kitchen cabinets. It was perched high above a winding graveled drive that led up to it and above several other small rental houses. A thick forest of trees embraced it, and in the distance they could see more mountains. The only thing Joellen didn't like was nighttime.

It was pitch black!

There were no streetlights with pools of light to alter the darkness. Without realizing it, she had become accustomed to them. Each time she had driven out to look at the house before signing the lease it had been daylight, and she had relished the country ambiance with its mountain stream flowing down below the winding road and the tall swaying trees with birds singing in them. After living in the city for the past seven years, she had come to appreciate the country but not at night.

Joellen lugged the living room chair across the hardwood floor, closer in to the cater-cornered television set, in readiness for the historical event to take place in just minutes. It was dark outside, dark and quiet, and she held Ryan close to her side. It was July 20, 1969, and at four seventeen that afternoon, the lunar module Eagle had softly touched down on the moon!

Televisions tuned in all over the country. New Yorkers had been crowded into Central Park since 7:30 PM to watch the moonwalk; thousands were packed in front of three huge screens to witness the unforgettable moment. In fact, the whole world was tuned in, united for a few short hours by their interest and concern for these men, who were farther from home than man had ever ventured.

The United States had finally accomplished what the Soviet Union had not. In most Americans' minds, they had won! They had beaten the Russians! Ecstatic reaction over the land erupted, and it was much needed. Midst all the troubles, the fighting at home and across the sea, this was a welcomed break, and Americans were so proud!

Apollo 11 had blasted off for the moon at 9:32 AM on July 16th, and its mission was exactly 102 hours and 46 minutes old when Neil Armstrong, the command pilot, radioed to earth his historic words *"The Eagle has landed."*

Mission Control in Houston responded with suppressed excitement, "We copy you on the ground. You've got a bunch of guys about to turn blue. We're breathing again. Thanks a lot."

The first men to reach the moon, Neil Armstrong, a thirty-eight year old civilian commander and his co-pilot Col. Edwin Aldrin, Jr. of the Air Force, had brought the ship to rest on a level, rock-strewn plain near the southwestern shore of the arid Sea of Tranquility. As the space crew began to prepare for the complex Extra Vehicular

Activity, the world tensely waited. Neil Armstrong and Colonel Aldrin made ready, while the third member of the team, Mike Collins, orbited the moon in the mother vehicle, Columbia. About six-and-a-half-hours later, the astronauts opened the hatch and aimed the television camera at the steps, which led down to the surface of the moon. Mission Control in Houston confirmed that all systems were go.

"Are they really on the moon, Mom?" Ryan asked excitedly.

Joellen nodded. "Yes...yes...let's watch!"

The little fellow slid down onto the shiny floor and scooted in closer to the television set, trying to grasp the memorable event at the tender age of six.

Houston radioed, "Okay, Neil, we can see you coming down the ladder."

"I'm at the foot of the ladder. I'm going to step off the Lunar Module now. That's one small step for man, one giant leap for mankind."

The world was hushed, as some six hundred million people back on earth sat glued to their television sets. The pictures of the bug-shaped lunar module and the man trampling about it were so sharp and clear that it actually seemed unreal. His initial steps were tentative tests of the lunar soil's firmness and of his ability to move about in his bulky white spacesuit and backpacks. He was also testing the lunar gravity, being only one-sixth that of the earth.

"The surface is fine and powdery. I can...I can pick it up loosely with my toe."

"He's walking on the moon, Mom!"

Joellen smiled at him, experiencing an overwhelming sense of pride to be an American. "That's right...he's walking on the moon…the same moon we look at every night!"

"Neil, this is Houston, we're copying."

"It does adhere in fine layers like powdered charcoal to the sole and sides of my boots," he said. "I only go in a small fraction of an inch, maybe an eighth of an inch. But I can see the footprints of my boots in the treads in the fine sandy particles."

About twenty minutes later, Colonel Aldrin joined Mr. Armstrong on the moon surface, and for fifty-one minutes they were busy setting up another television camera out from the lunar module, scooping up soil and rock samples, deploying scientific experiments, and hopping and loping about in a demonstration of their lunar agility. Then they planted the stars and stripes, and a powerful emotional feeling swept over Joellen as she watched in amazement with the rest of the world. The flag wasn't blowing like they were used to seeing on earth. In fact, a metal rod at right angles was added to keep it unfurled, but it was there for all the world to see.

Ryan fell asleep, and Joellen lifted him up and carried him off to bed. She tucked him in the small twin bed, pulling the covers up snugly around him, and hurried back to the living room. She was sleepy, as well, but she couldn't pull herself away from the television. This was history!

Mission Control interrupted the Extra Vehicular Activity at 11:47 PM. "Tranquility Base, this is Houston. Could we get both of you on the camera for a minute, please? The President of the United States would like to say a few words to you."

Then President Nixon spoke.

"Neil and Buzz, I am talking to you by telephone from the Oval Room at the White House. And this certainly has to be the most historic telephone call ever made. I just can't tell you how proud we all are. For every American, this has to be the proudest day of our lives. And for people all over the world, I am sure they, too, join with Americans, in recognizing what a feat this is. Because of what you have done, the heavens have become a part of man's world."

THE TUMULTUOUS SIXTIES, the divided decade, was finally coming to an end, going out in love-ins with riotous parties. One month after Neil Armstrong walked on the moon, it culminated in youthful rebellion with Woodstock, the infamous communal party where a half million young people, drugged and naked, danced in the mud. Most Americans were anxious to witness the end of the chaotic decade, wrought with violence and death. It had sadly seen the young president's assassination, that of his brother Robert, and Dr. Martin Luther King's assassination. These tragedies would forever blight the so-called love and peace decade. On top of these infamous events, the racial violence and controversial war were on-going plagues.

Joellen left the old Cotton Mill Building at 5:00 PM. She walked tiredly to the graveled parking lot and unlocked her car, quickly rolling down the windows to get some air. It was an oven! Driving out of the parking lot onto Carroll Avenue and onto the expressway, she headed for Aunt Myrtle's to pick up Ryan. She must hurry because church began at 7:00, and they had to grab some supper.

The summer revival was just starting and would last for two whole weeks with Jack Van Impe, the prophetic evangelist. Joellen would be singing in the choir every night for the entire two weeks. She was proud to be a part of it, but knew it was going to be a taxing week for her and Ryan.

It was late when they drove home, turned off the highway and down the dark country road, alongside the rushing mountain creek that paralleled it. Ryan was asleep in the back seat, and she was beat. It had been a long day. Tall trees sandwiched them in on both sides, lonely and spooky, and she couldn't see the moon or the stars through the dense canopy overhead. The dark creek waters murmured a ghostly, hypnotic spell. She loved living at the foot of the Tobacco Row Mountains in the daytime. But at night—that was altogether different! Her friend Miriam had laughed at her, but she couldn't control her feelings, and it didn't help any that a large mama bear and two cubs had been sighted prowling around.

At least it was much cooler, but it always felt cooler along this stretch of the road. Whether it was actually cooler or just psychological with the refreshing sounds of rushing mountain water, she wasn't sure. Regardless, she rolled up her window higher as the preacher's words came to mind. "Christians should do what they know is the right thing to do, and if they don't, it is sin."

To death do us part the creek waters murmured.

She had always believed in those words. Now she was a Christian and was supposed to do the right thing! Did that include making her marriage work? A marriage that seemed utterly impossible—was she supposed to go back with Dale?

She didn't want to!

She shuddered at the memory of the quarrelling and drinking and turmoil, but he promised that he had quit drinking. Could she believe him? She wanted to, but she feared the risk of getting back into that hopeless situation again. For the first time in her life, she was finally able to live peacefully and happily. She might be struggling financially to make ends meet…and she might be afraid of the dark—she glanced around at the shadowy trees—but no one was mistreating her. She approached the winding driveway and drove up the graveled surface beneath tall poplars and pines, parking as close as she could to the house. She shined the headlights straight at the back door.

"Wake up, Ryan…but wait till I get the door open. I'll come back for you." With that, she literally flew to the house, imagining every second to be accosted by something big and black.

"She doesn't need to be afraid."

"But she doesn't know that, Victor."

"Well, she ought to!"

IN LATE AUGUST, Dale arrived in Lynchburg, on leave for several weeks, still handsome, still possessing his James Dean guise—his brooding demeanor that had attracted her in the first place, but the years had changed Joellen. Too much life in a short period of time, and now a new life of faith had transformed her into someone entirely different. They had been apart for over three years, and she wasn't a teenager anymore. In fact, she wasn't the girl that he had married.

Dale studied her.

She looked the same on the outside, but she wasn't the same. He searched for the girl he had fallen in love with as a teenager, but the search was illusive. Just when he thought he saw her, she vanished, and someone else was with him—someone he didn't understand. He was baffled, but wouldn't give up. He wouldn't accept the change and decided that if he took her away, away from her job, away from her family and friends, away from it all, he would find her. He wanted his family back again in spite of their troubled past, and she said she would go.

CHAPTER SEVENTEEN

RYAN STOOD AT the upstairs window in rapt attention. The sweeping Minnesota sky held millions of snowflakes, and they slowly descended from its gray immensity, thick and feathery. They steadily fell, covering the spacious green lawn, the two long curving sidewalks that snaked out to the street, and the top of the small wooden garage out back. They laced the green shrubbery and tall trees that had yet to lose their leaves.

· He loved it, but it was October!

Just a few days prior they had moved into the large upstairs apartment of the older two-story weatherboard house. It faced Wadena's Main Street, which boasted of a few local businesses and a railroad crossing in the heart of town, then led out to the neat residential section. Joellen was thrilled to finally find a place. The first couple of weeks they had lived in a cramped efficiency motel, hardly big enough to turn around in. She studied the comfortably furnished apartment with long, ample windows facing all directions, but most of all she liked being upstairs. It was a unique experience, the ability to gaze out over the treetops and see the narrow streets winding this way and that, giving her a bird's-eye view atop the town. She certainly wasn't on top of her own life, she thought sadly. Used to working, making her own money, making her own decisions, she was now totally dependent and vulnerable. She wouldn't feel this way, however, if she had more faith in Dale.

The breakfast dishes awaited her, and she headed for them. Yesterday's sunshine had lit up the vivid green and yellow kitchen wallpaper, but today the sun was gone and there was snow. She reached for the Joy.

Dale was assigned to the Air Force Radar Station located about six miles out of town. A long straight road led out to it, and he had to report at six o'clock in the mornings. The small town of Wadena didn't offer any school buses, and this presented a challenge. With just the one car, Joellen had to awaken Ryan at five thirty, bundle him up in warm clothes, and they would all drive out to the base in the cold dark morning. Ryan slept in the back seat beneath layers of cover, and after dropping Dale off at the base, she would drive back to town. They would peel off their coats and wraps and gratefully crawl back into bed for another hour. Then get up again, and she would fix breakfast for Ryan and drive him the ten blocks to school.

She scrubbed at the dried sticky egg on the plate and glanced out the kitchen window, anxiously watching the snow fall. She had heard the tales of Minnesota blizzards. The dried egg held fast, and she reached for the scrub pad in the yellow frog's mouth that stared up at her with its whopping black eyes. Aunt Anna had made it for her. She scrubbed a little more, and then dried her hands.

"You ready, Ryan? Get your coat."

"It's still snowing, Mom!"

He raced up the school sidewalk, playfully swatting at the snowflakes, and waved to her as he entered the redbrick building. Joellen smiled and waved back, then returned home, pulled off her coat and sat down at the portable typewriter, one of the few things she was able to stuff into the Corvair when they left. It was good practice to type her letters back home, for who knew what the future held? Dale had come home drunk over the weekend, and sadly she realized that he had never quit. Suddenly there was a quick knock at the door, and she hurried to it.

"Hello!" A diminutive silver-haired lady stood there, radiating warmth with a smile that flooded her aging face, lighting it up to youthful vibrancy. Her animated persona created the illusion of a much larger individual than the tiny person standing before her.

"Hello," Joellen replied.

"I'm Mrs. Daniel, your next door neighbor. May I come in?"

Joellen stepped aside. "Yes, please come in." She motioned her toward the couch.

The little lady took a brisk step toward it, then stopped in her tracks. "Are you a Christian?"

Somewhat taken aback by the sudden, unexpected question, Joellen was momentarily speechless. "…why…yes, I am."

"Good," she retorted in her accustomed matter-of-fact way, smiling broadly. "Don't we have a wonderful Savior?"

"Yes ma'am…" She marveled at her candidness, but quickly felt at ease with her. Mrs. Daniel spoke with confidence and authority, but an authority coated with love, to which Joellen immediately responded. They sat and chatted for a while, and the old lady invited her to join their Tuesday Bible study held in her home. "Now if you ever need anything, just come on over to see me," she concluded as she rose to leave.

Suddenly life seemed brighter as Joellen watched the spry little lady, bundled up in a plain brown coat and black wool scarf, scurrying across the snow clad yard and the side street that separated the two old houses. She watched her disappear into the back door and stared at her small tracks as they slowly filled back in with snow.

Tuesday morning was a typical Minnesota winter morning, cold and snowy but sunny bright. Joellen squinted in the brilliant sunlight that danced over the crystallized yard, while trudging over to Mrs. Daniel's. It shimmered and sparkled, and she thought of pie meringue glistening before it went into the oven. She peered up into the tall trees, intricately coated, their branches and twigs frosty masterpieces, and stepped cautiously through the hard crusty snow.

They had done it again!

Every night when darkness fell, teenagers daringly raced through the small town on their speedy snowmobiles, pushing the snow back down onto the shoveled sidewalks and pathways. The town had outlawed it, but it was proving very difficult to enforce. They were just too fast to catch, having come and gone before anyone knew what was happening. Oh well, out with the shovel again!

She eased down onto the formal but austere dining room chair surrounded by the Bible study group—six elderly women all smiling at her through bifocals. Wrinkled and weathered from the severe Minnesota winters, they obviously were survivors, not only survivors, but conquerors.

"Let's have a word of prayer, ladies, before we begin," suggested Mrs. Daniel. Heads bowed, and they joined hands. Joellen felt a firm but warm clasp, and Mrs. Daniel prayed. Then they simultaneously opened their Bibles.

"We're just beginning to study the book of John," she spoke directly to Joellen. "So you have joined us at a good time." Sheer Bible pages rustled, and Joellen grabbed her own big black Scofield Bible that she had brought from Virginia and began flipping through.

"The Book of John is often called the love book," Mrs. Daniel began. "God's love letter to us, and we're going to take our time, not hurry through it. We will rightly divide the Word of truth." She paused and pointed to a crowded bookshelf behind them. "We have enough commentaries to help us, but we will concentrate on the Bible itself." She began to slowly read.

"In the beginning was the Word, and the Word was with God, and the Word was God...."

Joellen soon forgot the age difference as she joined in the study and discussion and also the ready laughter of the group of Midwestern ladies. She enjoyed the pleasant camaraderie each Tuesday morning and found the Bible study not only interesting but satisfying to her soul. She marveled at how they could spend an hour on just several verses, discussing them, comparing them, seeking further understanding through the many commentaries and leaving no stone unturned. She began to learn more than she ever expected and looked forward to the weekly meetings, the warm friendship of the ladies and the delicious snacks, especially the sweet rhubarb roll, scrumptiously tasty.

"I grow my own rhubarb, you know, but it takes a whole lot of sugar!" Mrs. Daniel laughed her ready laugh.

Dale was becoming more and more difficult, drinking frequently, and his old ways returned. His deep insecurities vexed him, and he couldn't get past the fact that they had been separated for three years, and she had had other relationships, even though he had, as well. He drilled her, and she cried in despair. As a Christian, she wanted to be completely honest and would answer his questions truthfully, but this only added fuel to the fire. It was a real dilemma. They argued, and he raved and threatened her, then stormed out, banging the door, only to return home late and drunk.

It was a cold night, the beginning of December, and his threats were unusually frightening. She quickly grabbed up their coats, and pulling Ryan along, they fled while he was in the bathroom, but once in the car, she didn't know where to go. She drove through town, past the darkened streets, past the shadowy houses with their warm yellow lights shining out onto crystal snowy lawns.

They had nowhere to go.

There was Mrs. Daniel, of course, but she didn't have the courage to go knocking on her door; besides she was too close to home. She knew Mr. Daniel would be there, too, and she was embarrassed to bring such solid hardworking people into her troubled world. How could they understand? A little park on the other side of town came to mind, and she headed for it. It was vacant, still and peaceful, and she parked but kept the motor running. It was cold, very cold.

"What're we gonna do now, Mom?"

She glanced into his big brown eyes.

"We're just going to sit here awhile…and wait for daddy to calm down…then we'll go back home." She leaned over the seat and hugged him. "Why don't you lie down here and go to sleep." She pulled the blankets up over him, glad that they kept them in the car. They had been instructed to do so as soon as they arrived, in case of emergencies, and, of course, they used them every morning on the long ride to the base. Almost immediately he was asleep, and she was glad. She wanted so much to protect him from the bad scenes.

But what could she do now?

She rubbed her flat stomach, pondering her condition. Could she be pregnant? She wasn't sure, but sick as she had been for the past few mornings, she highly suspected it. She leaned back against the seat, trying to calm her nerves and gazed up into the moonless sky that was partially covered with thick grayish-white clouds, hanging low and heavy.

A tear rolled down her cheek, followed by another and another. Why had she believed him? Leaving her home, her family, her friends, and her good job, now she was way up here in this freezing-cold country with nobody to turn to. What would happen to them? She wanted to break down and let the tears flow, let it all out, but she must be strong.

Snowflakes began to fall.

At first they were barely perceptible, then more and more descended from the darkened sky, frosty, white flakes floating all about them, dusting the windows before they instantaneously melted. Soothed by their presence, she also felt another presence.

"I will never leave thee, nor forsake thee."

A deep, satisfying joy washed over her, a feeling of profound closeness to God. Though a thousand miles from home, she knew she wasn't alone, and she whispered into the night as the snow thickened...

Praise be unto the precious One
Who gave me no peace in sin
Praise be unto the precious One
Who tenderly called me in
I didn't know who I was

Where I'd come from or where I was going
I sought my answer midst the stars
The seas and streams a'flowing

But praise be unto the precious One
Who showed me all things
Praise be unto the precious One
My heart will forever sing

LIFE IN THE tiny Midwestern town was quiet and simple, and Joellen settled in, determined to make a go of it. Days turned into weeks, and the winds blew stronger and the earth hardened, then froze, and Christmas came. She and Ryan cut out paper tree ornaments and hung silver tinsel on the cedar they had bought in town. They had ornaments back home, but were only able to bring what was necessary, which wasn't much. The rest of their belongings were stored above Aunt Ella's grocery store. Her store was larger than Aunt Anna's.

That winter turned out to be a record-breaking frigid and snowy winter for the Midwest, especially Minnesota. The digital temperature gauge, jutting out from the Wadena Main Street corner bank, regularly displayed a minus, even boasting forty degrees below zero, topping that of Alaska.

Joellen piled on layers of sweaters and coats, but still felt cold. Her weekly job, and sometimes daily, was to shovel the long sidewalks that curved out from the house in two opposite directions, linking to the wide public sidewalk out front. It was a city mandate that they be kept clear. She really didn't mind shoveling the light dry snow. At least it wasn't wet and heavy like Virginia snows, and the dazzling sun was always there. Being outside was undoubtedly invigorating and stimulating for her, but the freezing temperature was something else. Hot flumes of air rose from her nose and mouth into the frigid air, and she had to frequently take breaks to get back inside, holding her stinging hands over the steaming radiator while they burned and tingled. But still she loved the snow, in awe of how it just kept piling up, up, up.

The ground had been covered since the first of November, and they wouldn't see it again until late spring. City crews arrived, attaching long metal rods to the fire hydrants so they wouldn't disappear, and they got used to stepping over the extension cord draped across the side yard to the small garage, in order for the car to start. Joellen even got used to piling several layers of clothing on Ryan and herself before facing the raw elements, but the young lad seemed to enjoy it all, particularly walking on top of the hard, crusted snow, several feet high by midwinter. He was only disappointed that he couldn't build a snowman or make snowballs out of the fine powdery stuff.

God had answered Joellen's prayers on the long, long drive to Minnesota. She had fervently asked Him to lead them to a good Baptist church. She figured she'd better find a Baptist church because it was there that she had heard about God's saving grace, and she didn't know much about the others. However, after arriving, all they saw were Lutheran and Catholic churches. Dale wasn't too interested one way or the other, and she was about to give up when one popped up right in front of them.

It was twilight, just before Christmas. They decided to take Ryan walking in the snow to see the myriad lights strung from the rows of neat little houses along the city streets. They unhurriedly maneuvered down the winding sidewalk that Joellen had just shoveled and out onto the snow-packed street, their footsteps muffled as they walked hand in hand, the three of them midst the snow-blanketed streets. The whole town was silenced by the layers and layers of white, and edged with heavy snowdrifts in its corners. Only the bright-colored Christmas lights spoke of life and energy, shining out into the snowy fog with a blurred and misty radiance, reflecting off the white snow, softly etching a Currier & Ives painting. They walked on, almost reverently, absorbing the moment, happy for the present, and Ryan wished they could walk forever.

Unexpectedly, a small sign sticking up rather lopsided out of the snow caught their attention. *Southbrook Baptist Church.* Joellen stopped in her tracks, glancing all around for the church or a steeple rising into the foggy sky, but there was none. Then she noticed what appeared to be a *basement*—a cinder block basement heaped with snow. She studied the sign again.

"Well…this must be it. Southbrook Baptist Church…."

"Must be," Dale agreed.

"Is it a church, Mom?" Ryan questioned, staring at the rough gray cinder block.

"We'll find out come Sunday," she answered, squeezing his hand.

THE SMALL CONGREGATION heartily welcomed them, and they quickly became a part of a church in progress as it diligently and prayerfully worked toward building a new church further out of town. Joellen and Ryan responded to their sincere and caring Midwestern hospitality, though Dale soon slacked off. He was coming home later and later. Sadly Joellen realized that this had probably been his habit in the past, but she vainly tried to persuade him to change. Instead he insisted that if she really loved him and wanted to make him happy, she would go with him. Torn and confused, she finally gave in. Surely God wanted her to make this marriage work and to make her husband happy.

She would try.

The dreaded evening came. Ryan would stay with their neighbor up the street who had two little boys about his age, whom he enjoyed playing with occasionally. As they dressed, Dale whistled. Their first stop was the VFW, where apparently he usually began his night of drinking. The second stop was a regular bar, and Joellen sat miserably in the booth beside him, inwardly shrinking from the boisterous environment as he downed glass after glass. The loud music belting off the ceiling, the course talk, raucous laughter, and overall worldly atmosphere repelled her. She was amazed at how different it all was now—how different she was! Just like the Scriptures said: *Therefore if any man be in Christ, he is a new creature: old things are passed away: behold, all things are become new.* Once she had frequented such places herself and been a part of it, or had she ever really been a part of it? In fact, there had always been that nagging sense that she was out of place, but now she felt like a lamb in a lion's den! She wanted desperately to escape, but instead she forced herself to sit calmly beside her husband.

She would try.

He continued to drink.

"Excuse me. I need to go to the bathroom." She clumsily climbed over him and out of the suffocating booth. She pushed open the door to the empty bathroom and began rummaging in her pocketbook. She pulled out a Gospel tract and carefully propped it up in front of the sink beside the soap dispenser.

Celeste and Victor watched amusedly.

There, she felt better!

In spite of their limited space, she had wedged a large cardboard box into the back floorboard of the Corvair when they left. It was full of tracts given to her by her church, and she had secretly left a trail of them in the obscure and sometimes unseemly bathrooms of service stations and short order restaurants on their trip north. But she was convinced that if any place needed such hope it was the beer joints and night spots, and it also eased her guilty conscious. Should she really be here?

"Back already?" Dale joked.

Smiling half-heartedly, she climbed back over him. Finally they left, only to find another bar, and the same scenario followed. Dale ordered drinks for himself, and Joellen sat there beside him, drinking a Coke. She fumbled in her pocketbook and realized she didn't have any more tracts. "I forgot something in the car. I'll be right back." She jumped up.

He nodded, oblivious to what was going on. She returned with more tracts stuffed in her pocketbook. *If she had to go through with this, the least she could do was spread the Gospel!*

After three bars, Dale abruptly announced with unmasked irritation, "We're leaving…I'm taking you home."

"Why?" Obviously she had failed him.

"It's no fun."

"What do you mean?"

"I mean it's no fun when you're not drinking, too." He grabbed up his jacket and led the way to the car. Pulling on her coat, she hurried after with mixed feelings. She was ecstatic to be leaving but concerned about his sudden changed mood.

Dale was angry and confused. He knew she wouldn't touch the stuff. She had told him so, and he really didn't want her to. Dadgummit, he was so mixed up! He wanted her the way she was, but yet he couldn't enjoy *drinking* with her or going to the bars. The two just didn't mix. He wondered again if he had done the right thing in bringing them up here, but he wanted them. At least he thought he wanted them, sometimes he didn't know what he wanted!

She pulled off her warm coat and went to hang it up. "Why don't we watch television and..."

He was standing at the door.

"You're not going back out..." her voice trembled, knowing the tears were coming.

"I'll be back later...not too late," he replied callously.

The ready tears welled up. "But I thought we were coming back home and..."

"I said I was bringing *you* back!" He yanked open the door and left. Joellen sank into the nearest chair, tears flooding her eyes and running down her cheeks. She felt utterly helpless.

It was the only time she went with him. He didn't ask her again, and she was glad. However, his nights out continued and increased, as did his drinking. She struggled to be strong, but the fears and disillusionment more often than not won out, and she cried herself to sleep. *I have not turned him over to the Lord...I am probably putting him before the Lord...but I can't help it!* Distraught over it all, she begged God to change him, to make him stop drinking and carousing, to make him the kind of husband and father they needed.

But he didn't change.

It was on one of those lonely nights, way past midnight, Ryan was asleep in his room, and Dale was out. Joellen lolled on their bed alone, rubbing the slight swell of her belly, and miserably crying great heaving sobs. She knew she shouldn't cry so hard. It wasn't good for the baby, but she just couldn't help it. What was she going to do? She couldn't go back home! She didn't want to go back home, but where could she turn? Utterly sick to her stomach from so much crying, she began to shake. It was then that she heard the music coming from the downstairs apartment. Two young single schoolteachers from Wisconsin lived downstairs, nice enough girls, happy and carefree, but she hadn't befriended them. Their worlds were too far apart.

They were probably having a little party, she figured. The unusual strains of music drifted up to her, and she cried the harder, feeling like she was falling into a great abyss…and all alone.

Suddenly in the midst of her crying, in the midst of her despair, in the midst of her loneliness, the distant strain of music lifted her up and out of her wretchedness. It soared with her, but it wasn't the music. There was more—an embryonic warmth flooded her soul, a pervading sense of protection, a presence so overwhelming that she could only bask in its embracing depth as its intensity and yet its profound calmness enveloped her. She knew beyond any doubt that she was not alone. The presence held her and soothed her broken spirit…until she slept peacefully.

The next morning she arose with renewed hope but secretly pondered the strange experience.

THE UNRELENTING WINTER snows piled up, drifting higher and higher, and the howling winds raged on, rattling the clear plastic tacked over the windows…and the

252

baby grew silently within her. She was happy to be pregnant in spite of her bleak circumstances and prayed daily for a little girl, then felt guilty and simply prayed for a healthy baby. Dale had bought her two maternity outfits, two-piece polyester pants suits, one blue and the other green. She wore them alternately and hand washed them weekly until they were a faded blue and green. On Sundays, she wore her brown tent dress that she had brought from home, the only dress that she could still get into.

Ryan couldn't wait. He had always wanted a brother or sister, but in his childish world, time was eons. "How much longer, Mom?" he asked over and over.

"The baby won't come until after summer...when the leaves start to turn."

He looked out at the piled up white snow and sighed.

By the end of March, the snows still hadn't let up, nor had Dale's drinking. In fact, it was becoming worse. She knew she should simply let go and let God take care of the situation but couldn't. The strong Scotch-Irish blood flowing within her veins fought to take charge of the situation. Dale began to view her as a mother figure, chastising him when he was bad, scolding him, and making him feel guilty. He didn't need that! And this Christian thing! He didn't need to be reminded of what he was doing wrong. He knew right from wrong. He just couldn't help it if his desires were what they were, but how could he explain that to her?

APRIL GRADUALLY THAWED the solid frozen snow, heaped up several feet, covering all signs of budding life. Then the gray skies dumped even more, but it wasn't frigid as before; it was soft and wet. Joellen was glad for that as she briskly sloshed toward town clutching Ryan's hand so that he wouldn't fall on the slippery sidewalk. Dale had been gone a couple of days, and she was determined to find out what was going on! Usually she had no money, but the monthly Air Force check had arrived in the mail, and she clenched it in her pocket. She was going to find him!

She switched on the ignition to the rental car and looked to her left and to her right. Which way? Ryan stood in the back, excited to be going anywhere. It was Saturday, and he was out of school, and they were going out, but he didn't know where.

Nor did she.

Fully aware that this was a stab in the dark, a bona fide goose chase, she prayed for enlightenment. Once before she confided in her preacher and his wife, and they had decided to take her riding around the small town to see if they could find the straying husband, and that trip came up negative. Why shouldn't this one? But she *had* to find out what he was doing. She *had* to make things right!

The small town of Wadena didn't take long to cover as she drove up and down its familiar streets looking for his unmistakable car. Dale had traded in her little Corvair for a large red Pontiac. But there were other small towns nearby, and she knew he often ended up in one of them. She decided to branch out, but where?

North, east, south, west?

She considered going eastward to Brainerd where they sometimes went together to visit a friend of his. Bemidji was to the north, and they went there occasionally. She was familiar with it, too. Then there was Saint Cloud to the south. She was totally confused and felt quite foolish actually but couldn't stop herself, pushed on by a driving force.

But if she chose one, he could easily be in the other, and she certainly couldn't go to all of them!

"Tell her, Victor."

She turned south toward Saint Cloud, her determination and resolve growing. Though she was just about convinced that the trip was senseless, and she had been stupid to rent a car and stupid to spend the money, she pressed on.

"Where we going, Mom?"

"Just going for a ride," she replied, and the little fellow happily stared out the window at the passing scenery until he tired of it and sprawled out on the long back seat to play with his army men. It took awhile to get there, but she soon saw the sign. *Saint Cloud.* Slowing down as she came into town, she wound around a couple of streets, not knowing where they were, but all the while looking for the car and feeling rather silly.

It couldn't be!

She had come up right behind a large red Pontiac. It was smack in front of her! Astonished, she could hardly believe it, but it was him all right, and he was driving very slowly, very oddly, around and around in circles. She slowed down, too, not knowing what to do now that she had found him. He didn't seem to be going anywhere…just driving in circles, around and around. Then her heart sank.

"Ryan, stay down on the seat!"

"Why, Mom?"

"Just do as I say." Dutifully he obeyed. Confronted with the dire situation, she didn't know what to do, but she didn't want Ryan seeing either. Dale was following another car—following another woman. Joellen realized that the woman knew he was following her, and they were playing some kind of cat and mouse game apparently. Her hands began to shake uncontrollably, and she gripped the steering

255

wheel. Her heart beat faster, but determinedly she kept following, slowly around and around the corners. A fleeting thought occurred to her of the ridiculous scene—the threesome winding through the narrow streets of Saint Cloud, but rage boiled within her! It twisted and constricted, as her suspicions and fears were blatantly realized!

Then Dale glanced up into his rearview mirror.

He had seen her!

He immediately slowed his pace, then came to a complete stop, and she sped up beside him. "Now I know what you do!" she screamed out the window. "Don't you ever come back! I hate you...you hear...don't you ever come back!" She jerked the rental car into gear and sped off, hardly able to see the road in front of her as stinging tears flooded her eyes. She careened around the streets and out of town.

"Was that Daddy, Mom?" Ryan asked softly from the back seat.

Guilt flooded her soul.

At that moment, she was more disgusted with herself than Dale. She shouldn't have done it, shouldn't have yelled out what she did in front of Ryan. She shouldn't have lost it!

He was peering over the seat at her.

"Everything's going to be all right, son," she cried. "...don't you worry." She swiped at her tears and forced a smile.

He smiled back.

"Would you like to go to the park when we get back home...the one with the bear?"

"Uh-huh."

But she heard the uncertainty in his voice. Driving back to Wadena, she determined in her heart: I don't know what

I'm going to do, but I know what I'm not going to do. I will never go looking for him again!

DALE DID NOT come home for several days. Joellen tried to act normal, like nothing was wrong in front of Ryan, though he was used to his father being gone, and used to her being the central person in his young life. But after the first couple of days, she was distraught. Though she had dared him to come back, suppose he didn't? What *was* she going to do? Who could she turn to? She remembered Mrs. Daniel's offer, and she desperately needed somebody to talk to. She had tried turning it all over to the Lord, but she figured she just wasn't a good enough Christian. She still yearned for human comfort. Maybe it was because of her pregnancy, or because she was so far from home, or maybe it was just her. Would she ever be a strong Christian?

Standing on her neighbor's porch as the spring wind buffeted her, still raw and cold, she hesitated, ashamed of her plight. Then she knocked.

"Why, come on in, child," Mrs. Daniel's cheery voice welcomed her immediately. The elderly lady sensed instantly that there was trouble brewing beneath the surface and not too far beneath it at that. "Let's go into the dining room." She led the way into the sun-splashed room which also served the purpose of a family room, the same room in which they conducted their Bible studies. Joellen followed, fighting back the tears that were ready to flow.

"I can see you're upset." She patted Joellen's clenched hands as she stiffly sat down on a formal chair in front of her. Joellen nodded, but the flood of tears broke loose as she relayed her dismal circumstances.

Mrs. Daniel reached for her Bible. "Let's just see what He might have to say to us." She wisely turned the crisp tissue-thin pages to Psalm 91 and read softly…

> *He that dwelleth in the secret place of the most High shall abide under the shadow of the Almighty.*
> *I will say of the Lord, He is my refuge and my fortress: my God; in him will I trust.*
> *Surely he shall deliver thee from the snare of the fowler, and from the noisome pestilence.*
> *He shall cover thee with his feathers, and under his wings shalt thou trust: his truth shall be thy shield and buckler.*
> *Thou shalt not be afraid for the terror by night; nor for the arrow that flieth by day;*
> *Nor for the pestilence that walketh in darkness; nor for the destruction that wasteth at noonday.*

The rise and fall of Mrs. Daniel's soothing monotone voice and the comforting words of Scripture were a healing salve, lifting Joellen up and above the fears that had been crushing down upon her. She glanced out the window to the two-story house across the street, to the upstairs apartment. Why had she been so fearful? Hadn't He said, *"I will never leave thee nor forsake thee"*? She felt foolish. She must be stronger. She must learn to trust Him more. She must be more like Mrs. Daniel, who was still reading.

> *Because thou hast made the Lord, which is my refuge, even the most High, thy habitation;*
> *There shall no evil befall thee, neither shall any plague come nigh thy dwelling.*

Bit by bit, the heavy load fell from her shoulders, gently sliding down, down, down, and she straightened up. Had she forgotten all that she had learned? She stared at Mrs.

Daniel as she read. The old lady had experienced her own troubles in her life, hard times particularly living through the Great Depression. Joellen recalled the waxed paper hanging on a small clothesline in her basement to be re-used, a remnant of that past. The next words caught her attention.

"For he shall give his angels charge over thee, to keep thee in all thy ways."

IT WAS THE first of May, springtime in a new decade. The turbulent sixties were history and would make for controversial discussion for years to come. But for now, there was renewed hope. President Nixon had begun withdrawing forces out of Vietnam, pledging to bring back 150,000 before the year was out; however, the fighting was far from over.

With the withdrawal, the forces left were demoralized, and drug use was on the rise. Henry Kissinger, presidential assistant, was holding meetings in Paris for mutual withdrawal, and America was hopeful, but not everybody. Draft evaders hiding out in Canada remained there, and student demonstrations continued. On the fourth of May, a tragic event occurred at Kent State when one hundred National Guards fired their rifles into a group of demonstrating students, killing four and wounding eleven. The National Student Association and the former Vietnam Moratorium Committee leaders called for a national university strike of indefinite duration to protest the war, and more than one hundred colleges and universities across the nation shut down.

Integration was also forging ahead but not without resistance. South Carolinians stormed school buses to prevent it, and racial unrest was prevalent most everywhere. But in

Lynchburg, the final integration plan had been approved in April, which would have all senior high students, black and white, attending E. C. Glass in the fall. Dunbar, the black high school, was being relegated to one of three junior high schools in the city.

But things back home seemed far away to Joellen as she struggled with her own desperate situation in Minnesota. Unable to wholly trust in God, she grew more and more anxious as the baby grew within. Dale was drinking heavily, and the money was always short. At times the cupboards were practically bare—except for eggs—they always had eggs! Dale's friend, a dairy farmer in Brainerd, kept them supplied.

She knew she wasn't depending on the Lord as she should, but she couldn't just wait and wait and wait. She had to make him change! Her distraught state peaked one day the end of April as she cried and pleaded with him not to go. He ignored her and continued dressing. He must not leave again! She couldn't bear the thought of another night alone and the wretched crying. He grabbed his coat and started down the steps, anxious to be gone. She followed after, her face red and swollen, and standing at the top of the stairs, she begged him not to leave. Angrily he turned and glared up at her, then reached for the door.

Hopeless, she let go of the banister, tumbling down, over and over, and landed at the foot of the stairs in a crumpled heap.

"You took care of the baby?"

Victor glared at Celeste. "Well, of course!"

Dale stared at her. "You're crazy!"

The words rang in her head as the door slammed shut.

She cried herself to sleep that night, but the event proved that nothing would stop him, and more importantly, it proved to her that she was totally out of control. How could she have done such a thing? Such a dangerous thing! She was flooded with guilt. Suppose the baby, her precious baby, had been hurt?

"Forgive me, Lord! Please forgive me...and please make my baby okay! What's wrong with me? Lord...I need your help!" she cried. She saw her mother before her and wondered if she was headed down the same dark wretched path. Was that strain of emotional instability to imprison her as well? She thought of her grandfather, the man she had never met, the man who had lived his life in an institution. "Lord...please help me!"

Afterwards, she struggled for more faith. It was hard. It was more than hard. It was extremely difficult, and before long she succumbed again to the overwhelming desire to take control, to make things different. The snows were still on the ground, though it was May. Dale was dressing to leave. Usually when he left, she knew she wouldn't see him until the next day or sometimes the next. She begged him not to leave, not to get drunk. She tried to stop him; they quarreled, and in despair, she ran out of the apartment, down the steps and into the snowy darkness, oblivious that she was barefooted. She raced around to the back of the house. Standing on one foot then the other in the cold wet snow, her feet began to tingle. Suppose I get frost-bit? Surely he will come looking for me! She heard a door shut, and her hopes rose.

Then she heard the car start up.

He can't be leaving!

The Pontiac backed out of the little garage and disappeared up the dark street. Tearfully, but resignedly, she hurried back inside and sank down on the bed to pull on some warm socks over her cold wet feet. She sobbed and sobbed as she struggled with the socks, her awkward belly in the way, and then she felt a little hand patting her gently.

"It'll be okay, Mom…it'll be okay."

She sobbed even harder, ashamed to be crying, ashamed again of what she had just done, ashamed that her little boy had to comfort her. She wanted to be strong. She needed to be strong for him and the unborn baby, but she felt so weak.

WHAT OCCURRED A few days later launched a dramatic chain of events. In a drunken stupor, Dale fell down a flight of stairs in a bar and seriously dislocated his shoulder. The Air Force airlifted him to Wilford Hall Hospital in San Antonio, Texas. Therapy was going to be extensive and lengthy. Though the next few weeks were peaceful for Joellen and Ryan, she wondered what the future held. Then Dale returned for them. His orders had been transferred from Minnesota to Texas for the duration of his therapy.

It was a crossroads!

Should she go with him to Texas or return to Virginia? She struggled with the decision. All she could think of was *"til death do us part."* It was what the scriptures taught. It was the right thing for a marriage. It was what her parents had done, and besides there was Ryan…and another child soon to be. And she couldn't work now, and always in the back of her mind was the thought of returning home. Though she was frightened of the unknown, at the prospect of going to yet another new place with him, she kept coming back to these thoughts. She couldn't go back home.

CHAPTER EIGHTEEN

JOELLEN CAREFULLY PACKED their few belongings, and Dale drove them across country, one-handed, determined to prove he could. It was the middle of July, and the windows pulled in the hot humid air in potent gusts, but at least it was moving air, and they welcomed it.

"It's going to be a little girl," Dale announced and reached over to rub Joellen's swollen stomach.

"How do you know?"

"Wait and see."

She hoped so.

Dale glanced at Ryan in the back seat, his large brown eyes anxiously staring out the window. "Well, Ryan, what do you think of moving to the big state of Texas?"

His eyes lit up, obviously excited about the move. Texas sounded like a great place. He might even see some cowboys. "I'm glad!" he replied.

Dale was happy to be moving his family to Texas, and optimistic for a new start. He was going to really try this time. He had missed them, but even as the noble thoughts ran through his mind, his confidence waned. He wondered if he could. He didn't understand himself, never had. He remembered the youth group when the church was just starting, and he was part of that little group. He had been so proud to be a part of it, too. He remembered Reverend Falwell visiting him at home. He visited everybody in the neighborhood. He remembered his decision to follow the Lord back then. When did things change? He wanted to do what's right. He had tried! He really had, though he knew Joellen didn't believe him. Nobody did. But the pull to get away, the pull to drink was so strong! It always won. Deep down, he figured he wasn't good enough, not good enough to be what he should be anyway, not good enough for other people, and not good enough for Joellen. And she was seriously considering going back home. It had taken some begging and pleading to get her to come, promising that everything would be totally different. But could he keep that promise?

Thoughts of the wild parties in San Antonio raced through his mind…the exciting music, the stimulating drink, and the electrifying Mexican girls. He glanced over at Joellen studying the map, and Ryan glued to the window, and pushed away the strong temptations. Instead he thought of the little one coming. He had so much going for him—he couldn't afford to mess up again. He watched the wide open fields passing by and was glad to be leaving Minnesota, the freezing cold, the fierce winds, the piles of snow, leaving it all behind.

Texas was a new start!

Joellen's thoughts were similar as they drove into the tip of Oklahoma. She wiped her forehead again. It was getting hotter and hotter as the Pontiac sped down the straight highway with miles and miles of flat, horizontal plains stretching out in all directions. She leaned further out the window. She had never known such heat! Her body had acclimated to the frigid Minnesota weather and now was facing the exact opposite with no time to adjust, and she was seven months pregnant! Dale pulled over at a rest area, and she clumsily rolled herself out of the car. Her back ached, and her damp clothes stuck to her.

"Look, Mom!" Ryan called out as he energetically romped throughout the rest area, pointing up to the round concrete umbrella tops that shaded the concrete picnic tables. She nodded. Looks like we've landed on the moon, she thought irritably. No trees, no air stirring...and it feels like we just stepped into a giant suffocating oven!

They drove on through the evening as the scorching sun made its welcomed descent, bringing some relief. Its disappearing performance created a ghostly effect, casting a fiery-red path across the vast prairie, eerily outlining the myriad black oil drills that rhythmically pumped up and down.

Ker chunk...ker chunk...ker chunk.

The unique and ever-present pounding added to the strangeness. It was a melancholy sound, like an omen of sorts, as the blood-red sun rested upon the hard-baked plains.

The next day they drove out of Oklahoma and into Texas, but didn't witness any change. When they left the small modest motel, the bright morning sun bitterly confronted them, already simmering, pressing upward, promising another hot uncomfortable day of driving. At least she would enjoy the passing scenery. She had always loved traveling, seeing new places and things and people, like the Native Americans they had seen yesterday in Oklahoma when they stopped at the rest area. Cherokees, no doubt, and she recalled reading the disturbing book, *Trail of Tears.* Again her interest was piqued with the Native Americans as it had been in Minnesota. She lifted her maternity top, fanning it, hoping she could stand the heat another day. Already her belly was tight and sticky.

SAN ANTONIO—25 MILES...the large green overhead highway sign read. Life sure has its surprises, she thought, as she pointed to the sign for Ryan to see. He looked up at it and grinned. The little fellow was excited. It was an adventure for him. She only hoped life would be better for them here in the big city.

They drove straight to the base. Dale had attempted to describe Lackland Air Force Base to her, but still she was not prepared for its immensity. Sprawling out over 6,800 acres with large stretches of grassy lawns, winding streets, and lots of redbrick buildings that housed barracks, mess halls, and many other necessary military facilities, it was a town in itself. It had begun in 1941 as a World War II officer training school at Kelly Air Force Base nearby and became a separate base in 1942. It implemented basic training in 1946 but also served other purposes, including beginning training for officer candidates, English language instruction for foreign students, and training for security police. It took its name from Brig. Gen. Frank D. Lackland, who commanded the flying school at Kelly Air Force Base during World War II. Now it was a household name. It also boasted the famed Wilford Hall Hospital—the reason they were there.

Ryan's eyes darted all around at the awesome military presence, the scores of uniformed soldiers, and particularly the military planes. At seven years old, it was all making a lasting impression on him.

A base guestroom would be their temporary home until they found a place off base. Joellen walked into the small cramped room with its tiny adjoining bathroom and was happy to finally be able to breathe. It was air-conditioned! The noisy window unit was turned up high, humming loudly and erratically, but it was cool!

She set about unpacking their things.

"I need to run down to the base office," Dale said. "I'll be back in a few minutes."

"Can I go, Dad?"

"No, you stay here with Mom."

The few minutes turned into an hour, then two, then three. Joellen became anxious. *Surely he will come back!* But darkness fell and he did not return, and she realized that he was gone. How long, she didn't know. She stared at the bag of donuts on the nightstand, the only food they had, and she had no money. How could he do this? They had just gotten here! She didn't know anything about the place…she didn't know a soul on base or even in Texas, for that matter. She didn't know where to go or who to turn to if she needed to. Masking her fears, she talked about their new home in the big state of Texas, rambling on and on, and Ryan was unaware of their impending situation. She closed the blinds above the humming air conditioner and proceeded to tidy up the room, waiting and praying for his return. But he didn't return.

"I'm hungry, Mom."

"…I'm sure Dad will be back soon. I'll tell you what, why don't we eat these donuts?"

He nodded enthusiastically, pleased to have donuts instead of supper. Then he sprawled out on the little cot up against the big bed to watch the portable television in the corner. But just before bedtime, he repeated, "I'm still hungry, Mom. Can I have another donut?"

The words pierced her soul—she didn't know what to do. She knew he was okay for now but suppose Dale didn't come back in the night. "Why don't we try to go to sleep... and we'll get some food in the morning." She stretched out awkwardly on the bed. Covertly, she wanted to save the last two donuts for the morning because she knew he would be hungry when he awoke.

"Okay," he replied and was soon fast asleep, and she was thankful for that.

Her cumbersome body rolled over on the double bed, and she tossed restlessly, her thoughts straying to home, her church, and the story she had taught her Sunday school class before leaving—the Israelites wandering in the wilderness. She felt like she was wandering, too. The full moon climbed high in the wide-open Texas sky, and she cried softly.

Narrow shafts of pinkish light fell through the blinds and across the room. It was dawn. The spot beside her was empty. Fear seized her—what was she going to do? Immediately her eyes fell on the crumpled bag of donuts. That would be enough for Ryan for breakfast, but then what? She glanced over at his small sleeping form, and hoped he would stay that way awhile longer.

As she lay praying, she recalled seeing a sign that said *Chaplain* when they drove onto the base. Where was it? Maybe she could find her way back to it, but what would she say? She didn't want to get Dale in trouble, but she wouldn't let her son go hungry either. Deep down, she knew that wasn't all. She hated to ask for help—it went against everything within her! There it was again—her stubborn pride. She remembered her mother's words—*too much pride to be poor*. Well, lying there in the strange bed, all alone, she had to admit her mother was right. She hated like the devil to ask for help, to ask for something to eat. If only God would drop down some manna in the little room like He did for the Israelites. She smiled at the thought as the shafts of pink light gradually turned gold, then a bright glistening yellow.

Ryan sat up. "Mom?"

"I'm right here."

"Is Dad back yet?"

She shook her head.

"But I'm hungry, Mom." He tumbled out of bed onto the cool tile floor. Reluctantly, she pushed herself up to face the dreaded day, and handed him the donuts. The little fellow quickly devoured them. "I'm still hungry, Mom."

She had no choice. She sat down on the bed to pull on her blue maternity pants, then slipped the top over her head, and laid out Ryan's clothes.

His shoes!

They were still in the car. She hadn't finished unpacking before Dale left, and Ryan's shoes were lying on the back floorboard where he had left them. Well, he'd just have to go barefooted. She remembered how hot it was yesterday and hoped it wouldn't be as hot today. She glanced at Ryan, now occupied with the TV, and decided to wait awhile longer in hopes that Dale would return. She busied herself with straightening the small room and organizing their clothes. Soon it was nearing lunchtime and still no Dale.

"Mom, I'm hungry."

They left the redbrick building, hand in hand, walking toward the area where she thought she had seen the Chaplain sign. The climbing morning sun was already hot and pressing down upon them. Suddenly Ryan began jumping up and down.

"What's wrong?"

269

"It burns my feet, Mom!"

She bent down to touch the pavement and jerked her hand off. It was already blistering hot from the scorching sun, and drawing the tar substance to the top. It reminded her of when she was a kid and spent her summers barefooted, often doing dances on those hot rural roads. "Here," she pointed to the grassy lawn. "Walk over here on the grass." He hopped over on it, but immediately screamed out.

"Now what?"

"Stickers!"

She grabbed him up in her arms, stumbling under his weight and that of the unborn child, and suddenly realized that the appealing green grass was deceiving. It was full of minute sticky burrs, and they were stuck in his little feet! She sat down with him and gently began pulling them out, one by one, as he cried.

Victor looked sadly at Celeste.

His crying subsided as he struggled to be strong, and she pulled out the last burr. It was their first acquaintance with the Texas burrs, and the sprawling grassy lawns were literally filled with them. Now what? Shifting her purse to her other shoulder, she picked him up and carried him on her hip, but by the time she got to the end of the street, she was panting. Dropping him to his feet, she had to rest, but the hot pavement set his feet afire again and he jumped off into the grass.

"Mom!" he cried out again, and she grabbed him back up to pull out the sticky burrs, then started out once more.

"It'll be okay…now stop crying…." She soothed him while hefting him up on her hip and turned left at the intersection. She thought she remembered it was to the left.

She hoped so. The hot sun beat down upon them, and she began to feel faint, but she had to keep going. She had to find the place.

They trudged along, and every now and then a car passed by, and she was tempted to cry out for help, but couldn't bring herself to do so. She heard music drifting across the dry grassy turf from one of the buildings, one of the distant buildings that seemed to be made of liquid, its redbrick lines waving in the wretched heat, but she couldn't make out the words of the tune. The melancholy strains merely added to her loneliness. If only she could have heard the words…

When you're weary, feelin' small,
When tears are in your eyes,
I'll dry them all;
I'm on your side,

When times get rough
And friends just can't be found,
Like a bridge over troubled water
I will lay me down
Like a bridge over troubled water
I will lay me down

Intimidated by the large redbrick building with the Chaplain sign tacked overhead, she warily knocked at the door.

"Come on in," a throaty business-like voice answered.

Holding tightly onto Ryan's hand, she pushed open the door.

"Can I help you?" a tall, uniformed man posed, his face void of feeling. She supposed he was the chaplain. Two other uniformed personnel stood by staring at her, just

271

as impersonal, and she wished the floor would open up and swallow them. How could she ask *them* for help? How could she tell them her embarrassing predicament?

They waited.

"We…I need to talk with someone…."

"Step right in here," the chaplain waved them toward an adjoining office and followed, seating himself behind a large metal desk. He motioned to a couple of fold-up chairs.

"Have a seat."

She sat down before him and nervously pulled Ryan onto her lap. She needed him close. Stumbling awkwardly over her words, she briefly stated their reason for being there. The chaplain immediately began drilling her with questions concerning Dale's disappearance and when she thought he might return, questions for which she had no answers. She watched his eyes dart back and forth from them to a stack of papers on his desk, dully peering over his black-rimmed glasses. Then he concluded in his matter-of-fact way, "Here's what we're going to do. We'll give you meal tickets that you and your son can use at the mess hall. Just show these tickets at the door and you'll be able to eat your meals there." He thrust them at her. "…you can use them three times a day, and they are good for several days. When they run out, just come back to see me." With a pasted smile, he briefly gave her directions to the mess hall and stood up.

So did Joellen, letting Ryan slide down beside her. She wanted to ask him more about the directions, she wanted to tell him about the shoes, she wanted to find out what she should do if Dale didn't return, but she couldn't bring herself to ask anything. He was busy, and she couldn't wait to get out of there.

The door closed behind them, and the brilliant sunrays met them. They set out toward the mess hall with the scanty directions. She was surprised at how far it was and wondered why the chaplain hadn't thought of that. *Military is military, I guess, no matter if you're seven months pregnant, and your son has no shoes. We'll make it! God will take care of us!* She clutched the meal tickets in her hand and pushed them safely down into her pocket. At least they had food now.

They trekked back and forth across the sprawling grounds for their meals that day and learned how to detect the menacing stickers. Ryan walked on the pavement until it was too hot, then on the grass when there were no stickers, and she carried him when there were. She felt so small and insignificant on the mammoth base crawling with military personnel. *I know You're with me, Lord. Just give me strength, and give me wisdom to know what to do.*

That night, they had the small TV to watch, and she was glad enough that they had a place to stay and food to eat. Ryan actually thought it quite fun going to the large mess hall with all the soldiers. She tried to make it a game for him, laughing and playing as much as possible. Her only concern was what if Dale didn't come back? The dark cloud hovered over no matter how much she struggled to trust God.

If only I had more faith!

Dale returned on the third day, full of apologies but no answers. He had gotten drunk with the guys, he explained, and passed out. He didn't really remember much of it. Joellen's heart was broken that he could care so little to leave them that way, but other thoughts took precedence. She simply could not trust him for their safety or well-being; it was up to her, but not even her.

It was up to God.

CHAPTER NINETEEN

THEY DROVE OUT to the outskirts of San Antonio, past the busyness of it all where a few trees grew listlessly and wild grasses waved in the sultry breeze. They passed by the relatively new school named after Astronaut Neil Armstrong.

"That's where you'll be going to school, Ryan," Dale said.

He stared at it quietly as they passed by.

Then they turned into the modest subdivision and wound through it, both Joellen and Ryan wide-eyed. Up and over its slight knolls, over its newly surfaced streets already hot in the early morning, and they saw the realtor's car up ahead.

"Deep Valley," Dale read the street sign aloud as he turned in, and Joellen remembered the eerie sound of the oil drills as they drove through Oklahoma and Texas. *Ker chunk...ker chunk...ker chunk.* She pushed the haunting thoughts aside as Dale pointed to the lovely little house in front of them.

"This is it," he announced proudly.

"I like it!" Ryan exclaimed from the back seat. "I like it...it's got a big back yard."

They walked through the new house, blissfully taking in the shiny kitchen with its appealing cabinets, the bright living room with its double window facing the street, and the short hallway with three small bedrooms leading off it. Joellen especially loved the white tiled floors, so cool to the touch. It was simply beautiful, and she couldn't believe that they could actually be moving in!

She studied the smallest bedroom that was furnished as a nursery with delicate white wicker furniture including a white wicker bassinet. The curtains and accessories were a soft yellow gingham, and she had never seen anything so lovely in all her life. The house had been a display model for the subdivision. Now all the furniture had been removed except for the nursery. Was it possible that they were going to leave it?

They ambled through the house while the realtor patiently stood by and Ryan happily followed behind. It was brand new! Even the grass had just been sown, and Joellen couldn't wait to work on that. The new neighborhood was designed primarily for the transient military families, and Dale had surprised her. The military loan was already in process. She stepped into the small bathroom and flipped the switch. The overhead heater buzzed on, and she glanced up. "Yuck…what's that?"

"Oh…just baby scorpions," the realtor replied nonchalantly. "Don't worry, they're fried!" But Joellen cringed at the revolting spectacle. The little crawly creatures, with long tails caught in the wire fixture were absolutely the ugliest things she'd ever seen.

Virginia summers are hot, Joellen thought nostalgically. But the Texas heat was oppressive, stifling, and exceedingly humid. As soon as she went out, the curls in her hair immediately fell out, and her clothes would be clinging to her, damp and sticky, but the worst part was night. Back home, she reminisced, you could look forward to a cooling off in the evenings after a hot summer day. Virginians sat out on their porches when the sun went down and enjoyed refreshing evening breezes. Not here! It was just as hot at 12:00 AM as it was at 12:00 PM! There was nothing to do but stay indoors in the air condition, and she thanked God for it. Many of the Mexican Americans lived without it, she understood, and she couldn't imagine that. She had grown up without it, of course, but not in Texas! The elderly Mexican painter, who was putting some finishing touches on Ryan's bedroom, was busy brushing the last spot. Joellen stood in the doorway watching. "It's really hot out there," she began in a friendly tone. "Do you have air condition at home?"

He turned and embarrassingly gazed down at her from the ladder, motioning that he didn't speak English. She smiled up at him, trying to assuage his embarrassment, and left him to his work.

They had purchased the most inexpensive furniture they could find for the house, a maple finish, and all the rooms were now furnished except the nursery. It was empty. The charming white wicker furniture and its yellow gingham accessories had been removed right before they moved in, much to Joellen's disappointment. She understood, of course, that it didn't belong to them and really didn't expect it to stay, but every time she passed by the empty nursery, she couldn't help but see that beautiful wicker furniture and precious wicker bassinet. Each week she mentioned to Dale that they needed to get a baby bed, a bassinet or something.

"We will," he answered, but the nursery remained bare.

The breakfast dishes were done, and Joellen stared out the kitchen window. The same four ladies were sitting outside on the carport a few doors up. Every morning, they sat there, drinking coffee, looking like they were having loads of fun. She could hear them laughing and talking, and wished she had a friend, someone to talk to. She remembered Mrs. Dunford back in Lynchburg and how they used to talk. In fact, Mrs. Dunford was the first person to seriously talk to her about the Bible. She especially liked to talk about the "New Jerusalem" descending from Heaven one day. And Mrs. Daniel up in Minnesota, what a dear Christian lady. She wondered if maybe she might find another Mrs. Dunford or Mrs. Daniel down here in Texas.

It was the end of August, and she had watched Ryan hasten up the street to school with the other children. She decided to put on a pot of beans for supper, but discovered she was out of sugar. Pinto beans were no good without a little sugar to flavor them. Her mama always used sugar and so did Aunt Anna. She glanced out the window. They were still there, and she really needed that sugar! She changed clothes, brushed her hair and stepped out into the already rising temperature and headed toward them.

As she approached the ladies, they stopped laughing and talking. Curiously, they watched her, wondering about this new young neighbor. Most of them were over forty and obviously bored with their everyday existence.

"Come and join us," a gregarious redhead called out.

"Thank you, but I wondered if I might be able to borrow a little sugar until tomorrow. I was fixing some beans and discovered I was out." She stood before them, feeling miles apart. A rather tall lady, with short-cropped salt and pepper hair, snuffed out a cigarette and stood up. "Sure thing, I'll get it." She reached for Joellen's empty cup.

"Why don't you sit down and have some coffee with us," a heavyset lady suggested, but Joellen detected more curiosity than sincerity. "We've been wondering why you haven't joined us."

Reluctantly she eased down into one of the empty lawn chairs. "Thank you…but I don't care for any."

"You don't like coffee!" the redhead exclaimed as if she had committed the unpardonable sin.

She shook her head.

"Whoever heard of such! I thought everybody liked coffee!"

"Well…I tried to develop the taste for it once, actually twice, but I just couldn't…." She looked from one to the other, wondering why in the world she was explaining this to them.

"H-m-m-ph," the lady uttered, dismissing the subject.

Joellen looked up into the clear blue sky. "It sure is…a nice morning," she said haltingly.

"Guess you could say that. Gonna be hotter than hell before it's over."

"You can say that again, Marie," the heavyset lady laughed hysterically, sending rolls of fat jostling. The neighbor with the sugar returned. "How about some coffee, dear?" She handed her the sugar.

"She don't like coffee, Vivian," Marie answered for her.

"That so. Never heard of anybody didn't like coffee!"

"Just what I said!"

Joellen was anxious to leave. "Thank you so much for the sugar. I guess I better get back…."

"Don't run off. We're glad to finally meet you. Where you from?" Vivian asked, motioning for her to sit back down.

"Virginia."

"Virginia, huh. Well, I'm from New Jersey originally, but I've lived so many places I don't feel like I have a home."

She laughed at herself. "Marie here is from Maryland, not far from Virginia." The other two quickly added where they hailed from, then fell back to discussing the neighborhood gossip that Joellen's appearance had disrupted. She sat uneasily on the aluminum chair, and left as soon as she could without seeming too ungrateful.

JOELLEN'S HAPPINESS WITH the new house was short-lived. Nor did it halt Dale's path of destruction. She wondered where he was as she lay in bed rehashing the strange incident in Saint Cloud. With four directions in which to go, and randomly picking one, then to drive up right behind him! What were the odds of that happening?

She rolled her very pregnant body over and remembered the other time back in Virginia just before they left for Minnesota. It was Wednesday prayer meeting night, and she had gone over to meet Dale at his folk's house. They had planned to go to church, but he wasn't there, and his mother didn't know where he was.

She had not told anyone of the vague, unexplainable sense of direction she received that evening, but she had followed it and drove to the narrow downtown street. When she drove down it, she particularly noticed one of the old Victorian houses on her right, and at that very moment the door opened. Unawares, a woman came out with a man in uniform. Startled and hurt, she had spun out of the street, gone home and gathered up all his belongings and taken them over to his mother's. She dropped them down on the porch with instructions that she never wanted to see him again!

Two weeks passed.

Then he called, begging forgiveness. In spite of the disturbing development, in spite of what she had seen, Joellen wrestled with her decision to leave with him. Part of her still believed that she should try to make the marriage work. But looking back, she also had to admit that part of it was pride! Her stubborn pride! She had already given her notice at General Electric and at the Sunday school department and the choir. Everyone was happy for her and had told her goodbye, wished her the best and was expecting her to leave. Even Reverend Falwell had announced it after the evening service. How could she not go?

Lying in bed with the inky darkness closing in upon her, she wondered about these strange happenings? It was almost as if an unseen hand was directing her, or warning her, or seeking to protect her. She saw herself falling down the steps in Minnesota again, and cringed at the thought. She pondered—the Thaxton strength and the Conner instability. Did she walk a fine line between the two?

The next morning, she stepped outside to water the struggling wire grass that was grappling for life, sending out its weak tendrils in hopes of finding water. She noticed the women up under the carport again, as she turned on the water hose. She waved, but tried to appear engrossed in her watering.

"Joellen!"

She glanced up, and they motioned for her to come. Reluctantly she turned off the outside faucet and headed toward them. She didn't want to sit with them and listen to their gossip or answer their prying questions. She wanted to water her grass!

"How's your husband?" Vivian blurted out before she even reached them.

"Yes…how is he?" The redhead chimed in curiously, leaning over Vivian's shoulder.

"…he's fine," Joellen answered uncomfortably, unwilling to confide in these snooping women any of her problems.

"Fine!" Marie repeated loudly. Immediately Joellen knew something was wrong.

"But he was in a wreck!" Vivian exclaimed. "I saw it on TV this morning!"

Taken aback, Joellen struggled to stay composed. "…a wreck?"

"You mean you don't know!"

Marie scraped her lawn chair back and thrust a newspaper at her. "Haven't you seen the paper, my dear?"

Dazed, Joellen shook her head.

"I saw it on the news this morning, too!" another piped in as Joellen fearfully scanned the paper.

"…it was *your husband!*" Marie exclaimed. "I saw him!"

In small headlines, Joellen read where there had been a bad automobile accident during the night, involving a military man who was apparently drunk. The details were scant except for the fact that he was going down a ramp the wrong way and rammed into another car with a lady and a baby in it. She felt her knees going weak and her face growing hot, and she wanted to run away from these malicious women, and run away from it all.

BUT THE NEIGHBOR women were right. Dale was intoxicated, and he had driven down a one-way ramp the wrong way and collided with a Mexican lady and her small child. The youngster received a concussion and the lady two broken arms. He came out of it unscathed, but the car was totaled. Joellen didn't see him after the accident for several days, and when he did return, he wouldn't talk about it. Though she empathized with the poor Mexican lady and her little child, she simply didn't have the stamina

281

to dwell on it. It took all her physical and mental strength to care for Ryan and the unborn baby, who would be here all too soon. She could only pray for them.

Dale found himself without wheels; though not even this would deter his craving to get to a bar and drink. They had just bought Ryan a new bicycle when they moved into the house, and he dearly loved it. He loved anything mechanical, but especially his shiny green bicycle. It was his first "big boy" bike. He rode it constantly up and down the driveway and in front of the house. Sometimes he even rode it to school, proudly parking it beneath the school building, which was built up high on brick columns with an open area beneath so that the children could play outside on those blistery hot days. Joellen was glad to see him so happy.

Dale decided to ride the bike to the little country store a couple of miles away for cigarettes. Joellen didn't feel comfortable with it. He insisted there was no other way, it was too hot to walk, and he had to have a cigarette! But he didn't come back.

"Mom, my bike is gone!" Ryan cried when he got home from school.

She tried to explain what had happened, but big tears welled up in his eyes.

Sometime during the middle of the night, Dale stumbled in, but without the bike! The next morning she questioned him, but all he had to say was that it was gone when he went back for it. It must have been stolen while he was in the bar, he feebly explained. Joellen was furious as she watched Ryan sadly walk up the road to school the next morning. The little fellow was heartbroken.

She had to find his bike!

She quietly dressed while Dale slept off his drunk, tugging on her green pants, the thin stretchy top part fitting tautly over her large belly, and she set out walking through the subdivision and out of it. She turned right toward the long section of country road that led to the cluster of low cinder block buildings at the end of it. She had never been to the little store, but she had seen it once when they drove past. She was unaware that there was also a small bar next door; however, she might have known that Dale would know. The sun was fast climbing the wide-open sky, already beating down upon the narrow asphalt road that was hemmed in on both sides with tall Texas grasses subtly waving. She wondered why because there was no breeze that she could feel, only the hot baking sun. Was Dale telling the truth? With no money for more drink, she wouldn't put it past him to sell it, and she grew more and more angry. But then she thought of Ladia's two expensive Labrador pups that were stolen right out of their back yard, with its high Trojan fence, just two weeks ago. The Mexicans stealing over the border! Yes, if it's gone, it was probably stolen, she concluded, but it couldn't be gone! Maybe he was just drunk and didn't remember where he left it.

Her feet hurt terribly. She couldn't see them for her huge belly, but they were more swollen than ever, the hot pink flesh swelling over her tight black flats. It was the first time she'd put them on in awhile, but they were all she had to wear. She stared at the high weeds encroaching on the narrow road, waving, undulating, slightly distorted under the hot morning sun. She wondered if she should have come. But she had to find Ryan's bike!

Her feet ached even more, and she reached down to pull off the flats to walk barefooted, but the road was blistering. She quickly put them back on. The sun climbed higher and grew even hotter, and she began to feel faint. She rubbed her stomach, growing more afraid.

"She'll never make it," Celeste said.

"She shouldn't even be out here!" Victor frowned.

Sergeant Ray, who was married to the neighbor called Vivian, drove up to the crossroads and out of the blue decided to take a shortcut to the base. He hadn't driven down this way in a good while. He drove slowly along watching the edges of the road. The last time he'd come, he'd spotted one of those long slithering prairie rattlesnakes. He hated those things. He hated all rattlesnakes, and here he was in Texas where more rattlesnakes lived than any other state—ten different kinds in fact. But the prairie rattlesnake and the western diamondback were the worst! They were the aggressive ones, and you didn't want to come up on one. Sergeant Dearing did just last week. A diamondback came at him, chased him even. He studied the tall grasses and wondered how many were lurking within. The hot sun beat down upon his windshield, glaring off it and he strained at something up ahead. It couldn't be! No one walked this road! Why, they would be nuts! But as he drew nearer, he could see what appeared to be a woman.

"Oh my!"

He pulled up beside her, recognizing the young pregnant woman from their street. She turned and looked at him—her face beat red, streaked with perspiration, her large belly protruding underneath the limp green top.

"Ma'am," he tried to be calm. "What in the world are you doing out here?"

"I'm walking to the store," she replied, rather embarrassed at how she must look, suddenly feeling quite foolish.

"Don't you know you *can't* do this?" he blurted out, completely exasperated with the situation. "Don't you know that this area is full of snakes, rattlesnakes…they'll even chase you!"

"…I…I didn't know that." She glanced all around.

"Well, it's true! You should never walk this road! Here…I'll give you a ride to the store…come on…get in." He pushed open the door of the large Ford Fairlane. Awkwardly, she climbed in, sinking onto its soft vinyl seat, and pulled the door shut behind her, thankful to sit down, thankful to be off her feet, and thankful to be out of the hot sun. He drove on down the road.

"I'll wait for you and take you back home. You can't walk this road!" Though she felt silly and somewhat chastised by the sergeant, she was also grateful to him. When he pulled up in front of the small cluster of buildings, he added, "I need a few things myself. I'll meet you back here." She knew he was just being considerate, and she rolled out of the car. First she walked all around to find the spot where Dale said he had parked the bike. Maybe, just maybe…but it wasn't there. She checked behind the buildings with their garbage bins overflowing with flapping cardboard boxes, buzzing with flies. Disheartened, she searched and searched. Then she pulled open the door to the small dim lit bar, and a burly, bearded bartender peered over the counter at her.

"Have you seen a green bicycle? My husband left it here yesterday…leaning up against your wall outside he says… it's my little boy's bike…it's brand new, shiny green…."

He shook his head. "Ain't seen no bike 'round here, Ma'am…sorry."

She fought the tears. What was she going to tell Ryan?

Life was daunting there in the hot plains of South Texas, and a tangible darkness closed in around Joellen, a totally cut-off feeling, but there was a ray of sunshine…in the name of Mrs. Sato. She and her family had moved in next door. Mrs. Sato was Mongolian, and she murdered the King's English; in fact, it was a challenge to understand her at all. No less, she was a welcomed diversion for Joellen, daily cheering her up.

The old Asian woman had ended up in San Antonio via Turkey, and before that Japan, but originally from the small country of Mongolia that lay between China and the Soviet Union in east-central Asia. Mrs. Sato described it as a rugged land, full of towering mountains, not at all like San Antonio. But it also has the bleak Gobi Desert in the southeast, she added, and it was either very hot or very cold. Joellen figured that's why she didn't mind the hot temperature in Texas.

Mrs. Sato had fond memories of her childhood, and Joellen learned about it as she chatted away, describing how China had ruled Mongolia for hundreds of years until the Mongolians drove them out shortly after the turn of the century. Then they appealed to Russia for support, and soon after, fell largely under the control of Russia. The old lady explained to Joellen that she and her parents had to flee the country with nothing but the clothes on their backs. They fled to Japan, where she later met Mr. Sato, who had had a similar experience, and they married. But once again they had to flee the war-ridden country of Japan during World War II and ended up in Turkey.

The Satos had one daughter, Ladia, whom they raised in Turkey. Ladia, in turn, met an American soldier and married. She came with him to America and soon brought over her aging parents. Having been uprooted more than once and beleaguered by raging wars, never being able to put down solid roots, the old couple was delighted to finally be in America.

"I am being citizeen now…Amer-i-can Citizeen…no more moveeng…I am happy being Amer-i-can Citizeen… yes!" She nodded emphatically, grinning from ear to ear, and Joellen nodded with her, her jovial mood clearly contagious. On the other hand, Mr. Sato was quite the opposite, quiet and reserved. He stayed in his room much of the time, painting his charming pictures of old Mongolia and Japan, exquisite geisha girls and soft pastel oriental scenes with plentiful lily ponds. He was also proud of his new citizenship, but unlike his cheery wife, he became pensive when he remembered his boyhood days in the old country. And this big country, America—it was very strange, busy, everything so plentiful, so new! But he knew he must adapt. He would spend his last days here, and he would die here…far away from his own people. So the old man sequestered himself and labored over his art, lost in his memories. Ladia and her husband were gone much of the time, as well, leaving Mrs. Sato largely to herself, but she was not one to stay to herself too long. A gregarious and energetic person, she soon sought out Joellen.

Tap…tap…tap.

There was the familiar light tap on her kitchen door and the broad smiling face pressed up to the windowpane, with her twinkling eyes and her nose flattened against the glass. Joellen hurried to open the door.

"I be bringeen' you some good theeng to eat," Mrs. Sato articulated in her broken English. She held out a steaming pastry carefully wrapped in aluminum foil.

"Why, you didn't have to do that…."

Mrs. Sato nodded vigorously. "You be likeen' this...ee's good for you...an' the...." She waved at Joellen's large belly with a chuckle. "An'...number two son...eh?" She always referred to the baby this way. Of course, Joellen was happy to see her new friend and even more happy to see the pastry. Food was scarce, and she was tired of eating the same thing.

But Mrs. Sato's cuisine!

She had never tasted anything like it! Light fluffy pastry stuffed with all kinds of marvelous mouthwatering things—chicken, seafood, beef, and rice. Always the rice, and the tastiest rice she had ever put in her mouth. Sometimes the pastry was filled with sweets—jellies of all flavors, surprising and delighting Joellen. Having lived in so many places, Joellen wondered what kind of food she was eating. Mrs. Sato said it was Japanese with a few hints of the old Mongolian appetite because she had learned to cook in Japan as a young girl. Whatever it was, Joellen quickly developed a taste for it and looked forward to the frequent treats delivered with such affection. Mrs. Sato couldn't do enough for her new neighbor. She was happy to have a friend, someone who could understand her and actually talk with her. Her family was too busy. Ladia worked for one of the large department stores downtown, and Peter, her handsome Mexican-American son-in-law, was usually at the base.

Joellen placed the food on the counter. "Come on in, Mrs. Sato." She led the way to the small living room where they sat down opposite one another.

"Husband...'ees back?"

Joellen shook her head dejectedly, and the old woman mimicked her, shaking hers just so. She knew what was going on. There was no way of withholding the truth from such close neighbors. But unlike the meddlesome women up the street, Mrs. Sato honestly cared for her.

"Number one son...at...school...still, eh?"

Joellen nodded, and the old lady lapsed into a jumble of words that even Joellen couldn't understand. She excitedly but vainly gestured this way and that but obviously didn't know the English for what she was struggling to convey. Finally she gave up and pulled Joellen toward the door. "You be comeeng...eh? Ladia buy...I show...you be comeeng...." Short, stocky and slightly humped, she rocked back and forth on her heels as she lumbered toward the door. Joellen followed her out into the hot sticky morning. They crossed the hard-baked lawn with its straggling grass.

"I need to water...."

Mrs. Sato shook her head adamantly. "First...you be comeeng...you see...."

"I'm coming...I'm coming...."

It turned out to be a brand new entertainment center, television, stereo and the works. Mrs. Sato was quite proud of it and randomly punched all the buttons, some right and some wrong, sending forth a blaring assortment of disconnected sounds. Backing off, Joellen glanced into the bright, immaculate kitchen, and to its right was a small alcove with a gleaming yellow washer and dryer.

"These are new, too, aren't they?"

Mrs. Sato's face clouded over, and she shook her head vehemently. "No keep...they be comeeng back...take away."

"But why?"

"Why?" the old lady asked incredulously. "... you see... yellow...no yellow in Sato house! Veery...veery bad luck!"

SUNDAY MORNING, JOELLEN prepared for their church service at home since they had no way of getting to church. Dale was gone, and she settled down to read from the Bible. Ryan sat on the floor beside her.

And at midnight Paul and Silas prayed, and sang praises unto God: and the prisoners heard them.

And suddenly there was a great earthquake, so that the foundations of the prison were shaken: and immediately all the doors were opened, and every one's bands were loosed.

Ryan interjected, "Bands were handcuffs, Mom."

"I know." She smiled at him.

And the keeper of the prison awakening out of his sleep, and seeing the prison doors open, he drew out his sword, and would have killed himself, supposing that the prisoners had been fled.

But Paul cried with a loud voice, saying, Do thyself no harm: for we are all here.

Then he called for a light, and sprang in, and came trembling, and fell down before Paul and Silas,

And brought them out, and said, Sirs, what must I do to be saved?

And they said, Believe on the Lord Jesus Christ, and thou shalt be saved, and thou house.

"The big earthquake didn't really do it," Ryan concluded. "God did it!"

She nodded proudly. "Ready to sing now?"

"Can I pick?"

She handed him the little paperback songbook. They didn't hear the car drive up as they lifted their voices in song. The door opened and in walked Dale, but he wasn't alone. Thomas and Andrea followed close behind with their young son. Thomas was a tall black fellow originally from Alabama, one of Dale's Air Force buddies, and Andrea was his pretty blond British wife. She flounced in with a cavalier flair, immediately noticing the Bible and songbook. "Joellen, what are you doing?" she quipped in her lovely English tongue.

"We were…having church."

"Church!" she exclaimed with peals of laughter erupting as she tossed her blond head. "Why, who ever heard of such!"

Thomas smiled awkwardly, and Dale looked embarrassed.

"Why, you are right churchy, aren't you there, Miss Joellen?" Andrea teased, patting her on the arm.

"Yeah…she is right churchy," Dale agreed sarcastically, and Joellen felt terribly alone.

"Mom, can we go outside now?" Ryan asked.

She nodded, and he scampered off, followed by Anthony, a beautiful child with golden skin and shiny auburn hair that lay in subtle waves. He was the pride of their lives.

"But why *are* you having church?" Andrea persisted, finding the whole idea quite preposterous, as she sprawled out on the chair facing her.

"…because I'm a Christian." Joellen was growing more annoyed with the interrogation.

"Well, so am I," Andrea challenged, her constant laughter ringing throughout the small house.

"You are?"

"Of course; I belong to the Church of England."

Joellen stared at her. "But, Andrea…being a Christian doesn't mean belonging to a church."

"Of course it does. Like I said, I belong to the Church of England and my Mum…and my entire family back in Cambridge. What are you saying?"

Joellen twisted uncomfortably on the sofa. "One becomes a Christian by trusting Christ as their Savior. The word Christian comes from Christ."

Andrea continued to laugh. "Oh, Joellen, you are something. You *are* churchy. Come, let's go outside." She jumped up and grabbed Joellen's hand, already forgetting the conversation. "You must come to our new house, Joellen. It's simply lovely, and I'm so happy to be here in the big city of San Antonio!" They had recently been transferred to Lackland from another base in Alabama where Andrea had received a startling shock, which she had relayed to Joellen. Unaware of prejudice in America, she was totally unprepared for what they experienced. She didn't go into much detail, but obviously it was not welcomed. "In Britain," she explained to Joellen, "this is not the case. I had no idea! My friends, my family, my mum, everyone was taken with my strong black man! My girlfriends, they are too jealous. I did not know that anyone could not feel the same way about my Thomas…until we moved to Alabama!"

THE NIGHT OF September twenty-first, Joellen had an odd feeling, an uneasy sensation. Could it be time? But she had no pains. She went about her usual duties, helping Ryan with his homework, overseeing his bath, and tucking him into bed. Finally she lifted her heavy awkward body into the lone bed, wondering if Dale would be home soon. She didn't want to face it alone. Maybe it was just in her head, but she couldn't get to sleep and decided to get a glass of milk. It seemed she could never get enough milk, and pushed herself back out of bed. She padded barefoot down the hallway, over the cold tile floor to the kitchen and switched on the light. A strange dark object appeared out of the corner of her eye, and she glanced up.

A scorpion!

She gasped and fell backwards, clumsily bumping into the doorway. It was hanging onto the ceiling, and she had never seen one so large or wickedly ugly! It had to be at least eight inches long. It was black with large claws, but it was the long, curved, poisonous tail that sent shivers up her spine. She knew its sting was painful and dangerous. Frantically, she looked around. She had to kill it or she would never be able to go to sleep. Suppose that thing got in bed with her or Ryan?

She stood there, wildly contemplating how to kill it, and knowing full well that she would never be able to bring herself to get close enough to do it. She remembered the can of Raid, and rushed to the bathroom. There it was. A whole can. She grabbed it and raced back to the kitchen. It must not get away!

It was still there in the same spot; it hadn't moved. She dragged a kitchen chair over to the center of the room and awkwardly climbed up on it, praying she wouldn't fall and that she would be able to kill the thing1.

"You there, Victor?"

"Of course."

"You better watch her—she's pretty clumsy, you know!"

She stretched out her right arm as far as she could, aimed it, held her breath, and sprayed.

The scorpion didn't move.

She sprayed and sprayed and sprayed. Still it didn't move. Her arm began to tremble and her back ached as she precariously perched atop the chair. Then it very slowly began to crawl across the ceiling. She climbed down and pushed the chair closer, climbed back up and continued to spray. It stopped again, but determinedly hung on. The strong odor was beginning to bother her, and she didn't know who was going to win. She shook the can. Almost empty!

Stubbornly the scorpion clung to the ceiling.

Well, she could be just as stubborn! At least her daddy always said so. She sprayed and sprayed. Suddenly it let go and thudded to the floor. Afraid to get down, she stood there, her eyes glued to the ugly dark object as it slowly curled up and died.

Exhausted, she crawled back in bed, physically and emotionally drained, but too keyed up to sleep. She reached for her Bible and propped it up on her huge round belly. She was almost through Galatians in her determined effort to read and study the Scriptures through, with the help of all the commentaries that she had brought from her church back home. But she knew it was God's Word that had sustained her thus far. Suddenly the Bible began to move, first to the left, then to the right. It twisted and wobbled, jerked and shuddered. She silently laid it down beside her and watched her belly as the baby rolled and tumbled.

This is it, she chillingly thought. She glanced at the small wind-up clock on the dresser. Twelve fifteen. Where is Dale? "Please, Lord, bring him home...I don't want to go through this alone...."

"But she's not alone!" Victor grimaced. "She should know that by now!"

"She's scared," Celeste replied, "Just like her mama was, remember?"

They hovered over the bed.

"But when is she ever gonna learn?"

She picked up the Bible again and read, the words marching through her mind without comprehension. It was racing over the past, the present and the future—the scary future.

A sudden pain wrenched through her body!

She gasped and grabbed her belly. It was time—time for new life to enter the world, whether or not the world was ready, whether or not Dale was ready, whether or not there was a cradle for the little one to lay its head. The dresser drawer sat waiting. She had pulled it out last week and placed it atop the dresser. A soft yellow blanket lay over it.

Then she heard a key in the lock, and Dale stumbled in. Drunk. He fell down on the bed opposite her without a word. Now what? She knew she should probably go to the hospital, but how? He was in no shape to take her, and she didn't want to go alone, besides she didn't even know how to get there. Ladia and Peter had offered to take her anytime, but she couldn't bring herself to ask them, not yet, and she really did want Dale with her. As she struggled with her difficult plight, she decided she would take her chances and let him sleep it off. She had only had a couple of pains, and they were far apart. She eased back down to wait, and timed them as they slowly increased throughout the night. She timed them through fearful tears—fear of the pain, fear of the future, fear of bringing another child into such a home.

"I will never leave thee, nor forsake thee...."

The still small voice came to her as a gentle morning breeze stealing over soft green moss and fragile bluets.

TWO DAYS LATER Joellen returned home from the hospital with the precious bundle in her arms, the little girl she had prayed for, then stopped praying for, but God had answered anyhow. Sydney Rae Rodman—a tiny blessing midst turbulent storms. She stood over the infant and gazed down at her still sleeping form beneath the yellow blanket. She looked so small lying there in the large dresser drawer, so small and helpless, and Joellen determined in her heart that she would take care of her and Ryan, no matter what! And she knew she was not alone.

She thought of the morning just a couple of days ago when Sydney was born. She had timed the pains, those wretched pains as they steadily increased throughout the wee hours of the morning while Dale slept. She timed them and caught her breath with each searing throb, and she prayed. She prayed throughout those long, scary hours. About five o'clock in the morning, she knew she couldn't wait any longer. She couldn't chance it anymore, and she awakened Dale. She was disappointed to find that even then the alcohol held him in its grasp, lingeringly, determinedly. He aroused from his deep slumber in a jovial, carefree mood. He was a jolly good fellow and about to have another youngster—wasn't that just the dandiest thing! Joellen humored him, helped him dress, and he wanted to drive them to the hospital in the old car he had just bought, but she convinced him that Ladia and Peter were looking forward to taking them.

The drive to Wilford Hall Hospital was all but a daze in her memory, so intense were the pains by then. She vaguely remembered the kidding and joking back and forth between Dale, Ladia, and Peter. She knew it was for her good, to lighten her load, but all she could focus on were the pains and the ordeal ahead.

The sheer size of the hospital, the cold sterile environment, and the long room full of expectant mothers, all in varying stages of labor, moaning and crying, only added to her fears. It was not at all like Ryan's birth in the small, orderly Baptist hospital back home on the beautiful tree-lined street of Rivermont Avenue. Instead the place was enormous and very hectic with nurses, interns, and doctors rushing about, carrying on muted conversations of which she caught scary bits and pieces. Then a doctor or an intern, she didn't know which, stopped at her.

"This one ready yet?"

"Oh no…she just got here," a hurried nurse hastily replied. We've got several others ahead of her. But the doctor pulled down the sheet anyway and began examining her. Joellen's face flushed a crimson red before another contraction sliced through her, and she gripped the sides of the bed.

"I don't think so," he pronounced. "She's beginning to deliver!" With those words, there was a change of pace and a flurry of activity around her, but all was becoming bleary. The pains of birth were taking over. I just got here, she thought to herself as they wheeled her into the delivery room. *I just got here in time!*

"What about the saddle block?" a nurse questioned, whipping through the swinging doors.

"Too late for that!"

She was prepped and prepared for delivery, and stared up into the face of the strange doctor. "Won't be long now," he said encouragingly.

But it was. The contractions increased, twisting and manipulating her body, and draining every ounce of its energy. She cried softly…and prayed. Fifteen minutes passed, twenty, thirty, forty…an hour, and still the terrifying ordeal continued.

"What's the problem?" someone asked. "I thought she was delivering."

Problem? Her foggy mind reeled.

"I don't know," someone answered, obviously puzzled. "You take a look."

Take a look? What is this?

"Beats me. Looks like it ought to come on out."

"Dr. Fred...over here...this one doesn't want to come out for some reason."

Joellen fought her fears, blinking back salty tears, and looked up into several faces. Why so many? She was unaware that this was not unusual in the large military hospital. The interns were learning, but they were obviously baffled.

"It's turned the wrong way—that's the problem. You've got to turn it," Dr. Fred instructed and left the scene. They reached and probed in vain and then tried all over again. Joellen clutched the sheet and clinched her eyes shut.

"We can't reach it. Too far up."

Dr. Fred was back. "You're right," Joellen vaguely heard him say as the piercing pains racked her body. He leaned down close. "Mrs. Rodman, you're going to have to help us get your baby out."

Help? she wondered incredulously. How could she help?

"The baby is too far up to reach with forceps, and it's turned the wrong way. We have to get it turned before it can come down the birth canal."

Her fears escalated.

"Now I'm going to coach you, tell you what to do...all you need to do is follow my instructions...understand?"

She nodded feebly, and a young black intern extended his large dark hand. "Here, hold onto my finger," he said compassionately, and she grabbed hold.

"You've got to push the baby into position," Dr. Fred instructed. "There's no other way. I will count to three and

298

then say push. When I say push, I want you to push as hard as you can. When I say hold it, then hold it."

She listened, struggling to comprehend, thankful for the blessed relief between contractions, but suddenly her face tightened as another gripped her, and she cried out.

"Just follow my instructions," Dr. Fred coached, "... take a deep breath, now push...push...push...now hold it...now take another deep breath...now push...push... push...now hold it...."

Joellen pushed and pushed to no avail. The doctor nodded for the intern to give her some gas, some rest from the worst contractions, and she vaguely felt the mask slip over her face. Weird, fluid images began to wave across and around her, and bizarre voices slowed to a grotesque sound, and she felt strangely apart from everything, then relaxed, a heavenly calm. Then it happened all over again.

"You've got to keep pushing!" Dr. Fred's voice spoke somewhere in her frantic mind. More pushing, then the gas mask again. As it came toward her, she shook her head. "No, you shouldn't do that...it's not a good..." She tried to stop the intern, dreading the weird sights and sounds, but it covered her face anyway. Then lifted again, and the pains were there, even worse.

"Push...push...push...now hold it...now push." The wretched pushing continued. "Push...push...now hold it...." Dr. Fred used the gas sparingly, selectively, and his coaching reverberated off the sterile white ceiling until all her energy was gone.

I'm going to die, she thought...we're going to die...me and the baby...way down here in Texas....

"You've got to push!" the doctor demanded, his tone becoming harsh.

She couldn't, she didn't have an ounce of energy left. Her body was fading in and out of a twilight zone, vague and unbearable. When would it all end?

"This baby is definitely fighting to be born," Dr. Fred said to the interns, and the strange words rang somewhere in the corridors of Joellen's fuzzy mind. They reached down into her heart, down into her soul, hanging there precariously, and she thought it awfully peculiar to hear such a thing. She tried to envision it, and the image of a little baby fighting to be born took shape.

She must help!

"Push...push...push...now hold it...hold it...now push...push...push...."

From where she summoned the strength she never knew, but summon it she did...and pushed and pushed and pushed.

"It's coming!"

The head crowned.

"Push...push...push...."

"The head is out!"

And Joellen felt it with every nerve in her body, the hard thrust and then the sudden relief. Then another thrust. She felt every contour of the infant's form, its head, its tiny shoulders and its buttocks as it slid out the stubborn birth canal and into the light of the world.

"It's a girl!"

A faint smile appeared on her sweat-beaded face.

SYDNEY WAS ONLY two days old when her daddy left again. He got them home from the hospital and then disappeared. Joellen never ceased to be shocked at his timing. One would think that after awhile she wouldn't have been, but not so. Often when things seemed to be going well, he left, and he had been so happy with his new baby girl. How could he leave her?

One day passed, two days, three…four…five.

Alone and afraid, she prayed. She prayed in the morning, in the noon, in the evening, all day long and throughout the night. She prayed for strength. She prayed for wisdom, and she prayed for Dale—for God to change him! She knew God could change him, if only He would! But even as she prayed, she also knew down deep in her heart that God didn't work that way. He wouldn't make him change. It was up to Dale.

What did Dale want?

He said one thing but acted out another. She slowly rocked the baby and smoothed the soft fuzz on top of her little round head. Innocent scents of baby powder and baby oil permeated the room as she rocked and stared vacantly out the front window and up at a few wispy clouds languorously floating over. Probably too hot for even them, she thought. Why, it was the end of September and still no sign of fall. She loathed the stifling heat of Texas and dreadfully missed her beloved Virginia with its fresh invigorating autumns. If she were home, she would have her windows open, enjoying the rustle of maple trees in gentle breezes and the smell of mums and marigolds, and occasional chimney smoke nearby. But here the windows had to remain shut, and the air conditioner hummed relentlessly, turning everything cold. She was a prisoner behind its doors, and the white tile floors were too cold to go barefooted, the kitchen countertop was cold to her touch, her hands were cold and her feet were cold. She even felt cold inside.

She was lonely for family and friends, lonely for her church, and she felt so vulnerable, but staring out the window, His words came to her...

"My grace is sufficient for thee: for my strength is made perfect in weakness."

Another week passed and Mrs. Sato was knocking on her door, but she wasn't alone this time. Ladia was with her, an intense young woman always stalking ahead with defined purpose. Joellen pulled open the door with her left hand, while holding the sleeping baby in the crook of her right arm. "Come on in, ladies."

Ladia pounced in, her mother close behind. "Good morning to you, Joellen," she quipped, "...and how is the baby?"

"She's fine." She led the way across the small kitchen to the living room. "Have a seat." She motioned to the sofa, while easing back into the rocker.

Ladia frowned. "No word yet?"

Joellen shook her head, and Ladia shifted impatiently on the sofa. Her mother watched her for a clue, always following her daughter's lead. Being her only child, Mrs. Sato loved her dearly and depended on her not only for her material needs but for guidance in this big new country.

"What are you going to do?" Ladia demanded in her commanding way.

Again Joellen shook her head and smiled at the two women. She didn't know what to do.

Ladia was obviously irritated. "You cannot just sit and rock the baby all the time," she exclaimed in her rapid, flawed English. "... you rock the baby in the day...rock the baby in the night...always you rock the baby...besides the baby is sleeping. Why you still rock?"

Her words stung, but Joellen continued to smile. "I like to rock her."

"I know…but you must do something!" she goaded, hanging on the edge of her seat now, visibly aggravated.

"…but he always comes back."

"He is not coming!"

Joellen looked from her to Mrs. Sato, who uncomfortably dropped her head.

"It has been too long this time, don't you think?" Ladia persisted.

Joellen knew she was right. It had been longer than ever, but she didn't know where to turn.

"Maybe this time he does not come back!"

Joellen fought the ready tears.

"I have idea. We will take you to the base…tell them what's wrong?"

Joellen hated to give in and admit that maybe he wasn't coming back. She had been struggling against this thought every day, every minute of every day, but she knew Ladia was right. She needed to do something.

"We can go while your Ryan is at school. This is better, yes?"

Joellen agreed.

Ladia jumped up, pulling her mother up with her. "I am going for my handbag…then we will go. You will be ready?"

Reluctantly, Joellen nodded.

The austere military officer was brusque. Nervously Joellen sat before him, clutching Sydney to her breast, while Ladia and her mother waited outside. She didn't want to be here, she didn't want to hear what she might hear, but she knew it was what she had to do. After a series of methodical questions, the balding middle-aged sergeant stated, "Well, I know it's a bit morbid, but when we have a missing person, we always start with the morgues."

She nodded, and he began dialing.

She sat up straight and rigid. The sergeant called several morgues, stating his purpose in brief, matter-of-fact statements. "This is Sergeant Davis with Lackland Air Force Base. Do you have a body there by the name of Dale Read Rodman? We are missing Sergeant Rodman."

Joellen postured tensely on the edge of the hard wooden chair and anxiously waited each time as the sergeant listened to the voice on the other end. She hung on every word, watched each expression for any clue before he would hang up and shake his head. He soon exhausted the city morgues.

"Now the hospitals," he said wryly.

Again she listened as he made the routine calls and asked the same questions. Sydney began to squirm in her arms, and she gently rocked her against her breast. He wasn't in the hospitals.

"Now the jails." The officer continued to dial, and Joellen waited as thoughts reeled through her head. Where was he? It all seemed so strange, so surreal, and she hated it!

Finally the officer hung up. "No luck, but we will continue our search and be in touch with you as soon as we come up with something."

The next day Joellen arose tired and nervous. She hadn't slept and couldn't stay away from the window, always watching for him. She tried to hide her fear from Ryan, but knew he sensed the seriousness of this absence. The cupboard was sparse, and soon she would have to make a decision.

He strode up the street to school, slinging his backpack, and she watched him until he was out of sight, and then sat down to feed Sydney. She couldn't understand any of it. Why was she going through all this…since she had become a Christian? Why did life just get harder and harder? Why was everything such a mess! But she knew God was in control…even if she didn't understand any of it, and she clung to His word.

"And we know that all things work together for good to them that love God, to them who are the called according to his purpose."

There was a loud banging at the door, and she jumped up quickly with Sydney asleep in her arms. It was Ladia, rattling off words so fast she couldn't make out a thing she was saying. She was obviously excited.

"Slow down, Ladia. I can't understand a word…."

"News…I am coming with news…good news!" She grabbed hold of the countertop with both hands, completely out of breath. "We just get a phone call…a phone call from the base…you hear…and they are bringing Dale home…."

Her words caused mixed emotions. Why were they bringing him? He couldn't bring himself? Where had he been? What had he been doing? Was he okay? In some ways it seemed like they were bringing a stranger home.

"This is good news, yes?"

Joellen nodded blankly.

Three impeccably dressed soldiers in creased military uniforms brought him in. His demeanor was that of a stray dog that had been found, his face was dreadfully swollen and discolored, and he looked beaten, ashamed, and humiliated. She was shocked. What could she say?

She said nothing.

Sadly she realized that the tremendous bouts of drinking were not only wrecking their marriage and their home but also his health.

After days of endless drinking, Dale had awakened in Mexico, his old car stolen, his money stolen, his identification gone, and all he had were the clothes on his back. Though frightened and sick, he knew he had to get out of Mexico somehow, someway. He asked a young fellow to point him toward Texas, and he set out walking. He had no idea how he would get over the border with no money but pushed on. Fortunately an old Mexican man kindly gave him enough money to cross over. Slowly and feverishly, he kept walking and finally made it to Laredo. But after so many days of steady heavy drinking without eating, he was actually about to pass out. He spotted a police officer on a street corner and stumbled up to him for help. He was rushed off to the nearest hospital in Laredo, where he remained for days, being fed intravenously. Joellen was told that had he gotten to the hospital a few hours later, it may have been too late. Guiltily, she wondered if this would have been a bad thing.

Dale recovered from his drinking spree, and his dislocated shoulder also healed. He received orders to leave Lackland, orders to report to Shaw Air Force Base in Sumter, South Carolina. Joellen informed him that she and the children were going back to Virginia. He cried, he pleaded, he begged, "Please don't leave me. It will be different in South Carolina...I promise...we will have a new start. The Mexico thing did it! I've quit drinking for good!"

Half-heartedly, she listened to his pleas, and remembered her purpose when she left Virginia—to make the marriage work! Was it possible that the horrible Mexico thing had done it? She wanted so to believe him. After many hours of promises, she reluctantly agreed to go with him one more time. Maybe, just maybe, he was telling the truth. Besides, she still couldn't bring herself to call it quits. She had to make it work...somehow. And she knew the temptations in San Antonio were many. Hopefully things would be different in the small town of Sumter. She had to believe that.

CHAPTER TWENTY

THE LONG, RUMBLING passenger train jolted to yet another stop, and Sydney began crying again. Joellen rocked her back and forth against the hard seat and wished the train would quit stopping! Every time she was sleeping soundly, it would rumble, creak, jolt and jerk to another stop. Why, it must be stopping in every single small town between San Antonio and New Orleans, where they would switch trains. Joellen glanced at Dale and Ryan, both fast asleep and she was glad, but she wished she could get some sleep. Her eyes were heavy, and her nerves were taut. She nestled the tiny infant in her arms, once again feeling the joy of having a daughter. She brushed the fine hair atop her small head. Even if she did have troubles aplenty, she was blessed with the children. She gazed down at her young son's sandy brown head resting against her thigh, and her heart went out to him. He would have to start a new school again, and with each school being in a different state, what was he missing? Would the lack of continuity rob him of his primary start?

The baby kept crying, and she fumbled for the rumpled bag stashed between her feet and pulled out a small plastic bottle. Maybe she was hungry again. She seemed to be hungry all the time. She was glad that Sergeant Clayborn, her neighbor, was able to get all these sample bottles of formula, and they were disposable, too, perfect for traveling. Once again she marveled at how God always provided for their needs. Not only did she have Mrs. Sato on the one side, but Sergeant Clayborn had moved in on the other and worked at Wilford Hall Hospital. Although they didn't see much of each other and didn't know one another that well because both Sergeant Clayborn and her husband worked all the time, she came bringing this large box of disposable formula just before they left. Sergeant Clayborn was a few months pregnant herself, and Joellen figured this was why. Apparently, she had seen enough to piece together a pattern and felt led to help. But Joellen knew that it was really God who had touched her heart. "Thank you, Lord," she whispered as the baby sucked contentedly.

She rested her head against the stiff leather seat as the heavy train lurched forward again. It picked up speed, and she watched unfamiliar streets and buildings slip past. The unknown town was left behind as the great train swept on, gathering momentum, and soon the rhythmic sounds of its wheels scraping metal tracks lulled her into a dreamy half-sleep. She fought to stay awake as they passed through field after field and patches of trees here and there. They were rushing through wide open country, unknown country, and Joellen wondered what South Carolina held for her. At least they were leaving Texas. For that, she was glad. She knew it had a lot to offer, but to her, it would always conjure up pictures of hopelessness, pictures she chose to forget. The only good thing that she would carry with her from the great state of Texas now drowsily closed her eyes and contentedly slept to the rhythmic pounding of the heavy wheels, and the disposable bottle slipped out of her tiny mouth.

They reached New Orleans late at night, gathered up their belongings and quickly headed into the huge train station. Joellen was relieved to sit down in the terminal without rocking back and forth. She changed the baby and opened up another disposable bottle. Sydney sucked hungrily, while Joellen glanced around the busy station, but she couldn't wait to get on their way. A large black clock high overhead read 11:55 PM. No wonder she was tired and sleepy. So was Ryan. He was slumped over in the chair beside her, but his big brown eyes still roved over the teeming train station. She looked up to see Dale approaching with an odd look on his face.

"The train doesn't leave until tomorrow."

"Tomorrow!" she cried.

"Just what I said...we can't leave until tomorrow!"

Her heart fell, but she could tell he was irritated and frustrated. She glanced around at the crowded terminal. "Well...what are we going to do till then?"

"I don't know of anything but to stay here...we don't have the money for a hotel. You have any suggestions?" he flared back angrily.

The old familiar dread swept over her.

"Unless you want to go by bus," he added. "We can catch a bus in awhile they say. It won't cost as much either...it will take longer to get there, but at least we would be on our way...."

THE GREYHOUND SPED out of New Orleans, and Joellen watched the copious array of lights gradually fade into darkness. Though exhausted from the change-over, she was glad to at least be moving toward their destination. The bus was full but strangely quiet. Everyone was obviously tired and sleepy, trying to get some rest. They were seated near the back, and Ryan was already asleep beside her. Across the aisle, she could see that Dale's eyes were closed, as well. She stared out the darkened window and felt very alone.

Had she done the right thing?

It was too late now, no use wondering about it. She remembered hearing a sermon on making decisions, and the preacher said that we all make decisions in our lives, some good and some bad. She had certainly made enough bad ones! But once we have made the decision, he had expounded, we have to move forward and try to make that decision work. Well, that was her goal! They were heading fast toward a new home. At least it was closer to Virginia. That much was good. She had never been to South Carolina and had never heard of the small town of Sumter. Dale had said they would be staying in the "guest quarters" on base until they found a place to live, and that it was quite nice. It comforted her to know that they would have a place to stay when they arrived, at least for a couple of weeks. Her eyes felt heavy. She should have known that their money was limited, but caught up in the move and looking after the children, she hadn't thought of it. She stared at the shadowy forms all around her—in front of her, beside her and in back. They were all sleeping! Everybody was sleeping...everybody but her and the driver.

The Greyhound flew down the long stretch of highway, and she struggled to stay awake, afraid that she would drop the baby if she fell asleep. Suddenly she leaned toward the window—water! It was as if the bus was skimming across a vast body of water with no bridge! The sides of the bridge were not visible to her—only water—dark moving water, choppy and churning all around them. Fear seized her. She had always been afraid of water. Perhaps it was because she couldn't swim, or maybe because she almost drowned as a youngster in Betsy Creek. She didn't know, but she had never liked water and bridges. Surely they would be across soon, but the bus kept on and on, skimming over the dark waters.

It would take some time, for the Greyhound was passing over Lake Pontchartrain's new causeway that had just been completed with much ado the prior year. Now the world's longest bridge, it was twenty-four miles long! But Joellen didn't know that. Tense and rigid, she hugged Sydney closer to her breast and nervously held onto Ryan while the bus careened over the black brackish lake that looked more like the ocean to her.

THEY ARRIVED IN South Carolina very early the next morning and gladly exited the Greyhound to find the bus terminal cold and empty, but they would have to wait awhile for their ride to the base.

Groggy and sleepy, they vainly tried to get comfortable on the cold metal chairs. Joellen made a pillow out of their jackets for Ryan, and he curled up on two chairs and quickly fell back to sleep. Dale followed. Joellen still held the baby, fighting the inevitable. She kept nodding off, almost dropping the precious bundle more than once. Reluctantly, she placed her in the little white plastic carrier and slid her beneath her chair, draping her blanket around it so no one would notice her. The terminal was so quiet. She pulled her sweater about her shoulders and constantly moved from one position to another, struggling to stay awake.

A couple of hours later another bus arrived, depositing a roomful of wide-awake passengers. They seated themselves, curiously encircling the odd little family that was stretched out on the fold-up chairs. Joellen awoke suddenly to find strange eyes staring at them. Her heart leapt!

The baby!

She jerked up the blanket. Sydney was sound asleep.

Celeste smiled at Victor.

THE STAY IN the base guest quarters was beyond anything she had expected and soon found out why. It was actually the officers' guest quarters and certainly was a treat for them except for the constant deafening roar of the powerful jets zooming overhead, precariously close to their rooftop. But Ryan was thrilled with it. Shaw Air Force Base was much smaller than Lackland, and she was glad. After the second week, they located to an apartment in a sprawling brick complex. Like most such dwellings, the occupants cautiously guarded their privacy, coming and going clandestinely, and Joellen met no one.

Dale was back at work, and she was touched that soon after they moved in he had taken Ryan shopping for another bike. But as soon as her hopes lifted, they were dashed again. The second week after they moved into the apartment complex, he came home late at night, very drunk! Joellen's independent feisty spirit let go. "Where have you been?" she fired off. "How can you think of coming home drunk? You promised! We could be in Virginia…but, no, you promised…you…."

Wheeling around, he landed his fist into her stomach and stumbled off to bed. She gasped at the searing pain that knotted her into a ball, and she crumpled to the floor, struggling vainly to get up. But every time she tried, the pain was unbearable. She was unable to move.

"Please help me, Lord!"

After awhile she was able to slowly and painfully slide across the floor and crawl up to the couch. Still unable to straighten up, she thought the twisting pain would subside; instead it increased. Could it be because I'm only seven weeks from delivery, she wondered…and things are still tender inside. Another pain sliced through her, and she gripped the couch, wet with silent tears. She must not wake the children because she couldn't tend to them. She was scared, more scared than ever! Suppose she…?

But she couldn't!

"Please, God, please let me live to raise the children, to see this baby grown…."

Curled up in a fetal ball, the blurred night dragged on between searing pain and hazy prayers. She cradled her stomach and wished she hadn't fired off to him, wished she hadn't believed him in the first place, wished she had gone to Virginia instead of South Carolina! Toward daybreak, the pain gradually began to lessen, as the first rays of dawn filtered through the window in a lilac haze. Very cautiously she moved and found herself able to slowly sit up.

"Thank you, Lord," she whispered tearfully.

OVER THE NEXT few weeks Dale stayed gone most of the time, only coming home late at night, always drunk. Worn down like an old rug, Joellen felt whipped. She read her big black Bible daily, but still felt trapped and she worried far too much. She knew she shouldn't. She knew it was the opposite of faith, and she desperately grasped for a lifeline, and found it early one morning.

"Thou wilt keep him in perfect peace, whose mind is stayed on thee."

The words from Isaiah pierced her guilty soul. She searched for something big to write on, and uncovered a

314

discarded shirt box on top of the closet shelf, bent and crushed, but the lid was intact. She cut off the four ends, creating a flat poster board, and copied the powerful words in large print with Ryan's crayons. She propped it up on top of the bedroom bureau.

As she went about her chores throughout the small apartment, in and out of their bedroom where Sydney slept in her portable wooden crib, she always glanced up to the top of the bureau, and the brightly-colored cardboard sign reached out to her.

"...whose mind is stayed on Thee."

It worked!

Her worry dissolved like Minnesota ice in springtime, and peace flooded her soul whenever she obeyed and thought on Him. Just like Peter walking on the water. She knew the story well, having taught it to her Sunday school class. When he saw Jesus walking on the water, he wanted to go to Him and asked if he could. Jesus told him to come. Peter stepped out of the boat and walked on the water to Jesus. But then he took his eyes off Jesus and looked around at the boisterous winds and choppy waves...and he began to sink.

She must keep her eyes on Jesus!

It was Christmas Eve, unseasonably warm. Joellen sat out on the concrete stoop, barefooted and lonely. She was weary of carrying the load, trying to make sure they had enough food on the table before Dale wasted it all on liquor. Her nerves were frayed and taut, afraid of his unpredictable moods and drunken scenes, and she was tired, so tired. The weighted burden rested heavily upon her. She knew she couldn't stand much more, for her resolve and her strength were fading.

The darkening sky was stippled with dazzling stars, and she gazed up into it and yearned for something...anything different...a rest from her troubles. "Please, Lord, I just can't take it anymore...please change things, Lord, if it is possible...."

TWO WEEKS LATER Joellen and the children were headed for Virginia. She glanced out the back window at the small U-haul bouncing along behind with its splash of orange, containing their few belongings. The baby's crib that they had finally bought in Sumter was wedged in between Ryan's new purple bike, the dishes, pots and pans, and family pictures and other mementos she had dragged from one home to another, from one state to another. The gray Chevrolet sedan traveled up the highway leading north, heading home, and her daddy was driving. Daniel and Brian were sitting up front with him, talking incessantly about the flat countryside and sandy soil of South Carolina compared to the red clay of Virginia.

The Red Cross was sending her home, her and the children.

And they had come to rescue her. She stared out the window with mixed emotions, happy to be going home, though hating to go this way, defeated and broke. But she was still in awe of how it all came about. *God works in mysterious ways*, she thought silently, while holding the almost empty bottle in Sydney's mouth. She lifted it higher, and the baby sucked furiously. Ryan was glued to the window. Going home! He tried to remember what home was like, but it seemed vague and far away to him. He knew things weren't right, but as he listened to the constant drone of the "man talk" up front, he was happy.

The sedan sped straight up the highway, putting more distance between them and the little town of Sumter. They crossed the state line into North Carolina, and she thought of Mrs. Shoesmith back in South Carolina, the elderly lady that lived behind the apartments, a sweet Christian lady that she had met at the clothesline sometime after moving in. God always provided a little old lady in her path—Mrs. Dunford first, then Aunt Myrtle, Mrs. Daniel, sweet Mrs. Sato, and finally Mrs. Shoesmith. Though she didn't get to know Mrs. Shoesmith as well, the old lady certainly made a difference in their lives.

She was out back grabbing clothes off the clothesline one day when a sudden storm came up, pelting her with large raindrops, while a strong wind whipped the clothes back and forth out of her hands. Mrs. Shoesmith was doing the same thing. They hurriedly made introductions, then fled inside, but their kindred spirits rallied, and Joellen learned that she was a devout Presbyterian and attended the Presbyterian church in downtown Sumter. Mrs. Shoesmith found out that they had no way of getting to church and offered to help by having her niece pick them up on Sundays. Her niece, a Mrs. Harding, a matronly woman in her fifties, attended the Baptist church in Sumter. Joellen would have rather gone with Mrs. Shoesmith to her Presbyterian church, instead of being picked up by a complete stranger, but she was happy enough to finally have a way. Mrs. Harding gave them a ride every Sunday, but they never went beyond a casual friendship. The reserved lady dressed in fashionable clothes, sitting behind the wheel of a sleek Lincoln, didn't appear accessible.

But now they were headed home, and Ryan's sandy head was following the big trucks plowing by, keenly scrutinizing each one, particularly the dark smoke shooting up from their tall chrome stacks, shooting up into the sky. She watched him and remembered his tender step of faith at the Sumter church. He wanted to be sure he was going to heaven he said, and had asked to go forward, and she had walked with him down the aisle to accept Christ.

"Look, Mom!" He pointed to a jet zooming overhead. He loved all planes, any kind of planes, but especially the large military jets. She smiled at him, and he turned back to the window. She dreaded the fact that he was being moved yet again to another school. Three schools in three different states in his second grade!

"Y'all doing okay back there?" her daddy asked, glancing into the rearview mirror. Both she and Ryan nodded, and the conversation up front turned to automobile motors. Sydney had fallen asleep to the soothing motion of the car, and her thoughts returned to Dale and wondered what was going to happen to him…and to them.

What a strange turn of events.

A couple of weeks ago, she had gotten up in the morning, like any other morning, and helped Ryan get ready for school. She watched him ride off on his new bicycle down the street, and then picked up Sydney, who had been fussy all night and was still crying. She wondered if it was colic. Dale had been gone for several days, and she waited for his return—wanting him to come home, but dreading it at the same time.

But he didn't return.

That night there was a hard knock at the door, and she opened it to a tall attractive man in a decorated military uniform. His commanding presence filled the doorway, and a nicely dressed lady stood primly by his side.

"Mrs. Rodman?"

"Yes...."

"I am Colonel Wisener, Mrs. Rodman, and this is my wife, Katherine. May we come in?"

"Yes...of course...come in," Joellen stammered, awkwardly ushering them into the modest living room. It was apparent that he was a man of importance, high-ranking stature, and this wasn't just any visit. She grabbed up the baby blanket and diapers off the sofa. "Please have a seat."

Ryan edged in closer to her.

"Hello, young man," the colonel smiled kindly at Ryan, who smiled back uneasily.

"Ryan, you go into your room now and finish your homework." He looked at his mom and obeyed, but she knew he would be listening.

Colonel Wisener watched him disappear into the bedroom, and then shifted uncomfortably on the sofa, obviously finding this part of his job extremely difficult. His wife eyed him carefully. "The reason we are here...Mrs. Rodman..." He cleared his throat. "...is because...unfortunately...I have some bad news for you...."

She braced herself.

"Your husband is AWOL."

Joellen nodded slowly, not knowing how to respond. What would this mean for her and the children?

"He is in jail in Lynchburg, Virginia...."

"Lynchburg!" She was dumbfounded—anywhere but Lynchburg! How could he be in Lynchburg? Lynchburg was home! Where she should be...how could he be there?

"Yes ma'am. Apparently he drove to Lynchburg, was drinking and got picked up for driving under the influence.

319

Of course, you understand that means he's automatically AWOL."

Joellen continued to nod, but she didn't understand any of it. Her mind was racing ahead—what about them? What about the children?

Colonel Wisener awkwardly cleared his throat again. "As a result…Mrs. Rodman…this also means that his military compensation is cut off."

The full impact set in. "I see…."

"Do you have family back home, Mrs. Rodman?"

"Yes, sir." *But I can't go back home!*

"Do you have parents?"

She nodded, but thought of her poor daddy. He had all he could handle with her mama sick and the other children. She fought the ready tears. He can't afford to help us out, besides, *I don't want to go back home!*

"I can get a job," she blurted out.

Colonel Wisener and his wife exchanged knowing glances. "I don't think that would work out," he replied softly.

"But I worked back home…for years…I can get a job… I know I can and I can work and take care of us…."

"You see…Mrs. Rodman, there *are* no jobs to be had here in Sumter. Campbell Soup Company is about the only place here…and they are not hiring."

She looked frantically from him to his wife. "You mean… there is nowhere else…nowhere I could get a job?"

He shook his head. "I think you need to consider going back home…to where you have family that can help you…you and the children."

The baby began to cry in the bedroom. *But you don't understand, Colonel!*

"It's for the best," he continued.

"How long will he be in jail?" she asked resignedly.

"It could be some time, and as I said, there will be no money coming in. Going back home is the best thing…the only thing for you and the children to do."

Her fight was ebbing away. After all this time, almost two years of struggling to make it work, she would still have to return home—her marriage a failure.

"We will pay for sending you and the children home… actually the Red Cross will take care of it. You don't have to worry about any of that. Is there someone who could come and pick you up? Anyone we can call for you?"

"I…I don't know," she practically whispered. "I will call somebody."

That night Joellen cried long and hard, her head pressed into the pillow so that the children wouldn't hear. What was she going to do? She hated to call her daddy. He already had enough problems, and she couldn't go back home. But where would they go? Where would they live? She had no money. She began to pray, and then she remembered her prayer on Christmas Eve when she sat out on the concrete stoop.

Something was happening, and she had to trust God.

The next morning after sending Ryan off to school, she bundled up Sydney and headed out the door, across the back yard, and underneath the clothesline to Mrs. Shoesmith's.

"May I use your telephone, Mrs. Shoesmith?"

"Of course, dear, come on in."

During the wee hours of the morning, she had decided to call Aunt Anna and have her contact her daddy. She wasn't going to tell Aunt Anna her dilemma, just have her contact her daddy for her. Trembling, she dialed the operator. She hadn't spoken to Aunt Anna or anyone back home for almost two years.

"I want to make a collect call," she said timidly and gave the operator the number. Her anxiety increased with the ringing on the other end. Then she heard Aunt Anna's perky voice.

"Hello."

"Will you accept a collect call from a Joellen Rodman?"

"Yes...yes, of course." The comforting sound of her aunt's voice caused tears to well up, and there was a sudden tightness in her throat. She couldn't talk.

"Joellen?" Aunt Anna's kind voice called out across miles and miles of tautly stretched telephone lines.

She tried to speak, but couldn't, as she struggled to quell the sudden urge to bawl.

"Joellen, you all right?"

"Aunt Anna..." her voice broke.

"Is this Joellen? Are you all right?"

Aunt Anna's caring voice suddenly opened up the flood gates, and all she could do was cry.

"What's wrong, honey?" her aunt questioned, obviously alarmed and concerned. "Are you all right, Joellen?"

Between sobs, she managed to tell her.

"Don't you worry about a thing, honey," Aunt Anna soothed. "You just come on home...your room will be waiting for you."

It was if she had suddenly fallen into the arms of an angel, and a weight had been lifted off her that had been pressing down hard upon her, heavier and heavier every week, every day, and every hour. Joellen didn't have a room at Aunt Anna's. She had never had a room at Aunt Anna's. She had never lived with her except for when she was a baby and her daddy was away at war. But there were no words on earth that could have sounded sweeter to her than those kind and embracing words. Maybe there was hope!

CHAPTER TWENTY-ONE

PRESENT

THE TWO MAPLE leaves lying on the warm dash had already begun to curl up around the edges, and their dusty earthy fragrance slowly pulled Joellen back to reality. She sighed, the past is the past. One had to move on like the RV winding around the curving Parkway. But the past is part of us, she thought, just like the present and the future, the mysterious future. Yet the youthful past is indelibly engraved into our minds, our subconscious, so much so that we never escape its nostalgic web. Its joyful but painful tentacles reach out to us at the most inopportune times, hammering into our thoughts until we give in to its haunting cry.

She thought of Tab Hunter.

She had turned on Larry King just before they left—and there he was! Though certainly still handsome for his age, Tab Hunter was an old man! He was seventy-four years old! And something within her had resisted the image before her. Where was the young, virile, innocent-looking boy? Where was *the* Tab Hunter that had thrilled her heart as a teenager and compelled her to clip his pictures out of movie magazines and plaster them into her scrapbooks?

The poster boy of the fifties, the heart-throb of us silly, love-sick girls, and he's gay! How ironic. Life is deceptive, she pondered. What a dream-world we lived in, what a fragile fairyland—the fifties!

Pensively, she stared out the window at the colorful tree branches stretching out over the Parkway from both sides, clasping one another. She was glad that Elvis was not around! She wanted to remember him with a head of thick dark hair, dressed in a colorful jump suit and singing his heart out, glad that she would never see him seventy-four years old!

Bright yellow leaves were strewn all over the sides of the road, vivid iridescent yellow. They were glistening jewels midst the fog, contrasting with the otherwise hazy gray mist enveloping the Parkway. They had already passed Goshen Creek, following its rushing mountain stream quite a ways, and Blowing Rock, too. She remembered visiting there years ago in their first camper. Said to be North Carolina's oldest travel attraction, all the way back to the thirties, she just remembered the huge cliff.

"How high is that cliff at Blowing Rock, Wade?"

"H-m-m-m, let's see. Four thousand feet, I believe, hangs over the Johns River Gorge."

She could always count on him for facts and statistics. He had just that kind of mind.

"Wasn't there some kind of a legend attached to it... something about a Cherokee brave and Indian maiden?"

"Yeah...the Cherokee brave supposedly jumped from the rock...and the maiden prayed every day until a gust of wind blew him back up to her. They say from that day on a constant wind blows up to the rock from the valley below."

She marveled at his memory.

They passed on by Julian Price Memorial Park where they had camped before, then approached the Linn Cove Viaduct, the last part of the Blue Ridge Parkway to be completed. A modern wonder that skirted around the rocky perimeter of Grandfather Mountain and off it in a sweeping "S" curve, it was just finished in 1987. Wade wheeled the RV onto the viaduct, and out over the side of the massive mountain over four thousand feet high, an awesome feeling. Joellen didn't particularly like it, but at least it wasn't over water!

As they left Grandfather Mountain, Wade joked, "Well, that's one thing I'll never do again!"

She smiled at him. He wasn't referring to the viaduct, but to the popular mile-high swinging bridge that they had walked over on their honeymoon years ago. Like her fear of water, his was height, but he had omitted to tell her. When they began walking over the swinging bridge, his fear was immediately realized. She was strolling across, enjoying the unique sensation and rattling on, when all of a sudden she realized that she was talking to herself. Wade hadn't responded for some time. She glanced back, and there he was at the beginning, slowly and cautiously stepping across the swinging bridge. She waited for him to catch up, and they had never gone back.

"We all have our fears," she kidded as they left the viaduct behind.

"I made it across, didn't I?"

"Yes, you did."

"Look over there!" He was pointing to a groundhog sitting nonchalantly on the side of the road, munching on a small green apple, totally oblivious to them or anybody.

"Some people call them woodchucks, you know. I was just reading about them in the *Parkway Milepost.*" She flipped to the page and pointed to the picture. "See. With front teeth so long and chisel-like, they look like they're bucktoothed. Can you believe people used to eat them?"

"Nope, but I think they're cute. Would you like one?"

"No thanks."

"Well, I think we have one anyway...living under the garage back home."

"Great...that's what's been trampling my cosmos down."

Wade chuckled, "Everything's gotta be somewhere."

They entered Pisgah National Forest and the heavy fog persisted, adding to Joellen's thoughtful mood. The hazy fog's illusion that they were all alone in the world, wheeling along in their man-made capsule, was virtually surreal.

Pisgah particularly interested Joellen. Before leaving on their trip, she had just finished reading in the book of Deuteronomy where God called Moses up into the mountain of Pisgah, another Pisgah, of course. A small mountain range in central Jordan, it rises east of the River Jordan. God called him up to view the Promised Land after forty years of wandering in the wilderness, but He wouldn't let him go in.

Wade interrupted her thoughts, "I picked up that brochure on Pisgah National Forest at the visitor center." He motioned toward the sofa. "Thought you might like to read it."

She reached for it and read quietly.

"Anything interesting?"

"Says a preacher named the mountain."

"Makes sense," he said.

"A Scotch-Irish, gun toting, Indian fighting Presbyterian preacher, who accompanied General Griffith Rutherford's expedition against the Cherokee into western North Carolina way back in 1776, and his name was Reverend Hall."

"H-m-m-m."

"…says he was impressed by the French Broad River when he saw it from the mountain."

"I can understand that. It's beautiful, that is when you can see it without the fog. All of it, there's over half a million acres of forest here, and that's a lot of land by anybody's calculation!"

She nodded. "…it says that George Vanderbilt began accumulating property around his estate, and that's how it started. You know, he was the grandson of the big railroad baron. It was sold to the government when he died."

Wade sipped his coffee and set it back in the cup holder on the dash. "I wish we could do this for weeks and weeks."

Joellen laid the brochure down. "You know, when I finished reading the book of Deuteronomy the other night, I felt sorry for Moses."

He glanced at her. "Why?"

"Well…after all he'd done, being God's spokesman, leading the Israelites for years, going to bat for them over and over when they complained and sinned, God still punished him when he struck the rock disobediently, and he wasn't allowed to go into the Promised Land after that. Instead he died there on the mountain top called Pisgah."

"H-m-m-m."

"Makes me realize He's a God to reckon with!"

Wade nodded.

"Everybody talks about Him being a God of love all the time…and He certainly is that, of course. But He's also a God to be feared!"

"You're right about that."

"I think we've forgotten…maybe conveniently forgotten. But if you read the Old Testament, you really see what an awesome God He is."

"You don't hear much on the Old Testament these days."

"It speaks of Him being a consuming fire!"

"That's something you don't hear, for sure."

"I know, but over and over it tells how God killed hundreds, thousands of people that sinned against Him, just like that!" She snapped her fingers. "By opening up the ground and literally swallowing them up! Or with plagues or by fire that shot out from Him and consumed them. Even two of Aaron's sons were killed that way when they offered incense against His commands. Fire went out from the Lord and devoured them."

Wade reached for his coffee again.

"The beginning of knowledge is the fear of God," she added, staring out the window. "That's what the Bible says. There's a lot of knowledge today, but little fear of God, and we're all guilty."

They fell into a contemplative silence as they passed by Linville Falls, crossed over the Linville River and soon pressed on through another darkened tunnel, the Little Switzerland tunnel. Its damp irregular walls were rough, exposing the jagged coarse mountain rock. "Hard to believe they could build the Parkway through all this," Wade commented.

"Thank goodness for the CCCs, but it must have seemed like an impossible task."

"I'm sure they never imagined so many people would be enjoying it."

"Well, it's one good thing that came out of the Great Depression."

Wade pressed the accelerator, climbing higher into the dense fog. Quietly they enjoyed the colorful leaves, drooping with rain and forming another tunnel. The glistening wet color encircled them, but a curtain of fog shrouded the distance and the otherwise haze-encased world that lay beyond.

"You know, there was one thing really special about Moses' death."

He was surprised that she had switched back to Moses. "What's that?"

"God buried him."

"He did?"

"That's what it said in the last chapter of Deuteronomy. He buried him in a valley, and no man knows to this day where he's buried."

They pulled into Crabtree Meadows Campground just as dusk fell and backed up into a cozy leafy site, and settled in for the night. The large can of Brunswick stew and hot buttered sourdough bread that they had purchased on the Parkway made the perfect meal. After washing the few dishes and sticking them in the doll-size plastic dish drainer, Joellen curled up on the sofa with an afghan. Wade hunched over the booth-style table contentedly reading his trade paper. The fog had culminated into a soft drizzling rain, a gentle pitter-patter on the aluminum roof, a soothing dreamy sound.

"This is the life," he sighed, bent over his paper.

"It sure is," she agreed. *But it was not always this way.*

SHE REMEMBERED COMING home to Virginia with Ryan and the new baby. Aunt Anna's home was an oasis, truly a sanctuary in the midst of her troubles. It was quite small—a cozy cottage perched on a hillside in Madison Heights. There were two bedrooms, one was Aunt Anna's, and the larger one had been made ready for them. She and Ryan slept in the full-size poster bed, with Sydney in her crib beside them.

Aunt Anna had been a widow for over ten years, living alone and finding herself lonely more often than not. After her husband died, she sold the grocery store and worked at General Electric, the same place Joellen had worked. She was a warm, compassionate soul, a people person, who looked more like her mother, Grandma Thaxton, every passing year. But she didn't possess Grandma Thaxton's strict discipline and rigid compliance to order and spotlessness. Instead, she enthusiastically embraced life, seeking out the newfangled ideas of the time and throwing herself wholeheartedly into them. She was either creating jingles for prize money or braiding rag rugs, or ordering the most unique gadgets from her many catalogs.

Obviously, the unexpected arrival of Joellen and the children presented her with a looming challenge, but also with new purpose in life. Aunt Anna was delighted with their company, especially caught up with little Sydney. "Mama always said the way I loved babies, I'd probably have a dozen of them," she repeated often with her ever-ready chuckle, though she had only given birth to one son.

Immediately Joellen sought work, not realizing that it, too, would be difficult. It took several months to land a job, stressing both her and Aunt Anna, although they guardedly kept their feelings to themselves. The sudden increase from one mouth to four caused Aunt Anna considerable concern, and Joellen's remorse over not being able to find a job to help was daily taking a toll on her. She hated that Aunt Anna had to take care of them. She wanted to work, and she prayed and prayed for a job.

Ryan was enrolled in the third school for his second grade. Uprooted and confused, he never complained. Like the miniature plastic soldiers he played with day after day, he stoically pushed forward. A young family with two sons about his age lived directly behind Aunt Anna.

"Where's *your* daddy?" one of them asked his daily question.

"At work," Ryan answered as always.

"When's he comin' home?"

He shrugged his slender shoulders and headed for the house.

"Where you goin'?"

"Inside…gonna play with my G.I. Joe."

He pulled open the kitchen door and heard the soft drone of his mother and Aunt Anna's voices in the living room. He didn't know where his daddy was, but he wasn't going to tell them that! He knew he had been in jail—that's why they had come back to Virginia, but Mama said he was out now, but she didn't know where he was. He secretly watched the neighborhood boys' daddy come and go every day to work, and sometimes he watched him fly out of the house, pulling on a uniform, going on a rescue call. He must be mighty important, Ryan thought, and wished he had a daddy like that. He slipped into the big bedroom and peered over the crib at the baby. He wished she'd hurry and grow up so they could play together.

"Ryan," Joellen admonished, "don't bother Sydney. She's still sleeping."

Quietly, he edged away from the crib and knelt down to find his G.I. Joe and pulled him out from under the bed. He carefully ransacked through his pile of trinkets and grabbed hold of the old diaper he had been saving. Actually, it was one of Sydney's Pampers that was too small. He eased out of the bedroom, holding onto the diaper and scooted into the kitchen for Aunt Anna's scissors. She always kept them in the third drawer beside the sink, and they were always there. He scurried to the bathroom and began tediously cutting up the Pamper into smaller pieces.

Joellen peeked through the cracked door. "What're you doing, Ryan?"

"Making something...something for my G.I. Joe...but I need a needle and thread."

"Wait a minute." She went to Aunt Anna's sewing box and retrieved a large needle and some coarse white thread.

"What's he need that for?" Aunt Anna asked, somewhat puzzled, remembering the time she'd gone into the bathroom and there was white string running up and over and around, loop to loop, from the commode to the roll of toilet paper, and she couldn't sit down!

"I don't know. He's making something for his G.I. Joe." She was proud of her young son's ability to amuse himself for hours in such activities. "Here you go." She handed the needle and thread through the door, and the little fellow proceeded to stitch up the diaper material.

"What's it going to be?"

"A sleeping bag for my G.I. Joe...like Justin has. He's got three that he got for his birthday. I'm gonna make me one...see?"

She stood in the doorway as he carefully ran the needle back and forth through the inflexible, plastic-like material. Justin was his cousin, and with mixed emotions she watched, proud of his resourcefulness and creativity, yet saddened.

AFTER THREE LONG months, Joellen finally found a job as a secretary with the Jim Walter Homes office located on the south side of Lynchburg. She readily accepted, delighted to at last have a source of income and not be such a burden on Aunt Anna. It was the answer to many prayers.

Ryan completed his second grade after struggling through yet another school. He would soon enter the third grade, and Joellen was fervently praying that he would be able to attend the brand new Christian school started by their church. Aunt Anna looked at her skeptically when she mentioned it. "How in the world are you going to pay for it?" she questioned.

"If it's God's will for him to go, then He will provide." She had no doubts of this, and yearned for Ryan to be able to attend the school and get a good Christian education. If anyone deserved it, he did. She prayed and waited for an answer, but as the summer waned, so did her hopes.

Just before the end of summer, her manager casually mentioned that he was looking for someone to clean the display models on a weekly basis, and if she knew of anyone, to please let him know. Her heart leapt at the opportunity, but she said nothing. She made a call to another Jim Walter Homes location in a nearby city and discovered that their secretary was doing that very thing. Why couldn't she? She waited all day for the right time to approach her manager but none came, and he was getting ready to leave for the day. He had his hand on the doorknob.

"Mr. Drake...I wanted to talk to you about something."
He glanced around impatiently.

"I...I would like...the janitor job."

He spun around. "*You?*"

She nodded, holding her breath. The janitor job held the key to the Christian school for Ryan.

"Why would you want to do that?" He frowned. It was totally ludicrous to him, not to mention disgusting. Who would want that dirty ol' job? To him, Joellen was a charming young lady, and he couldn't fathom her sweeping out those dusty models, taking out the trash, and cleaning the bathroom for gosh sakes!

"I need the money."

"Well...yeah...but a *janitor!*"

Bob Drake was new to Lynchburg, transferred from Florida and had already raised concerns for Joellen. Though recently married for the third time, he obviously still considered himself a playboy. Joellen took an immediate dislike to him but struggled to conceal it. It had taken her three long months to land this job, and she wasn't about to jeopardize it. The former manager, a decent sort of fellow, had hired her and immediately afterwards accepted another position himself, leaving her to the obnoxious imaginations of Casanova.

"I need the money to pay for my son's school," she persisted.

He shook his head incredulously but finally agreed, much to Joellen's relief. Now she could send Ryan to Lynchburg Christian Academy! Weekly she began cleaning the three dusty models plus the finished model that served as their offices, and emptying the trash. Aunt Anna kept Sydney on Saturday mornings while she cleaned, and Ryan usually accompanied her, happily sprinting through the empty models, playing his pretend games, or helping her clean, but today she was alone.

IT WAS ALREADY hot, even though it was relatively early in the morning. Joellen pushed the heavy broom back and forth across the rough wooden sub floor, stirring up thick dust particles that swirled around her in a foggy brown cloud. Her chest felt tight, and she began coughing. She stopped to rest, wiping her wet forehead, realizing too late that she had probably smeared it with dirt from her grimy hands. Oh well!

Her hands resting atop the broom, she stared out the cloudy window, up into the distant clear blue sky. *He sees me down here in the middle of all this dust...and He cares!* Again she marveled at how God had provided the little job, right down to the penny! It paid twenty-five dollars a week, and the school bill was one hundred dollars a month. A rush of warmth flooded her soul to think that the great God of the universe was taking care of *her!* She heard a car drive up and anxiously waited for it to maneuver slowly through the parking lot and on out again. She breathed a sigh of relief. *Silly, that's what the models are here for,* she chided herself. But ever since last Friday she couldn't help but feel a bit uneasy.

She had been engrossed in typing up a lengthy deed of trust, rushing to get it done for the week's sales, when the manager came in. The model, transposed as the office, was fairly small, and the main front room doubled as a lobby and her office. One adjoining room was the manager's office, and the other was the finance officer's; however, the finance officer was seldom there—he was out of town a lot. The last room served as a small kitchen. At any given time, however, there was usually someone coming or going, carpenters, painters, electricians, plumbers and the like. But on that particular Friday morning, there was no one there but her.

Swinging open the front door, her manager stood preening, as if to say I'm Romeo and you're Juliet! Immediately, she was apprehensive, but sought to conceal it, pretending not to notice. Her fingers pounded the keyboard, struggling to concentrate on the wordy deed of trust. She loved to type but had never liked typing sale papers, full of legal jargon and plat descriptions which made no sense at all to her. *Beginning at a point in the center of Pine Road; thence along entrance road S. 33 degrees 56' N. 162.12 feet, N. 63 degrees 39' E 21.9 feet, thence W. 64 degrees 03' S. 70.5 feet to a post; thence leaving entrance road S. 20 degrees 46' N. 54.27 feet to a stake; thence S. 46 degrees 10' S. to a point—*

A shadow fell over her.

Without looking up, she knew that he was standing immediately in front of her, nothing between them but the bulky Royal typewriter. She pounded the stiff keys harder. What was he up to? This was the moment she had dreaded. He was going to make a pass, and she was going to stop him. It would mean her job! In fact, she had already talked to Aunt Anna about it, and was so relieved that she supported her and knew she must do what she had to do.

He clasped his hands together and slowly raised his arms above his head as if stretching, but his objective was to encircle her. With a sly grin upon his arrogant face, he proceeded to gradually come down with his arms just above her head.

"Bob."

He stopped—his arms in midair.

"Don't do that."

His arms still hanging in the air, he retorted, "I know what you're going to say—that you're a Christian, and you don't like this sort of thing."

Images raced through her mind of Ryan in the nice Christian school and little Sydney at the babysitter's and Aunt Anna at work…and all of them needing her job. With great trepidation and fighting the tremor in her voice, she replied, "I know you don't mean anything, and you don't think this is anything…but it is to me. I am a Christian… and you must not do this!"

His arms dropped to his sides, and he backed off. She didn't dare look up for fear of what he was going to say. Her face burned hot, she was trembling, and she waited for him to fire her.

Instead there was silence.

Then he turned and walked away. "Okay, if that's the way you want it."

He had not bothered her since. She pushed the dirt, sweeping it into a neat pile, and pondered such a great loving God that had heard her prayers. She had begun asking Him to protect her job as soon as she knew what kind of man Bob Drake was, and Aunt Anna prayed, too. She knew God had intervened, for Bob Drake was not the type to take a putdown.

"*Thank you, Lord,*" she whispered in the dust-filled model.

Bob Drake wasn't the only challenge. The motley crew of carpenters, painters, electricians, plumbers, some with rowdy lives and loose tongues, presented her with her own mission field. Though puzzling, they quickly grasped her Christian stand, and treated her with high regard, awkwardly stumbling over their habitual blunders.

"…'cuse me, ma'am…didn't mean to say that, just slipped out, 'cuse me."

Amused, Joellen would smile. "That's okay. I know you didn't mean it." She grew fond of the odd group of workers and sought every chance to be the Christian example before them.

"...and ye shall be witnesses unto me."

She realized that nothing happened by chance in a Christian's life—that God either caused it or allowed it for a purpose, and she looked for the purpose in her being there. The workers began to question her about her beliefs, baffled at a young attractive lady, separated from her husband, that wasn't interested in dating, only in church things!

The long hot summer was coming to a close, fall was in the air, light and crisp, and she was happy to be back in Virginia, anxious for the leaves to turn.

"Lord, please live through me and speak through me today," she prayed on the way to work. It was the same prayer she prayed every morning, while driving down Wards Road. She glanced at her watch. She must hurry. Today was trash day, and she had to get it out to the incinerator before time to open the office.

About an hour later, the manager arrived as she was finalizing another deed of trust. Suddenly the sky clouded up, dark and ominous. Then the rains fell hard, hammering the roof of the model home. Bolts of lightning flashed, crisscrossing through the windows, and thunder rolled loud and boisterously, seemingly shaking the foundation. Bob came out of his office and sat down uneasily on the couch facing her desk. What was on his mind? The pounding rain increased, washing the windows in waves of water, and Joellen typed furiously.

"You really believe in this God, don't you?"

Surprised, she looked up and realized he was serious. "Yes, I do."

He stood up and grabbed the stapler off her desk, waving it in front of her face, and slammed it back down. "Okay…if there really is a God like you say, then ask Him to move this stapler!"

Shocked, she stared in disbelief from him to the stapler.

"Go on…tell Him…tell Him to move it…see if He can!"

"No…."

"Didn't think you would…because you know He can't!"

"I didn't say that."

"Go ahead then…tell Him!" He pushed the stapler back at her.

"The Bible says we're not supposed to tempt God."

"What do you mean?"

"When Jesus was led up into the wilderness…the devil tempted Him…took Him up and set Him up high and…" She struggled to remember the scripture. "…and the devil said to Him, *'If you're the Son of God, throw yourself down: for it's written, He shall give His angels charge over you….'*"

Bob listened.

"…but Jesus answered the devil, *'It is written…Thou shalt not tempt the Lord thy God.'* "

Bob looked at her strangely and backed off. He slumped down on the couch and muttered, "I never met a real Christian before…."

She remembered what he had told her just last week. How he had played backup music for a popular gospel group in Florida when he was young, and how they behaved when the concerts were finished, how they drank and caroused behind closed doors.

He ran his hand uncertainly through his trendy styled hair. "I'd like to believe what you say, but I don't know... I've been about as sorry as they come...ever since I can remember...ever since my pa taught me how to lie and steal money from little old ladies."

Joellen vividly recalled that story. His father used him in deceiving poor people out of their money. He had described to her just last week how his father pretended to be in the termite exterminating business, and how he would go up to a house and knock on a door. He would ask the resident, more often than not some old lady living alone, if she would like for him to check under her house for termites. He would add that there was no cost for his inspection unless he found termites and then only if she wanted him to do anything. While busy talking, young Bob, only four or five years old, would sneak up under the house, crawl on his belly in the dirt and cobwebs until he found an old, damp piece of wood to pull off. Then he would take his little box of termites out of his pocket, open it up, and the hungry varmints would flood over the damp wood. He would then wait for his father, who after a short so-called inspection, would hurry back out with the piece of damp wood crawling with termites. Shocked and afraid that her house was about to fall in on her, the little old lady would readily give him whatever he asked to treat the house.

Bob Drake sat staring at the floor.

"No one is too sinful for God to save."

He looked up at her. "Don't you remember me telling you about my old man being in the bootlegger business, and I was the lookout...and that's small stuff compared to what I've done since…oh well. Like I said, I'm too sorry…."

"No one is too sorry for Him to save," she repeated. "All you have to do is read the Bible and you'll see. God called David in the Old Testament a man after His own heart, but yet David committed adultery and murder. Still God used him mightily, used him to write the beloved Psalms in the Bible."

He stared at her.

"Then there was Paul, saved on the road to Damascus by the blinding light that God sent down, and he had been a persecutor of Christians," she continued. "There are so many stories like that. God said, *'For all have sinned, and come short of the glory of God.'*

"But He also says, *'For whosoever shall call upon the name of the Lord shall be saved.'* "

Bob stood up, shaking his head. "I don't know," he said and walked back to his office.

JOELLEN AND THE children lived with Aunt Anna for about a year-and-a-half, and they were planning on staying longer until they could manage to move out on their own, but what transpired late one night after they had all gone to bed changed things.

The phone rang.

It was a well-respected layman from the church. "Joellen, I'm sorry to call you at such an hour…but I'm here with Dale…and he has something to tell you."

She stiffened.

The phone was handed over to Dale.

"Joellen…."

"Yes…."

His voice strained, obviously emotional, he proceeded to tell her that he had turned his life over to the Lord and that things were going to be different now. She was silent. The layman took the phone back.

"Joellen?"

"Yes."

"I'm not calling to ask you to take him back, but I believe he has truly gotten things right this time. Just watch and wait, give him time, but I believe he is a new man."

She hung up, and Aunt Anna asked, "Who was that?" Joellen repeated everything and returned to bed with mixed emotions.

Dale began to call regularly, beseeching her to come back to him. Aunt Anna was openly skeptical and troubled, but she could see that Joellen was choosing to believe what she wanted to believe. Actually she was torn—afraid to go back to him, afraid not to. He wanted her, and he was her husband, the father of her children. Besides, she had taken the oath—*to death do us part.* Surely God would expect her to make her marriage work if he had truly changed. Wouldn't He? She didn't feel at liberty to discuss it with Aunt Anna or with anyone in the family, for that matter, for she knew how they disapproved. They could only see one side, hers and the children's safety and welfare. But suppose he was a new man?

After a couple of months she gave in, and they moved into a terrace apartment at the foot of Thomas Road, just below the church and its embryonic Christian school. Joellen was happy for that; now Ryan could walk to school, and just a short walk, too. She hated that he had had such a disrupted start and sincerely hoped that the Christian school would make up for it, giving him a strong, stable foundation, one rooted in God's principles. In fact, it was her foremost desire to raise both Ryan and Sydney in the school.

For the first few months things went well. Then it happened. Lying on the sofa, she waited...nine o'clock...ten o'clock...eleven o'clock. The familiar knot formed in her stomach, and she questioned his decision for the Lord. Was it simply a ploy or was he just not capable of change? She was confused, she was angry, and she was embarrassed. How could she face Aunt Anna...her daddy...the world?

She strained to hear his car in the driveway...twelve o'clock. Still no sound. All was quiet except for the occasional muted movement of the children as they tossed in their sleep. The minutes crept on while she painfully recapped the past. How could this be happening again?

Tears welled up and ran down her cheeks, thoughtlessly bloating her eyes and face a puffy red. She thought she was doing the right thing when she took him back. The more she cried, the more upset she became, but she must get hold of herself. She had to get up early for work, but she only sobbed harder.

I just don't understand.

The Bible lay on the end table where she had laid it after church, and she reached for it, flipping through its pages, searching for something, anything to hold onto. She scanned the Psalms, but her mind was too agitated. She wiped her eyes and continued turning the pages through Proverbs, and an underlined verse suddenly lifted from its tissue-thin page.

Trust in the Lord with all thine heart; and lean not unto thine own understanding.

CHAPTER TWENTY-TWO

PRESENT

SUNSHINE FLOODED THE RV, streaming through the large window over the bed, and Joellen stared up into golden hickories towering over them, their leaves translucent, pierced by bright sunrays. The fog had lifted.

They ate hot biscuits, ham, and apple butter, and then Wade pulled back onto the Parkway. Joellen checked her cell phone. *Roam.* She placed it beside her to keep an eye on it as they wound around the mountainside. She waited for *SunCom* to appear as they rounded the other side of the mountain and then dialed.

"Hello."

"Katy?"

"Yes. Where are you?"

"In the mountains of North Carolina."

"Figured it." Her sister laughed cheerfully.

"How's Mama?"

"Well…she's not doing so good."

"Still hallucinating?"

"Yes."

"Do you think we need to come back?"

"No. Y'all go on and have fun. There's nothing…you… can…do h…ere."

"You're breaking up."

"I know…don't worry. Have…fun…." The phone went dead as they rounded the mountain.

She laid it back on the dash and glanced at Wade.

"Everything okay?"

"Katy said for us to have fun." The mockery of life, she thought. The baby that she had prayed not to be born had turned out to be an integral part of her life. Katy was the most giving person she had ever known, and she loved her dearly.

The Parkway stretched out ahead in the glowing morning sunshine, washed in the rains, clean and beckoning. They could see its curving ribbon for miles and miles up ahead, winding around the awesome mountains. Autumn leaves floated down all around them. She lowered her window to inhale the pristine air, and gazed at masses of dark shining rhododendron, clumps and clumps of them banking the road. A sugar maple dominated the upcoming curve, its wet black bark starkly contrasting with its transparent yellow leaves, tipped a fiery red.

Little Switzerland the sign read.

"Oh, let's stop here," she suggested, recalling the unique mountain village they had visited on previous trips, and especially the used bookstore and its treasures. It was immensely popular with the tourist traffic and literally crammed with books, all kinds of books…and she loved books. An avid fisherman, Wade also enjoyed old bookstores, always seeking rare and appealing books on the art of fishing and waterways. He skillfully maneuvered the large RV around the sharp curves and steep inclines.

It was understandable why it was called *Little Switzerland,* built on craggy ridges, steep and picturesque, with sweeping vistas of misty mountains and deep valleys, imparting a sense of being transported far across the vast seas. To the west rose Mount Mitchell, to the south Linville Mountain, to the east Grandfather Mountain and to the north was Roan. Wade found a narrow parking spot. "You might want to watch out back."

Joellen hopped up, shot to the bedroom and crawled up on the bed. "Come on back," she directed, while scanning the cluster of interesting shops and the little café. She eyed the unique inn with its chalet character that unquestionably looked the part, just what she would expect in the Swiss Alps.

"That's it." He shut off the engine, and they climbed out, glad to stretch their legs, and headed for the bookstore. It was almost an hour before they emerged.

"Feels good to be back outside." Wade inhaled the breezy mountain air, "...but I found a couple of good books."

"So did I." She clutched her stack, most of them she had read before and cherished. She glanced down at the small book on top—*Gift from the Sea* by Anne Morrow Lindbergh, a little treasure, and a copy of *Jane Eyre* by one of the Bronte sisters. She had read all of their books and always got the sisters mixed up. Then there was a copy of *Bury My Heart at Wounded Knee* by Dee Brown, another treasure, and lastly a small copy of *Pilgrim's Progress* by John Bunyan. It had been many years since she had read them, but they were classics, and she couldn't resist them. The new book, *Windows of the Soul*, was the only one she hadn't read. They filled their cups with coffee and iced tea respectively and continued on their way. Joellen leafed through the books.

"You're gonna miss all this beauty," Wade warned.

Glancing up at the vibrant forest, she was torn between enjoying it or reading, but she knew he wanted to share it with her, so she reached around and stacked the books on the sofa. "I'm glad I found that old copy of *Pilgrim's Progress*. You know when America was first settled they only had two books, the Bible and *Pilgrim's Progress*."

"That's all they needed. Now, there are way too many."

She frowned. There could never be too many books for her. "I picked up one that looks quite interesting, called *Windows of the Soul* by Ken Gire. It's about God reaching out to us. Listen to what it says... *His search begins with something said. Ours begins with something heard. His begins with something shown. Ours, with something seen....*' "

Suddenly all was dark. They were passing through one of the many tunnels along the southern end of the Parkway.

Wade chuckled. "Wish Brook was here."

She smiled.

"Remember how she used to tease you?"

How could she forget? Brook was their baby daughter, the child that God had given her and Wade. She was thirty-nine when Brook was born and thought that she was too old to be having a baby. Funny, she reflected, how time changes things. Now thirty-nine seemed young to her! And Brook was grown! But they had shared many Parkway trips, and the memories lingered around every curve, up every mountain. The child had literally grown up in the camper.

"Mom, read me this book!" she would cry out excitedly, thrusting it at her and stifling a giggle.

Playing along, she would read until suddenly it was pitch black, then yell out, "Who turned out the lights?" She could still hear Brook's peals of childhood laughter filling the moving camper. The memory was sweet and sad at the same time. Bittersweet, she thought, like the striking autumn vine climbing profusely up the trees.

They emerged into the piercing sunlight, only to approach another. The two were called twin tunnels, and she studied the roughhewn rock enclosing them, wet and dripping from underground springs. Again they surfaced into the brilliant sunlight and welcomed its soothing warmth.

WATCH FOR FALLEN ROCKS

Joellen glanced at the sign and up at the rocky cliff with vivid red Virginia creeper climbing it. Breathtaking!

"Hope they stay up there!"

"Me, too," she laughed. In all their years of traveling the Parkway, all the hundreds and hundreds of miles, they had never seen a rock fall, but they knew they fell, of course. The evidence lay alongside the winding road.

"Milepost 347."

Wade enjoyed announcing the mileposts. A great idea on somebody's part, not only keeping travelers abreast as to where they were located in these remote mountains, but they could break the monotony sometimes. Of course, in the peak of autumn, there wasn't much monotony, but some people thought so, she had been told. Apparently they were people in a hurry. Everybody was in a hurry nowadays, but you can't appreciate the mountains in a hurry, she thought to herself. You have to slow down and let them speak to you, and they will share their gentle beauty. However, sometimes they will frighten you with their intense harshness. Either way, they will challenge you, and present you with something greater than yourself... strength...time...and their Creator.

They drove through the bleak darkness of Rough Ridge Tunnel and again surfaced through the arch into startling sunlight, heightening their senses. Mount Mitchell was ahead, the highest elevation east of the Rockies, rising more than a mile high. Part of the towering Black

Mountain range, Mount Mitchell, was a favorite destination for many. As they ascended, the forest makeup drastically changed. Thick groves of dark spruce and fir popped up, and heavy, grayish-white clouds rested atop their shadowy forms. A dense fog was blowing across the summit, and the temperature dropped noticeably. The climate, said to be more like Canada than North Carolina, seemed to actually transport them there, leaving behind the colorful fairyland. The shifting blanket of heavy fog rolled and waved through the thick stands of evergreens as the RV pulled up the towering mountain.

Six thousand, six hundred and eighty-four feet.

This was not a record-breaker in the scope of things, not in the family of mountains worldwide, but here on the east coast and even in America, it was nothing to sneeze at! As they neared the summit, ghostly tree skeletons marched over the ridges, matchstick remnants of spruce and fir, victims of insect diseases and acid rain. Their pale-white images were veiled by the constantly moving fog, depicting a melancholy scene.

"Dr. Mitchell, the mountain's namesake, actually died up here!" Wade said, adding to the brooding mood.

"Really?"

"Buried up here, too, read it in one of the brochures. While hiking across the mountain, he fell down a cliff above a waterfall, was knocked unconscious, and drowned in the water. "

He pulled the camper over to the side, and Joellen stared down the steep precipice. "Boy, it is w-a-y down!"

"Come on, let's get out." He was anxious to explore the summit.

They trudged up the graveled pathway and stone steps, flanked by rocky ledges, firs, and myriad plants. Cold water dripped off the layers and layers of jagged stones, and high winds pounded them. Joellen zipped up her warm fleece jacket.

Caught in a swirl of fog, the summit was surreal as they stood solemnly before the stone crypt. *"Here lies in the Hope of a Blessed Resurrection, the body of the Rev. Elisha Mitchell, D.D...."*

"Well, he was buried on the place he loved," Wade said softly as others milled around them.

"But it seems so desolate up here, so far up, and all alone."

He nodded.

"One thing for sure, in the resurrection, he won't have as far to go," she concluded. "Come on, let's climb to the observation deck."

The stone building eerily echoed their footsteps as they slowly ascended the curving steps and exited the door on top. Fierce cold winds immediately buffeted them as they grabbed hold of the railing, peering down on masses of firs and spruce, and out into miles and miles of foggy distance, miles and miles of mountain ranges, row after row.

Comfortably back in the RV, warm and dry, visitors hurried past as they devoured barbecues and chips and watched the fast-moving fog continue to churn around them. When they descended Mount Mitchell and were back on the road, they passed through several more tunnels, Craggy Pinnacle, Craggy Flats, and Tanbark Ridge, and soon entered the Grassy Knob tunnel, the longest one yet and very smooth. "I like them better rough on the inside, seems more natural."

Wade announced, "Milepost 400. Only sixty-nine more miles to go."

Before reaching the campground where they would spend the night, they passed through seven more. "All these tunnels really do remind me of little Brook," Wade thought aloud. "She sure did grow up fast."

"They all did," Joellen replied. And from the corners of her mind she drew out their pictures, one by one…Ryan, Sydney, and Brook, all three of them, and silently studied them. Twilight brought shadows down upon the RV wheeling around the mountainside and inevitably darkened the colorful forest into a mysterious and foreboding place. A pensive mood settled down upon her.

Where did all the years go?

She was too busy to notice them slipping away. Quite subtly, they disappeared before her very eyes. And though she was proud of all her children now and enjoyed them as grown-ups, there was an element of sadness in the whole scheme of things. That sweet little boy, so stoic and uncomplaining, and those precious little girls, one a tomboy, the other an animal lover—they were gone.

The campground was a welcomed sight, and Wade pulled in to register. They prepared for bed, but the poignant mood prevailed. When at last she curled up beside Wade, sleep did not come. Instead the memories, so many memories, filled her sleepless mind.

AND SHE REMEMBERED the night when Dale didn't come home, after she had reluctantly left the haven of Aunt Anna's. She thought again of the verse that God had given her during that troubling time, and she still held it close to her heart.

Trust in the Lord with all thine heart; and lean not unto thine own understanding.

He had actually given it to her twice, making sure that it sunk in. Shortly after that night, they had a visit from two men from the church. She and the children were home alone, and they stood out on the porch to talk. She was well aware of the heart-wrenching story of one of the men and wondered if maybe he could give her a word of encouragement, a word of hope that she so desperately needed. They knew about Dale and his problems, and they were hoping to catch him at home.

"We're sorry we missed him…but how are *you* doing?" the man with the story asked. His question conveyed concern and compassion.

"Okay."

"I know it's hard," he smiled at her, "but God's grace is sufficient."

"I'm sure you have learned that firsthand."

He nodded and stared off into space. For a moment there was an awkward silence except for the distant barking of a dog.

He quickly recovered and replied, "When my wife died during childbirth, leaving me with three small children, I couldn't understand for the life of me why God would let it happen, why he would take a young mother away from three helpless children, a devout Christian mother at that! I was utterly distraught…and sought God over and over for answers. You know what He told me?"

Shaking her head, she waited for his answer. The other gentleman stood by quietly listening.

"It's what kept me going during those dark, dark days."

She anxiously waited.

"A Proverb… *'Trust in the Lord with all thine heart; and lean not unto thine own understanding'.*"

It was the same verse!

"I couldn't keep the children and work, too," he continued. "I had to pawn them out to family members and friends, one here, one there. It broke my heart to see them separated…and I struggled to understand it all. But God was teaching me to trust Him instead," he concluded with a serene expression upon his face that struck Joellen.

That night she rehashed the visit and thought again of the man's story, recalling how his young wife was found to have cancer while pregnant. As her pregnancy grew, her cancer grew, placing the baby in grave danger. The doctors diagnosed that she might die before she delivered, causing the baby to die also. Though she was told that if they took the baby early, it would probably mean sudden death for her, she chose to give the baby life. They operated and took the infant boy, and she died.

If this poor man was able to overcome such dire circumstances, surely she could do the same!

And God blessed him for his faith. He was a testimony to God's grace in their church and entire community. After awhile he was able to bring the family back together under one roof, and then God sent him another lovely Christian wife, who became mother to his children with a devotion to admire. Joellen watched the romance bud and blossom. She had watched the young father sit out in the pew during choir practice, and she saw them make loving eyes at one another. And when they married, God blessed them with more children. It was a sad story, but a story with a happy ending, and she thought of Job in the Scriptures.

Though He slay me, yet will I trust in Him.

After that, she didn't dwell on trying to understand things so much. In fact, she had little time to dwell on anything. She was busy with moving two more times, busy with the children, with a new job at an employment agency, and her ministry—teaching children in Sunday school about God and His love. It would have been a fulfilling life, a happy life—except for Dale.

But she didn't know the constant hurt and mental anguish that he carried with him daily. All she could see were the lost jobs, the infidelity, bare cupboards, and his empty chair when they sat down to eat or the empty bed when she rose up in the morning. And she was tired of moving. If only they could have a real home to call their own, a place to settle down and stay. The children needed roots.

Secretly, she had begun saving five dollars a payday for a down payment. She didn't dare let Dale know as she stared down at the little blue bank book with its stamped balance that had slowly grown to seventy-five dollars. She privately put it back in the zipped side compartment of her purse, and it gave her a warm feeling, a hope that someday they would have a home!

AFTER JOELLEN BECAME a Christian, the church was a stabilizing influence for her, a rock, a compass in her Christian walk, but suddenly the rock was trembling. The church found itself floundering, sinking in deep, unfamiliar waters. It was facing a fiery trial. The U.S. Securities and Exchange Commission was bringing legal charges against it, claiming that it had used fraud and deceit in selling millions of dollars in bonds to investors. It claimed that the church was insolvent in that its assets were not sufficient to meet its obligations as those bonds became due and payable. Thomas Road Baptist Church would later be exonerated of those charges, but at the time it was very troubling.

The church had grown so rapidly from thirty-five members to thousands in just a short period of time that it found itself in a mess, after making financial mistakes to keep up with its phenomenal growth, and trying to underwrite its growing television ministry and its embryonic university. Unfortunately, the church was tried and convicted in the newspaper headlines before it even went to court, which was very discouraging to its members, including Joellen. The possibility that the church might be forced into bankruptcy, put in receivership and the sanctuary padlocked, spread like wildfire throughout the congregation and Lynchburg.

Joellen didn't understand how all this could have happened, but she believed it was God's house, and He was in control. There was a depressing gloom over the church, and members were willingly giving their support and their savings to help. Some even took out mortgage loans. But it needed millions! What was going to happen?

The first court date was set. Joellen decided to go and took off from work, along with other members, for moral support. As she sat in the cold, austere courtroom, realizing that their church doors could actually be closed and padlocked, she thought of her seventy-five dollars.

She didn't want to give it up. It had taken so long to save. She didn't want to give up her hope for a house! And she knew if she took the money out, she would probably never be able to save it up again, especially now that things were becoming even worse at home. But God's house was more important, she decided, and the next day she went to the bank and drew it out. She called the church office to speak with the church secretary. "Mrs. Hogan, I have some money for the church. Should I bring it over to your office?"

"That will be fine, Joellen."

She carefully placed it in a white envelope and drove over to the church. She pulled open the heavy door, climbed the stairs to the church office and handed over the envelope. When she descended the stairs, she felt absolutely wonderful!

THE CHURCH WASN'T the only thing in trouble. So was the nation. Watergate was shaking its very core. It had arisen from a break-in at the Democratic Party headquarters in the Watergate building complex in Washington, DC, and stunned the country with the biggest political scandal in US history. It dragged on and on, and the president was in the middle of it all. The investigations continued, then impeachment hearings began. By the summer of 1974, the House Judiciary Committee finished reviewing the evidence and voted for impeachment, charging the president with obstruction of justice, attempting to hide the identities of those who ordered the break-ins, and abusing presidential powers, and lastly of disobeying subpoenas. Knowing he faced certain impeachment, Richard Milhous Nixon, the 37th President of the United States, announced his decision in a nationwide television address and resigned on the ninth of August.

At noon that day, Vice President Gerald R. Ford was sworn in as president.

It was the talk of the nation, but at home there was something else going on. Katy was getting married, and Joellen was preparing for the wedding. She and Janet were to be Matrons of Honor, and Sydney was excited about her role as flower girl. Aunt Anna was busily making Sydney's little white dotted Swiss dress.

The wedding came off beautifully, and Bennett walked his last daughter down the aisle, all the while cautiously watching Meredith as she sat despondently in the church pew, her face downcast with heavy bags beneath her eyes.

"WHERE'S DADDY?" SYDNEY asked her mother.

"He's probably still at work." Joellen always provided her and Ryan with an answer, but an answer that she knew wasn't sufficient. That's what hurt the most, seeing the children without a father even though he was there.

Their last move had taken them out to the rural part of Campbell County, outside of Lynchburg, to a small four-room house built on a slanting hillside with a large yard encircling it, but it was the rent that drew them, rent that Joellen felt she could afford, one hundred dollars a month. Dale's drinking and erratic behavior grew even worse, and he became more and more hostile toward her. How could he love her and resent her at the same time? she wondered and so did he.

Too embarrassed to approach her family, she kept quiet. Even if she could have gone to her father, she didn't have the heart to now. He had taken her mother to a hospital in Roanoke for shock treatments, hoping this would give her some peace. Joellen wondered about the shock treatments. She knew an electrical current would somehow be sent through her mother's brain to hopefully shock her out of the extreme depression. She certainly hoped it would.

Bennett waited behind closed doors and thought of all the times he had done so. Five times for their babies, and the last one, Katy, had just gotten married. He didn't have any more babies at home, and he was glad they were grown, and he didn't have to worry about them or worry about Meredith trying to care for them, though he missed them terribly. But this time was different. He didn't like the sound of the whole thing either, but the doctor had advised it, saying that he thought it would help. Please God, let it help, he prayed silently.

Meredith lay unconscious, under anesthesia and pretreatment medications so that she wouldn't feel the electric current or the resulting seizure, and to reduce the chance of vertebral fractures. She was hooked up to an IV and to an EKG machine and the EEG machine. A rubber gag was in her mouth, and electrolytic-conducting jelly was smeared on her temples and into her thick dark hair. The doctor stood nearby ready to push the red button, and two male assistants were pressing down on her shoulders and thighs to prevent the powerful jolt from dislocating her arms and legs.

Click.

A hundred volts coursed through her body for less than a second, but the convulsing lasted for a minute or so. A few minutes later she awakened on a thin rubber mattress, completely stunned and exhausted. The electroconvulsive current that had traveled through her body seeking to annihilate whatever was holding her captive had also temporarily stolen her memory. She glanced around, wondering where she was, and stared at the IV and the other cords hooked up to her. Frightened, she looked for Bennett. Where was Bennett?

"Mrs. Thaxton, do you know what just happened to you?" the doctor asked.

She stared vacantly at him and then slowly remembered.

Bennett jumped up when they wheeled her back into the room and rushed to her side. He patted her arm. "You're gonna be all right now, Meredith...you're gonna be all right...."

She looked up at him with fear in her eyes.

"You'll be able to go home tomorrow the doctor said... and see the children...they'll be happy to see you."

What children? Her mind reeled. What was he talking about?

The scattered pieces of her memory would gradually assimilate into a pattern, and she would understand. However, it was all a jumble now, but there would be permanent voids left from the powerful shocks, voids like Katy's wedding that she would never again remember.

DALE LOST HIS driver's license again for DUI, this time for ten years, but still he was coming in later and later at night, if he came in at all. He would stumble clumsily through the door in a quarrelsome mood. Concerned for the children's safety, Joellen began putting little Sydney in bed with Ryan whenever Dale wasn't home, and charged Ryan to keep her there. She despaired in hearing young Sydney cry when Dale was loud, cursing and abusive, but still she insisted they both stay in the bed. She didn't know what else to do.

It was one of those nights that initiated the inevitable chain of events. Dale had been gone for a couple of days, and Sydney was in bed with Ryan. He staggered in just after midnight and right away became argumentative. Joellen's temper flashed, and she flared back. He grabbed her around the neck, and she cried out. He swore at her, and hysterically she broke away, running to the bathroom. He followed, waving back and forth in his drunken stupor.

Sydney was sobbing loudly in the background, and Ryan was frantically trying to hush her up. Then he jumped out of bed, listening at the doorway to the quarreling and cries coming from the bathroom, with Sydney trembling and hanging onto him. Dale stormed out of the bathroom, raving and cursing, and they flew back to bed.

The next morning, as Joellen drove the children to school, Sydney was happily chattering away, resilient as any four-year-old, but Ryan was silently staring out the window. Then he spoke. "Mom, I did what you told me to do last night. I didn't come in there, and I kept Sydney with me like you said…but the next time Daddy comes in like that and hurts you, I *will* get up, and I *will* stop him!"

Fear seized Joellen. She knew that if he did such a thing, he would get hurt. And maybe badly hurt for when Dale was drunk he would hurt Saint Peter if he tried to intervene. "You must not do that, Ryan!"

He looked at her somberly. "I will, Mom."

And in that instant, she knew he would. The young, wiry twelve-year-old was becoming a man all too soon, and she knew he would try to protect her. What was she to do?

CHAPTER TWENTY-THREE

PRESENT

A LARGE BLACK bear with two cubs pushed through the brush seeking the tantalizing autumn berries found abundant in the Blue Ridge Mountains. Suddenly coming upon a sizable shiny obstacle on wheels in its path, the heavy mother bear snorted, shook her head, and wobbled off in another direction, her cubs obediently following.

Joellen stirred and awoke to the heavenly warmth of the bright sunshine spilling through the RV window. Cascading through giant treetops, it splashed an imaginative design atop their quilt. She yawned and turned over, staring up at a huge oak embracing them with sturdy outstretched limbs, festooned with a royal array of golden leaves. She raised up on her elbows. *If only I could stay here forever.*

"What do you see?" Wade asked, slowly waking up.

"A fairyland...an autumn fairyland!"

He lifted himself on his elbows to join her. "You're right. Thank you, Lord, for all this beauty."

Back on the road again, they were passing through Frying Pan Tunnel. "Funny name."

"There are lots of unusual names up here," Wade remarked. "You wonder about their origin...Milepost 411."

She smiled.

"How's this place for breakfast?"

She nodded.

"Cradle of Forestry Overlook, where it all began." Wade looked around.

"Ham and eggs?"

"Sounds good to me. Look at that fog rolling up from the hollows, would you?" He maneuvered the RV into the pull off, lining it up for the best view. Joellen jumped up, pulling out pots and pans from under the sink. He shut off the motor and got out to stretch his legs.

Waves of fog were rising and falling around them while they ate. "Mighty good," Wade complimented. He loved a good breakfast, especially when they were camping, and he spread the gooey strawberry preserves on his thick slice of sourdough bread.

"Thank you. I'll wash the dishes, and then you can read the Bible." It was Sunday morning.

"The Proverbs of Solomon the son of David, king of Israel;" Wade read reverently, and Joellen listened as the fog swirled around.

> *A wise man will hear, and will increase learning; and a man of understanding shall attain unto wise counsels:*
>
> *To understand a proverb, and the interpretation; the words of the wise, and their dark sayings.*
>
> *The fear of the Lord is the beginning of knowledge: but fools despise wisdom and instruction.*
>
> *My son, hear the instruction of thy father, and forsake not the law of thy mother.*

After reading the first three chapters in the Book of Proverbs, they prayed and started on their way again. Wade thoughtfully sipped his coffee and Joellen reflected on the eighth verse. She thought of her mother and how she had instilled God's law in their childish minds even though she herself was so sick. But as a rebellious teenager, she had forsaken that law and later on, as a young woman in her early twenties, she had again forsaken it. Thank God, He didn't give up on her!

She wondered how her mother was doing. Katy said she seemed to be resting better, but how could she rest with those relentless fears? And where did they come from? What mysteries lay veiled behind her large doe-like eyes? Mysteries she had most likely blocked out early in life, mysteries that the shock treatments had perhaps concealed forever.

Sadly, Joellen recalled all the bitterness that she had had toward her mother, a bitterness akin to hatred during her teen years. It didn't leave her when she escaped home either. All the dreams, nightmares really, that had plagued her, dreams of returning home. After becoming a Christian, the bitterness left, but there was always that gulf between them, the impassable gulf. Though it had diminished over the years, little by little, subtly breaking down, it was still there.

But now that her mother was at the end of her life, things looked different, and Joellen grappled with her feelings. Maybe if she had tried harder? Maybe if she had made more of an effort to understand her? Strangely enough, but not strange really, she had always seen *herself* as the victim ever since she was a young teenager, and that mindset had stubbornly lodged itself and stayed with her throughout life.

Until now.

Now that her mother's strength had ebbed away, now that age had transformed her into a pitiful specimen of life, now that those ever-present fears had caught up with her, hurling her into snake pits and chasing her with knives to cut off her head, Joellen realized that her mother was the saddest victim of all!

But it was too late.

Or was it?

They would be back home in a few days.

The RV moved onward, swaying around sharp curves, pushing and pulling up the never-ending inclines and sprinting too fast down the mountainsides until Wade thrust it into second gear. She studied the host of colors, deep crimson black gums and dogwoods and golden hickories and striking yellow maples contrasting vividly with lush dark pines climbing the sharp ridges.

They passed the East Fork of Pigeon River, and Joellen gazed at a huge rock wall, wet and slippery. Sounds of water trickling down its rocky sides could be heard dripping off the bottom, beautiful chimes of nature, calming, hypnotizing. Her mind soothed to its music and wandered back again to the past, and she thought of Ryan.

IT WAS THE light bulb flashing! The moment the young fellow had spoken those words so many years ago.

I will get up, and I will stop him.

The inevitable impasse, the ultimate catalyst for change, it made her realize that they were living in a dangerous, volatile situation, and she had to do something before it was too late. She couldn't bear to think of Ryan being hurt. And what if she were hurt? Who would take care of them? There was no way out! The cold hard fact that she had been hiding from was suddenly illuminated by the courageous words of a young boy.

And Dale made it easy for her, though certainly not intentionally. After that climatic night, he left the following morning and was gone for several days, blowing all of his paycheck. Then he called and asked her to come and pick him up. Expecting the call, she summoned up all the courage she could. "I will come and pick you up," she replied gravely, "...but I will not bring you home. I'll take you someplace for help if you want me to...either Elim Home or Arise," both in which he had already been before.

There was silence on the other end. He sensed her resolve and reluctantly agreed. It was a place to go, and he had no choice. She picked him up and took him to Elim Home for Alcoholics, another ministry of their church.

It was the end of the troubled marriage.

Dale stayed on at Elim Home awhile, then left and moved to Roanoke, fifty miles west, to be near his brother. The Veteran's Hospital was also conveniently located nearby, where he found himself off and on with his drinking addiction. Life was certainly more peaceful for Joellen and the children, but the financial struggle continued. They didn't even have the small amount that Dale had sporadically provided.

She was thankful for her new job which paid better, still it wasn't enough. Seeking ways to supplement her income, she heard of a national insurance company that was advertising for candidates to schedule appointments via phone with prospective clients, paying five dollars per appointment. Excited about the opportunity and the fact that she could do it at home with the children, she readily accepted. The calls mostly fell on deaf ears or sometimes rude ears, but it did provide a meager extra income.

Joellen was finally learning to trust God, and her faith grew. They never went without food. She bought the basics and learned to stretch them. Ryan and Sydney complained about the powdered milk but drank it anyway. Aunt Anna always sent them home with opened boxes of food items that she "just happened" not to like. It was a blessing, she knew, not only from Aunt Anna. She bought no clothes for herself and very few for the children, but God provided. Her good friend Miriam gave her a new khaki trench coat when she saw that she needed one, and when Miriam bought herself a new refrigerator, she gave her old one to them. Miriam also took them out to dinner occasionally, a rare treat for Ryan and Sydney. Nan, another friend, handed down all of her daughter's pretty little dresses to Sydney, and Sydney received shoes galore through Aunt Anna's neighbor, who worked at Consolidated Shoe Company. The tiny display samples fit perfectly. Joellen learned how to cut off Ryan's shirt sleeves after winter and hem them up for summer shirts. And their landlord gave seeds to them to plant a small garden: tomatoes, cucumbers, squash and a small crop of pumpkins in the fall, which they mostly gave away. This was even better, enabling them to give for a change.

THEY REMAINED IN Campbell County for a while after the separation. Then Joellen began looking for a place to rent closer to Lynchburg, but most were not within her means. That's when she learned of the government loans for qualifying candidates, and they didn't require down payments. But it seemed too good to be true! When she mentioned it to her friend at work, she was immediately discouraged.

"I'm concerned for you, Joellen. Buying a house is a major undertaking, and you already have the children in the Christian school. Do you think you can handle both?" her co-worker asked worriedly.

Joellen didn't honestly know whether she could or not. She prayed earnestly, seeking God's will and direction. The modest homes, being built in small clusters in rural areas, were like a dream.

Could they possibly have their own home?

She warily filled out the paperwork, pushing down hard on the ink pen, carefully and legibly, almost afraid to think about it, afraid the opportunity might vanish! She waited and prayed and waited. "Lord, if it's thy will, please let the approval go through, but if it's not thy will, then stop it."

It was in His hands.

Still she couldn't help but hope. A real home, a home for the children, a home they could call their own. She remembered the last apartment they had looked at, the only one within her means, but it was pitifully shabby, a terrace apartment in an old rundown house. The yard was teeny, scraggly and ugly, but it was the look on Ryan's face. He was getting older, and he would be ashamed to live there. It convinced her to reach higher, to step out on faith.

The word came. They qualified.

"Thank you, Lord!"

The first step was taken, now the second. Which company? Which house? She looked, and researched, and finally selected one, and met with the representative, then cautiously filled out more paperwork. How could she turn back now? The children were so excited.

THE PHONE RANG. It was her daddy. "You haven't done anything on that house have you?" he asked anxiously.

"No. I'm still waiting."

"Good…don't do anything yet," he advised. "I just saw Buddy Harrington today, and he has his house for sale." Obviously excited, her daddy rattled on breathlessly, "You know the little brick house on Wright Shop Road that Uncle Clayton built…on our old home place site?"

Of course she knew. She had watched him build it, she and Betsy Jeanne standing there under the oak tree with cherry popsicles dripping down their bare arms, wet and sticky. It was a darling little house, but it was the yard that came to mind immediately. Her papa's yard with the long straight sidewalk that ran out to the steps, and the small white pillars that he had built. She and Janet and Daniel and Betsy Jeanne and all their cousins had spent hours playing on them. She remembered all the large family gatherings, too, beneath the shade of the oak trees, Papa and Grandma Thaxton, her mama and daddy, Aunt Anna and Aunt Ella and all the other kinfolk. She remembered playing croquet in the sweeping yard, hitting the hard wooden balls through the little wire wickets placed strategically throughout it. Uncle Clayton, her daddy's oldest brother, had bought the home place from Grandma Thaxton when she grew too old to keep it up, and not long after, it had burned to the ground. That's when Uncle Clayton decided to build the small brick house. Suddenly she was as excited as her daddy.

"How much is he asking?" she blurted out.

"Nineteen thousand and five hundred dollars."

"Why, that's less than the homes I've been looking at…."

"...and not built nearly as good!" her daddy added. "Clayton put the best materials in this house! Call him up. Call Buddy!"

JOELLEN LAY VERY still, listening to the night, the steady hum of cicadas, the far-off howling of a hound, and the muted sound of an occasional automobile passing out front. The familiar outlines of her bedroom furniture took shape in the soft light of the half moon. Sydney was pressed up against her, sound asleep, and Ryan was asleep in the small bedroom across the hall. She glanced at the digital alarm clock, its bright red numbers radiated twelve fifteen, but she couldn't sleep! She had been lying there awake for over an hour.

It's ours!

Mine and Ryan's and Sydney's. She basked in the new-found feeling, its warmth and magic. No one can tell us to move. The deep satisfying emotion was a balm, and she really didn't want to go to sleep. She wanted to savor it as long as possible. She thought she heard Ryan turning in his bed and wondered if he was really asleep or perhaps experiencing the same thing. He was thrilled, both he and Sydney. It might be small, only two bedrooms, a kitchen and living room, but the yard made up for it with its sturdy oaks. The sidewalk was gone, but the concrete steps and pillars were still there, though chipped and leaning. She couldn't wait to talk with Brian to see if he could possibly straighten them out. Then she was going to paint them white like they used to be.

It was a perfect home for them, and it was also filled with perfect memories. Not only had she and her sister and brother and cousins played in its grassy yard, but so had her daddy and Aunt Anna and Aunt Ella and all the Thaxtons.

Bennett was only six years old when Papa Thaxton built the home place. She smiled to herself. No wonder he was so tickled with the idea that it was back in the family.

And without a down payment!

She pondered the seventy-five dollars that she had given to the church while Sydney snuggled up close to her back. *God does work in mysterious ways,* she thought again as a cow lowed in the distance, and she pulled the blanket up close.

Her thoughts switched to the basement and what Ryan had mentioned when they were moving in. "One day, Mom, when we can afford it…we might fix up a room down here for me. Then Sydney can have my room." She stared out the window at the white oak silhouetted in the half moon and vaguely remembered her papa's woodshed that used to sit beneath it and the chicken house beside it. She had sat mesmerized for what seemed like hours, entranced with the baby chicks that chirped and nudged one another aside to get closer to the warm brooder light, and she remembered waking to the sound of the rooster crowing.

You can't go home again Thomas Wolfe said.

She knew technically it was true. But yet, it was the deep yearning in one's heart to return to their childhood, to return to the nostalgic memories carried with them throughout life. And she turned over to sleep, to wait for the rooster's crowing.

CHAPTER TWENTY-FOUR

PRESENT

"MILE POST 421!"

Early morning sunrays streamed over the mountainside, illuminating a startling vista as far as Wade could see. Lush foliage glistened, wet with dew. Vibrant colorful trees and thick tangled underbrush embraced the winding Parkway as the RV pushed up the incline and on through Devil's Courthouse Tunnel.

"Lots of spruces," he remarked with a yawn. "Uh-oh." He was staring down at the instrument panel.

"What is it?" Joellen stared at it, too.

"The rear ABS light just came on."

"What's that?"

"The automatic breaking system."

"That doesn't sound too good."

Not wanting her to worry, he replied, "Oh, it's nothing to be concerned about. It'll be all right."

She didn't know anything about an ABS light, must be something else new. Every time she turned around there was something new cropping up as if she didn't have enough already to deal with. Newfangled cell phones that took pictures, new voting machines, internet banking, and they kept pushing her to pay her bills on it. Well, she just wasn't ready for that! There was a certain satisfaction in writing out a check, sticking it in an envelope, stamping it—though she had to admit she liked the self-sticking stamps—and dropping it in the mailbox. There! Another one paid! And just the other day, before coming on the trip, she had sat down to the computer to research some old dances of the sixties. While caught up in a soothing, nostalgic mood, suddenly the thing spoke.

"He-l-l-o!"

She had practically come up out of her chair. She didn't care for inanimate objects talking to her. There was enough with people!

They wound around the seemingly endless road and approached Haywood-Jackson overlook. Wade swerved into it. "Elevation 6020," he read and shut off the motor. Joellen hopped out to take some pictures of the beautiful mountain ash. Then they continued on, passing through one of the longest tunnels, Pinnacle Ridge.

"I'm going to miss them," she said, realizing they were nearing the end.

"The tunnels?"

"...and the mountains. There's a peace up here like no-where else." They drove on quietly for a while, her mind returning to the little brick house, and to the small side porch with the two rockers that Brian had found in a dump and given her. She had painted them white, and at night, after working all day, after the children were in bed, she'd sit down in one to spend a little time with God.

> *...and the voice I hear*
> *Falling on my ear*
> *The Son of God discloses*
> *And He walks with me*
> *And He talks with me...*

RYAN AND SYDNEY flourished on Thaxton's Lane. They roamed the same forests and pastures that she had as a child and her father before her. They waded the same creeks, they climbed the same trees, and they rode their sleds down the same sloping snowy hillsides. They especially looked forward to Saturdays! For on Saturday mornings Granddaddy Bennett stopped by to pick them up for the day. Bennett was retired now and looked forward to it, as well. It broke his heart to see Ryan and Sydney without a father. Dale was no longer in the picture, having removed himself not only physically but emotionally. Bennett could not understand such a man.

He knew, of course, that Joellen was the one who had finally severed the relationship, and he was glad for that. It was long overdue. Still he couldn't understand how Dale could totally cut himself off from the children, but Joellen understood. Dale saw them as a unit—she and Ryan and Sydney—and he was unable to separate them.

Joellen hammered the nail into the two by four. They were downstairs working on Ryan's room, her daddy, Daniel, Brian, the children and her. Deep in thought, she was pondering how to buy the carpet since it was to be a fairly large room. She had already spotted a red plaid carpet with vivid yellow lines crisscrossing through it, horizontally and vertically, and hoped she could afford it. It would match the soft yellow paint and certainly brighten up the room in the basement. A small radio perched between the open framing blared statically with lively country music, drowning out the hammering. Ryan beamed with pleasure. A teenager now, he needed his own space. Sydney raced in and out between the studs and beneath the ladders. When it was finished, she would have Ryan's room, and she couldn't wait!

Bennett skillfully pounded away, his stained, wrinkled nail apron stuffed with eightpenny nails. Joellen watched him. He was getting old. She didn't like to think about that. He had had a hard life with her mother's sickness, but he was happy today, helping with the room. It was his expertise that made it possible. He supervised, and they followed his directions. It was what made him tick, doing for others, and he was especially happy to be working on the little house, taking pride in it like it was his own.

"Granddaddy, can you take me to K-Mart?" Sydney nagged, scooting under his ladder.

"How am I gonna do that and build this here room?" he teased, all the while enjoying the warm sense of being needed.

"When you finish, will you?" she persisted.

"We'll see. I 'spect we'll be here all night though."

"No you won't!"

"*OUCH!*" Brian yelled out.

"Mash your finger?" Daniel mocked.

He nodded, wringing his sore finger in the air. Suddenly the music stopped.

We interrupt this radio program for breaking news. Elvis Presley, the King of Rock and Roll, has died....

Joellen stopped hammering. *It couldn't be!* Not Elvis...so full of life...just past forty. She was stunned.

"You can put the hammer down, Joellen," Daniel said, and she realized she still had it suspended in air.

Elvis can't be dead!

Bennett thrust the nail back into his apron. "Did y'all hear that?" Everyone nodded quietly, almost reverently.

375

"Gosh, that's hard to believe." Brian stared at Joellen. "And he was scheduled to come to the Roanoke Civic Center soon."

A strange emotion gripped Joellen, a profound sadness, a sense of loss.

"Did you have tickets to see him?" Brian asked, watching her oddly.

She shook her head.

"Did you ever see him in person?"

Again she shook her head.

"Why not?" Brian was curious, knowing that she had loved Elvis as much as he had loved the Beatles.

"Because...I...well, as a Christian, I don't think we should idolize other humans...and I was concerned how I might act myself...if I ever saw him."

He nodded understandingly.

"I'll be back." She hurried up the stairs, and Brian looked at his father, who went back to hammering.

THREE YEARS PASSED, three happy years. Sydney grew into a full-fledged tomboy, climbing trees, and keeping up with Ryan and the other neighborhood boys. Joellen watched them out of the big picture window, a whole gang of them, not much different from the *Little Rascals* in some ways—all ages, but bonded together in one merry group. Ryan was the oldest, and would be the first to leave. He was starting his senior year and had more important things on his mind now.

Joellen's paycheck had steadily increased, receiving salary plus commission, and she was able to buy Ryan several outfits for his senior year, the first time he had received this many new school clothes at one time.

"All these!" he exclaimed. "You're going to buy them all?"

"You're a senior this year, and you should have more clothes." His handsome young face beamed.

"What about me?" Sydney pouted, standing beside him. "Do I get this many, too?"

"Not this year. But after Ryan finishes, it'll be your turn."

"Shucks," she turned and scooted off.

But just when things were looking up, her car broke down.

"Gonna cost'ya fo' hundred dollars, Miss," the auto repairman said.

Joellen caught her breath. *Four hundred dollars!*

Suddenly the floor beneath her feet was being pulled out from under her. Where in the world would she get four hundred dollars?

"I kin fix'er up for ya' temporarily. Might keep'er goin' another month or so, but it's playin' out like I told ya'. Gonna cost'ya fo' hundred dollars for the new part and labor."

She left the car, feeling mired down in quicksand and sinking deeper and deeper. It might as well be four thousand dollars! She couldn't think of anyone to go to for help, certainly not her poor daddy. And she couldn't go to Aunt Anna. She had already helped her far too much; besides, she didn't have that kind of money either. There was her friend, Miriam, but she couldn't ask her. It was just too much! What was she going to do? That night she picked up her Bible and turned to her favorite chapter in Philippians to read… *Be careful for nothing; but in every thing by prayer and supplication with thanksgiving let your requests be made known unto God.'*

And she prayed.

The next morning she caught a ride to work. Always the first one to arrive, she usually unlocked for the others, but when she reached into her pocketbook for her key, she realized she had left it on the key ring. And the key ring was at the auto repair shop.

She glanced at her watch. She would have to wait about a half hour before someone else arrived, and it was cold in the foyer. The minor irritation following her car dilemma suddenly brought tears to her eyes, and she sank down on the concrete steps in the enclosed stairwell, fighting them. The magnitude of her plight was overwhelming. She was barely making it as it was with the added costs of Ryan's senior year, and she knew it was no use in going back to court for child support. It never did any good. Dale either wasn't working or he avoided it. She had made it so far without it but now four hundred dollars! She must not cry! Her makeup would smear, and everyone would know she had been crying. She must be strong! God would help her. Hadn't he always?

Then why was she feeling so low? So hopeless? She stared out the huge plate glass window in the stairwell, flanked by tall green shrubs pressing in against it. Why was life so hard? Always so hard? She crouched there on the steps, feeling sorry for herself, and stared into the thick shrubs with teary eyes. Suddenly a small bird flew into them. It perched there quietly, directly in front of her.

His eye is on the sparrow....

It was as if God was pointing out His sovereign care, reminding her of His promise. Everything was going to be all right—she knew it was going to be all right! *His eye is on the sparrow...and I know He watches me.*

WHEN SHE WENT back to the garage, she was in for a surprise.

"Was able to fix'er up without the new part...think she might be all right for a while longer. Can't promise ya' though...might act up again. If'n it does, ya' gonna need that part I was tellin' ya' 'bout."

"Thank you, Lord," she sighed as she climbed into the car.

Just like he said, it did all right for a couple of weeks. Then one day when she went out for lunch, it wouldn't start. She tried and tried, but it would only grind and grind.

"*R-r-r-r.*"

Her boss, Mr. Norberg, privately watched from his upstairs office window. He knew he should go to her rescue, but he didn't know anything about cars! So what could he do? He turned back to his paperwork but couldn't concentrate. He leaned over to the window again.

She was still down there.

Doggone it! Why did she have to have that old clunker anyway? But he knew why. She couldn't afford anything better. Mr. Norberg was a fine man and a kind man, but he had so much already to look after! His father, God rest his soul, a successful inventor, had left him a wealthy man, and it was up to him to preserve it, and he struggled to do just that, to protect the family fortune and hopefully increase it. There was a lot to tend to!

R-r-r-r.

The struggling grind of the sick motor drifted up to his window. There was always someone needing something! But Joellen did try, and he appreciated her loyalty to his small business. He leaned over again to peer out the window.

R-r-r-r.

Well, he might as well go down there! Reluctantly, he stood up and headed for the door and down the steps. He didn't know what in the world he could do, but as her boss, as a man, he had to at least try.

R-r-r-r.

"What's the matter with it?" he asked awkwardly, standing there in his immaculate suit and tie.

Joellen looked up embarrassed. "It won't start...I guess it's that same problem...."

"Here, let me try it."

She got out, and he sat down in the bucket seat, stretching himself backward to get a proper position....

BANG.

Mr. Norberg was lying prostrate, his head on the back seat. "What...what...what happened?" he gasped, struggling to get up.

"I'm sorry," she laughed, unable to restrain herself. "I don't mean to laugh, but you look so...so...."

He crawled out, obviously frustrated. "What happened?"

"The plank fell out."

"The what?"

"The plank." She reached down in the back for the rough-hewn plank that had slid out from behind the seat. "I have to use it to prop the seat up because the seat's broken." The astounded look on Mr. Norberg's face told all.

"Ah…Joellen…how about coming back up to my office…we need to talk." He hurriedly marched back to the building, shaking the dust off his suit, and shaking his head as he ascended the steps. *Never in all my life!*

She followed. Once in his office, he smoothed back thin wisps of graying hair. "Joellen, you know you've been doing quite well with your sales, commendable, in fact, and I have been thinking of starting you on a quarterly bonus program as compensation. I was planning on beginning next quarter…but…well, I think we need to do something sooner!"

She remembered the little bird in the bush.

"I think you need to look for another car."

"Yes, sir…."

"Do you have anything in mind?"

Her heart leapt for joy. "No, sir, but I can look."

"Why don't you do just that. I don't think you should worry about fixing that old…I mean your car up. You need something else…more reliable."

She nodded, hardly able to conceal her happiness.

"I'm going to write you out a check for your first bonus…and I hope it will help."

"MILE POST 440. Just twenty-nine more miles to go." Wade pulled over to an overlook. Immediately they were invaded by swarms of ladybugs encircling the RV, alighting on the windshield and windows.

"O-o-o-h…just look at them!" The tiny orange hard-shelled bugs with black spots were everywhere.

"Leave them alone." Wade settled back in his seat. "They've got to be somewhere, too."

"But I don't want them in the RV!"

He pulled back onto the Parkway. "It's still on."

381

"What?"

"The ABS light."

"I thought you said it was okay."

"It is…I hope so anyway."

Joellen decided it was time to pray. She certainly didn't want to break down way up in the mountains. Even though she would love to stay forever, there were things and people awaiting her down in the valley. That's life, she thought, mountains and valleys. Though she had experienced many deep dark valleys, especially in her younger days, God had opened up glorious mountaintops for her, as well. She recalled all those mountaintop experiences. It was around the time that she bought her new car that things began to look up. She smiled at the memory of Sydney and how she had tried to help.

They had pulled into the Amherst Chevrolet dealership late one evening, and she was showing the dealer her old car, hoping for a good trade-in. Sydney was quietly sitting in the back seat. The dealer seemed interested.

"Well, looks like a pretty good car," he commented, straining to make a proper assessment in the fading light.

Suddenly Sydney came running around the side of the car, lugging the large metal piece that had fallen out from the seat months ago—the reason for the plank. "And here's another piece that goes with it, too," she said proudly.

Joellen wanted to disappear.

THEIR LIVES WERE changing, and Joellen saw God's hand in it all. How could she ever thank Him for all His blessings?

It came to her while visiting an old lady across the road from their house. Mr. and Mrs. Willows, way past eighty,

lived there, but one day Joellen noticed a funeral arrange-
ment posted beside their door.

Mr. Willows had died.

She called on the elderly lady and listened to her story.
A story worthy to be told, the legacy of a couple sticking
together through thick and thin, until one passed on into
eternity. Mrs. Willows' husband had been less than a model
husband, a boisterous, drinking man, but the old woman
had loved him and stuck with him.

Joellen returned home with a passion.

It wasn't a new passion, but a renewed one. She had
always wanted to write a book. Now she had the story! It
wasn't Mrs. Willows' story exactly, even though she had
inspired it. Joellen felt a need to write such a story. Perhaps
because of her own failed marriage, perhaps because the
story just needed to be told—whatever the reason, she was
going to write it.

THE OFFICE BUILDING was quiet. It was eight o'clock
in the morning, and Joellen had another thirty minutes before the others showed up. Rain poured outside, and she
slipped a blank sheet of paper into the new IBM Selectric
typewriter. The drone of the rhythmic raindrops beating
against the large plate glass windows lulled her into a contemplative mood. She had always loved rain. Maybe it was
a good omen, and she scooted the rollaway chair up close
and began to type.

To Death Do Us Part

There! A good, sound title. As the rain washed down
in slanting sheets, the keys banged away, and Joellen was
transported into another world—a world of words, a creative world to lose herself in when times got hard, and a

world that no one could alter but her, no one could mess up but her.

Once started, she couldn't stop. Every morning she rushed to the office in order to work on her book before the regular day began. Evenings, she proofread and corrected. It got her up in the morning and put her to bed at night.

"You're writing a book?" her co-worker inquired skeptically.

She nodded.

"But how do you know how to write a book?"

She didn't have an answer.

"It just seems like a big undertaking, if you ask me."

Afterwards, she kept quiet about it, besides it was just between her and God. If He wanted her to do it, she would, and she believed that He was guiding her to do so.

"Lord, please give me the words," she prayed daily when she sat down at the typewriter. Days passed into weeks, weeks into months, the manuscript grew thicker and her passion grew stronger. The story took on a soul of its own, breathing life into its characters. She couldn't wait to get back to it, to find out what they wanted to do next! Her excitement mounted, and she wished she could share it with someone but was afraid to. Suppose they didn't like it?

Mr. Norberg retired, and the employment agency was swallowed up by an international firm, and, in turn, her job was restructured, significantly reducing her salary. The timing couldn't have been worse, right in the middle of Ryan's senior year, already a taxing time. It drove her to her knees. She was struggling to make the house payment, the school payments and help Ryan buy a secondhand car, a shiny gold Duster that he wanted very badly. They had bought an old rusted-out Mustang for his first car, for a small fee, but this one was more. Ryan was already working two part-time jobs to help out. They decided to have a yard sale.

"I'll sell my gun, Mom…and my bicycle."

The rifle had been his Christmas gift, and he cleaned and polished it regularly. And he loved his bicycle; he had always loved bicycles, but Ryan was growing up. She remembered what the school dean said, "You know, Ryan's the only one in the class who really knows what he wants to do with his life!" That's why she had agreed for him to join the Air Force the beginning of his senior year on what they termed "the delayed entry program." This way, he explained, it would give him a jump on his military career.

After the employment agency was taken over by the international firm, and after they had lived through the stringent cutback in her salary, things changed. Joellen received a decent promotion in just ten months into sales, and then quickly into management, which offered more opportunities than she ever imagined. God's blessings abounded, and she found herself in some of the most exclusive resorts in the country on weeklong business trips and conferences, experiencing a side of life that she never dreamed of. It reminded her of what Paul had to say to the Philippians.

For I have learned, in whatsoever state I am, therewith to be content. I know both how to be abased, and I know how to abound…

CHAPTER TWENTY-FIVE

PRESENT

"IT'S DEFINITELY A true fall day," Wade attempted to alleviate Joellen's concern. She watched the crisp leaves somersaulting to the pavement in front of them, their shimmering yellow leaves descending in dazzling sunlight. They resembled shiny nuggets of gold, and the RV speared right through them.

"Balsam Mountain," he read.

They passed through Lickstone Ridge Tunnel and on by the Qualla Indian Reservation. "Reminds me of those Indian Reservations in South Dakota," he kidded. "The things you get me into."

She smiled at him, remembering all those miles they drove through the Standing Rock Indian Reservation and the Cheyenne River Indian Reservation in research for a book, and they didn't find out until later that it wasn't exactly the wisest thing to do. There are often bitter sentiments, Joellen was later enlightened by a South Dakotan, and if one were to break down, he might just stay broken down way out in the middle of those vast plains.

She looked over at Wade and doubted it could have happened to them. In the middle of the wind-swept prairie that stretched for miles and miles all around, they were suddenly stopped behind a line of vehicles at a roadblock. Their large boxy camper jolted to a stop, and all eyes were upon them. Wade rolled down his window and thrust out his hand. "Hello there, buddy…problem up ahead?"

The Indians looked up in surprise, carefully surveyed the RV with Virginia tags and its gregarious driver, then smiled back. "It's okay. You'll be on your way soon."

"Beautiful country," Wade continued.

They nodded, and soon he was engaged in deep conversation, enjoying himself immensely. The engines started up, and the vehicles began to slowly inch forward. Wade stuck out his hand to shake the nearest hand, and suddenly was vigorously shaking several. Just as the Bible says, she thought, to have friends, you have to be friendly. And everyone was Wade's friend.

"Milepost 462," he announced.

Soon they were entering Rattlesnake Mountain Tunnel. "Don't like that name!"

Joellen agreed.

"Well, mountains are full of them," he added. "…no doubt about that, all these mountains, Virginia, North Carolina, and the rest."

"But we don't see them most of the time, and I'm glad. My Minnesota friends often asked, 'How do you guys stand living with all those snakes?' I guess they envisioned snakes crawling all over the place."

Wade chuckled. "Snakes don't want to meet up with us anymore than we want to meet up with them. Think this might be the last one. Sherill Cove Tunnel."

"Really?"

"Don't have much further to go." They entered the dark tunnel, and when they emerged back into the piercing sunlight, Joellen noticed a lone ladybug still clinging to the windshield. "She's going home with us, I guess."

Wade didn't say a word, but waited for the next pullover, and she knew exactly what he was up to. He pulled over, got out and ever so gently lifted the ladybug off and carried it over to a clump of tall grass. "Now, little lady, here's a new home for you."

She smiled in wonderment again. A rugged man, a strong man, "primitive," the kids called him in jest, but he had a unique tenderness about him.

Thank you, Lord.

Wade Farrar was definitely an answer to prayer.

THUNDER ROLLED AND lightning flashed, streaking the blackened sky above the small brick house on Thaxton's Lane. It was two o'clock in the morning, and Joellen lay still in her bed.

She hoped the children would stay asleep. There was no sound from Sydney's bedroom across the hall or from Ryan downstairs. He usually slept soundly but not Sydney. Another bolt of thunder reverberated throughout the house, sending chills up her spine, and she pulled the blanket up snugly about her, remembering her daddy's frequent declaration. *"I believe there's something in the ground here that draws the lightning!"*

She felt uneasy.

She had heard his story repeated more than once about lightning striking the old gum tree at the end of the back yard when he was a mere boy. "Split it right down the middle and fire flew out like nothin' you ever saw!"

Then there was the time right after she and the children had moved in when lightning blew up their television, and it wasn't even on. A few months later, it burned out wires on their kitchen stove. So at the least hint of a storm, she raced to unplug everything. Had she missed anything? She went down the list: the television, stove, refrigerator…another bolt of lightning lit up the bedroom. Thunder crashed, seemingly shaking the foundation of the house, and Joellen sprang out of the way as Sydney careened around the doorway and vaulted in beside her.

"It's all right." She hugged her tightly as another boom of thunder resounded, then blaring sirens! Joellen jumped up with Sydney clinging to her.

"Let go, Sydney. Let me see what's going on." She peeled off her hands as red blinking lights flashed throughout the dark house, alternating with streaks of lightning.

"Mama!" Sydney was terrified. She grabbed her hand and flew to the door just in time to see a long red fire truck pass across her back yard and yellow-suited firemen whipping all over the place.

Alarmed, she ran to get Ryan, but a fireman was knocking at her door. "Ma'am, it's not your house…but the one beside you!" She was immediately relieved, but thought of poor Mrs. Carlson, the elderly widow next door. She dashed to the living room window and could see the fiery glow before she jerked the curtains aside. Raging flames were shooting high into the stormy night, into the heavy rain. Sparks were dancing dangerously close to their house and into the tall oak tree between them! She raced to the stairs.

"Ryan, get up! Mrs. Carlson's house trailer is on fire!"

Grabbing her trench coat out of the closet, she pulled it on. "Sydney, get your coat!" They fled outside into the driving rain and around the corner of the house as the back yard streaked with jagged lightning. Already the firemen were battling the hot flames with their massive wriggling hoses that bulged and writhed like huge pythons. She stood there in the rain, hugging Sydney close to her beneath the umbrella, and watched as they efficiently went about their business, putting out the fire. Mrs. Carlson had gone next door when the storm started and was still there.

The storm eventually subsided, and the lightning ceased. Only an occasional thunder could be heard, as it rolled and rumbled off into the distance. Joellen breathed a sigh of relief, while staring up into her oak tree for damage.

"Hi, you're Joellen, aren't you?" The tall fireman appeared out of nowhere.

"Yes," she nodded, staring at the water dripping off his fireman's hat.

"I'm Wade Farrar. We went to school together. Remember?"

IT WOULD BE more than a year before she met up with Wade Farrar again, and a lot happened that year. Ryan graduated from the Christian school and prepared to leave for the United States Air Force. His dream from the time he was a boy, he was happy to be fulfilling it but couldn't shake the sadness of leaving his mother and little sister.

Who would take care of them?

Filling the role of man of the house since his youth, it bothered him to leave them alone now. It was a balmy spring day, and he watched his mom as she weeded the small strawberry garden at the edge of the back yard. Her friend Miriam was helping.

"This is killing my back!" Miriam stood up, stretching. "You need to have a man doing this!" she kidded.

"Yeah, Mom, you do," Ryan agreed.

Stunned, both she and Miriam stared at him.

"It's true, Mom. If you don't hurry up and find somebody, you'll be too old!" he kidded, but she caught the underlying seriousness. Ryan had always insisted that she not date ever since his father exited their lives. Not that she ever wanted to, but he had made it clear that he was man of the house. Even had she wanted to date, she wouldn't have because of his strong feelings. He had been hurt too much, and she would not add to it.

"Well, well, well," Miriam chided him. "What's this all about?"

"Just what I said, she's not getting any younger!"

Miriam winked at Joellen, who continued pulling the strangling weeds from her delicate strawberry plants, but Joellen understood that it was his way of letting her know that it was time. She had no intention of dating, but it was good to know that if anything ever did happen, he was okay with it. She looked up from the strawberry patch. "Well, you've done a one-eighty!"

"Like I said, you're not getting any younger," he repeated, laughing awkwardly. She smiled at him, enjoying the tender moment of understanding between them, but dreading the thought of him leaving. He had been a part of her since she was a teenager!

THE TRAILWAYS BUS pulled out of the Fifth Street terminal in downtown Lynchburg, and Joellen fought back the tears. She must be strong. She clutched Sydney's hand and sought to control the swirling emotions within. She watched Ryan's smiling face as he waved behind the closed window. Then the bus drove off. With a trembling hand, she waved back. She waved frantically as if by waving it would bring him back.

But the bus disappeared.

A void, a deep, wide void filled her being. *He was gone.*

How could he be gone? Just yesterday he was playing with his little green soldiers at her feet. And he was riding his skateboard up and down Thaxton's Lane; just yesterday he was sleigh-riding down the hilly pasture. How could he be gone?

Tears stung her eyes.

"We gonna go now?" Sydney asked.

She nodded and glanced behind her, to where the old, yellow tenement house used to stand on Clay Street, to where Ryan had ridden his little red fire engine up and down the long common hallway. She stared at the spot where the tiny back yard with its black dirt used to be, where he pushed his little trucks.

How could he be gone?

Slowly she turned to walk back to the car. Sydney followed and jumped in the front seat beside her. She switched on the engine.

"Why's he going to Richmond, Mom?"

"Because that's his orders, what he was told to do. He will fly out of Richmond to Texas where he will go through basic training."

"And he's going to San Antonio where I was born, right?"

"That's right."

"It's hot in here!"

"Roll your window down. It'll get cool once we start moving." She drove down Fifth Street, feeling only half alive. Part of her had been wrenched away on that Trailways bus. She wondered if he would remember the base. It had been so long ago, and he was just a little fellow. Would he remember those Texas burrs? An enormous guilt swept over her. Had she spent enough time with him? Had she played with him enough? Had she loved him enough?

Tears rolled down her face. All she could think of was that she had been so busy making a living for them that… the years had silently slipped away.

And she couldn't go back!

Sydney was staring at her. "You crying, Mom?"

"I'll be all right. It's just sad, you know…your brother leaving…."

"But he was happy, Mom. I could tell. He wanted to go in the Air Force."

"I know, Sydney…I know…."

They crossed Williams Viaduct, crossed the placid waters of the James to Amherst County. They climbed the steep hill, the same steep hill that her father had climbed for many years, and his papa before him in his horse and buggy. A brooding, pensive mood settled over her. Was this what life was all about? Always loving, always leaving? Had her father felt this way when she left home? Had his papa before him?

She pulled into the driveway, and Sydney jumped out and scampered off down the road, anxious to see her friends. Joellen reluctantly turned the key in the lock, the metallic sound louder than usual. She opened the door, listening to the familiar squeak that magnified itself, and entered the kitchen, acutely aware of the silence. She stood there. The tiny, almost imperceptible, faucet drip echoed throughout the still house. Drip…drip…drip. She passed through the small hallway and into the bathroom.

It was bare!

His brush was gone, his shaving crème, his cologne… everything was gone! The countertop was empty, and she cried.

THE STACK OF Ryan's letters was lying on the dresser. Joellen stared at them. She would have to write him tonight. They corresponded regularly, but not as much as during those first days when he was in basic training at Lackland. Then she had written him every day. But now he was growing more away from her and didn't need her daily letters as much. It was as it should be, she sighed. She wouldn't have it any other way, but still it saddened her.

He was stationed in England at Alconbury Royal Air Force Base. She had been awfully upset when he received the orders and had personally made a visit to the Recruitment Office to question the recruiter. "*Why would you send an eighteen year old way across the ocean all the way to England for two years? Why not send the older ones?*"

The handsome young recruiter had smiled indulgently and explained that it would be the best thing in the world for him. Well, maybe, she thought. But how would he deal with being gone for two years? How would she deal with it?

It had been six months already.

She opened her closet again, scanning the neatly hanging outfits. She would tell Ryan about the class reunion in her letter tonight and wondered what he would think of it. She wondered herself.

Twenty years!

Had it been twenty years since she walked down that aisle? She wondered about Bill...and Diane...and Harry. Everybody! What would they look like? And what would they think of her? What would she wear? My goodness, she thought, what *will* I wear?

It was going to be a relatively small group, of that much she knew. Everyone was coming as couples, most were married couples, but they would all be paired up. All but her! Every time she thought of that, she got cold feet.

Grabbing a black dress and white jacket out of the closet, she knew she had to go. She couldn't back out now. She was on the committee! Anyway, it didn't matter. She was used to going places by herself. She had been doing so for almost eight years now. Laying the dress and jacket on the bed, she studied the effect. Oh well, it would work. She turned back to the mirror, immediately pulling her shoulders back, and crept in closer, then stretched her eyes wide open. It was those crow's feet...the ones that Virgie had teased her about. She'd predicted this! Way back when they were welding coils together at General Electric, she'd predicted it. She remembered how she had begun giggling and couldn't stop.

"What's so funny?" she'd asked.

"It's those crow's feet...." Virgie kept giggling.

"Those what?"

"You know, the wrinkles in the corners of your eyes! By the time you get old, you'll be all dried up."

"...and I suppose you won't!" she had retorted.

Virgie shook her head and laughed even harder. "We don't dry up. I'll still be looking young when you're all wrinkled! Just you wait and see." And sure enough, the last time she had seen Virgie, she looked as young as she had at General Electric years ago. Not fair!

She smiled at herself in the mirror, recalling that time. It was Lydia's wedding, Virgie's oldest daughter, and Ryan had accompanied her. She was proud of her tall handsome son. The wedding was held at Scott Zion, Virgie's church, and she and Ryan were probably the only white people there. The church was packed, and for the first time she realized how Virgie must have felt all her life with the tables turned.

She leaned in closer to the mirror to smooth out the crow's feet, but they only sprang back when she removed her fingers. *Virgie was right!* Well, I probably won't be the only one. We're all in the same boat.

AUTOMOBILES SWEPT BY in the fast lane, careening around long curves in the dark night. Joellen nervously gripped the steering wheel, her hands hot and sweaty, wiping first one, then the other on her black dress, then taking long deep breaths, inhaling and exhaling. It was the night.

The 20th High School Class Reunion.

Why was she so anxious? It was only a small group of old classmates, and she had certainly attended far more important and more stressful events, but the tense feeling wouldn't ease. In fact, the more she concentrated on it, the more it increased. This was ridiculous. She tried to divert her attention, noticing the constant traffic sweeping past and the darkness enveloping her, which only caused her to feel more alone. She glanced up into the rearview mirror and wondered if her makeup looked okay. Did she have on too much? Maybe she should have applied a little more. It was nighttime after all. Oh well, too late now.

How did I get myself into this?

I'd rather be going anywhere than to this class reunion! I must be nuts! Anyplace at all! Even to work…or to the doctor…or the gynecologist. Anyplace…well, maybe not the dentist! She kept inhaling and exhaling as she sped down the expressway, then looked up into the night sky. Large white clouds sailed across it like Spanish galleons out of history.

"Lord, I don't like going to this class reunion all alone! In fact, I get tired of always being alone. It sure would be nice to have someone on this earth to be with me…the way You meant for it to be. But if You want me to be alone, I accept it, Lord. Thy will be done. Just please give me a full life…."

SHE PULLED INTO the already crowded parking lot and shut off the engine. Well, here goes. She could handle it. She was used to putting on a face and smiling and pretending. She was used to exuding confidence, even if she didn't feel confident. It was part of her job. We all learn that basic principle in the business world, she reminded herself, comparing it to a Shakespearean drama with myriad characters acting out their respective roles, donning their particular costumes, incognito, hiding behind their individual masks, the real people mysteriously hidden from view. Who were the real people?

She was one!

Briskly and self-assuredly, she clutched her shoulder bag and marched into the Sheraton Inn, making her way to the assigned dining room. Before pulling open the door, she could already see a crowd. Her confidence quickly dwindled, and her knees went watery. She fought her ever-present enemy, feeling the rush of blood sprouting upward to transform her face into a flaming turnip before the 20th High School Class Reunion.

"Joellen Thaxton…my, my…it's been years!"

Who in the world? Oh my gosh! It's Shirley McDonald!

"It sure has," she responded as quickly as possible. "Well, looks like we have a good showing so far." Awkwardly she glanced around the room full of strangers, who slowly and subtly were reverting back into teenagers, teenagers from the fifties and sixties, teenagers with many added pounds, teenagers with different color hair or no hair!

Laughter and joking merged with the soft background music, gradually relieving some of her tension. And there was Miss Mavis! She hadn't changed a bit. Looking old as Methuselah, but no older than when she was her homeroom teacher. She glanced from one to another, struggling to make the proper connections, but her head was spinning. It was quickly apparent that tonight would be a night to remember.

She had no idea!

IT WAS AFTER midnight, and she tossed and turned in a creepy, bizarre world. Images of teenagers flitted across her path, with bulging stomachs, balding heads, and youthful skin now weathered and wrinkled. They danced before her foolishly with peals of laughter, weirdly throwing pencils, erasers, and literature books high into the air. The path was littered with them, and she knelt to pick them up, especially the literature books. There were so many! Why must they throw the literature books away?

She sat up. What a crazy dream!

She must get some sleep. It was over, finally over. After all the anxious anticipation and all the daily dreading, it wasn't so bad after all. In fact, she had enjoyed it for the most part, particularly winning the little contest for *The Least Changed*. Of course, it was understandable. All the girls who had boasted the Annette Funicello figure in high school now bulged in their skirts. At last there was some advantage to being the skinniest kid in class. She had finally caught up!

She pulled the blanket up around her and stared out the window beside her bed, into the wee morning hours. It's strange, she thought, gazing up at the quarter moon, how those few high school years played such an integral role in her life. Certainly, she had experienced much since then, traveled many miles, seen a lot and met a lot of people. But, yet, those few high school years had had a greater impact on her than any of the others. It was as if time stood still during those years, like an old picture that had posted itself within a corner of her mind to go with her throughout life.

She peered at the alarm clock on the dresser. Twelve forty-five! My goodness, she must get some sleep. Tomorrow was Sunday. If only she could quiet her hectic mind and escape the class reunion. She glanced once more out the window. The moon disappeared behind a fast moving cloud, and she closed her eyes and fell asleep reciting the nostalgic poem she had written for the night.

What is that ringing…familiar ringing?
School bells? Is it school bells?
But the old school house has long been gone
And with it the old, old bells

What is that rustling, familiar sound?
Could it be the pages turning?
Revealing knowledge to be found
But there is no one learning

What is that laughing that we hear?
Echoing off the worn old halls,
The laughing youth of yesteryear
Jubilant, excited, one and all,
Who is that dressed in blue and gold?

So young and very bold,
Could it be the class of '62
My tearful eyes behold….

WADE FARRAR TUMBLED into bed, and thought of the small dark-haired lady who had read that touching poem. She was dressed in black and white, quite petite, and he had made up his mind. He was going to call her even if she did turn him down.

Not only was she small and dark-haired, she was a church-going girl. She met his criteria. He had carried this picture in his mind for years, the girl that he might one day marry. Wade was an eligible bachelor and until recently had lived at home, the only child of elderly, adoring parents. He didn't live at home all those years because he had to, but for economic reasons. Wade liked to make money, not spend it. He had inherited the frugal spirit of his parents.

As he rolled into a ball of tangled blankets, he remembered the first time he had seen Joellen, really seen her. It was the night of the fire over a year ago, and his interest had been stirred then. She was in that khaki trench coat, huddled beneath a big black umbrella, as the rain poured down in sheets midst thunder and lightning. It was the first time he had seen her since high school, when she and her friends had hung onto the backdrop of the ball field watching them play. Cute little girls, he thought to himself, and she was still cute.

Gosh, he couldn't wait to call her.

Joellen jerked off her shoes, the first thing she did every day when she got home. Boy, what a Monday! She was tired already and had four more days to go. Though she knew she shouldn't, she lived for the weekends. She couldn't help it. Aunt Anna said she was wishing her life away. Oh well, you had to have something to look forward to, and this weekend was it. She didn't have to fret about any old class reunion now. She could stay up late Friday night, and lie on the sofa with a book in her hand as long as she wanted. Sydney would fall asleep, and she would lie there long after twilight had turned to dusk and dusk to night. She would lie there reading to her heart's content and fall asleep with the book spread open on her stomach. Usually it was one or two in the morning, but that was okay because she could sleep in late. It would be Saturday. How could she not wish for the weekends?

She reached for the leftover pot roast in the refrigerator and stuck it in the preheated oven. The congealed grease soon bubbled over, and its savory fragrance filled the kitchen. So often on a Saturday she'd put one on, sometimes even getting up before seven to cut up the potatoes, carrots, and onions, and cram them into the crockpot with a chunk of beef and a little salt and pepper. She'd set the timer to slow cooking and then climb back in bed for another hour or two. She enjoyed working in the yard all day, coming into the house filled with its delicious aroma, and anticipating dinner. Ryan had loved it, too.

"When's it gonna be ready, Mom?" he'd ask repeatedly.

She wished she could scoop up a steaming helping for him now, but she was glad that he was finally adjusting to life in England. Though he complained of how *old* everything was, at least he seemed to be enjoying a few pleasures in his off time. His letters described canoeing down the rivers and streams with his friends, biking for miles and miles over rolling countryside, and generally experiencing the British life. It sounded like lots of fun.

She grasped the head of lettuce from the refrigerator bin and carried it to the sink, holding it under the surging faucet. Sydney liked salads. Rinsing the lettuce, she glanced out the kitchen window at the old house across the road... her inspiration for *To Death Do Us Part*. Guilt hammered her again. She needed to get on with it, do something with the bulky manuscript stuffed in a bedroom drawer. But time was sweeping her along, and she just couldn't seem to get to it! There was always something to do, and soon it would be grass cutting time again. Then she would really miss Ryan. And there were the porches that needed painting. She had already bought the paint and….

The phone rang.

Wiping her hands on the dishtowel hanging from the junk drawer, she grabbed it. "Hello."

There was a pause. "Is this Joellen?"

It was a man's voice. *Who could it be?* "Yes."

"This is Wade Farrar."

Even before he finished saying his first name, she knew it was him. But he had been with someone else at the reunion. Why was he calling her?

"I saw you at the class reunion," he began slowly, cautiously. "It was a nice reunion, wasn't it?"

"Yes, it was…a good turnout." *Why is he calling me?*

Chatting briefly about their old classmates and the children, Joellen's mind kept racing. *Why is he calling me?* There could only be one reason, and she dreaded having to tell him. Finally he popped the question.

"Joellen, I would like to take you out."

"Well…I…that's very nice of you," she stammered. "I appreciate you calling…but I…well…I don't date." There, it was out!

There was silence on the other end.

She frowned, feeling like a heel, and he seemed like such a nice guy, too. Seeking to fill the awkward silence and salve her guilt, she explained, "You see, I haven't dated in all these years. I've tried to give the children all my time…of course, my son, Ryan…he's gone now, stationed in England like I told you…but I still have Sydney, who is eleven…and…well…it would be a big decision for me, you understand. I would have to give it a lot of thought…yes, a lot of thought….." She was running out of words.

"Well, I wish you would…"

"Would what?"

"Give it some thought."

"Oh…yes…well, I will…and if I change my mind…I'll call you…yes, I'll call you." *Now that was stupid! She would never call him. She just needed something to say because he wasn't talking. Why was he so quiet? He was making her rattled.*

Wade analyzed, *she says she hasn't dated for years. The chances of her calling me are pretty slim.* "Do you mind if I call you instead?"

Doggone it, I'm getting deeper in! "I…I guess that'll be okay." Feeling more cornered by the minute, she was becoming annoyed, but at the same time keenly aware of how nice this Wade Farrar seemed to be.

"…would you mind if I called you…say at the end of the week?"

End of the week! Why, I haven't dated in eight years…this is a monumental step…and he expects me to make up my mind in a week! She was in a dilemma, but she didn't want him to think her a simpleton, not able to make a decision.

"That…that will be…I think that will be okay." All she wanted to do was get off the phone! She hadn't felt this disconcerted since she was a teenager. She hung the receiver back on the wall phone and stared at it like it was a black coiled snake, then slumped down on a kitchen chair. "Oh my."

Obviously flustered with the whole affair and definitely confused, still she couldn't help but notice how lightheaded she felt. He *was* interested in her, and it felt good. It felt very good. And he had a nice deep voice. Yes, a real nice deep voice.

For the next few days Wade Farrar was constantly on her mind. What was she going to tell him when he called? She pulled out her old MHHS yearbook and studied his high school picture, but that didn't help. He didn't look at all like the young boy with the crew cut. In fact, he looked quite handsome, she thought again, recalling the class reunion, but she didn't have any desire to go out with him or with anyone, for that matter. She hadn't dated since her marriage to Dale ended, and that had been almost eight years! Why break her record now? She preferred things the way they were—no hassle, no emotional entanglements. It had taken a long time to get here, she acknowledged to herself, to get her life running smoothly, and she liked it…most of the time anyway. Sure, there were those times when she missed having someone. Especially in church when she couldn't help but notice the husbands wrap their arms around their wives' shoulders, and times like the class reunion, but she wouldn't be going to anymore of those for a long time, maybe never. And for the most part, she was too busy to be lonely.

Aunt Anna and Katy were delighted to hear about her dilemma, and encouraged her to go out with him, but she knew they were biased. She knew they wanted her to have someone to look after her, but she didn't need anyone to look after her! She was doing all right on her own. She decided to decline Wade Farrar's invitation.

The rain was coming. She could feel it in the air as she drove home from work. A few scattered splashes smacked her windshield, then steadily increased to a full-fledged downpour, and her wipers dashed back and forth. She strained to see the bleary lines bisecting the narrow road and dreaded the inevitable phone call at the end of the week, and having to tell him that she didn't want to date him. Suddenly she remembered her prayer—the prayer that she had prayed on the way to the class reunion. How had she forgotten?

It sure would be nice to have someone on this earth to be with me...the way You meant for it to be.

Suppose...just suppose?

Could it be? If she didn't go out with him, she would never know. She might miss God's plan. Her mind raced back and forth, keeping pace with the rhythmic wipers as the pouring rain beat down, pounding the little car, and the lines in the road all but disappeared. Oh, what was she going to do? She wished she hadn't gone to that 20th High School Class Reunion! She wouldn't be in such a predicament. She pushed the thoughts out of her mind. It was Wednesday night, and they had to get ready for church. She was glad. It would take her mind off the matter.

After church, Joellen flopped down at the kitchen table and poured herself a tall glass of milk and sliced a nice chunk of chocolate cake. She did feel better. The services always lifted her spirits. Sydney was already in bed, and she reached for her book.

The phone rang.

Now who in the world could that be? It's nine o'clock!

"Hello."

"Joellen?"

It's him! But it's only Wednesday, her mind calculated. *Why is he calling me on Wednesday? Wednesday is not the end of the week! Wednesday is hump day!* And he was asking if she had made up her mind! Totally flustered and even more irritated that he had upset her usual Wednesday evening relaxation, not to mention getting the day wrong, she wondered how to answer. Oh well, if she was ever going to find out if he was sent by God…or the devil…she might as well say yes.

That night she lay quietly in bed staring out the window. "Lord, if You are sending this Wade Farrar into my life, please give me a peace about it."

And He did.

A wonderful peace settled upon her on their first date and infused their brief courtship from then on. Initially she was confused when he lit up a pipe, and even more when she discovered that he had never trusted the Lord as his Savior. How could God be sending her such a person?

It was their third date, and they were sitting in a beautiful peaceful garden atop a mountain in Waynesboro, a part of Lao and Dr. Walter Russell's marble palace. A serene statue of Christ hovered in the center, and soft spiritual music wafted over sweet-smelling spring flowers. Joellen had to find out!

"If you were to die today, do you know where you will spend eternity?"

Taken aback by this sudden, straightforward question, he gaped at her, unable to speak, then stammered, "Well… I've always tried to lead a good life…and…."

Wrong answer!

She gazed up into the cloudless blue sky and wondered. Why would God send her someone who wasn't even a Christian? *And he smoked a pipe!*

Wade stared at her. Obviously his answer wasn't the right one, but who was she to ask him such a thing after all?

"I…I don't think it's fair for you to ask me such a personal question…."

She jumped up from the stone bench where they were sitting. "I'm sorry you feel that way. I just had to ask, that's all." She leaned over to touch a budding yellow rose.

"Why don't we go for a walk?" he suggested, grabbing her hand, anxious to change the subject. The rest of the day was spent totally immersed in each other's company, but the unfinished subject remained between them.

CHAPTER TWENTY-SIX

PRESENT

"MILEPOST 467," WADE announced, "only two more miles to go...uh-oh!"

"What is it?"

He didn't answer, but Joellen knew something was wrong. "What is it?"

"The brakes...."

"The brakes!"

"They're not working well...." But the look on his face implied more. She panicked and glanced down at the tremendous heights.

"...how will we get down?"

He pulled over and shut off the motor. Must be that ABS, he said to himself.

"But what are we going to do?"

"Don't know yet. We'll wait awhile...give her a chance to cool down. Then we'll try."

"How?"

"I'm thinking."

She began praying.

"I'm going to get out and stretch my legs while she cools down. Want to come?" He opened his door.

"No, I'll just wait here." She was too anxious to do anything else. She watched him walk over to the rock wall and stare off into the far distance, and she wondered if he was as concerned as she was. Hadn't God always taken care of them? He would get them down off the mountain!

Victor smiled.

She watched Wade sit down on the wall and decided he was more handsome now than when they married. His dishwater blond hair had whitened to a soft uniform blond, and his broad shoulders seemed even broader. She smiled as she recalled their whirlwind romance that astonished everyone, including her. The first week he asked if he could come over on a Wednesday night, and she told him she would be going to church.

"Would you mind if I come with you?"

And from that night on he accompanied her to church three times a week, smoking his pipe all the way there and back. She was puzzled, but still she had a peace.

At each service when the invitation was given, Wade Farrar raised his hand for prayer. But Joellen made a point to remain neutral. She wasn't going to make the same mistake twice. If he was serious, and if something was going on between him and God, she would be still and watch God work. She did not want him to do anything for her or to please her. It must be real. Week after week they went to church, and week after week he raised his hand.

She kept her head bowed and prayed.

One month later Dr. Falwell ended another service. "If there is anyone here who has never accepted the Lord Jesus Christ as your personal Savior and would like to today, just pray this prayer with me. 'Lord, I acknowledge that I am a sinner. I have sinned against you, and I ask for your forgiveness. I repent of my sins and ask You to come into my life...into my heart'."

The service ended, and Joellen jumped up, ready to bolt for the door to beat the crowd.

"Wait a minute, honey." Wade grabbed her hand.

She looked at him questioningly.

"I just prayed that prayer...and I want to talk with someone."

"WELL, WE'RE GOING to try it." Wade climbed back into the RV.

"What if the brakes don't work?"

He turned the key in the ignition, pressed the emergency blinkers, and put it in second gear. "I'm going to drift very slowly to the end of this pull off, then brake. In case they don't work, that curbing will stop us."

The RV began rolling, and Joellen prayed. Just before hitting the curb, Wade braked, and the RV stopped. "They're working so far. Just pray we can get down off this mountain."

"I'm praying!"

With the emergency lights blinking, they slowly descended the mountain in second gear while multihued autumn leaves fell, and brilliant sunrays danced off the hood. Down, down, down they went.

"Milepost 468," Wade breathed softly, touching the brakes lightly. "So far, so good."

Joellen glanced over at the ABS light and prayed that they would make it all the way down. She saw a sign up ahead, Oconaluftee River, and remembered visiting the Oconaluftee Indian Village some years ago with little Brook. She remembered her panning for gold in Cherokee, excitedly looking for that real nugget.

"Still doing okay?" she asked.

He nodded quietly and gravely.

"There it is!" she exclaimed.

"What?"

"The end of the Blue Ridge Parkway."

Wade reached across for her hand. "Thank you, Lord, for bringing us down off the mountain."

To every thing there is a Season…

PRESENT

JOELLEN PAUSED ON the concrete steps, glancing up at the tall oaks that towered over Guggenheimer Nursing Home, their thick bounty of leaves fluttering in the light autumn wind. She inhaled the crisp coolness, and then pulled open the heavy door. Stepping into the hospital-like environment, she was unwillingly transported into another world, a world she would rather not know, but it was reality. The receptionist greeted her warmly, and she headed down the sterile corridor to her mother's room, automatically stopping and listening at the door.

Silence.

Meredith Thaxton was asleep. Lying there in the hospital bed, she looked unusually old but peaceful to Joellen, as she eased down in the chair that was pulled up beside the bed. Though almost eighty, her mother's face was barely wrinkled. She recalled her boasting often about the family's fair skin that came from Grandma Isabelle's side. Grandma had it, of course. Joellen remembered how youthful she appeared even as an old lady, and most of her children, and some of her grandchildren had inherited this characteristic. She stood up and peered into the small mirror above the stainless steel sink. Well, she used to have it. Her mother had often mentioned strolling her as a baby and hearing people's compliments. It was the one thing she had inherited from her mother, though she had always seen herself more like the Thaxtons, especially her daddy. Small and thin like him, she had his deep-set green eyes and fine straight hair. She had often wished she had her mother's thick wavy hair, but Katy got that.

She eased back into the chair and prepared to wait. They all took turns coming and going, sitting with their mother. Not that she actually needed them, for the efficient staff of the nursing home took good care of her. But they knew her time was short, and they wanted her to know that they were with her.

And they needed to be with her for themselves.

Joellen needed to be with her.

She didn't understand her own feelings, but daily she was drawn to the nursing home, even when it wasn't necessary, even when the others were there, she was still drawn like a magnet. They didn't talk. Usually Meredith was sleeping, and even when she wasn't, they didn't really talk. Sitting there beside her, Joellen wished she could talk to her, but the chasm between them had solidified over the many years, and the words wouldn't come.

But she wanted to.

She reached out and smoothed the white hospital blanket that lay crumpled upon her breast and stared at her mother's swollen crooked fingers, and suddenly remembered the ugly slap that night so many years ago. She withdrew her hand from the blanket and stared out the window at the glowing sun and the gently swaying leaves.

Why couldn't she forget? The utter humiliation still stung more than the slap itself. That dreadful night was stamped into her memory forever. Her mother was staying with her for a couple of weeks, which she often did. She and Ryan were living up in the mountains, and it was around about the time that man walked on the moon.

She had just gotten home from work, checked the mailbox and received her phone bill, which was way over a hundred dollars. She had gasped. She didn't have that kind of money! Her mother had called her sister in California and ran up the bill. She went to her and asked her to please not make such expensive long distance calls, explaining that she could not afford to pay them. Meredith lost it and slapped her in the face. It was a hard slap, immediately sending Joellen back to her teens, back to the little cinder block house down in the country.

"Mama, get your coat. I'm taking you home," she had said, and did just that. But on the way Meredith opened the door to jump out of the car. Joellen hollered for her to shut the door, afraid that Ryan would also fall out of the big door on the Corvair. He was in the back seat. When she mentioned him, Meredith shut it. But as soon as she pulled up in the driveway, Meredith jumped out and ran off into the dark woods. Everyone went looking for her. They were afraid she might venture too far and fall into those old copper mines that were a couple of miles back behind the house—big open pits. And Joellen felt responsible and guilty for bringing her back home that way, so guilty.

But they found her, and Joellen would never forget the look—the look of hatred in her mother's tormented eyes, the look of hatred for *her* when they brought her back into the house. She could still see her seated on the chair with her daddy and the others around her, soothing her, but all the while her mother stared at her with that look of hatred. Not only had it scared her, but it reached way down deep inside and twisted itself into a permanent hurt. Her daddy suggested that she leave, that maybe it would be best, and she remembered how she felt driving out of the country that night, so alone.

She learned later that her mother screamed all night long, and Brian had to go out and sleep in the car. The next morning her daddy took her back to the hospital.

Joellen pushed the memory away and watched a dark cloud forming to the north. Maybe it would rain. They needed rain. She glanced back over her shoulder. She was still sleeping. She wished she didn't have those memories. She doubted her sisters did. Katy and Janet seemed so relaxed with her. They kissed her and talked to her easily. Why couldn't she? Even her brothers were better at it than she was.

She slumped back in the chair, listening to her mother's slight snoring. A nurse peeped in on them, cheerfully winked, and moved on down the hall. She reached down to her purse and pulled out the new gospel tape and laid it on the little bedside table. She would play it for her when she awoke. Her mother liked the tapes she had brought so far. It wasn't much, but it was something. Of course, she had made her mother happy through the years, taking her places, buying her new dresses and jewelry. Amazingly, they enjoyed the same taste, and Joellen loved to buy things for her. It was the easy way of reaching out, of showing her that she really did care, much easier than saying it.

One day when she was still in the hospital before she was moved to Guggenheimer's, her mother had asked a favor of her. Looking up at her with those liquid-brown eyes, she half whispered, "Joellen, would you buy me a dress...a nice dress, to lay me away in?"

"Let's don't talk about that, Mama," she'd quickly replied. "We don't want to think...."

But Meredith Thaxton shook her head authoritatively, "No, I want you to go to town and buy me a dress, a pretty dress. Will you do that for me, Joellen?"

It was a pleading look, but a look of confidence in her. Her mother trusted her to do this, to buy the dress. Joellen remembered the event with mixed emotions, but she was proud that her mother had chosen her to buy the dress, her last dress. She didn't ask Katy or Janet.

She'd hurried out to the mall, to Belk, Hecht's, Penney's, Sears. She rummaged through dozens of racks, stuffed with size twenty-two, for just the right dress. It had to be navy blue, of that much she knew. Her mother had always loved navy blue, and she liked a classic look, nothing tawdry. One thing about her mother—she may have been sick all her life, she may have battled unknown fears and sunk in bottomless pits of depression, but she had class. Joellen found the dress, the perfect dress—a dark navy blue with a delicate scarf attached to the neck, a soft silk scarf of pastel blue and pink. She knew her mother would be proud of it.

It was hanging in Joellen's closet.

"Joellen Grace…."

She jumped. Her mother was staring at her with those frightened eyes. "Joellen Grace," she repeated. Joellen stood up and moved closer to the bed to hear her soft whispery voice and detected the urgency in it.

"Yes," she answered, wondering why she called her by both names. She had just begun doing that in the last week or so. She had never called her by both her names before. Never. Was it something out of the past? Had she possibly called her that when she was a baby?

"Will you stay here with me?" she pleaded.

"I'm here, Mama."

"Don't leave me." Her eyes darted back and forth to the open door. "…if you do…he'll come back….and he will

419

kill me...." She pulled the white blanket close up under her chin like a small child.

"No one's going to hurt you, Mama. The nurses are out in the hall. They won't let anyone hurt you, and I'm here...."

Frantically her mother tossed her head from side to side on the flattened pillow. "No...no...no...you don't understand...he'll come back...."

Before Joellen could figure out what to say next, her mother's eyes closed again, and she was asleep. Joellen sighed and fell back into the chair to wait.

AS THE DAYS shortened, so did Meredith Thaxton's life. Her aging body was attacked by a series of mini-strokes, the last of which took her out of the world of consciousness, and she lay with slitted eyes as the children crept in and out, talking to her like she could hear and understand everything they said.

Joellen sat by her bed alone. Katy was on her way to relieve her, and the others would be there later. But now, it was just her and her mama. She patted her swollen hand, bruised and blue from all the I.V.s, and sadly realized she could be more demonstrative now that her mother didn't know she was there.

Or did she?

She smoothed her damp gray hair from her forehead and wondered what it would have been like if she hadn't been sick all her life, if she hadn't lived in that dark world of anxiety and depression? Maybe they could have had girl talks like some of her friends had with their mothers...or they could have laughed and giggled in the night. Grandma Isabelle had laughed and giggled in the night with her once when she spent the night with her, and it was so much fun. But Mama wasn't like Grandma Isabelle.

She supposed she was more like her father, the mystery man who sent the dreaded letters and boxes of stale candy, but Joellen wondered. What secrets lay in the past? The writer in her sought for answers. What happened to the little girl that happily skated on the downtown streets of Lynchburg? What happened to the child that spent her days sitting in the Isis or the Paramount watching the same movies over and over? What had happened to throw her into such an abyss? Had she simply inherited his genes, or was there more?

She quietly studied her mother, the slit in her closed eyelids vaguely revealing those doe-like eyes now clouded over, and she suddenly realized that she would never know! Meredith Thaxton would take her secrets to the grave.

THE PHONE RANG.

Joellen picked it up.

It was Janet. "Joellen…."

She was crying, and Joellen knew what she was going to say.

"…*Mama just died.*"

She wished she had been there. She and Katy had just left the nursing home an hour before when Janet and Daniel showed up. But it was best, she thought. It was best that Janet was there, and Daniel. She knew that they wanted to be. She hung up the phone and sat down.

It was over.

Her mother was finally at peace, out of her prison, out of the dark abyss. No more fears!

And it was over for her, too.

She didn't have to struggle with the strained relationship anymore, but there was a deep sadness slowly filling her soul. She wanted to go back, back to that little girl swinging in the homemade swing, back to the carefree days of summer, back to her mother rocking her in the old creaking rocker. If they could just start over...maybe it would be different.

But she knew in her heart it wouldn't. Her mother was born Meredith Conner and she Joellen Thaxton. And though they were mother and daughter, and they really loved one another, they were never able to cross the chasm.

And Joellen cried.

THE FUNERAL PROCESSION lined up outside Joellen's home, and they slowly shuffled down the long driveway, and down the road and onto the expressway and on to the funeral home, the same funeral home where her daddy had been a few years prior.

Quietly wedged in between her sisters, she thought about how automobiles and vehicles play such prominent roles in one's last days. She remembered following behind the ambulance when her daddy was taken away.

Here she was again. The driver slowly and methodically turned into the driveway of the funeral home. She stared at the modern brick building, relatively new, but exuding a bleak presence for all concerned. She hated funeral homes even more than hospitals and nursing homes. She wanted her mother to have a nice funeral, but she was anxious for it to be over. The last few days were one big blur with people coming and going, and phone calls from sympathetic family and friends, and lists of things to do and arrangements to make. She had been busy with all the preparations and glad for it, thus taking her mind off her mother and off her inner turmoil. But still she felt like a fluttering autumn leaf, unable to land on the leaf-strewn earth, yet unable to reattach itself to the big oak.

It fluttered and fluttered, hanging helplessly in the air.

There was no closure. There was so much left unsaid, undone. She glanced from Katy to Janet. She doubted they felt this way. But they had always been closer to her. Why? She never knew. Perhaps it was due to timing. They say everything is timing. Maybe that was it. When she was a teenager, her mother was at her worst, sunk deep in depression.

But that wasn't all. She wished it was, but she knew better. It was probably also due to her own willful, independent nature. Katy and Janet were different, easier to love, most likely. They were caretakers, but she could never bring herself to care for her mother when she was hurling names at her. She wasn't made like Katy and Janet, and that was the reason for the rings. Their mother had only two rings: her wedding ring and the mother's ring they had given her one mother's day. When they were all sitting there in the cramped office at the funeral home, struggling among themselves with those final, difficult decisions, she had insisted that Katy and Janet take the rings. With a choke in her throat, she knew she was feeling sorry for herself, but couldn't help it. Her mother would have wanted it that way, too, she thought, as the driver pulled up to the side door of the funeral home.

She grabbed her purse, and they filed into the gloomy interior, a rush of heavily scented roses and carnations welcoming them in a sickening, pungent way. As much as Joellen loved flowers, she despised flowers in a funeral home. They should be outside growing in the loamy earth, soaking up the warm sunshine, blowing in the cool breezes—not here!

She followed behind Katy as they approached the open casket and was soon staring down at her mother for the last time. But it wasn't her mother! She hated this American custom of open caskets. Her mother was gone, her spirit lifted high, soaring in the heavens…with her daddy and the Lord. It wasn't her!

But then her eyes fell upon the navy blue dress with its soft silk scarf of pastel blue and pink, and a calming spirit settled upon her.

The family stiffly arranged themselves upon the metal fold-up chairs behind the privacy wall for the service. Joellen glanced around at her siblings with bowed heads, respectfully wiping their eyes. She felt like crying, but couldn't. She wished she could bolt for the door, away from it all, away from the unwanted thoughts whirling around in her head, bouncing like a volley ball. Then she saw her old friend Virgie rise and move to the podium, and she began to sing in her beautiful resonant voice.

…like a Bridge over troubled water…I will lay me down. Like a Bridge over troubled water…I will lay me down…When you're weary, feelin' small, When tears are in your eyes, I'll dry them all….

Joellen relaxed. Everything was going to be all right. Mama wasn't here anyway. She glanced up at the ceiling and on beyond, and she was sure her mama was watching. She had crossed over those troubled waters now, she thought as she listened to her friend's lovely voice, so many troubled waters in those eighty years.

...like a Bridge over troubled water...I will lay me down. Like a Bridge over troubled water...I will lay me down...When you're weary, feelin' small, When tears are in your eyes, I'll dry them all....

The funeral procession stretched out down the narrow rural road leading to the country cemetery, and the words of the poignant song kept ringing in Joellen's ears. It conjured up memories of the past, another time, another place, sending her back to Texas again—she and Ryan walking across hot pavement—and he didn't have any shoes to wear, and his little feet were burning. Truly God had been the *Bridge* over troubled waters for her back then and for all these years...for both her and her mother.

She glanced at Janet, Daniel, and Katy to see how they were holding up. Brian wasn't there. He would probably meet them at the cemetery the way he had at their daddy's funeral. Brian, the sensitive one, couldn't deal with hospitals and funeral homes. She wondered why. There are so many unknowns in life, she thought. One could speculate, imagine, even presume, but it was all a mystery. She thought of last night. Brian hadn't come to the family night either. Instead he had offered to house-sit at her house to make sure no robbers looted while they were all gone. They had been told such things do happen. But when they returned from the funeral home, they found Brian out on the porch, sitting in the dark.

All was quiet after everyone left for the funeral home, he related almost reverently, but instead of watching television like he usually did, he had switched off the lights and gone out to the front porch to sit. Meredith had lived with Brian and his wife Karen for the last year or so before she was taken to the hospital, and he just wanted to be alone and quiet. The autumn night was still without a hint of

425

breeze, he described, the only movement was that of a few fireflies.

"Mama," he'd spoken into the solid darkness that night. "Mama, I miss you…and I'm sorry, Mama, that I didn't spend more time with you…instead of watching TV… watching the ballgames." He choked up. "I'm sorry, Mama! I wish I could go back…and…talk with you just one more time…."

There in the dark on the front porch, Brian poured out his heart to her, and though he didn't say it, Joellen knew he must have been crying. Then all of a sudden, he explained in a hushed voice, the heavy wind chimes hanging on the end of the long porch began to chime. With a start, he had jumped up, realizing there was no breeze. It was eerie, he said, and he went back into the house, feeling quite uneasy. But then he returned to the darkened porch, slowly, very cautiously.

"…if that's you, Mama, please let me know…."

And the chimes rang again.

Joellen reflected on his unusual story as the funeral procession climbed the hilly terrain, but she wasn't surprised for she had heard such stories before, and she believed in the spirit world. God is a Spirit, she thought…and now so is Mama…and Daddy. One day, we will all be. And there was so much out there that humans didn't know and couldn't comprehend with such finite minds. She thought of Brian again and wondered if her mother had been reaching out to him…or maybe it was God or one of his angels. Brian would be the one that needed that special touch.

The funeral limo was grinding up a narrow, graveled drive sandwiched between two cemeteries that were separated not only by the rutted road but also wire fences.

Joellen glanced to her right to the small Jewish cemetery that had held such a mysterious aura and piqued their childhood curiosity. They didn't know any Jews out where they lived and never saw any in the cemetery, though they had always watched for one to see if he looked like Jesus. The two cemeteries were distinctly different. The high gates to the Jewish cemetery had been invariably shut and locked, its grounds always immaculately manicured, unlike theirs with its untidy trash pile of discarded flowers and that often needed mowing. She leaned toward the window remembering the small smooth stones that often graced the Jewish gravestones. She didn't see any.

The funeral limo halted at the entrance of the cemetery where most of her deceased family rested, then slowly maneuvered through the narrow rusting gateway. She saw Brian nervously waiting. The engines shut off, one after another, and they began to awkwardly pile out of the vehicles and slowly amble toward the green canopy.

Joellen glanced around the familiar old cemetery. It hadn't changed much except that the trash pile was gone. She remembered how she and Betsy Jeanne would stop here on their way back from the country store on those sweltering, hot summer days, sucking on ice cold cherry popsicles. The memory of the warm sun on their backs as they rummaged through the pile of discarded and faded plastic flowers, the sweet smell of summer grass and hot tar from the hilly road winding through the graveyard, the drone of crickets, and the buzz of honeybees all came flooding back to her.

She took her place under the green canopy, fighting off the hodgepodge of nostalgic emotions and overpowering grief.

CHAPTER TWENTY-SEVEN

PRESENT

"THEY SAY TIME heals," Joellen talked to herself as she drove west on State Route 460 out of Lynchburg.

"Maybe so." Several years had passed since her mother died. A Mack truck roared past, the burly driver curiously staring down at her, perhaps wondering who she was talking to. But time does give one the opportunity to put everything in perspective—she decided to converse silently—and things have a way of becoming strangely clearer. She was able to understand her mother more in the few short years since her death than during all the years of her life, and the hurt and the pain seemed to diminish with each setting sun and each dawning day. The good memories were choking out the bad, and she wished she could have focused more on the positive than the negative while she lived. She remembered what her mother told Brian in her last year. *"I know I wasn't the best mother, but I did the best I could."* Joellen pressed the button to open the passenger window, bringing in the dry leafy air, and thought to herself, that's all any of us can do.

It was the end of October, and soon it would be winter. In fact, they had already experienced a few hints of it with blustery winds and cool temperatures at night, but today she had a reprieve, perhaps the last one. It was one of those glorious Indian summer days! As she left behind the

bustling traffic of Lynchburg, rolling green hills and picturesque meadows embraced her. She sighed and pushed the
somber thoughts away, thoughts of her mother, thoughts
of her children all grown up, thoughts of life in general
and the passing of time. She inhaled the invigorating autumn air and relished the sweeping vistas on both sides of
the smooth highway that rolled and dipped over southern
hills.

She was headed to Bedford, not to work this time, but
just to spend a leisurely day in the mountains before all the
leaves fell. Already they were mostly gone, but those that
clung on were worth seeing, vibrant vivid color glowing in
the dizzying sun. She would take a hike all alone. Seldom
did she have time to be alone, what with such a busy life,
her growing family, children, grandkids, and her books. She
couldn't help but remember that prayer she had prayed on
the way to the 20th High School Class Reunion.... *"It sure
would be nice to have someone on this earth to be with me...the way
You meant for it to be. But if You want me to be alone, I accept it,
Lord. Thy will be done. Just please give me a full life...."*

Well, He had done it!

Not only had He given her such a wonderful husband,
but He had also given her a full life! "God is so good," she
began to sing the little song that she had so often taught
her Sunday school class. She sang it loud and clear out the
open window. "...God is so good...God is so good...He's
so good to me...."

Wade had gone fishing with the guys, and the children
were all occupied with their busy lives, the grandchildren,
too. And Aunt Anna was gone, also—having died the previous January. Joellen was all alone, and there was no one

429

to talk to…but the Lord. So, she decided she would go up into the mountains…and have a talk with Him.

She could see them now, the majestic Blue Ridge, vividly outlined, their familiar ridges rising in the distance, rimmed against the clear blue sky. *Sharp Top* pierced it, and *Flat Top* more gently bumped up against it. How many times she'd climbed them, but today she wouldn't climb them. She just wanted to aimlessly take a walk in the woods, and embrace it all. She couldn't wait to get there. Moving along, she suddenly shot up behind a large lumbering truck.

Great!

A concrete crypt was loaded on its back, held down by heavy iron chains, on its way to a final destination. She frowned. Perhaps the deceased person was waiting for it in some funeral home or perhaps not. Maybe the owner was full of life somewhere, with absolutely no clue that his or her crypt was flying down State Route 460. Creepy! She pressed the accelerator, swinging around the hulking truck, while pushing the button to her stereo. She could use a shot of optimism. Poking the button repeatedly underneath her steering wheel to reach the right CD, she was thankful Ryan had installed this complicated thing. She didn't like gadgets, never had, probably because she didn't understand them. Simplicity—that's what she liked. Suddenly the SUV vibrated with the great sounds of yesterday…

> *Come on let's twist again like we did last summer*
> *Yea, let's twist again like we did last year*
> *Do you remember when things were really hummin'*
> *Yea, let's twist again, twistin' time is here*

Singing along, she ignored the passing cars—she didn't care who saw her! Transported back to the beguiling fifties by Chubby Checker, she was filled with youthful energy,

swept back to *Bandstand* and teenage hops and youth…
ah…youth.

How she had loved the twist! She had loved being on
the cutting edge of the rock and roll era when it exploded, sweeping her along with it. She figured it was in her
blood, that Scotch-Irish blood. She remembered Grandma
Thaxton telling her that even she had loved to dance. Hard-
working, strait-laced Grandma! When she heard music as
a young girl, she would hide behind the door and dance.
Now that was a thought!

And her own mother, Meredith, had often nostalgically
boasted of doing the Charleston when she was a young girl
in downtown Lynchburg.

Yes, it's in my blood! The rhythmic music jammed the
SUV as it flew down the highway, and she was that spirited,
young girl of fourteen again with excitement and enthusiastic anticipation of what life held in store! Her head reck-
lessly bobbed to the familiar beat and her hands hammered
the steering wheel…

> *Yea round'n around'n up'n down we go again*
> *Oh baby make me know you love me so then*
> *Come on let's twist again like we did last summer*
> *Yea, let's twist again, twistin' time is here*

The song ended.

She glanced up into the rearview mirror, and the pensive mood returned. She couldn't go back, even though
she didn't feel any different, even though she was the same
person on the inside!

She couldn't go back.

Out of the blue she remembered that little old man
from her past. *My gosh, I must have been only about twenty-one
at the time!* She had been driving down Langhorne Road

one beautiful sunny spring day, the birds were singing and youthful blood pulsated through her veins. Exuberant and full of life, she was ready to conquer the world, when suddenly her eyes had fixed upon the old man slowly ambling down the sidewalk; very gingerly he walked with a cane, unsteady, testing each step before he took it. The stoplight caught her, and he toddled by.

She watched him.

Stooped and shriveled—decrepit was the word that had come to mind. But once he was a young man, she had thought, perhaps a strong handsome young man. Most likely he had loved and been loved by some pretty young girl, maybe a dynamic romantic love.

It was a startling insight for her. To realize that he was the same person on the inside—only trapped within that aging body, and her heart went out to him.

That had been a long time ago. Now she was entering the autumn of her own life and fully understood the poignant scenario from the past. She was changing, she had changed, yet she was still Joellen Thaxton on the inside, but nobody knew it but her!

It's me! She wanted to yell out the window to the oncoming cars. *I'm still here…it's Joellen…Joellen Thaxton!*

Frustrated, she punched the stereo button over and over until she heard those old familiar words reverberating again…and she sang louder over the hum of traffic, over the rush of the autumn wind…

> *Let's twist again like we did last summer*
> *Yea, let's twist again like we did last year*
> *Do you remember when….*

Route 43 rose before her, climbing upward, curving around, back and forth. She silenced the stereo for the mountain ambiance as she ascended. All was quiet now except for the rustle of crisp oak leaves scudding across the pavement and across the shiny hood of her SUV. Already its abiding strength was filling her soul, refreshing her busy, hurried mind.

October was definitely her favorite month, not only for its matchless beauty, but a lot had happened in this transition month of beauty and death. She recalled walking down the church aisle way back in 1968, and her life was never the same. She thought of her marriage to Dale, and though he was gone now, claimed by alcohol at the age of fifty-one, he had given her two wonderful children, Ryan and Sydney.

Then there was Wade and their marriage on the twenty-second of October, and exactly one year later, on their first anniversary, she had gone into labor. And their precious little Brook was born the next day. What a blessing she had been to both of them—a beautiful child in their old age, but they weren't old! She smiled to herself and remembered Mr. Wilson, her science teacher at old MHHS. He was fresh out of college and fancied himself with a bounty of knowledge for all those little rural kids, wet behind the ears, and he had been especially fond of the word "relative." Einstein's theory of relativity must have impacted him immensely while in those college halls. He used the word practically in every other sentence. Of course, Einstein's theory had caught the imagination of the average person more than any other physical theory in history, especially that of relativity and time. It was certainly beyond her how a clock moving relative to an observer appears to run slower than a stationary clock. But when it comes to age, well, she understood that! It depends on which end of the spectrum you're on, she thought to herself, as she pulled up the curving mountain road.

Mr. Wilson had certainly been a handsome science teacher, a welcomed addition to the drudgery of school life, not too much older than his bored students. They were enamored with his sleek sports car parked right out front of the old building. She wondered what he was doing now. Was he still alive?

"The brevity of life," she whispered into the bracing autumn air that was blowing her hair every which way, but she didn't care. Those were Billy Graham's words. She remembered the famous preacher saying those very words the day he came to Lynchburg for the graduation of his grandson at Liberty University. He was also the commencement speaker that day and related a story about someone asking him a question.

"Now, Reverend Graham, since you are past eighty, what do you have to say about life?"

"The brevity of it," was his answer.

She wheeled the SUV around the never-ending curves, reminiscent of that day. In preparation of the special event, the church minister of music had asked for volunteers to make up the huge thirteen-hundred-member choir that would be up front in the large stadium, and she had readily volunteered. What a privilege it would be! But it was even more than that, enabling her to give back just a drop of what Billy Graham had done for her during that television crusade—the spark he had ignited when she was just a mixed-up teenager.

The day turned out to be cool and rainy. She recalled awakening to the soft pitter-patter of raindrops pelting the back gutter of the house. She stretched to look out their bedroom window just as night gave way to dawn, and a cold drizzly rain trickled down the foggy windowpane. Oh no, she hoped it would stop or they might all catch pneumonia in the outdoor stadium. At least she was glad that she had bought that poncho. The weatherman had been right.

She had jumped out of bed and rushed to the bathroom and leaned her head over the bathtub, sticking it under the surge of gushing hot water from the faucet. With squinted eyes and water drooling over her face, she fumbled for the shampoo sitting on the edge of the tub. Her friend Nan was going to meet her there, and she was just as excited as she was. This wasn't just any choir, she thought, while rubbing the suds into her hair. It would be a day to remember.

Crowded on the damp bleachers, chilled but awed, they watched the large stadium quickly fill up in the drizzle of rain. She pulled her yellow poncho tightly up under her chin, afraid she was going to freeze before it was all over. But the moment the mammoth choir stood up to sing, she forgot the rain and the chill and all the discomfort. There was electricity in the air. And it wasn't just the overall exhilaration, it wasn't just the fact that she was singing in Billy Graham's choir. It was the realization of what God had done for her once she walked around that kitchen table on Clay Street in downtown Lynchburg.

How can I say thanks for the things You have done for me?
Things so undeserved, yet You give to prove Your love for me.
The voices of a million angels could not express my gratitude;
All that I am and ever hope to be—I owe it all to Thee.

THE SUV LEVELED off as it topped Route 43, and she veered right to the Visitor Center, still humming *To God be*

435

the glory, to God be the glory, to God be the glory for the things He has done. The parking lot was almost empty, much to her surprise. It must be because it's Monday, she thought. It was probably full yesterday and Saturday. The famed Peaks of Otter always drew crowds in October. She climbed out, locked the doors and headed for the tapered path that paralleled the Parkway for a ways before coming to a crossing where one either continued on to the popular Johnson Farm Trail or headed off toward Harkening Hill, the third mountain of the Peaks. She crossed over the wooden footbridge, pausing briefly to gaze into the clear pebbled mountain stream, and then began hiking the familiar trail. So many early mornings she had hiked it when she was working on her last book.

She walked through the fading autumn forest with translucent shafts of sunlight falling through its feeble canopy, feeding on every sight and sound, and its absolute beauty humbled her. She recalled the words of the Norwegian Philosopher, Arne Naess. *"The smaller we come to feel ourselves compared to the mountain, the nearer we come to participating in its greatness."*

So true, she thought and repeated the Psalmist— *"...what is man, that thou art mindful of him?"*

But she knew...down deep in her heart, she knew that He was mindful. Not only from the Scriptures did she know, but she knew from experience. *I will never leave you nor forsake you.*

"Thank you, Lord," she whispered into the forest.

There was the sign pointing to Johnson's Farm Trail, the restored farmstead built in 1854 and occupied into the forties. It was a favorite trail in the area, complete with homestead, barns, old farming equipment, a springhouse, and all the other paraphernalia that went along with a small farm in those days. But she didn't want to sightsee today. She wanted to meditate and turned left toward Harkening Hill.

She stooped and picked up a discarded walking stick and trudged up the mountainside, recalling all the many times God had been with her—back when she was young and just starting out on her journey, on Clay Street with its growing-up pains and fears; in the cold, snowy plains of Minnesota, sunk in loneliness; and the hot deserts of Texas, her wilderness; in the lowlands of South Carolina where He had reached down and healed her body. God had been with her when she visited Ryan in England when he was stationed at Alconbury Royal Air Force Base, and she was three months pregnant with little Brook, and suddenly the bleeding came while touring London. So far from home and frightened, she didn't know what to do but pray. And He answered.

She stared at the almost skeletal tree-lined ridges. And He had been with her all these years in the mountains of Virginia. The remnant leaves floated about and acorns dropped, pinging off rocks and fallen decayed trees. A gurgling mountain stream could be heard up ahead, and she hastened toward it. It was making its own mysterious music as the clear cold water spilled over smooth round stones on its eternal path.

But she heard another song...familiar words wafting high above and scaling the perilous mountain ridges, floating through the forest, over moaning stark branches prepared for winter, over oaks and poplars, hickories, and maples. A young girl stood on rickety wooden steps of an old auditorium, in a white cap and gown with a gold tassel...and she was singing with all her heart, the words becoming clearer and clearer....

When you walk through a storm, hold your head up high
And don't be afraid of the dark,
At the end of the storm is a golden sky
And the sweet silver song of a lark,

Walk on through the wind,
Walk on through the rain,

Tho' your dreams be tossed and blown
Walk on, walk on, with a hope in your heart,
And you'll never walk alone,
You'll never walk alone!

The song faded into the still forest, where only a few leaves hung on. Soon they, too, would fall, and the trees would face the winter rigid and naked, but with strength and dignity they would face it. She watched an oak leaf turn loose, brown and curled, and it slowly parachuted through the air, exhibiting a supple somersault, gently fluttering in the breeze, and then it landed gracefully on the leaf-strewn earth.

The winter—a time to contemplate, a time to reflect, to think about the past—the flowers would soon wither and die, the grass would turn brown, and the bird's song would cease, but spring would come again, and there would be new life!

To everything there is a season....

438

Song, Poetry and Literature Credits

"Shake, Rattle and Roll," p. 3 – Elvis Presley Lyrics

"I'll Fly Away," p. 30 – Copyright 1932 in Wonderful Message. Hartford Music Co., Owner. Copyright 1960 by Albert E. Brumley and Sons, renewal

"How much is That Doggie In The Window," pages 31 and 123 – Words and Music by Bob Merrill

"Whatever Will Be, Will Be," p. 55 – Words and Music by Jay Livingston and Ray Evans. Copyright 1955 Artists Music, Inc. (ASCAP); Copyright 1978 Artists Music, Inc.

"Young Love," p. 71 – Written by Carole Joyner and Ric Cartey, recorded by Tab Hunter (1957)

"The Stroll," p. 79 – The Diamonds Lyrics. Clyde Otis and Nancy Lee

"Mack The Knife," p. 108 – Lyrics: Brecht, Blitzestien. Music: Weill

"Have I Told You Lately That I Love You?" p. 115 – Words and Music by Scott Wiseman. Brook Benton Lyrics

"Annabel Lee," p. 116 – Edgar Allan Poe

"Macbeth," p. 120 – William Shakespeare

"*Teach—now.*" – "To a Skylark," p. 125 – Percy Bysshe Shelley

"The Twist," p. 128 – Chubby Checker Lyrics

"Canterbury Tales," p. 129 – Geoffrey Chaucer

"I Believe (For Every Drop of Rain That Falls)," p. 138 – Written by Irvin Graham, Prime Artist – Frank Sinatra

"You'll Never Walk Alone," pages 139 and 438. Words by Oscar Hammerstein II; music by Richard Rodgers

"She Loves You," p. 165 – Beatles

"I Want To Hold Your Hand," p. 166 – Beatles

"Love Lifted Me," p. 201 – James Rowe and Howard E. Smith

"Lord, I'm Coming Home," p. 203 – William J. Kirkpatrick, pub. 1892, copyright: Public Domain

"Just As I Am," p. 220 – Charlotte Elliott, 1836; Sir Joseph Barnby, 1893

"I'll Tell The World," p. 223 – Baynard L. Fox, copyright 1958, 1963, renewal 1986 by Fred Bock Music Co./ASCAP

"Bridge Over Troubled Water," pages 271 and 424-425 – Words and Music by Paul Simon, copyright 1969

"In The Garden," p. 374 – Words and Music by C. Austin Miles. Copyright 1912 by Hall-Mack Co., The Rodeheaver Co., Owner, Renewed 1940

"His Eye Is On The Sparrow," p. 379-380 – By Charles H. Gabriel.

"Let's Twist Again," p. 430-432 – Chubby Checker Lyrics

"My Tribute (To God Be The Glory)," p. 435 – Words and Music by Andrae Crouch. Copyright 1971 Lexicon Music, Inc.

Additionally – Scriptures taken from The Holy Bible, King James Version

Carolyn Tyree Feagans grew up in Amherst County,
adjacent to Lynchburg, at the foot of the
Blue Ridge Mountains.
(P.O. Box 10811,
Lynchburg, Virginia 24506)